PRAISE FOR

A Murderous Procession

"An exhilarating whodunit and my favorite book of the year. I'd like to crown Ariana Franklin Queen of the Historical Mystery."

—Tess Gerritsen

"A high-spirited series of romantic suspense."

—*The New York Times Book Review*

"Fans of historical fiction and mystery readers will be rewarded."

—*Publishers Weekly*

"Sprinkled with fascinating historical facts about the medieval period, Franklin's plots always intrigue." —*Library Journal*

"Historical details are many, and add an extra layer of atmosphere."

—*Booklist*

PRAISE FOR

Grave Goods

"Let's not analyze why we love women who cut up dead bodies. Let's just enjoy *Grave Goods*, the third adventure in Ariana Franklin's dynamic series of novels featuring Adelia Aguilar. . . . Science and romance vie with superstition and barbarism in this richly detailed, almost indecently thrilling mystery."

—*The New York Times Book Review*

"The author excels at creating complex and often contradictory characters, and Adelia accepts the bad as well as the good in people with equanimity. . . . Franklin's prose is admirably clear and crisp, as contemporary-sounding to the reader as her characters' conversations would have sounded to each other." —*The Denver Post*

continued . . .

"Re-creates a living, breathing past populated with entertaining characters." —*Library Journal* (starred review)

"A rich and entertaining story." —*Contra Costa Times*

"[A] highly entertaining series . . . With Franklin, history is fun and games, as well as terribly suspenseful." —*New York Daily News*

"Excellent . . . Eloquently sketched characters [and] bits of medieval lore flavor the constantly unfolding plot." —*Publishers Weekly*

"Well-researched, colorful, sometimes comical, and often engaging." —*Kirkus Reviews*

PRAISE FOR

The Serpent's Tale

"Captivating . . . This excellent adventure delivers high drama and lively scholarship." —*The New York Times Book Review*

"An impeccably researched tapestry of murder most foul, regal intrigue, and heady feminism . . . refreshing." —*Entertainment Weekly*

"[Franklin] brilliantly captures the heated tension between king and queen, evoking jealousy as the root of political and personal turmoil." —*Los Angeles Times*

"An enjoyable romp . . . A warm, promising continuation of the series." —*Kirkus Reviews* (starred review)

"Mesmerizing . . . brings medieval England to life . . . A colorful cast of characters, both good and evil, enhance a tale that will keep readers on edge until the final page." —*Publishers Weekly*

PRAISE FOR

Mistress of the Art of Death

Winner of the Ellis Peters Historical Dagger Award

"Great fun! Franklin succeeds in vividly bringing the twelfth century to life with this crackling good story. Expertly researched, a brilliant heroine, full of excellent period detail."

—Kate Mosse, *New York Times* bestselling author of *Sepulchre* and *Labyrinth*

"[A] vibrant medieval mystery. Outdoes the competition in depicting the perversities of human cruelty. Adelia is a delight, and her spirited efforts to stop the killings . . . add to our appreciation of her forensic skills. But the lonely figure who truly stands out in Franklin's vibrant tapestry of medieval life is King Henry—an enlightened monarch condemned to live in dark times."

—*The New York Times*

"It's hard enough to produce a gripping thriller—harder still to write convincing historical fiction that re-creates a living, breathing past. But this terrific book does both. . . . *Mistress of the Art of Death* is wonderfully plotted, with a dozen twists. . . . It's a historical mystery that succeeds brilliantly as both historical fiction and crime-thriller. Above all, though, Franklin has written a terrific story, whose appeal rests on the personalities of the all-too-human beings who inhabit it." —*The Washington Post*

"Smart and sophisticated . . . A rollicking microcosm of budding science, medieval culture, and edge-of-your-seat suspense."

—*USA Today*

"This is one of the most compelling, suspenseful mysteries I've read in years. Adelia is a wonderful character and I cannot wait for her next adventure."

—Sharon Kay Penman, *New York Times* bestselling author

continued . . .

"The bold, brilliant heroine of *Mistress of the Art of Death* is the medieval answer to Kay Scarpetta and the *CSI* detectives. This is a compelling, unique, and vibrant page-turner."

—Karen Harper, *New York Times* bestselling author of the Elizabeth I mystery series

"Thanks to Franklin's research and evocative prose, the reader not only enjoys a good whodunit with exceptionally well-formed characters but also learns much about medieval England. . . . Franklin weaves a frightening story of serial killings with a cautionary tale of ethnic and religious hatred." —*Richmond Times-Dispatch*

"Intriguing historical fiction. A fabulous read . . . irresistible."

—*New York Daily News*

"Will surely please mystery fans as well as lovers of historical fiction." —*Library Journal*

"Franklin delivers rich period detail and a bloody good ending reflecting the savagery of the times." —*Booklist*

"Had Ellis Peters's Brother Cadfael been born a few decades later, he might have found a worthy associate and friend in [Adelia]. . . . Franklin has developed a skillful blend of historical fact and gruesome fiction that's more than sufficient to keep readers interested and entertained." —*Publishers Weekly*

"*CSI* meets *The Canterbury Tales*. Franklin hits commercial pay dirt with this criminal investigation drama set in twelfth-century England. A potentially winning formula, delivered with panache."

—*Kirkus Reviews*

TITLES BY ARIANA FRANKLIN

A Murderous Procession

Grave Goods

The Serpent's Tale

Mistress of the Art of Death

City of Shadows

A

MURDEROUS

PROCESSION

Ariana Franklin

BERKLEY BOOKS
New York

THE BERKLEY PUBLISHING GROUP
Published by the Penguin Group
Penguin Group (USA) Inc.
375 Hudson Street, New York, New York 10014, USA
Penguin Group (Canada), 90 Eglinton Avenue East, Suite 700, Toronto, Ontario M4P 2Y3, Canada
(a division of Pearson Penguin Canada Inc.)
Penguin Books Ltd., 80 Strand, London WC2R 0RL, England
Penguin Group Ireland, 25 St. Stephen's Green, Dublin 2, Ireland (a division of Penguin Books Ltd.)
Penguin Group (Australia), 250 Camberwell Road, Camberwell, Victoria 3124, Australia
(a division of Pearson Australia Group Pty. Ltd.)
Penguin Books India Pvt. Ltd., 11 Community Centre, Panchsheel Park, New Delhi—110 017, India
Penguin Group (NZ), 67 Apollo Drive, Rosedale, North Shore 0632, New Zealand
(a division of Pearson New Zealand Ltd.)
Penguin Books (South Africa) (Pty.) Ltd., 24 Sturdee Avenue, Rosebank, Johannesburg 2196,
South Africa

Penguin Books Ltd., Registered Offices: 80 Strand, London WC2R 0RL, England

PRINTING HISTORY
G. P. Putnam's Sons hardcover edition / April 2010
Berkley trade paperback edition / March 2011

Berkley trade paperback ISBN: 978-0-425-23886-8

The Library of Congress has cataloged the G. P. Putnam's Sons hardcover as follows:

Franklin, Ariana.
A murderous procession / Ariana Franklin.
p. cm.
ISBN 978-0-399-15628-1
1. Aguilar, Adelia (Fictitious character)—Fiction. 2. Women physicians—Fiction. 3. Henry II, King of England, 1133–1189—Fiction. I. Title.
PR6064.O73M87 2010 2009036949
823'.92—dc22

PRINTED IN THE UNITED STATES OF AMERICA

10 9 8 7 6 5 4 3 2 1

To my brother, Roger, and my sister-in-law, Ann

ONE

One

BETWEEN THE PARISHES OF Shepfold and Martlake in Somerset existed an area of no-man's-land and a lot of ill feeling.

Just as the nearby towns of Glastonbury and Wells were constantly at odds, so did these two small villages dispute over whose pigs had a right to graze on the beech mast of the intervening forest, which stream was diverted to irrigate whose crops, whose goats trespassed over the boundary and ate whose laundry, etc., etc.

Today, Lammas Saturday, after a fine summer that had enabled the harvest to be brought in exceptionally early, the two sets of villagers, everybody who could walk and even some who couldn't, faced each other across this strip of ground on which had been erected a dais to accommodate Lady Emma of Wolvercote (her manor was in Shepfold), her husband, and Sir Richard de Mayne (his manor was in Martlake), the two parish priests, an Arab doctor, his attendant, an elderly woman, and a ball the size of a good pumpkin consisting of tough leather stitched over a globe of withies stuffed with sawdust.

Father Ignatius (Shepfold) made the last of many appeals to prevent what was going to happen.

"My lady, Sir Richard, it is not too late to avert this evil and send all home. . . . The sheriff has specifically banned . . ."

His protest fell on stony ground. Staring straight ahead, Sir Richard said: "If Shepfold is prepared to be humiliated yet again, who am I to disappoint it."

Lady Emma, also refusing to turn her head, breathed heavily through her pretty nose. "This year it will be Martlake who is humiliated." Master Roetger, the tall German leaning on a crutch beside her, gave her an approving and husbandly pat on the back.

Father Ignatius sighed. He was an educated and civilized man. Tomorrow, Sunday, he thought, these people will dress in their best to bring sheaves and fruit to church and give thanks to God for His infinite bounty as was right and proper. But always, by some hideous tradition peculiar only to them, on the day before Harvest Festival they revert to paganism and turn the eve of a Christian festival into something resembling the excesses of a Lupercalia. *A madness.*

Adelia Aguilar sighed with him and mentally ran through the medical equipment she'd brought with her—bandages, ointments, needles, sutures, splints.

It would be nice to think they weren't going to be needed, but hope was outweighed by experience.

She looked up at the tall Arab eunuch standing beside her. He shrugged, helplessly. Sometimes England baffled them.

They'd traveled a long way together. Both of them born in Sicily, that melting pot of races; she, an abandoned baby, probably Greek, rescued and brought up by a Jewish doctor and his wife; he, later taken into the same good household to be her attendant, once a lost boy with a beautiful voice whom the Latin Church had castrated so that he might retain it.

Circumstances—well, that damned King Henry II of England really—had plucked the two of them away from Sicily and dropped them down in his realm. And now, seven extraordinary years later, here they both were, on a bare piece of land in Somerset with two villages out to maim each other in what they called a game.

"I just don't understand the English," she said.

Gyltha, standing on the other side of her, said, "Somerset folk ain't proper English, bor." Gyltha was a Cambridgeshire woman.

"Hmm."

For God's sake, she was a trained doctor, a specialist in autopsy, a *medica* of the Salerno School of Medicine in Sicily—probably the only foundation in Christendom to take women as students—*and this is what I've come down to*.

It wasn't even that she could officially practice her craft. In England? Where the Church regarded a woman with medical knowledge as a witch?

Ostensibly Mansur had to be the one attending the wounded while she must seem to be carrying out his orders—a thin pretense but one that saved her from ecclesiastical punishment; also one to which, trusting them both, the two villages paid affectionate lip service.

The crowd was becoming restive. "For love of Mary, get *on* with it," somebody called out, "afore us bloody melts."

It *was* getting hot, early morning though it was. The sun that had ripened wheat and barley so beautifully was now slanting on yellow-white stubble in which rooks pecked up such corn as the gleaners had left them, brightening the forest beeches where some leaves were already showing autumn colors. On the balk strips, bees and butterflies were making free among trefoils and cornflowers.

Father Ignatius gave in and turned to his fellow priest, Father John. "To you the honor this year, sir, if honor it be."

Father John, a Martlake man and therefore a lout, picked up the ball, raised it above his head, shouted: "God defend the right," and threw it.

"That wasn't straight," Father Ignatius yelled. "You favored Martlake."

"Bloody didn't."

"Bloody did."

Nobody paid attention to the scuffling priests. The game had begun. Like great opposing waves, and with much the same noise, the two sides crashed together, their women and offspring skittering around the edges, screaming them on.

A Martlake boy emerged from the scrum, the ball at his twinkling feet, and began running with it in the direction of the Shepfold parish boundary, a mob of howling Shepfoldians at his back. Lady Emma, Sir Richard, and Master Roetger followed more sedately, while Adelia, Gyltha, and Mansur, carrying their medicaments, accompanied by Adelia's six-year-old daughter and Emma's four-year-old son, Lord Wolvercote, brought up the rear.

They paused at a safe distance to watch the scrimmage as the Martlake lad was brought down.

"There goes his nose," Mansur remarked. "Is it not against the rules to kick in the face?"

"Better get the swabs out," Gyltha said.

Adelia delved into her doctor's bag. "What rules?" There were supposed to be some; no swearing, no spitting, no picking the ball up and carrying it, no gouging, no biting, no fisticuffs, no women nor children nor dogs to partake, but Adelia hadn't seen any of them observed yet.

Gyltha was lecturing Adelia's daughter. "You listen to me, dumpling, you get into a fight this time, an' I'll tan your little backside."

"That's right, Allie," Adelia said. "No brawling. You and Pippy are not to take part, do you understand me?"

"Yes, Mama. Yes, Gyltha."

By the time she'd dealt with the Martlake broken nose, children, ball, and contestants had disappeared. Distant howls were suggesting that the match was now in the forest. On its edge, Adelia's old friends, Will and Alf, were lounging against a tree, waiting for her to come up.

"Go home," she told them—they were Glastonbury men. "Don't get involved, I won't have enough bandages."

"Just come to watch, like," Will told her.

"Observers, we are," Alf said.

She looked at them with suspicion; they'd been hanging around her a lot lately. But there was no time to inquire; screams from amongst the trees suggested that there were wounded. They followed her in.

A broken leg, two twisted ankles, a dislocated shoulder, and five scalp wounds later, the supply of injuries temporarily dried up. Mansur hoisted the protesting broken leg over his shoulder and set off to take it home to its mother. Gyltha was mopping up Allie. The noise had dwindled to isolated shouts. People were beating the undergrowth.

"What are they doing now, in the name of God?" Adelia asked.

"Lost the ball," Will said, laconically.

"Good."

But her eye fell on a Martlake woman with a bulging midriff under her smock who was wending her way smartly along a nearby badger track. "Where are you going, Mistress Tyler?"

"Back home, in't I? 'Tis too much for I what with the baby due and all."

For one thing, Mistress Tyler had shown no sign of pregnancy while in church on the previous Sunday. For another, the badger track led in the direction of Shepfold. For a third, Lady Emma was Adelia's good friend—so that, despite her pretension to neutrality, Adelia really wanted Shepfold to win. "You put that ball down," she shouted. "You're cheating."

Mistress Tyler, holding tight to her protuberant and wobbling waistline, began to run.

Adelia, chasing after her, failed to hear the *whoomph* of an arrow burying itself in the tree beside which, a second before, she'd been standing.

Will and Alf looked at it, looked at each other, and then hurled themselves in the direction from which the flight had come.

It was useless; the marksman, having chosen a clear shot,

had made it his only one before melting into a forest in which a hundred assassins could be hiding.

Returning to the tree, Will pulled the arrow out with some effort. "Look at that, Alf."

"We got to tell her, Will."

"We got to tell somebody." They had a high regard for Adelia, who had twice saved them from a desperate situation, but, though agonized for her safety, they'd also wanted to preserve her peace of mind.

They advanced to where she was tussling with Mistress Tyler. At that moment, the ball fell to the ground from under the Martlake woman's skirt—and was spotted.

Before the two Glastonbury men could reach their heroine, she and her opponent had been overwhelmed by a pile of players. In trying to get her out, Will and Alf lost their temper and put their fists and boots at the disposal of the Shepfold team.

So did Adelia . . .

Some five minutes later, a familiar voice addressed her from its height on a magnificent horse: "Is that you?"

Muddy and panting, Adelia extricated herself to look up into the face of her lover and the father of her child. "I think so."

"G'day, Bishop," said Mistress Tyler, trying to restore order to her smock.

"And a good day to you, madam. Who's winning?"

"Martlake," Adelia told him, bitterly. "They're cheating."

"Is that the ball?" Seated in his saddle, the Bishop of Saint Albans pointed to where a round object shedding pieces of bracken had flown up from a group of fighting players.

"Yes."

"Thank God, I thought it was somebody's head. Hold my horse." Dismounting, flinging off his cloak and hat, Rowley waded in. . . .

THAT NIGHT THERE was weeping and gnashing of teeth in the parish of Martlake while, three miles away in Shepfold, a limp piece of leather was carried high on a pole into the great barn of Wolvercote Manor with all the pomp of golden booty being brought back to Rome by a triumphant Caesar.

Outside, carcasses of pigs and sheep turned on spits and hogsheads spouted the best ale to all who would partake of it. The lady of Wolvercote herself, limping slightly, deftly flipped pancake after pancake from the griddles into the hands of her villagers while her husband, who had used his oak crutch with effect during the match, poured cream onto them.

The bard, Rhys, another attachment to Lady Emma's household, had abandoned his harp for a vielle and stood, sweating and bowing away, in the doorway so that parents and children danced to his tune in long lines around the victory fires. Beyond, in the shadow of trees, young bodies rolled in celebratory copulation.

Inside the barn, Adelia sternly regarded the Bishop of Saint Albans sitting beside her daughter—and his—on a hay bale, the resemblance between father and child enhanced by the black eye sported by each. "Look at you. I hope you're both ashamed of yourselves."

"We are," Rowley said. "But at least we didn't kick Mistress Tyler."

"*Did* she?" Allie was charmed. "Did Mama kick Mistress Tyler?"

"Hard."

"I'll fetch some pancakes," Adelia said, and then, over her shoulder: "She kicked me first."

While she was gone, Will, holding a mug of ale, came up to ruffle Allie's hair and doff his cap to her father. "I was wondering if as I could have a word, Bishop. Outside, like . . ."

Adelia took Allie back to bed through the weave of dancers, bidding good nights, throwing a kiss to Mansur who was executing his sword dance for Gyltha, the love of his life and Allie's nurse.

For perhaps the first time in her life, she realized, she was content.

When, eight years ago, the King of England, who was troubled by a series of unexplained killings in his county of Cambridge, had sent to his friend, the King of Sicily, begging for a master in the art of death from the famed School of Medicine in Salerno, it was Vesuvia Adelia Rachel Ortese Aguilar who'd been chosen to go.

It had occurred neither to the Sicilian king nor to the school that they had made an odd choice; Adelia was the best they had.

However, her arrival in England, where women doctors were anathema, had caused consternation.

Only by the subterfuge of Mansur pretending to be the medical expert and she merely his assistant and translator had Adelia been able to do her job by solving the murders—and done it so well that King Henry II had refused to allow her to return to Sicily, keeping her as his own special investigator.

Damn the man. True, England had given her the happiness of friends, a lover, and a child, but Henry's requirement of her had more than once put her in such danger that she'd been deprived of the tranquillity with which to enjoy them.

The Church had driven her and Allie, Mansur, and Gyltha from Cambridge, but Emma, out of gratitude for being allowed to marry as she pleased—a boon that Adelia had successfully begged the king to grant his rich young ward—had built her a house on the Wolvercote estate, thus giving her the first home of her own she'd ever had.

Gyltha and Mansur had settled down together—to everybody's surprise but Adelia's.

(In Sicily, it was not unusual for eunuchs to have a happy sexual relation with a woman—or another man, for that matter; castration didn't necessarily mean impotence. In England, where eunuchs were a rarity, that fact was unknown; it was thought merely that Mansur had a peculiarly high voice, and that he and Gyltha were just . . . well, peculiar.)

And for the last two years, Henry II had not interrupted this idyll by asking Adelia to do anything for him, might perhaps—oh joy—have forgotten her.

Even her fraught relationship with Rowley—begun during an investigation, and before the king had insisted on elevating him to a bishopric—had settled into a sort of eccentric domesticity, despite his extended absences as he toured his diocese. Scandalous, of course, but nobody in this remote part of England seemed to mind it; certainly Father Ignatius and Father John, both of them living with the mothers of their children, had not seen fit to report it to Adelia's great enemy, the Church. Nor was there a doctor for miles around to be jealous of her skill; she was free to be of use to suffering patients in this part of Somerset—and be beloved for it.

I have found peace, she thought.

She and Allie put the hens away for the night and released Eustace, Allie's lurcher, from the confinement that had been necessary to keep him from joining in the football match. "We beat Martlake, we beat Martlake," Allie chanted to him.

"And tomorrow we shall all be friends again," Adelia said.

"Not with that bloody Tuke boy, I won't. He poked me in the eye."

"*Allie.*"

"Well . . ."

The door to their house was open—it usually was—but the creak of a floorboard inside brought back unpleasant memories and Adelia clutched her daughter's shoulder to stop her from going in.

"It's all right, Mama," Allie said. "It's Alf, I can smell him."

So it was. Beating off Eustace's enthusiastic welcome, the man said: "You ought to keep this old door o' yours locked, missus. I saw a fox getting in."

Considering that it was dark and that Alf had been in the barn a hundred yards away, Adelia marveled at his eyesight. "Is it still there?"

"Chased it out." With that, Alf lurched off into the night.

Lighting a candle to escort her daughter upstairs to bed, Adelia asked: "Can you smell fox, Allie?"

There was a sniff. "No."

"Hmm." Allie's nose was unerring; her father had remarked

on it, saying that she could teach his hounds a thing or two. So, sitting beside her daughter, stroking her to sleep, Adelia wondered why Alf, most honest of men, had chosen to tell her a lie. . . .

IN EMMA'S ROSE GARDEN, the Bishop of Saint Albans held the arrow Will had given to him so tightly that it snapped. "*Who is it?*"

"We ain't rightly sure," Will said. "Never got a glimpse of the bastard, but we reckon as maybe Scarry's come back."

"Scarry?"

Will shuffled awkwardly. "Don't know as if she ever told you, but her and us was all in the forest a year or two back when we was attacked. Fella called Wolf, nasty bit of work he were, he come at her and Alf. He'd've done 'em both but, see, she had this sword and . . . well, she done him first."

"She told me," Rowley said, shortly. Jesus, how often he'd had to hold her shaking body to fend off the nightmares.

"Well, see, Scarry was there, he was Wolf's lieutenant, like. Him and Wolf they was . . ."

"Lovers. She told me that, too."

Will shifted again. "Yes, well, Scarry wouldn't've taken kindly to her a-killin' Wolf."

"That was two years ago, man. If he were going to take his revenge, why leave it for two years?"

"Had to fly the county, maybe. The king, he weren't best pleased at having outlaws in his forest. Cleaned it out proper, he did. Had 'em in bits hangin' off the trees. We hoped as Scarry was one of 'em, but now we ain't so sure acause if it ain't Scarry, who is it? She's well liked round here, our missus."

"And he's trying to kill her?"

"Don't know so much about that. He'd a'be wanting to frighten her to death first, that was more Scarry's style. Me and Alf, we been watchin' out for her, and we found an animal pit somebody dug along a path she takes often. Covered it was, but us filled un in. An' then Godwyn, him as owns the Pilgrim and takes her out regular to Lazarus Island to tend the lepers, well, last week, his punt began to sink when they was halfway there and the both of 'em had to make their way back on foot across the marshes, the which is always chancy acause of the quicksand. Alf and me, we poled out later and raised that punt to look at her and found a neat hole in her bottom, like someone'd taken a gimlet to her. We reckon as whoever it was'd filled the hole with wax, like. And then there was . . ."

But the Bishop of Saint Albans had left him and was striding toward Adelia's house.

Alf met him at the door. " 'S all right, master, I checked the rooms afore she came. Ain't nobody in there."

"Thank you, Alf. I'll take over now." And he would, Christ's blood he would. How many times did he have to rescue the wench before she saw reason?

The fear Rowley felt when Adelia was in danger always translated itself into fury against the woman herself. Why did she have to be what she was? (The fact that he might not have loved her if she hadn't been was invariably set aside.)

Why, when they'd been free to marry, had she refused him? Her fault . . . a babble about her independence . . . an insistence that she would fail as wife to an ambitious man . . . her damned fault.

No, she'd had it her own way and Henry II had immediately pounced on him, insisting that he become a bishop—well, the king had needed *one* churchman to be on his side after the murder of Archbishop Becket—and he, in his resentment and agony, had acceded. He still blamed her for it.

They'd been thrown together on investigations since and found that neither could live without the other—too late for marriage, though, celibate as he was supposed to be, so they'd finished up in this illicit relationship which gave him no rights over either her or the child.

But this was the end of it. No more investigations for her, no more touching the sick, no more lepers—*lepers*, God Almighty. She must finish with it. And for the first time he had the means to see that she did.

Raging though he was, Rowley had enough sense to consider how he would break it to her and stopped in the doorway to consider.

The two Glastonbury lads were right; she should not be told that there was an assassin after her—but they were right for the wrong reason. Rowley knew his woman; an assassin wouldn't scare her away from this country hole she'd dug herself into; *she'd refuse to go*. She'd spout her bloody duty to her bloody patients.

No, though he had an iron fist, he'd put a velvet glove on it, give her King Henry's orders as if they were inducements . . .

But he was still very angry and he didn't do it well. Going into her bedroom, he said: "Start packing. We're leaving for Sarum in the morning."

Adelia had prepared herself for something else. She was awaiting him in bed and, apart from a strip of lace over her dark blond hair, she was naked, bathed, and scented. Her lover was able to visit her so rarely that their encounters in bed were still rapturous. In fact, she'd been surprised to see him arrive on a Saturday; usually he was preparing for the next day's service in some far-flung church or another.

In any case, he never shared her bed on Sundays—a ridiculous decision perhaps, and certainly hypocritical, but one which, knowing how it weighed on him to preach abstinence to his flock while not practicing it himself, Adelia was prepared to countenance . . . and, after all, it wasn't midnight yet.

So, bewildered, she said: "*What?*"

"We're leaving for Sarum in the morning. I came to tell you."

"Oh, *did* you?" Not for love, then. "What for? And anyway, I can't. I've got a patient over in Street who needs me."

"We're going."

"Rowley, I am *not*." She began to grope for her clothes; he was making her feel foolish without them.

"Captain Bolt is coming to escort us. The king wishes it."

"Not again, oh God, not again." *Le roi le veult*. For Adelia, the four most doom-laden words in any language; there was no appeal against them.

Drearily, she poked her head through her smock and looked at him. "What does he want this time?"

"He's sending us to Sicily."

Ah, now that was different . . . "*Sicily?* Rowley, how wonderful. I shall see my parents. They can meet you and Allie."

"Almeison will not be coming with us."

"Of course she will, of *course* she will. I won't leave her behind."

"No. Henry's keeping her here to make sure you come back to him."

"But, Sicily . . . we could be away for a year or more. I can't leave her that long."

"She'll be well looked after. She can have Gyltha with her, I've seen to that. They'll be lodged with the queen at Sarum." This was both *suggestio falsi* and *suppressio veri* on Rowley's part. Henry Plantagenet would have been perfectly content for Allie to stay where she was, at Wolvercote in the care of Emma. It had been Rowley who'd begged him to allow the child to move in with Eleanor, and then got the queen to agree.

It was the only thing king and queen did agree on. Since Eleanor of Aquitaine had joined the rebellion—the *failed* rebellion—of the two older Plantagenet princes against their father, things had, to put it mildly, been strained between royal husband and wife.

Adelia put her finger on it. "Allie can't stay with Eleanor, the queen's in prison."

"It's a prison anyone would be happy to be in; she's denied nothing."

"Except freedom." There was something terrible here; he was frightening her. Panic restricted her throat and she went to the open window to breathe.

When she'd got her voice under control, she turned around. "What *is* this, Rowley? If I have to go . . . if I must leave Allie, she can stay here with Gyltha and Mansur. She's settled, she's happy here, she has her animals . . . she has an affinity with animals."

"My point exactly."

"She has an instinct, a genius . . . Old Marly called her in the other day when his hens got ill; she cured Emma's palfrey of the stifle when Cerdic couldn't. What do you mean . . . '*my point exactly*'?"

"I mean I want my daughter to have the feminine arts that Eleanor can teach her. I want her to become a lady, not a misfit."

"What you're saying is that you don't want her to grow up like me."

In his fear and anger and love, that was what it came down to. Adelia escaped him, she always had; there must be something of his that wouldn't get away.

"No, I don't, if you want to know. And she's not going to. I have a responsibility for her."

"Responsibility? You can't even publicly acknowledge her."

"That doesn't mean I don't care for her future. Look at you, look at what you wear . . ." Adelia was now fully clothed. "Peasant dress. She's a beautiful child, why hide her light under that dowdy bushel? Half the time she goes about barefoot."

It was true that Adelia was in homespun; she had agreed to become the bishop's mistress but, when it came to it, she'd drawn the line at being his whore. Though he urged money on her, she wouldn't take it and dressed herself out of her small earnings as a doctor. She hadn't realized until now how much that irritated him.

This wasn't about Allie, this was about her.

But she fought on the ground that he'd chosen, their daughter. "Education? And what sort of education would she get with Eleanor? Needlework? Strumming a lyre? Gossiping? Courtly blasted love?"

"She'd be a lady; I'm leaving her money; she can make a good marriage. I've already begun looking around for suitable husbands."

"*An arranged marriage?*"

"Suitable, I said. And only if she's willing."

She stared at him. They had loved each other desperately and still did; she thought she knew him, thought he knew her—now it appeared they understood each other not at all.

She tried to explain. "Allie has a gift," she said. "We couldn't exist without animals, to plough, to ride, pull our carriages, feed us. If she can find cures for what makes them ill . . ."

"An animal doctor. What life is that for a woman, for God's sake?"

The quarrel degenerated. When Mansur and Gyltha entered the house, it reverberated with the yells of two people verbally disemboweling each other.

". . . I have a right to say how my household should behave . . ."

". . . It's not your household, you hypocrite. The Church is your household. When are you ever here?"

"I'm here now and tomorrow we go to Sarum and Allie comes, too. . . . The king's ordered it. . . ."

". . . You made him do that? You'd give her into slavery . . . ?"

Gyltha hurried to Allie's room in case the child should be listening. Eustace, the lurcher, lifted his shaggy head as she came in, but Allie was sleeping the sleep of the innocent and unknowing.

Gyltha sat by her bed just in case and glanced with despair at Mansur, shaking his head in the doorway.

". . . I'll never forgive you. Never."

". . . Why? *You want her to end up killing a man like you did?*"

If he'd been in his senses, Rowley would not have said it. When the outlaw called Wolf had tried to kill her and she'd been forced to kill him instead, it had hung a millstone around Adelia's neck; time and again Rowley had reassured her that the monster was better dead; she had saved Alf's life as well as her own, there was nothing else she could have done, but still it weighed on her that she, who was sworn to preserve life, had taken one.

After that the voices stopped.

Gyltha and Mansur heard the bishop clump down the stairs to make up a bed for himself on a settle. Distressed beyond measure, they went to bed themselves. There was nothing to be done now.

The last revelers in the barn went home. Emma and Roetger returned to the manor house, their servants scattered to their various sleeping places.

Silence descended on Wolvercote.

ON A WATER BUTT *outside Adelia's window where it has been crouching in shadow, a figure stretches its cloaked arms so that, for a second, it resembles a bat unfolding leather wings ready to fly. Noiselessly it jumps to the ground, overjoyed with what it has heard.*

His God—and Scarry's god is not the Christians' God—has just granted him the boon of boons, as Scarry was sure He would, sooner or later. He has poured the elixir of opportunity into Scarry's hands.

For Scarry's hatred of the woman Adelia is infinite. During two years' enforced exile from England, he has prayed to be shown the means of her destruction. Now, at last, the stink of his loathing has reached Satan's nostrils and its incense has been rewarded.

Once, in a Somerset forest not too far from here, the woman killed Scarry's joy, his life, his love, his mate, his Wolf. And Scarry has come back, with Wolf howling him on in his head, to rend her to pieces. How stupidly he has done it; how ineffectual. Arrows, pits, attempts to frighten her; she hasn't even noticed; the two oafs who watch over her have seen to that.

Unworthy of an educated man, which is what Scarry is. A way of passing the time, really, until the true and only God should show him the way. Which he has, he has. Dominus illuminatio mea.

Wolf never killed a female until she was squirming in terror and pain—the only state in which Wolf, or he himself, could have sexual congress with the creatures. Timor mortis morte pejor.

"But now, Lord, in Your infinite wisdom, you have manifested to me all that I need to hear and see and learn that Your will and Wolf's may triumph. The woman shall be reduced by slow torture, so much more satisfying, chop, chop, piece by piece, a capite ad calcem.*"*

At this point Scarry is out of the view of the house, and he twirls as the shimmering, hot night enfolds him.

How curious that she didn't ask her lover why the king was sending her to Sicily.

But he, Scarry, knows. By a great coincidence—no, not coincidence but, manifestly, by the workings of the Horned God in whose hand he rests—Scarry is intimately cognizant of the journey the woman is about to take.

And will be going with her.

Two

Emma stood in Adelia's room wincing as she watched her friend furiously bundle clothes into a saddlebag. "My dear, you can't go in rags like those."

"I don't want to go at all," Adelia shouted. "I'll never forgive him, never." A veil tore on a buckle as it was pushed in with the rest.

"But you do realize *where* you're going?"

"Sicily, apparently. And without Allie."

"And *why* you're going?"

"God only knows, some scheme of Henry's. I tell you, Em, if I could take Allie, I'd stay there and never come back. Holding a child hostage . . . that's what they're doing, king and bloody bishop. I'll never . . ."

"You'll be accompanying Joanna Plantagenet to her wedding, so Rowley says." Seeing Adelia's incomprehension, Emma blew out her cheeks. "Henry's daughter? Marrying the King of Sicily? Lord, 'Delia, even you must know that. We're all being taxed for it, damn him."

A king was entitled to tax his people to pay for his daughter's wedding, but it didn't make him popular.

Adelia, whose few accounts were handled by Mansur and who listened to her patients' physical complaints rather than their excise grumbles, didn't know it.

She paused for a moment. "Joanna? She's just a baby."

"Ten, I believe."

"Poor little devil." The thought of another poor little devil to be groomed for a good marriage broke Adelia's anger and she sat down on her bed, almost weeping. "I'll not forgive him, Em, he's taking her away from me, and me away from her. Putting her in prison. And it *is* a prison, in more ways than one. My little one, my little one."

"Rowley has his reasons, I'm sure." Emma knew what they were—she'd heard them from the bishop himself only a few minutes ago.

"Oh, yes, marvelous reasons. He wants Eleanor to turn her into a . . . a prinking doll, drain her of all initiative."

Amused, Emma sat down beside her friend. She smoothed the silk of her gown over her swelling stomach. "My dear, whatever we think of a queen who fomented a rebellion against her king, we cannot accuse her of lacking initiative. Yet with it all, Eleanor keeps her femininity. She can teach Almeison a great deal."

"What, for instance?"

"To keep her fingernails clean, for one thing. Courtesy, poetry, music. These things are not unimportant. I yield to nobody in my admiration for your daughter, but . . . I have to say it, 'Delia . . . she is becoming farouche."

"*Farouche?*"

"She spends too much time with animals. During the football game, she punched one of the Martlake boys so hard he lost a tooth. A baby tooth, I grant you, but . . ."

"He blacked her eye," Adelia said, defensively.

"Yes, but . . . my dear, you're limiting her, don't you see?" This was a lecture Emma had been meaning to make for some time; now she settled down to it. "It may be that when Allie's older, she will want to marry well. The fact that she can deliver a punch is not recommended in politer families. Children must be prepared for their adult position. In a year or two, Pippy will have to leave me to become a page to the De Lucis and learn the skills of a knight. I shall miss him, miss him terribly, but it must be done if he is to take his place in society."

"It isn't the same," Adelia said. When young Lord Philip grew up, he would have the choice to explore his gifts, lead the life he wanted; his wife would have none.

Emma was fortunate in that this, her second marriage, was happy—her first had been enforced—but legally Roetger, as her husband, controlled the wealth she'd brought to it. Again legally, he could turn her out without a penny, was entitled to beat her—as long as he used only reasonable force—take her children away, and there would be nothing she could do about it. That Roetger wouldn't do any of these things rested solely on the fact that he was a decent man.

And while Emma's life of household management and entertaining suited her, it wouldn't suit Adelia. Nor, she knew, would it suit her daughter.

"We're helpless, we women," she said, defeated.

Emma, who didn't feel helpless at all, patted her. "It's only for a year, then you can be reunited—Rowley has agreed to that." She stood up, brisk. "Now there's just time to furnish you decently for the journey. I'm going to pack some of my own clothes for you in a proper traveling box. My dear, you'll be voyaging with a princess of England in the company of very important people. We don't want to appear shabby, do we?"

So it was that at midday Adelia, looking elegant for once, and her daughter, considerably less so but with clean fingernails, rode out from Wolvercote Manor with an escort of Plantagenet soldiers, Gyltha, Mansur, and a lover to whom she still wasn't speaking.

Emma, standing with Roetger at the great gates to wave her off, was beset by a sudden qualm. "Pray God in His mercy send them safe."

In the lane outside, watching the departure, two Glastonbury men heard her prayer.

"Amen to that," Will said, crossing himself.

SCARRY IS RIDING *along the same road that Adelia Aguilar is taking at that moment, though well ahead of her. Unlike her, he is not heading for Sarum but for Southampton, where he will join the company that she, too, must join before they take ship for Normandy.*

Scarry hates that company, as he has hated his father, his mother, the prior of his seminary, everybody who hated him in turn for not being an ordinary mortal and taught him to hide it under his brilliance. Once more, he must mop and mow and play the idiot. Once more, he will know the constriction of assumed piety.

But for the moment, he is smiling because he is passing the spot where he first encountered his Wolf. His Road to Damascus, this road between Glastonbury and Wells. Then he'd been going the other way, on a dreary pilgrimage with his prior and other dreary souls to worship Glastonbury's saints. As always he was concealing his hatred like a shameful, tumescent pustule, while a worm nibbled his brain, and the voice in his head chanted other, profane words to the hymns they sang as they went.

Yes, my lord prior, no, my lord prior, let us kneel before each wayside shrine as we go, praising a Deity that undoubtedly exists but not in the form you say he does; a God who knows only how to condemn, whose loving Word is a lie.

They had been benighted, the road longer than they'd reckoned; they'd been afraid of the dark forest around them and were reciting Psalm 91 to avert the terror by night, as if regurgitating falsehoods however beautiful, however reassuring, could protect the credulous. When had their God ever shown the mercy He promised?

Then, out of the dark trees had come the terror, not blackness but light in the form of capering, semi-naked men, outlaws bearing torches and swords, laughing as they robbed and killed.

In recollection, Scarry laughs with them. Some of his fellow pilgrims had got away but he'd stood still, bemused, not so much terrified as amazed by the killers' liberation from the restraint that Christianity demanded.

Their leader—Wolf, my darling, my zest—had stuck his sword into the prior's belly and, as he stripped the jeweled cross from the neck, had looked up, grinning, into Scarry's eyes.

Recognition had leaped between them, two souls connected since long before the Great Pretender had been crucified, a lightning bolt that had burst the pustule and released Scarry from its pain.

The demand had been made. Scarry can no longer recall whether it issued from Wolf's mouth or was spoken by this new God manifesting Himself in the mingled shrieks of mirth and terror of that moment.

Come with me and I shall set you free. *What blasphemy, what a glorious overthrowing. What liberation.*

And he, Scarry, had answered the call. With his eyes fixed on those of this wild and marvelous creature, he had lifted his knee and stamped his boot down hard into the face of his whimpering prior, silencing the old fool and his God forever.

Then he and Wolf had danced away, the others following with the booty, leaving the road for a scented, untracked forest where they could suck the honey from each other's body, and where no law ran except their own, no rites but those due to the satanic leaf-green, goatlike God they worshipped. Male maenads they had been, ad gloriam, *horned beasts of a horned deity, rending living animals and humans into pieces, raping, robbing, unstopped, unstoppable, feared and unfettered, their psalms the shrieks of the dying, their altar a butcher's block.*

Until she came. She and the jackasses with her, searching for erstwhile, lost companions that had been rotting in the leaf mold of a glade where they'd been slung days before, once he and Wolf had finished with them.

He can see her in that glade now, can Scarry; innocuous, worthless, like all females, yet, like all females, inspiring the godlike, lustful, exultant rage that must be slaked on her flesh as he'd wished to slake his on his mother.

Mirabile visu. *A fawn caught in the thicket.*

"First me and then you, eh, Scarry?" Wolf had said lovingly.

"You and me, Wolf, you and me." It was how it had always been.

And, while Scarry pranced and watched, Wolf advanced on the offering, telling her what had been done to those she'd come looking for; the enter-

tainment they'd provided before they'd died, the rapture of their bleating. Is agnus, ea caedes est.

Then, unbelievably, a piece of iron had connected her and Wolf, not a penis but a sword she'd had hidden. It linked them, the hilt in her hand, its point in Wolf's chest.

Now Scarry, as he rides, weeps and whispers what had been his cry as he'd gathered the coughing, bubbling, beloved body in his arms. "Te amo. *Don't leave me, my Lupus. Come back.* Te amo! Te amo!" *But Wolf died that night, and the Horned Being with him.*

Later, she'd sent soldiers who'd cleared the forest and hung severed pieces of Wolf's pack from its branches.

Not Scarry, though. Using the woodcraft Wolf had taught him, he'd slipped away, to track and kill her who'd expelled him from his Garden of Eden. But she'd been too well guarded.

Eventually, desolate, a lost lamb, he'd been forced to return to the fold of the Christian God who'd triumphed, pretending he'd escaped from the outlaws' attack on the pilgrimage, so jarred by its savagery and the murder of the good prior that he'd become a hermit in the wilderness for a while, beseeching mercy for himself and the souls of the dead.

They'd believed him. They'd rewarded him for his piety. His high connections had given him responsibility in which he had acquitted himself.

For, see, Scarry is now a shade that can adapt itself to its surroundings, blending with the devout, his prayers more pure than any others, his rant against sin louder than a trumpet. He feigns a naïveté that charms.

For two years he has played his enforced role as an innocent in the virtue of Christian life, suffering it, hating it. But horned Gods do not die, and neither do their Chosen Ones. These last days, in his return to the forest, Wolf has taken up residence in Scarry's brain, reminding him of their glorious abandonment and of the woman who ended it. "Bring her down," Wolf says. "Kill her in My Name. You have the means."

"I have, beloved. I shall."

IT HAD BEEN ARRANGED between bishop and king that they should meet at Sarum Castle, but, as Rowley's party rode along one of the straight Roman tracks that led to its hilltop across a wilting Wiltshire Plain, they saw a rider galloping toward it on yet another, with more men on horses tearing after as if they were pursuing him before he could reach its safety.

His clothes were nondescript, and in the speed of his going, his short cloak was blown parallel to his horse's back.

"Henry," Rowley said with admiration and dug in his spurs to meet up with the King of England.

By the time Adelia and the others joined them, the two men had dismounted and were in conversation. Adelia saw no reason to interrupt them and stayed on her palfrey, but the king strode over, took its reins to lead her apart.

He didn't greet her, he rarely did, as if there was a special relationship between them that found courtesy unnecessary; it had little to do with sexual attraction—though there was a breath of that—more with the sense of equality he extended to her. Which could be charming but which Adelia, chafing under it today, decided was spurious; he merely had a regard for those who proved useful to him.

As she always did when he called on her, she thought: *I'm a Sicilian, I am not his subject. I can refuse to do what he wants.*

And knew, again, that she was helpless; she was in England, he was its king and refused to give her a passport, thus imprisoning her in a country that had trapped her even further during the years she'd spent in it by winding tentacles of love and friendship around her.

He extended a calloused hand and helped her down from her horse. "I gather the good Bishop of Saint Albans hasn't told you why you're summoned."

"No." Damned if she was going to "my lord" him, being no more pleased with him than she was with Rowley.

"Lovers' quarrel?" Henry showed his ferocious little teeth; he delighted in her illicit relations with his favorite bishop.

Adelia said nothing.

He kept on walking so that they progressed farther and farther away from the group behind them. "You're to accompany Princess Joanna to her wedding in Sicily."

"If I can take my daughter with me, I shall be delighted," she said. Get the rules established from the beginning. Then, because she couldn't resist knowing, she said: "Why?"

"To keep an eye on her health, woman, why else? I'm investing a lot in this marriage. I want the child to arrive in Palermo not only safe but well."

"The princess surely has her own medical adviser."

Henry II snorted. "She's got Eleanor's. As I remember he's the fat bastard who cut out the fistula on my arse when we were in Poitiers and turned it putrid. Couldn't ride for days. Eleanor has no judgment when it comes to doctors; she's never been ill in her life."

"There must be better ones."

"There's you. Or rather, officially there's Mansur. You two

can play your usual game. Winchester will be leading the party, a saintly man, and a good bishop, but not broadminded enough to accept a female as a doctor."

"He's broadminded enough to accept an *Arab?*"

The king displayed his teeth again. "He balked a bit, but I told him. 'You wait 'til you get to Sicily,' I said. 'You'll be hobnobbing with Jews, Saracens, plus various other heretics—and all of them government officials. Get used to it,' I said."

Aha, she'd found the weakness in his plan. She said: "What you have overlooked, Henry, is that when I pose as Mansur's assistant, most people take me for his mistress—and the Bishop of Winchester's not likely to let a trollop near the princess."

"Oh yes he will. I've preserved your virtue . . ." He paused. ". . . such as it is. I've told him that the Lord Mansur is a eunuch with a perfectly respectable female assistant who interprets for him. Our good bishop needn't be made aware of the fact that Mansur speaks better English than he does. The poor old bugger blinked, but he knows eunuchs aren't capable of pleasuring trollops—or any other woman come to that."

"They are, actually," Adelia said.

The king ignored her. She received a nudge in her ribs. "I'm even giving you and Mansur a nice fat purse of money to go with you."

That was a novelty. Henry counted every coin.

When she didn't respond, he said: "Thought of everything, haven't I?"

"About my daughter . . ."

Apparently, he didn't hear her. "There's another matter I

want you to keep an eye on. . . . You remember a certain sword you found in a cave on Glastonbury Tor two years ago and gave to me?"

"Excalibur?"

"For God's sake, woman. Hush, will you?" The king looked back, but the two of them had progressed out of earshot of the group behind them.

"Excalibur?" Adelia said more quietly.

"Yes, well, that's proved another pain in the arse. I should never have put the damned thing on display. The new Abbot of Glastonbury wants it back, Canterbury says it's theirs, the Welsh are wittering for it, even the Holy Roman Empire is claiming it as a right, God knows why. And the Pope wants me to go on crusade with it, as if waving it around will bring the bloody infidels to their knees saying sorry."

Despite herself, Adelia was disarmed; he could always make her laugh and admire; only this Plantagenet could call the most famed sword in Christendom a pain in the arse.

So far he'd managed to resist papal attempts to make him join other rulers fighting in the Holy Land; he said he had enough trouble holding together an empire of which England was only a small part, the rest of it running from the border of Scotland to the Pyrenees.

He'd told her once: "Go on crusade and some bugger pinches your throne whilst your back's turned."

Adelia's acquaintanceship with Excalibur had been equally fraught. Not realizing at the time that the skeleton she'd found in a little tomb deep in the rock of Glastonbury Tor was King

Arthur's—knowledge and proof had come later—nor that the sword lying nearby was his, she'd been holding the dirty, encrusted but still sharp weapon when she'd been attacked.

She'd raised it to defend herself—it had seemed to leap in her hand of its own accord—and Wolf, that would-be rapist and killer, had speared himself on it.

In the end, they'd left Arthur's quiet bones undisturbed, but Excalibur she'd given to Henry, another king who, for all his faults, was bringing an enlightenment and order to his little realm of England which, apart from the Kingdom of Sicily, her home, existed nowhere else in the world.

The murder of Thomas à Becket, apparently at the king's instigation, had cast a shadow over the Plantagenet's reign but, in the opinion of some—including Adelia—that intransigent archbishop had deliberately sought martyrdom by opposing every reasonable reform Henry had tried to introduce for his people's good. If anybody should inherit that symbol of the Arthurian legend, she'd thought at the time, it was Henry II.

Now he would give it away.

However, she saw that he was in difficulty, and said so.

"I hope you do," he told her. "That artifact conveys power. It's like the Holy Grail. Anybody who has it can claim to be the descendant of Arthur, defender of Christianity against the forces of darkness, and have thousands flocking to his banner." He paused and for the first time in their acquaintance, Adelia saw him embarrassed. "There are . . . princes . . ." He took a breath. "Certain princes who'd like to get their hands on it, a contingency that would be . . . unwise."

Princes? And then she thought: *Dear God, he means his sons.*

Young Henry had already made one attempt to overthrow his father and it was said that the younger boy, Richard, was even more ambitious for power than his brother.

The king became brisk. "Anyway, I'm sending it with Joanna to give to my future son-in-law and good luck to him. He's an ally, bless him, and he's fighting the same enemy as I am. He'll need Excalibur. . . ."

"What enemy?" She hadn't heard that Sicily was at war with anyone.

He hesitated, then he said: "It's a battle of wills, not arms. You'll see when you get there."

"Very well, my lord," Adelia prompted. "But why is this my concern?"

"Because you're taking it with you. Well, not you personally; I'm having it put inside a cross and given to someone else to carry." Adelia got another royal nudge in the ribs. "I'm told you'll be pleased by my choice of crucifer. He's a surprise for you."

"Thank you. But, again, how is that my concern?"

"You're to use your wits, woman; you've got plenty of them. It's going to be a hazardous enough journey with all the treasure I'm sending to William as dowry . . . God's entrails, but this wedding is ruining me." Henry winced in pain; he hated expending money. "However, politically, the one thing I *cannot* afford is that Excalibur should fall into the wrong hands on the way."

"But if you're disguising it . . ."

The king turned to look across the sun-drenched sweep of the plain to the sudden rise of ground on which stood the towers that imprisoned his wife. "The world is changing, mistress," he said, and his voice was bleak. "The numbers of those I can trust are dwindling. Spies and ill-wishers gather to bring me down, some of them in my own household." His energy came back. "I hope that the only ones who will know what the cross contains are you, Saint Albans, of course, Mansur, Captain Bolt, and the crucifer himself. Five of you. But we can't rely on that."

"My lord, I still don't see . . ."

"Well, I do," he said. "You have a nose, mistress; it can smell a rat in the privy better than any I know. Should there be anyone in Joanna's train, *anyone*, with an untoward interest in what the crucifer is carrying, I want him sniffed out and reported to Bolt so that my good captain can string him up by his balls and find out who he's working for."

Adelia glanced sideways at him, curious and a little alarmed. This was Byzantine reasoning; the revolt of his wife and son was making him overly suspicious if the only one he could put his trust in was her disadvantaged self.

However, she might as well capitalize on obsession. "I shall keep a keen lookout, my lord, and who will suspect me if I am accompanied by my daughter . . . ?"

"Oh, no, you don't," he said. "I'm keeping that child as an assurance . . ."

"A hostage," she shouted at him.

". . . an *assurance* that you'll come back. She stays. You go. *Do you understand?*"

Le roi le veult. She floundered in helplessness, never resenting anyone so much; no wonder Eleanor and Young Henry had rebelled. He wasn't *her* king, either; she was a Sicilian subject.

Perhaps he realized it, for he began wheedling. "Rowley

has arranged for her to stay with Eleanor while you're away, so think how the child will prosper; Eleanor has a way with girls." He pointed to a small figure that had rambled off. "Is that her? Introduce me."

Allie had found a dewpond and was kneeling in it, studying something on one of the rushes while the dog Eustace cavorted in its water.

"That's a pretty butterfly, isn't it?" Henry said. If Eleanor was good with girls, he was awkward.

Without looking up, Allie hushed him. "Not a butterfly. It's a damselfly, a common blue," she said, "eating a leafhopper."

Oh dear. Retrieving her dripping child, Adelia thought defiantly: *Well, how many little girls can identify insects?*

And heard Emma's reply: *How many would want to?*

IT WAS SAID that the giants who'd built Stonehenge had also raised the great circular earthwork on which Sarum stood. If so, they had commanded the River Avon in a panorama that spread for miles in every direction and which no enemy could approach without being seen.

To climb the opening that led steeply upward between high, stepped banks was not only to leave a world of grass for that of stone but to pass from one sort of air to another. Where, below, the women's veils had drooped, up here, on the bridge waiting for the portcullis to be raised, they fluttered in a strong breeze. It was always windy at Sarum.

Though the cathedral rose higher than the castle, only the

gargoyles on its roof and soldiers patrolling the ramparts had the advantage of a view; at ground level the surrounding walls blocked in the little city as if they held it captive.

Certainly the cathedral's monks felt that they, like Queen Eleanor, were imprisoned. As the portcullis went up for the king, a number of them tried to rush under it to gain the bridge outside. They were held back, none too gently, by sentries.

A richly dressed, rock-faced official bowed to the king. "Welcome, my lord."

"All well, Amesbury?"

"All well, my lord." The castellan looked venomously toward the monks. "Except for them. They keep trying to get out."

"Why shouldn't they?"

Amesbury was taken aback. "Because . . . my lord, because they are against us, *you*. The cathedral favors the queen; they could be taking secret messages to her supporters, engineering her escape, anything."

Henry strolled over to the most vociferous of the monks. "Where do you want to go?"

"The river." The man waved a fishing rod. "It is Friday, we need fresh fish, the dear queen needs it. All that monster there allows us is dried herring."

"Off you go, then."

The monk stared for a moment, unbelieving, and then, with his companions, bolted for the bridge. Amesbury hissed with disapproval.

Engineering the queen's escape would be a considerable feat, Adelia thought as she and the others followed Henry Plantagenet across a moat, under the shadow of portcullises, and through guarded gates until they reached the castle bailey and the heart of this tiny city. Like all town centers, it contained a busy market but, again, Adelia felt suffocation; only the wind was free, managing to swoop over the palisade to rattle the calico covers of the stalls and send the Plantagenet pennant on the roof beating against its pole as if it hated it.

Eleanor met them on the steps to the keep. "My lord."

"My lady."

King and queen gave each other the kiss of peace with apparent affection.

"Maudit." Eleanor snapped her fingers at Amesbury. "Refreshment for my guests."

"Amesbury, madam," the castellan pleaded. "I tell you, my name is Robert of Amesbury."

"Really?" Eleanor looked interested. "I wonder why I keep thinking it's Maudit."

Adelia felt Mansur touch her arm. "Maudit?"

"It means accursed," she muttered back.

"Ah."

The queen and the Bishop of Saint Albans were long acquainted, but her greeting to him was coldly formal—he was the king's man and always had been.

She was kinder toward Mansur: "My lord, I have instructed my daughter's doctor to welcome your opinion. I have held a high regard for Arab medicine ever since I went on crusade with my former husband."

The former husband had been the King of France—Eleanor, Duchess of Aquitaine, didn't marry just anybody. Ostensibly, the dissolution of that marriage had been because she'd given

Louis two daughters, not an heir, but Adelia privately thought that Eleanor had been too much of a handful for that pious and indecisive French monarch.

The queen waited until Adelia translated and Mansur had bowed, then turned to Adelia herself with warmth. "I recollect you very well from our time in Oxfordshire, Mistress Adelia. Together, we overcame demons, did we not? It is a comfort to me that you will be in attendance on my child for her journey. And this is to be my little ward whilst you are gone, is it?"

Allie, who'd been carefully instructed, behaved well and curtseyed as she should, though her mother could have wished her less wet and muddy.

Careful not to touch her, Eleanor smiled at the child before addressing the king. "Henry, our dress allowance will have to be raised."

The queen looked better than on the last occasion Adelia had seen her when, disguised as a boy, she'd been trying to escape her husband's soldiers; then male attire had accentuated her fifty-one years as opposed to Henry's forty. Despite having given birth to a total of ten children, she was once more elegant, slim, and poised. There was no complaint that she, consort to two kings, who'd ruled the great duchy of Aquitaine in her own right and traveled to the Holy Land with an entourage of Amazons, was facing a lifetime's incarceration; she might have been welcoming them to one of her own palaces.

Adelia knew her to be an impulsive, erratic woman with none of her husband's intellectual power—but what pride was here, and what stoicism.

The chilled white wine brought to the keep's second-floor

apartment was excellent, as were the accompanying little biscuits. A harper sat in one corner, singing a love song.

It was a fine room, to which Eleanor had contributed touches of color with Persian carpets, cushions, and Flemish tapestries, but candles had to counter the shade provided by the outside walls that kept the sun from its windows.

A pretty cage for an exotic bird, Adelia thought, but still a cage.

Her heart bled for her own nestling now to be confined in it—and for Gyltha, a woman who had lived her life under sweeping and untrammeled horizons as an eel-seller in Cambridgeshire's fenland. In fact, if Gyltha had not agreed to stay here with the child, Adelia would have bolted with both of them but, when consulted, Gyltha had said: "Little'un's too young to be lollopin' round foreign parts, bor, and I'm too old. Reckon as the queen'll have to put up with the two of us."

Immensely comforted, Adelia had kissed her. "She'll be lucky to have you."

And, indeed, as it turned out, Eleanor's staff had been so reduced that she welcomed Allie's nurse as an addition to it.

There was a sharp contrast between the two girls about to change places; Princess Joanna was a small facsimile of Eleanor in both dress and looks but without the lightning-bolt energy of either of her parents. Her little face was immobile. She kept close to a large, comfortable-looking woman in plain traveling dress, presumably her nurse.

There was a difference, too, in their leave-taking. Queen and princess kissed each other good-bye without emotion. Eleanor blessed her. "May your marriage be a happy one, my dear child, and may God and his sainted martyr Thomas à Becket have you in their keeping."

This was a shaft at the king and Eleanor drove it home with a happy smile at her husband. "Saint Thomas is our daughter's especial saint. She prays to him every night, do you not, my child?"

"Yes, madam."

Adelia and Allie's parting had to be equally short—the king wanted to reach Southampton next day. Adelia was nearly undone by her daughter's stricken facc; she'd tried to prepare the child during the journey to Sarum, but it was obvious that the reality had only now sunk in. Kneeling down so that they were on a level, she said: "Allie, I love you more than anything in the world. I wouldn't be leaving you unless I had to. The queen has much to teach you but always remember that you are already splendid in my eyes."

Oddly enough, it was Amesbury, with unexpected kindness, who saved them both from breaking down. Adelia had seen Rowley talking to him.

Lapsing into a Wiltshire accent, the castellan bent down toward Allie as she fought to keep her lips from quivering. "Do ee know what I got in the palace mews, my beauty?"

Allie shook her head.

"Kestrel. Fine young brancher and looking for a young lady as'll train un to the fist."

Allie held her breath. "I could do that, I help our austringer at home. I helped him mend a peregrine's tail feather with an imping needle."

"Did ee now? You're the one, then." The castellan/jailer

looked at Adelia. "I've got a young un, six he is, a keen falconer. She could come out to fly the bird with him and me across the plain."

Unable to speak her gratitude, Adelia grasped the man's hand.

Nevertheless, it was terrible to turn around as she rode away and see that small figure with Gyltha at her side, waving from the ramparts. Mansur didn't look back at all, but his silence suggested another parting that had been equally hard.

Rowley tried to engage her in encouraging conversation, but she wouldn't speak to him.

SCARRY IS ALREADY at Southampton; he can move fast when he wants to, can Scarry. He's wearing clerical dress today and is sitting in a back-street tavern near the Church of Saint Michael where, since it is a watering hole popular with the town's clerics and their visitors, he passes unnoticed.

In any case, he looks unremarkable because he's put on his bland face, the one he wears when he is involved in an act of betrayal. (Scarry has learned that to have no allegiance to kings or countries, or anyone but Wolf, can be profitable.)

Another man, not unlike him in dress, approaches the settle and table he has chosen in a dark corner of the tavern, says: "Good evening, master. Have you come far? May I join you?" His Latin has an accent from a country warmer than England. He calls for ale, a flagon for himself and one for Scarry, sits down, and taps his fingers on the table in a complicated rhythm.

Scarry taps back.

"We understand that Excalibur is on the move," the man says, like someone commenting on the weather. "The king is sending it to Sicily with his daughter."

Scarry inclines his head as if agreeing that it has indeed been a fine day.

"We want to . . . intercept it."

There is a pause while a tapster slams two tankards on their table, slopping them both, wishes them health, and waits.

"And this for you, my man," the agent says. "God bless you." A copper coin is passed over, neither of too much value nor too little.

"The treasure chests will be heavily guarded," Scarry says when the tapster goes.

"It won't be in the chests. At least, we don't think so. Too open to attack on the way. No, it's to be carried separately. Find out by whom, and there'll be a hundred gold pieces for you, twenty-five now and the rest on delivery."

With a slight thump, a purse slides down the man's sleeve and onto the table where it is instantly covered by his hand. Scarry puts out his own in an apparent pat of approbation and the switch is made.

"You understand? The sword is simply to disappear. It will not reappear until such time as its new owner is ready to unsheathe it. You will be contacted."

Scarry nods amiably. His companion is one of Duke Richard's agents; therefore, Scarry knows who, among the many people desirous of Excalibur, the new owner is to be. He doesn't care much. What are earthly kings and dukes to him? Mere purveyors of money. He has his own king.

He isn't even surprised that he is uniquely fitted to carry out the instruction; he is becoming used to his God's bounty in making easy arrangement for him.

For, two years ago, when, in his agony at Wolf's death, he was tracking the woman Aguilar, did he not see her coming down the Glastonbury Tor, reputed home of Arthur of Britain, with a man he now knows was the King of England?

Coiled in the long, warm grass, like an adder, he'd watched them.

The other man finishes his ale, stands, says loudly that he's happy to have made Scarry's acquaintance, and leaves.

Scarry doesn't watch him go. He is smiling, remembering . . .

Chatting like old friends, they'd been that day, Adelia Aguilar and Henry Plantagenet.

And King Henry, who'd gone up the hill unarmed, had come down it with a sword in his hand. . . .

Three

HENRY II WAS SAVING money; only Joanna's immediate court and servants would be sailing the Channel with her; the horses, grooms, cooks, laundresses, even some of the knights, soldiers, and others that were to form her marriage cavalcade overland were awaiting her in Normandy, the duchy Henry had inherited from William the Conqueror. It was cheaper than ferrying all of them over from England, though some of the treasure chests containing part of the dowry raised from the English would accompany her on the crossing.

He had, however, ordered Southampton Castle to lay on a farewell banquet for his daughter before she and the company caught the outbound tide. Even this, though, was less opulent than it might be—not so much because Henry had stinted, but because the castle servants and cooks knew, as did everyone else, that the king regarded time spent on eating course after course of food as time wasted.

Nevertheless, such dishes as were served at the great table in the castle's hall that evening were simple by most banqueting standards but of fine quality. So was the wine. From a gallery came the notes of viol and rebec as they accompanied a pure countertenor in song.

Halfway through, Henry Plantagenet stood up to raise his glass to Joanna.

"My lords, my ladies, gentlemen, may I commend to you this dutiful and excellent princess of England, Normandy, Anjou, Touraine, Aquitaine, Gascony, and Nantes who shall honor us and the Kingdom of Sicily by combining in her body these two great empires. May God be with her."

Everybody rose. There was a shout: "To Joanna."

The dutiful and excellent princess smiled her thanks.

The guests prepared to sit down again, ready to tuck into the spiced beef with oysters and battered egg dumplings that had arrived on the board.

But their king hadn't finished with them; he was still on his feet; they must remain on theirs. "As you know, our most beloved Bishop of Winchester will be leading the journey to Sicily . . ."

He bowed to a small, round, richly dressed man who was breathing hard from what appeared to be agitation, but stopped shifting long enough to bow back.

". . . and our well-beloved Bishop of Saint Albans with him."

Rowley bowed.

"Most of you in this company are well and happily acquainted with each other," Henry went on, "however, we have guests whom you have not yet encountered. I recommend to your friendship the Lord Mansur, who is highly versed in Arab medicine *and will be assisting our good Doctor Arnulf in everything connected with my daughter's health.*"

Henry had eyes that flared when he was particularly intent.

They flared now as they looked from the impassive face of the Arab to that of Eleanor's Dr. Arnulf, who wasn't taking this well.

But it was Father Guy, one of the Bishop of Winchester's two chaplains, who stood up, quivering with outrage and courage. "If I do not mistake me, my lord, the man is a Saracen, a *Saracen*. Would you give your daughter's well-being to one whose race is even now trampling the Holy Places?"

There was a general intake of breath, but Henry looked toward Mansur. "Lady Adelia, be so good as to ask my lord doctor if he has ever trampled a Holy Place."

Adelia translated.

"Tell that son of a she-camel to go and commit adultery with a monkey," Mansur said calmly, in Arabic.

Adelia turned back to the king and saw that, beside him, the Bishop of Albans, another Arabic speaker, was covering his mouth with his napkin.

"The lord doctor has never been to Jerusalem, my lord; he is Sicilian."

It wasn't *quite* true, but Henry didn't want the truth. Anyway, since the age of eleven Mansur had been brought up in her foster father's house in Salerno and was as Sicilian as she was.

"There you are, Father Guy," the king said. He turned to Dr. Arnulf. And waited.

After a little difficulty, Dr. Arnulf managed a smile and a bow. "Of course, my lord. Delighted, my lord. The Lord Mansur shall be consulted on all medical matters."

"*Yes, he shall*," Henry said with emphasis. "Unfortunately, as you see, Lord Mansur speaks no tongue apart from his own, but in this regard, I have been most fortunate to procure the service of the Lady Adelia, longtime a friend to myself and the queen, who speaks Arabic and will be present to interpret between you all. She was born in Sicily, as was the Lord Mansur, and therefore both of them will be able to provide guidance, which *I trust you to call on* when you reach that country."

Now it was the turn of Joanna's ladies-in-waiting to be flayed. "Since we were able to reach Lady Adelia only at the last minute when, due to misfortune, she was without an attendant, *I know that I can call on you*, Lady Beatrix, Lady Petronilla, and Mistress Blanche, to share your maidservants with her and provide her with all affection and daily comfort in your power."

He had given Adelia what status he could, but the stiff smiles and bows being accorded to her from across the table suggested that the three women who gave them weren't going to clasp her to their bosom any more than Dr. Arnulf intended to be Jonathan to Mansur's David.

"Also," the king said, "may I present to you the man who will sail you down the Mediterranean when you reach it, the Lord O'Donnell of the Skerries, my admiral. . . ."

Here was another stranger who'd been attracting glances of curiosity through dinner. With his black, curly hair tied in a plait and more showing at the open neck of his jerkin, the man didn't look like an admiral; he looked like a pirate. He had curiously long eyes as if he could face forward yet still see to the side; they had rested on Mansur with interest and even longer on Adelia, making her uncomfortable.

The company welcomed Admiral O'Donnell and prepared to sit down at last. But . . .

"It is by God's grace that the Lord O'Donnell was in this

country on business," continued the king, mercilessly. "We have not seen him these two years, yet in the past he and I have sailed through storms that would have foundered a lesser shipmaster. His fleet will be awaiting you at Saint Gilles, when you reach it, to sail you down the coast of Italy. And while on board, *he shall be obeyed in all maritime matters*."

Good. Good. The man looked a fine rogue to be accompanying them overland, but if his ships were sound when they reached them . . . And now could they proceed with dinner?

No, they couldn't.

"We owe our deep gratitude to our esteemed John, Bishop of Norwich, not only for his time and accomplishment in concluding the arrangements for our princess's marriage with Sicily but in traveling the route that you will be taking and choosing the hostelries and monasteries to accommodate you on the way, an endeavor that has taken him no less than two years."

Ah, their accommodation, yes, that was important. The company was pleased to toast the Bishop of Norwich. And now . . .

"*Also*," Henry said—he was enjoying this—"his nephew, Master Locusta Scaresdale, who accompanied him. Though Bishop John is returning to his diocese, Master Locusta has consented to be your outrider, going ahead to inform your various hosts of your arrival. I commend him to you."

Locusta? In Latin it meant lobster.

A dark-haired young man groaned. "William," Adelia heard him whisper. "My name's William."

"*Also*," the king said, "out of our charity and in the service of God, we have given our permission to certain devout pilgrims to the Holy Land that they may cross the Channel with you this evening and travel by land in the safety of my daughter's train."

Adelia's mouth twitched. Henry *loathed* pilgrims; they were exempt from paying any tax for the pilgrimage's duration and left a hole in his revenue.

The guests, however, nodded their heads at their monarch's piety even as they looked longingly at the board. . . .

"And, of course," the king added, "they will be on board the ships that take you into the Mediterranean. *I am sure* they will be extended every Christian kindness."

He took time with his head cocked on one side, seeming to wonder if there was more to say, reluctantly decided that there wasn't, and at last waved his guests to their food.

It was too late; the beef was cold and the dumplings had shriveled.

Even after the meal, the king's guests were expected to mingle amicably, which, under his gaze, they tried to do. Face after face appeared in front of Mansur and Adelia. Two of Henry's knights, Sir Nicholas Baicer and Lord Ivo of Aldergate, were gravely courteous; both of them weighty, more diplomats than fighters, they seemed unsurprised at Henry's choice of a Saracen doctor for his daughter—close servants of the Plantagenet eventually stopped being astonished at what he did.

Most of the other guests said polite things with a smile that didn't stretch to the eyes; ladies-in-waiting, the pirate-admiral, clerics.

Father Guy didn't bother to smile, though his colleague, Father Adalburt, did—but he smiled at everything to the point of simple-mindedness. He had never been out of England before, he told them.

"Is not this exciting? But how can you both be Sicilians when you are different colors?"

Adelia tried to explain the many cultures and races that the chaplain would encounter in Sicily. "You will find it a very different country from this, Father."

"Will I? But everybody there worships our Lord, I hope."

Patiently, Adelia explained that there were as many forms of religion as there were races.

This upset him. "*Ultima Thule*," he exclaimed. "And we take our dear princess there to marry? *Salvam fac reginam, O Domine*."

As they watched him scurry away, the Bishop of Saint Albans came up, grinning. "I see on your faces the look of people who've been talking to Father Adalburt."

"Where does such a buffoon come from?" Mansur asked in Arabic.

"Scar Fell, I believe. Somewhere in the Lake District, anyway."

"And why?"

"The Bishop of Winchester is his godfather and employs him out of charity. The thing to do is regard him as a holy fool and enjoy him. I do."

With meaning, Adelia said, "I am not enjoying anything."

"Not forgiven me yet, then?"

"No."

"You will. I'm too charming to withstand for long." He winked at her and walked off to talk to Lord Ivo.

The trouble is you are, Adelia thought. He was in plain clothes today, which suited him better than a bishop's regalia: thigh boots, swirling cloak, a peacock's feather in his cap. Big, strong, she never knew if he towered among other men in fact, or only in her eyes. Though, in working for the Plantagenet, they'd been through hell together, he'd always been able to make her laugh.

But not this time. In any case, their meetings and conversation would be restricted from here on in; he could hardly be seen to single out a woman who was apparently nothing to him. *Well, that suits me.*

The friendliest reception given to the Arab and Adelia came from Bishop John of Norwich and his nephew; having sojourned in Sicily for so long, they were eager to exchange experiences with two of its natives.

They'd made maps of Joanna's forthcoming route, which they were distributing, long thin scrolls of parchment like scarves on which were drawn each accommodating castle or hospice, the roads between them marked with the bridges, borders, and tolls to be encountered. Adelia and Mansur were asked for their approval.

Pleased to be consulted, the two Sicilians studied the map. "We're not going via the Alps, then?" Adelia asked.

That was the most straightforward route. Coming to England, she'd traveled it in reverse, by boat from Salerno up the Italian coast to Genoa, through the Mont Cenis pass into France and thence to the Channel.

Now, she saw, they would be going overland via the extreme west, hugging the edge of the Atlantic, down through Aquitaine, to Saint Gilles on the Mediterranean coast, where they'd board ship for Sicily. It would take longer and involve somewhat more time at sea—Adelia still remembered with discomfort the

Mediterranean storm that had nearly capsized the boat taking her to Genoa; she didn't like ocean voyages.

"We decided the route through Northern Italy would be a little too exciting for the princess, didn't we, my lord bishop?" Locusta said.

His uncle smiled back at him. "We did indeed. The peace between the Lombards and Barbarossa is a little too fragile; we can't allow Joanna into a war. From Saint Gilles you will travel by ship all the way to Sicily."

"I see. Then I think, my Lord Mansur thinks, that you have done excellently."

"Thank you." The bishop looked at his nephew. "Let us hope it goes according to plan for you, eh, Locusta?"

The young man sighed. "*Homo proponit, sed Deus disponit.* We can only hope."

Adelia smiled at the young man. "Locusta?"

"I was christened William, lady." He shook a finger in mock disapprobation at the bishop. "But it seems I emerged from the womb so angular and covered in black hair that my good uncle here nicknamed me for a lobster before it is boiled. Locusta I was and Locusta, I fear, I must remain."

At the door, the Bishop of Winchester was agitatedly telling Admiral O'Donnell, "But they are the wrong sort of boats. . . ."

Hearing disputation, Henry approached them. Adelia, about to leave the room, stopped to listen.

The bishop appealed to the king. "This person, my lord . . . I have been to the harbor . . . this person is taking us over the Channel in the wrong sort of boats."

"Wrong sort of boats, O'Donnell?"

The seaman shrugged. He was very tall. "My lord, what's wrong is the wind. If it fails to rise, my oarsmen will be rowing us across the Channel." He looked down at the bishop. "The little fella here is complaining at the lack of castles. . . ."

"Indeed, indeed," the bishop said. "There should be castles, turrets on our boat, it is too plain. One at the front, one at the back, for defense against pirates . . ."

"I believe 'fore and aft' is the correct expression," Henry said. "What pirates? Are you aware of any pirates in my Channel, O'Donnell?"

"I am not, me lord. Didn't you and I clear it of the bastards long ago? However, if the little fella wants castles, he can have castles, for they're a marvelous way of capsizing a boat in a storm—but not on my fokking ships he doesn't."

Henry took the bishop by the elbow. "You see, my lord, Admiral O'Donnell may be a foulmouthed, disrespectful, opinionated limb of Satan and, what's worse, an Irishman, but at sea he's Neptune and nobody knows the English seas better—nor the Mediterranean, come to that." He turned back to O'Donnell. "Is that where you've been these last two years?"

There was a gleam of white teeth. "*A mari usque ad mare*. And in Christian company, sure enough. Enriching me soul ferrying crusaders to the Holy Land."

"Enriching your pocket, you mean. God's eyes, I should have been a bloody sailor. Well, let us go and see if we can whistle up a breeze."

O'Donnell saw Adelia watching him and gave an elaborate bow.

So this man would be accompanying them overland on their

journey to the Mediterranean, would he? She wished he wasn't; he made her uncomfortable; she didn't know why; there was something about him. . . .

On the way out of the door, she was accosted by the princess's ladies-in-waiting. They were young, beautiful, and exquisitely dressed—Adelia was glad she was in Emma's pretty bliaut and cloak—and might have been sisters except that Mistress Blanche, as her name indicated, was fair, the other two dark. Suddenly friendly, they spoke as if of one mind, like triplets. "My *dear*," trilled Lady Petronilla in an Aquitanian accent, "you have no maid with you? Such a misfortune. How did it happen?"

"Allow us to remedy that situation for you," said Lady Beatrix, another one from Aquitaine to judge from her speech. "We can, can't we, Blanche?"

"The moment the king mentioned your lack, it came to us." Lady Petronilla snapped her fingers at a slight figure standing in the doorway. "*So* fortunate that we have such a one who is surplus to our requirements. The girl was attached to the household of my sister-in-law, Lady Kenilworth, you know, who no longer has need of her."

"We gift her to you," Lady Beatrix said, barely suppressing a giggle.

The gift came forward, tripped over its overlong skirt, and fell down.

"English, I fear," Mistress Blanche said in a stage whisper, "but we are sure she will suit you admirably."

"Thank you," Adelia said, bewildered.

That was too much for them; they turned and walked away, their shoulders shaking.

Adelia helped her new maid to her feet. "What's your name?"

"Boggart, ladyship, I'm Boggart."

"Boggart? It can't be your *name*."

Here in England, a boggart was a clumsy and malicious household sprite that caused milk to sour, objects to disappear, and animals to go lame. This child, only fifteen if she was a day, looked innocent enough with her round, freckled face and wide blue eyes.

"I think so, ladyship," Boggart said, cheerfully. "Never known no other."

"But what were you christened?"

"Don't know as I was, ladyship."

Oh, dear. Adelia regarded her new acquisition; the girl was clean but her small hands were those of an unlikely lady's maid, being calloused and with grime in the wrinkles of the knuckles that no scrubbing could remove. Yet a lady's maid was required on this journey, if only to provide Adelia with necessary status. "Well, um, Boggart, are you willing to enter my service?"

"Eh?" From the girl's look of incomprehension, it seemed she was puzzled by being given an option. "What'd I have to do?"

"Lord, I don't know." Adelia, never having had a lady's maid as such, was flummoxed; Gyltha had run her household with a rod of iron and such efficiency that Adelia's requirements had been seen to almost without her noticing. What *did* ladies' maids do?

"I could clean your boots," Boggart said, eagerly. "I'm a wonderful boot cleaner."

Adelia sighed. The Aquitanian ladies had given her a pig in a poke. They'd wanted rid of this child; the wonder was why they'd brought her along in the first place. But the sudden hope in the poor little thing's eyes made rejection of her unthinkable.

"I belong to you now, then, do I, ladyship?"

"You don't *belong* to anybody. I'm asking you if you'd like to enter my employment."

Again the look of incomprehension. Nobody had told Boggart that slavery had been abolished in his lands by William the Conqueror, that she was not a parcel to be passed from hand to hand. "I'm a wonderful boot cleaner," she repeated.

Adelia gave another sigh. "I suppose that'll do to start with."

With Boggart trailing behind her like a puppy, she followed the rest of the guests out onto the ramparts.

Southampton had become a major port, trading good English wool with Normandy in return for wine, and today its harbor was busy with ships coming in and those waiting to go out once there was wind.

The Bishop of Winchester, still complaining to the king, was pointing out the two vessels allocated for the princess's crossing; one for Joanna herself and her court, the other for the lesser mortals attached to it.

Adelia rather sympathized with the frightened little bishop; to her inexperienced eye the two boats, though freshly and brightly painted, were lower slung, with one bank of oars, two masts, and less ornamentation, than the becastled vessels she'd been in before. Only a limp royal Plantagenet pennant showed which was the princess's flagship.

O'Donnell was insisting that the company spend the night aboard. "Me Turkish friend here thinks he scents a sou'westerly breeze on the way, do you not, Deniz?"

He referred to a squat, strong-smelling goblin of a man in wide sailcloth trousers and a waistcoat that showed bare, brown arms with muscles like iron balls.

Deniz grunted.

"*Denise?*" Adelia whispered to Mansur. They were strange names she was encountering today.

"*Deniz*. In Turkish it means 'the sea,'" Mansur told her.

The O'Donnell's eyes slid in their direction. "Indeed it does, master," he said. "For it's the sea I fished him out of, and there's nobody understands it better."

He speaks Arabic as well as Latin, Adelia thought. *We must be careful.*

"And the breeze'll come up tonight," he was saying, still looking at her and Mansur, "so we can catch the tide at dawn, and I'll not be missing it in the kerfuffle of getting all the fine ladies and gentlemen to their berths that early."

It was kerfuffle enough as it was. Horses were kicking at being led down into the hold. Shouting dockers loaded chests of treasure and clothes, followed anxiously by the ladies-in-waiting, holding up their skirts. Priests and clerks teetered on gangways and argued with the sailors about which boat should take them.

All very well, Adelia thought, *but where is our protection?* The treasure they were carrying with them en route would surely attract robbers; women, servants, and clerics were unlikely to be able to fend them off.

Then, in the distance, she saw the tall figure of Captain Bolt briskly ushering his men aboard the second ship—and was comforted. She and the good captain had made each other's acquaintance during one of her previous investigations. As well as showing himself to be an excellent soldier devoted to his king, he'd been kind to her. He was the one who, at Henry's command, had cleared the Somerset forest of the late Wolf's remaining outlaws, and, afterward, had the bodies of those she'd so desperately searched for disinterred and given Christian burial.

Disengaging Boggart from a hawser she'd fallen over and managed to become entangled in kept Mansur and Adelia momentarily delayed on the quayside.

Again, the Bishop of Saint Albans casually strolled over to them. "Who is this?"

Adelia finished brushing Boggart down. "It's my new lady's maid."

"Good God." He turned to Mansur. "My dear doctor, is that box yours?" He pointed to a large packing case waiting with others at the end of the quay to be loaded.

"No, my lord."

"Really? I thought it might contain your medicaments. Perhaps you should make sure." He bowed briefly to Adelia and returned to the group of clergy.

"What was that about?" Adelia snapped, looking to Mansur. Their box of medicaments had already been taken aboard.

"Let us see. Tell that clumsy female to stay where she is."

"Stay here," Adelia told Boggart.

Together she and the Arab went to investigate, encountering an odor that was at once strong and familiar to Adelia's nostrils. "It's Ward," she said, clutching Mansur's arm.

"The dog? How can it be?"

"I'd know that smell anywhere." She hurried to the packing case. Behind it, hidden from the quay's hubbub, stood a young man holding a piece of string to which was attached a small, unsavory-looking dog. Both were happy to see her but, while the animal bounced its welcome, the youth kept his face straight and his East Anglian speech lugubrious.

"Ain't supposed to be seen with you two, am I? Disregarded, that's what I gotta be, so Prior said."

Adelia collapsed on him. "Ulf, oh *Ulf.* It's you. What are you doing here? I am so *pleased* to see you. Oh, *Ulf.*"

Gyltha's grandson had grown since they'd first encountered each other in the Cambridgeshire fens. The truculent, ill-favored child he'd been then, one she'd come to love—and had saved from a terrible abductor—was now considerably cleaner except for the light stubble on his chin. His unruly hair was hidden by the wide-brimmed hat of a pilgrim, but like most fenmen, he still pretended to a gritty dispassion.

"Get off," he said, wriggling out of Adelia's clutch. He nodded at Mansur, who nodded back; neither face showing pleasure at the meeting, though their eyes were glad.

"And Ward, too." Adelia cupped her hands round her dog's face, careful to wipe them on her kerchief afterward. "What are you both doing here?"

"Me, on the king's orders. I'm incognito, I am. And that there stinker's here a-cause the prior a-reckoned as you'd need him."

Adelia smiled. "I'm in no danger this time." Prior Geoffrey of Cambridge, her first friend in England, always worried for her safety, had given her Ward's predecessor, an equally smelly hound, so that, should she be at risk, she could always be traced by its scent.

As it had turned out afterward, the dog had indeed saved her life and lost its own in doing it. When, to her regret, she'd been forced to move from Cambridge, Ward had been one of the friends she'd had to leave behind.

"Prior don't think so," Ulf told her, " 'That girl's born unto trouble as the sparks fly upward.' That's what he said. 'You take that odiferous bugger to her and tell her to keep him close,' he said. And that's what I'm a-doing."

"But what's all this about the king's orders?"

Ulf tutted at her ignorance. His gaze directed itself deliberately on a large, plain wooden cross leaning beside him against the packing case. "Cos o' that."

Adelia looked at it for a minute before it came to her. "My God," she said. "*You're* the crucifer. So the king consulted Prior Geoffrey—how wise of him."

"*He* don't have to heft it," Ulf said with feeling. "That's heavy, that old bit o' wood, considering it's hollow and what's inside it don't weigh too much. Story is I'm a-taking my grandpappy's cross to Jerusalem to put on the Holy Sepulchre so's to account for Grandpappy's sins." He grinned.

She smiled fondly back. His grandfather *had* sinned. Prior Geoffrey, leader of Saint Augustine's in Cambridge, where Ulf was now learning law, had, as a young priest, formed a happy but illicit relationship with the equally young Gyltha, a liaison that, in the second generation, had produced this wonderful grandson.

The subterfuge was clever. It was quite usual for those who couldn't go on crusade themselves to send something of their own by proxy to the Holy Land. Henry, that crafty, *crafty* king, obviously with Rowley's help, had remembered his friendship with the prior, and the two of them had worked out this plan for

Excalibur's secret journey. Who would expect such a stripling to be carrying inside his cross the sword that all Christendom would kill to lay its hands on?

"And when we gets to Sicily," Ulf said, looking round to make sure nobody could hear, "old Rowley is to crack open the wood and give you-know-what to you-know-who. Pity as you can't see it now, bor. That's a sword and a bit, I can tell you. That's got magic, that has."

"I've seen it," Adelia said. Magical or not, she didn't want to see it again.

Ulf handed the dog's lead to Adelia and heaved the cross onto his shoulder. "I better get aboard, and you remember as I'm incognito. Us holy pilgrims don't have nothing to do with you gentry." He peered out, found the coast clear, and went off, pretending to stagger as he went.

Adelia untied the string from Ward's collar and replaced it with her kerchief, which looked slightly better. Neither of her new acquisitions today was going to improve her standing in the princess's train, but she was so glad of them. And even if she and Mansur could not be seen talking to Ulf, they would at least have one loving companion on their travels—two, if you counted Ward. The boy—she supposed she must now think of him as a young man—had the solidity and common sense of his grandmother; they would be taking something of Gyltha with them.

In any case, would the coming year be so bad?

The disgusting phrase she'd heard men use about rape—"Lie back and enjoy it"—came to her mind. Yes, she was being used, forced to accede to a demand against her will. On the other hand, Allie was as safe as she could be and had Gyltha to look after her, while she herself was about to set out on a journey she'd been wanting to make for years and in a style that, apart from the inevitable dangers of all travel, was as safe as possible under the circumstances.

Adelia took in a breath of air in which the seagulls were gliding for the pleasure of it. She touched Mansur's hand. "Oh well . . ." she said.

He inclined his head; he knew what she meant, he always did. He was another who was going home.

NIGHT HAS FALLEN *on the harbor. It is hot, uncomfortable, and crowded in the cabins of the royal vessels as they wait for the wind that will come with the dawn tide, but the passengers are tired so that, one by one, their lanterns—no naked flame is allowed on board—are extinguished. Except for their riding lights, the ships are mere shapes, like two dragons in the darkness. . . .*

No, one lantern is still burning. One man prefers the deck to his cabin and has wedged himself against a hatch so that he can commune with his Messiah in peace—or as much peace as the Messiah gives him.

"We have been introduced, beloved." Scarry's mouth moves but no sound comes from it. "I managed to abide her, for so I must. Even close to, she is no beauty—except for the smile, which she gave once, and then . . . well, I confess it: suum cuique pulchrum. *The skin is dark blond like that of a Greek. You would have enjoyed chewing on it.*

"Her eyes, which are brown, show an insult to all men. I am anyone's match, they say, I have knowledge. What presumption, what challenge.

"I have employed a minion to search her luggage. There is no sign of

Excalibur, but of a certainty she knows where it is. To whom else would the king have entrusted it but her, who led him to it?

"Keep your temper, my joy, my love, as I do. We have time, we have a thousand miles. We shall have the sword, and she shall be brought down. But slowly, piece by piece, a pedibus usque ad caput, *chop, chop, until the wits go.*

"For you, Wolf. On your altar. To you who were the equal of a god."

Four

A STRONG BREEZE came up, as the little Turk had said it would.

The Bishop of Winchester performed the usual ceremony, committing the boats and everyone in them to the mercy of God. To his concern, however, the admiral performed a ceremony of his own. Standing on the prow of his flagship, he raised his arms and spoke to his waiting crews in Irish, his voice traveling easily from ship to ship: "*Amach daoibh a chlann an righ.*"

Adelia asked one of the oarsmen what he'd said and was told, "It's the words Eva the witch says to the Children of Lir when she turns them into swans: 'Out with you on the water, ye children of the king.'"

"Isn't that a curse?" It was certainly pagan.

"Maybe, maybe, but swans do float and keep a-floatin'. And it's with us sailors, d'ye see, that we'd rather have a curse from himself than a blessing from the Pope."

Whatever it was, the oarsmen were able to take their ease while the vessels proceeded smartly over the Channel under sail, heeling slightly with the wind a-beam.

WORD ISSUED FROM Joanna's deck cabin. The princess was seasick. Dr. Arnulf, looking none too well himself, was being called to her side.

"And we attend, too," Adelia told Mansur firmly. "Not that I know of anything to help seasickness, but if he goes, we go."

The precedent that Arnulf was not Joanna's *only* appointed doctor must be set.

The royal cabin was crowded, dark, and smelled of vomit. The sufferer was hidden in a cluster of people who hung on to beams and, occasionally, one another to keep upright. From the midst of anxious ladies-in-waiting and maids, the new arrivals heard the voice of Dr. Arnulf: "The bile is blackish, the princess should be bled at once. Fetch me my leeches."

"Ginger." This was Joanna's nurse, Edeva. "Ginger's good."

"Surely . . ." It was the Bishop of Winchester's turn. ". . . a bone of Saint Erasmus attached to her stomach would be more efficacious; I think we have one in the ossuary we brought with us, haven't we, Father Guy?"

Which of the saints was Erasmus? Adelia had a vague remembrance of Somerset herdsmen invoking him to cure cattle pest; presumably he turned his spiritual hand to maritime upsets as well.

Father Guy pushed past her without greeting, hurryi
his box of bones. His colleague, Father Adalburt, A
was also here, using an aspergillum to spr
anyone he could reach which, because o
and the ship's brisk motion, did not includ

"The nurse speaks well," Mansur said quietly in Arabic. "Ginger is good, but the child also needs fresh air."

Adelia was taken aback; it was rare for Mansur to prescribe, but he probably knew more about ***mal de mer*** than she did; in his sad youth among the monks who'd castrated him he'd been sent on the long voyage to sing in Byzantium.

She raised her voice. "The Lord Mansur wishes to see his patient."

There was a reluctant movement that gave them both passage through to where Joanna lay shivering and uncomplaining, her pointed little face livid under a swinging lantern—an object that, Adelia thought, couldn't be helping matters. The girl looked up at Mansur without interest, raised herself, and was sick into a bowl.

"So much for ***him*** comin' yere," her nurse said, vengefully. "Don't do no good at all, do he? Bloody Saracen."

"Tell them," Mansur said. "Some powdered ginger, wrap her up warm, and take her on deck."

Adelia told them. Obviously, the child would mend once she was on land, but this wasn't about seasickness, it was a test to see whether or not she herself could do her job should the princess ever become truly ill. Would they listen to Mansur?

They didn't. Fortunately for the princess, it was discovered that Dr. Arnulf's leeches had been wrongly stowed in the other ship.

However, a saintly knuckle was bound to Joanna's midriff and nger administered, but only on the nurse's say-so. Disregarded, lia and Mansur left the cabin.

elia lurched over to the ship's side. "Damn, damn, ***dammit***."

"Trouble?" The Bishop of Saint Albans was behind her.

She didn't look round. "They're not taking any notice of us."

"We'll see about that."

A minute later, she heard his voice coming from the princess's cabin; the name of the king was mentioned several times.

"He will right things for us," Mansur said.

"He does everything right," Adelia said bitterly, "except parting me from my daughter."

"It will not hurt her." For the first time Mansur showed that he, too, thought Allie had been allowed to run wild. "Nor could he permit you to stay with Lady Emma. You were at risk."

"*Eh?*"

He told her everything. Of the danger she'd been in while in Somerset from an unknown assailant, of Rowley's desperate concern.

Because she'd been unaware, she had difficulty in believing him. Or Will and Alf, for that matter; good men but not the most reliable of sources.

Anyway, in Mansur's rippling Arabic it sounded like a tale from *One Thousand and One Nights* . . . a demon attempting to kill her, two faithful *fellahin* looking out for her . . .

"But who? *Why?*" She had no enemies.

"The Will and the Alf believed it to be the wolf man's beloved . . ." Here Mansur spat into the sea. ". . . the one called Slurry? Sparry?"

"Scarry?" She hadn't spoken the name in two years; she remembered the Latin lament that had shaken the trees as he'd cradled the dead Wolf in his arms. *Te amo. Te amo.*

"Oh, that's nonsense. The man's dead. If you remember,

Captain Bolt cleared the forest." And without mercy. Bits of the outlaws had hung from trees for days.

"The bishop does not think so. He believed the Will and the Alf."

"Why didn't Rowley *tell* me?"

Mansur shrugged. "He only told me on the way to Sarum."

"But why didn't he tell *me*?"

"You would not speak to him. Perhaps it is better in any case that you did not know until we reached Normandy, you might not have left."

"Of course I wouldn't have left." Always supposing there *was* a maniac after her . . . "He wouldn't hurt Allie, would he?"

The Arab looked down at her. "Why should he do that? You imagine vain things. Allie is safe enough in Sarum, where her father has put her."

Logic had little application to fear, but Adelia tried to apply it because, at one level, she knew her friend was right.

"Now you will forgive the bishop," Mansur said.

In the sense that Rowley had placed their daughter in the charge of Queen Eleanor against the wishes of herself, nothing had changed. But if there *were* an assassin roaming Somerset—and Adelia still had trouble believing it—Allie was safely out of his way.

What was explained was Rowley's anger that night; he'd always shown fury when he was frightened for her. Stupid man, she thought, as her own anger drained away.

Which left the dilemma that when they could have been friendly together, she had refused. Now that she would, they had no opportunity to; she dare not compromise him, nor could he compromise himself.

"Oh, damnation," she said, wearily.

A shivering princess emerged on deck, wrapped round by a thick cloak and her nurse's arm, to be helped to windward—presumably because it was the farthest side from Mansur and Adelia.

At that another voice took command. "No, no, the little one will be better to leeward, d'ye see," Admiral O'Donnell said. "Over this side what comes up tends to fly back in your face."

Joanna was helped across the deck and her hands placed about a cleat. "Hang onto that, ***mavourneen***, and fix your dear eyes on the horizon. Is that better now?"

Wanly, the princess nodded that it was.

"But maybe," the O'Donnell said, sliding his eyes toward Adelia, "we should dispense with the little dog."

Adelia glanced down at her feet where Ward, looking as wan as the princess, had put his head on her shoes and was exuding a smell that competed against the freshness of wind and sea.

There had already been complaints about him from the ladies-in-waiting with whom Adelia had shared the night—"He'll give *our* little dogs fleas." "*Our* little dogs are perfumed."—and she'd been compelled to shut him outside on deck where, tied to a stanchion, he'd whined away the hours at being parted from the mistress with whom he'd only just been reunited.

Shrugging, she turned away, Ward staggering after her on unsteady legs.

So the battle of the doctors had been won—with Rowley's help.

Adelia wondered if the royal nurse, obviously a powerful figure in Joanna's life, would prove an ally now that Mansur's advice had triumphed.

It appeared that she would not. Across the width of the deck, Edeva, her substantial Irish figure looming over her charge, could be heard stating in a loud mutter that "darkies" would only lay hands on "my darling" over her dead body.

AT THE MOUTH of the Orne, a galloper was sent ahead to Caen while the two ships stopped to pretty themselves. Sails were taken down, the salt of the Channel cleansed from woodwork, gilding was polished, bunting was spread, musicians readied their instruments, oarsmen settled into their benches. The company arrayed itself on deck. A recovered Joanna, dressed in white and gold, was placed on a raised throne and the sun shone on her.

Father Adalburt was expressing his surprise at Normandy's similarity to England. "Look, look," he kept saying, "fields and . . . and reeds. And *there* . . . wading birds just like those at home. Who would have thought it? Dear Lord, how wondrous are Thy works."

Slowly, with oars dimpling the water in unison, and to the sound of flute and tabors, they began to glide down the river from which the Norman warships of William the Conqueror had set out for England more than a hundred years before.

On the banks, reed cutters dropped their scythes to watch,

and herdsmen left their cows, calling to their wives and children to come and see these unearthly swans go by.

As the ships entered the harbor, the musicians on board changed their instruments to trumpets and blew a fanfare that was answered by a line of tabarded heralds on the quay.

Dressed in its best, Caen's entire nobility had turned out to greet its Plantagenet princess.

It might have saved itself the trouble; Joanna had no eyes for anyone but the young man robed in peacock colors in the forefront of the crowd. Showing animation for the first time, she bounced, squeaking with pleasure. "Henry!"

Crowned eight years ago when his father had feared for the succession, the Young King was glorious, resembling his mother in his beauty and his father not at all.

And kind, Adelia thought, as Joanna ran across the lowered gangplank to be picked up and whirled around in her brother's arms, both of them abandoning royal dignity. Here was someone showing more care for the girl than the parents who had let her go so easily.

And charming. Everybody on board the royal boat, from bishop to oarsmen, was thanked for his sister's safe arrival in Normandy. He was gracious to Mansur . . . "My lord, your fame in medicine precedes you." To Adelia he said: "Mistress, we are honored by a lady so knowledgeable in Arabic. Have you spoken it long?"

By the time Adelia had risen from her deep bow and was ready to reply, he had passed on to the next recipient of his attention. She didn't mind; it had been nice of him to distinguish her by asking. But she was left with an impression of lightness, an easiness without depth. A fine prince, maybe, but not a king. A symbol, not an administrator.

There was the trouble, she thought. When he was this boy's age, Henry Plantagenet had fought for and won the throne of England and already given it a stability that was the envy of monarchs everywhere.

Young Henry, on the other hand, had been passed an easy crown without responsibility, because he himself either had none or wasn't ready for it, leaving him with the trappings of kingship and no means to apply them, a situation that, egged on by Eleanor, had caused resentment and, eventually, rebellion.

Father and son had since exchanged the kiss of peace—but at a price. According to Rowley, Young Henry's return to the fold had been bought with the enormous stipend of a hundred pounds of Angevin money a day. Which, from the look of it, he was spending. His retinue as they progressed toward the Abbaye-aux-Hommes and its church of Saint Étienne for a service to greet Joanna included at least fifty noisy young knights complete with squires, all gorgeously dressed and mounted. To the disapproval of the staid Sir Nicholas Baicer and Lord Ivo, they chattered and laughed throughout the ceremony so that it was difficult to distinguish the words of the mass. Nor did their Young King attempt to quiet them.

Adelia, however, was encouraged; with an escort as large as this, she thought, the safety of the journey to Sicily was ensured.

She said so to Captain Bolt as she emerged from the church to find him and a troop of his men waiting outside, ready to escort her and the ladies of the party from the Abbaye-aux-Hommes to the Abbaye-aux-Dames, where they would spend the night,

Caen being unique in having two great convents, one for men, one for women, standing on either side of the city; the first built by William the Conqueror and the second by his wife, Matilda, both in expiation of their sin of marrying each other against the law of consanguinity—they'd been cousins.

"*Them,*" Captain Bolt responded with all the contempt of a professional soldier for men who paid for the land they held of the king by a knightly service that allowed them to go home after thirty days. "No discipline. See how they behaved in church? Shocking it was."

WARD SPENT THE NIGHT somewhere in the bowels of the nunnery with Boggart. Dog and maid had become delighted with each other, Boggart because, for the first time in her life, she had something, however smelly, on which to lavish affection, and Ward because Boggart, though lacking skill as a lady's attendant, was a marvel at stealing food from kitchens with which to feed him.

That's one problem solved, then, Adelia thought, as she climbed wearily into the large bed already containing Lady Beatrix, Lady Petronilla, and Mistress Blanche. *Dear Lord, keep Allie safe and don't let her be missing me as much as I'm missing her*.

THE MORNING BROUGHT its own problem, a larger one.

The ladies of the party had risen early to be escorted across Caen to the Abbaye-aux-Hommes, where they were now gathered in its courtyard waiting for the great journey to Sicily to properly begin.

And waited.

Loud and angry voices could be heard coming from inside the monastery, the Bishop of Saint Albans's louder and angrier than anyone's.

At last he emerged, flanked by Lord Ivo and Sir Nicholas Baicer, both looking nearly as thunderous as he did. He bowed to Joanna. "My lady, I must inform you that the Young King has gone to Falaise. For a tournament, apparently. And all his knights with him. He begs you to expect his return in a few days."

What the princess replied was inaudible, but Adelia heard Lady Priscilla exclaim, "A tournament, how I adore tournaments. Oh, that he might have taken us with him."

A few days? It might not matter to that young woman how long the journey took—she had no child waiting for her to come back.

As for the Young King . . . it was known that he was addicted to tournaments, but this was irresponsibility; what an abrogation of duty.

Adelia had been present at a tournament once during a visit to Emma's Normandy manor near Calais and, for her, that had been one tournament too many. They were called entertainments, two teams of knights hacking away at each other in what was supposed to be a mock battle, but during the melee at Calais four young men had been killed and fifteen others permanently maimed.

The attraction for the victors was in holding the defeated to ransom, along with their armor and horses—a way of earning so much money that as many as several hundred eager knights would take part, not only wasting precious lives but trampling peasants' crops for miles around. Henry in his wisdom had banned them from England but here, it seemed, under the nominal rule of the Young King, they were still legal.

She saw Captain Bolt talking with Rowley and, when he'd finished, went up to him. "What can be done?"

"Nothing." Bolt was tight-lipped with fury. "We wait."

They waited for four days, during which Caen's welcome to the princess and her large company began to drain away—like its resources.

On the fifth day a messenger was sent to Falaise to ask the Young King when he was expecting to return.

Again, Adelia approached Captain Bolt. "What's happened?"

"The messenger had to go on to Rouen. That young b . . ." Bolt took in a long breath. ". . . the Young King's heard as there's another big tournament there and he's off to fight in it."

"Rouen's, what, eighty miles away. What are we going to do?"

"I dunno, mistress. The bishops and Sir Nicholas and Lord Ivo are in conference about it."

Master Locusta, it appeared, was frantic that his arrangements with the castles and monasteries scheduled to receive them on the way would be put out. "I've no wish to speak ill of the Young King, but *really* . . ."

"I think you're justified in speaking ill of the Young King this time," an impatient Adelia told him.

The conference lasted another day. On the seventh, it came to a decision. Another messenger was sent to the Young King at Rouen to tell him that Princess Joanna and her train were finding it necessary to set off for Aquitaine immediately in the expectation that her brother and *his* train would catch up with her en route.

So the next morning the citizens of Caen lined the road to the southern gate to cheer and wave off the marriage cavalcade, partly to honor it and partly in relief that it was going. After all, it numbered nearly one hundred and fifty people who, with their animals, the city had been forced to accommodate and feed at its own expense.

Riding with Mansur near the head of the column, Adelia glanced back at the long, long line following behind her, and was encouraged; nobles, clerks, musicians and squires, personal servants, laundresses, grooms, luggage, and treasure, all were accommodated in carts or on mule- and horseback, a luxury that required nobody to walk, thereby speeding the journey.

As the procession reached the countryside and began passing through isolated little villages, their inhabitants came out to marvel at something to be seen once in a lifetime; the golden princess and ladies in their gilded palanquin, riders cloaked in crimson cloth or silk, horses in their rainbow caparisons, the shine of armor—like a jeweled dragon come glittering out of the age of myth to prance its way along the muddy high streets.

Captain Bolt's practiced eye, however, saw it differently. Pausing beside Adelia as he rode up and down the line to make sure his soldiers kept their posts along it, he cursed Young Henry and his lack of duty.

"Aren't we better off without him?" she asked.

"Maybe. But my men've got a princess with a mort of treasure to guard and, if so be it comes to an attack, we're mightily overstretched."

"THE JOURNEY BEGINS *to be unlucky for them; Young Henry has deserted us. That great fool, the Bishop of Winchester, complains of it,* mala tempora currunt, *yet I see in it our Great Master's hand. We are being shown the way, Lupus mine. Send us more misfortune,* O deo certe, *that I may contrive to have the blame for it heaped on the head of the woman we are to bring down."*

Five

It was Adelia's contention from personal experience that riding sidesaddle was bad for the back. Not a good horsewoman, she also thought it dangerous to be hanging on at a twisted angle should one's mount shy or bolt. Yet riding astride was denounced everywhere as unladylike, a style for peasants, especially by the exalted company in which she now found herself.

If King Henry's strictures to the three ladies-in-waiting had been properly observed, she should have traveled in the *de luxe* cushioned cart in which they and Joanna passed the journey by teasing their perfumed lapdogs, playing cards, and watching the scenery they could see through its gilded and ornamented bars. Adelia's only experience in it, however, was her last.

It wasn't that the little princess herself was unfriendly, merely withdrawn. Lady Beatrix, Lady Petronilla, and Mistress Blanche, on the other hand, had a curve to their lips as they questioned her about her "Saracen friend." ("*Do* tell us, dear—is his skin naturally that color or is it against his religion to wash?") And inquired after her new maid. ("We hope *so* much that the Boggart is proving satisfactory, how nice that she's taken to your *interesting* little dog.")

After a morning of it, Adelia reverted to the sidesaddle on the palfrey allotted to her. It was a pretty but very hard wooden *sambue*, a contraption resembling a three-sided box with a pommel that allowed her right leg to curve gracefully over her left, both of her boots fitting above each other into stirrups of disparate heights. At an amble the posture it demanded was uncomfortable; trotting was torture.

Bumping along on it beside Mansur, Adelia found her mind dwelling with admiration on the Empress Matilda, Henry II's mother, who had ignored opprobrium by riding astride during her war with her cousin, Stephen, for England's throne. "The Plantagenets would never have won if she'd had to go sidesaddle," she grumbled in Arabic.

"It gives elegance to a woman," Mansur said, approvingly.

"It gives her curvature of the damned spine."

"And modesty."

That was it, she supposed. Men didn't like women to have their legs apart unless they were in bed; yet how much more fittingly the female frame had been designed to ride astride than that of the male, with its protruding dangly bits.

She groaned. "A thousand miles of modesty, I'll never survive it."

"Then return to the royal cart."

"With those three harpies? I'm hardly welcome there."

At least this way, she didn't have to restrain herself from

punching ladies of the nobility in the mouth. Also, she could ride farther back in the procession among the lesser members of the household and occasionally give advice on their health problems, ostensibly through Mansur's pronouncements.

Their arrival at the great Benedictine abbey of Mont-Saint-Michel was to set the tone for what, Locusta hoped, would be their reception at every stop on the journey. He had gone ahead with a servant to alert the abbot of their coming and then returned to lead them on. "Thank God the tide's out," he said, as they approached the island causeway. "It took all my mathematics to time our coming exactly. I was afraid our delay would miss us another eight hours."

"Let us hope the tide stays out," the O'Donnell said. "For I'm told it comes in with the rush of a galloping horse."

In fact, water was beginning to swirl around wheels and hooves as they crossed to the strange mount on which monks had been laboring for one thousand years to complete an edifice that the Archangel Michael had instructed their first bishop to build.

They hadn't labored in vain. From a distance the top of the mount gave the impression that it had been set with enormous candles that had dripped wax into contorted and beautiful shapes.

It had been a hot day. August was going out with all the heat it could muster. The climb up the escalier street was hard on beasts and humans who'd already had a long and sweaty journey of it, but the prospect of rest in the cool of the lovely building above them spurred them on, as did the dizzying glimpses of the bay with a breeze coming off it, and the Normandy coast under the rise of a harvest moon.

Abbot and clergy waited to greet them; there would *always* be a crowd of clergy, *and* introductions *and*, invariably, a service of thanksgiving for Joanna's safe arrival, *then* a banquet under vaulted ceilings *and* toasts, before the poor little princess and her yawning following were accommodated in their beds. Next morning she had to see the graceful cloisters, the gilded statue of Saint Michael, kneel before precious relics, until the time came to remount and set off again.

It was to be the pattern.

We'll proceed by inches, Adelia thought in despair. *Allie, oh Allie.*

AT THE END of the fourth day's journey, while Mansur was helping her to dismount—a clumsy business at the best of times—her horse made a sudden movement and Adelia's right foot became entangled in its stirrup; Mansur staggered under her unexpected weight, and for a moment she was sent topsy-turvy with her veil dragging in the dust.

Lady Beatrix, Lady Petronilla, and Mistress Blanche stepped down the little ladder attached to their cart and clustered about her with delighted sympathy. "Are you all right, you poor soul? My dear, how *embarrassing*."

It was. For an instant, before Mansur helped her up again, a small crowd of men, including Captain Bolt, Father Adalburt, Admiral O'Donnell, and the Bishop of Saint Albans, were treated to the sight of Adelia's white thighs and a burst of good fenland invective against horse riding in general and sidesaddles in particular.

Next morning, limping out to the stable yard for another day's suffering, she found Captain Bolt putting a different saddle on her palfrey. It was a small affair and cushioned in red leather, high at the rear in order to support the rider's back.

He interrupted her explosions of gratitude. "Been made for a boy, I fear, mistress. You'll have to go astride."

"I don't care. Where did you get it from?"

"Weren't me. We passed a saddlery away back and somebody . . ." He lowered his voice; Bolt was an old friend of the bishop's and Adelia's, and aware of their situation. ". . . *somebody* found this as had been ordered for a young lord as'd never come for it. So he bought it for you."

Rowley. Oh, God bless him.

Tightening the cinch, the captain said: "And I'll spread it about as Queen Eleanor herself did sometimes ride astride. I know as she did; that time she escaped from the king and I had to chase her to bring her back—God help us, I had trouble a-catching her."

"Thank you. And please thank the somebody."

Bolt heaved her up onto the palfrey. "I was to say as it's to stop you breaking your neck as well as the Third Commandment." He shook his head in admiration. "Gor, lady, you can't half swear when it comes to it."

AT THE NEXT MONASTERY there was a kerfuffle in the middle of the night; a woman screamed, men's voices were raised, there was movement in the inner courtyard. The sounds incorporated themselves into part of a dream Adelia was having and, being exhausted from that day's journey, she didn't wake up but, like the three ladies-in-waiting with whom she shared a bed, merely groaned and stirred in her sleep.

Yet it was obvious next morning that something had occurred; Lady Beatrix, Lady Petronilla, and Mistress Blanche in their cart were to be seen in conversation more earnest than was usual with them while, all down the line, there was a frisson of talk, head-shaking, and, among some of the men, laughter.

"Do you know what's happened?" Adelia asked Mansur. Thinking the Arab did not understand them, people were looser with their talk in his presence than hers.

"It has something to do with the Sir Nicholas Baicer and shoes, but I can gather no more than that."

"*Shoes?*"

Isolated as she was from the general gossip, Adelia appealed to Captain Bolt as he rode past her on one of his checks up and down the procession.

He was uninformative, even defensive. "Nothing for you to worry about, missus. He's a fine soldier, Sir Nicholas, I've served with him."

She, too, liked what she knew of the man *and* Lord Ivo. Both knights were courteous whenever their paths crossed hers; they paid attention to all well-being, not just that of the higher echelons, Lord Ivo with gravitas while Sir Nicholas had a more hail-fellow-well-met approach and would talk to anybody about his family in England and Normandy with as much affection as he did about his hounds. Both men were lovers of the chase; indeed, one would occasionally veer away from the procession with his dogs and other enthusiastic hunters to pursue a stag through a forest, but always leaving the other by the princess's side. Like Captain Bolt, they inspired a confidence that, militarily, everybody was in safe hands.

Boggart, who, being Adelia's maid, was still as *persona non grata* in this closely knit traveling community as she was, could gather little more than her mistress, except that it was "summat to do with Sir Nicholas and shoes."

And with that, since there was no opportunity to talk to Rowley on anything but a passing and polite level, Adelia had to be content.

IT HAPPENED WHEN they were passing through the *Bocage*, that woody and rich farming area of southwest Normandy where cows grazed knee-deep in grass behind high hedges dotted like sprigged muslin with rose hips and light green hazelnuts.

Adelia, who'd been riding high and comfortably on her new saddle, had her attention diverted from lichened cottages and tiny, towerless churches by her horse. The horse had been acting bizarrely for the last two days, staggering occasionally and yawning. Now, the palfrey kept stopping to rub her head against any fence post they passed.

"I think Juno's ill," she said.

Mansur beckoned to the nearest groom, who came up.

Adelia dismounted so that the man could examine the mare. "Is she tired? Have I been riding her too hard?"

"Not you, mistress—you ain't but a puff of wind on her

back." His name was Martin, and he liked Adelia, who'd successfully treated a toe damaged when a horse had stepped on it. He walked around the mare, running his hands down flanks that had been becoming thinner, then took her head between his hands.

"Hello, hello, what's this here?" He pointed to the bare patches around the eyes and nostrils where the skin appeared inflamed.

Adelia peered with him. "It looks like sunburn. How can that be?" She'd never heard of a horse getting sunburned.

"It *do* look like sunburn," Martin said, and called for the head groom. "Here, Master Tom, what d'you make of this?"

There was a good deal of head scratching by both men, more questioning of Adelia about the horse's behavior, more examination during which the animal remained listless.

"You thinking what I'm thinking, Master Tom?" Martin asked.

The head groom sucked his teeth. "Ragwort."

"That's what I reckon."

Master Tom turned on Adelia. "You been letting this poor beast graze on the verges while you been on her back?"

"No, well, not much. Not where there's ragwort." She knew the plant; the ubiquitous bright yellow weed had to be avoided by humans and, it seemed, by horses as well. "I certainly wouldn't have let her eat it if I'd seen it."

"Well, some bugger's been givin' it to her—and lots of it over a fair old time for her to get into this state. She was fit as a flea when we left Caen."

"In her feed at night, you reckon?" Martin asked.

"Could be, could be," Master Tom said. "She'd not likely've touched it while it was growing. . . ."

"But that loses its taste when it's dried," Martin finished for him.

"Still and all, what bastard would do that to a horse?"

"What can be done for her?" Adelia begged. Inattentive as she was to the equine world generally, she and the mare had gone this far on the journey together and it was painful to see the animal in such distress. *Allie would know what to do*, she thought.

Master Tom shrugged. "Nothing. Not with ragwort poison. Put her out of her misery. Nothin' else *to* do."

Juno was led into woodland and her life ended by a quick and expert slash across the throat. The Bishop of Saint Albans immediately began an inquiry—as it turned out, an unsuccessful inquiry—to find out who was responsible for what must have been systematic poisoning of the horse in its nightly stable over the course of several days, something that inevitably pointed to a person belonging to the princess's train.

"The poor beast," Lady Petronilla said loudly to Adelia across the dinner table that evening. "You must feel *dreadful* now that you were so cross with her when you tumbled off her the other day."

"I was cross with myself, not the horse."

It was no use pointing out, as Captain Bolt and Rowley did, that Mistress Adelia invariably handed over her horse to the grooms to stable when the cavalcade reached its destination for the night, and was thereby absolved from feeding it ragwort. The company was left with the impression that she had cursed her horse and that, alone among all the other horses, it had subsequently died.

As Scarry tells *Wolf that night: "It begins."*

Adelia was finally vouchsafed an explanation of the "Sir Nicholas and the shoes" mystery when there was another disturbance at night, this time at the Abbey of Saint-Sauveur de Redon on the approach to Aquitaine, the duchy that had once belonged to Queen Eleanor and had passed to Henry Plantagenet on their marriage.

Again, she and the ladies-in-waiting, in their sleep, heard an alarmed feminine shout and male activity coming from somewhere beyond their room.

On this occasion, however, they were roused by their door crashing open and Lady Petronilla's maid, Marie, rushing through it, whimpering.

"In the name of God, Marie," said Lady Beatrix, querulously. "What is it?" She glanced at the hours candle on the bedside table to see that only half its length had burned down. "It's the middle of the blasted night."

"He done it to *me* this time, m'lady," Marie sobbed. "Terrible frit he gave me. And *look* what he done." She lifted her leg to display the fact that one of her feet was without its shoe.

"Who did? And where have you *been*?" (The maids slept on palliasses in the same room as their mistresses.)

"There was this noise in the passage outside, m'lady, and I got up to open it, thinking as one of the dogs had got shut out, and there weren't nothing there so I went down the passage a bit, and, oh m'lady, it weren't a dog at all, it were Sir Nicholas."

"Oh, dear," said Lady Petronilla. "Well, never mind. And *you*, mistress, stay here, it's nothing for *you* to concern yourself with."

But Adelia had already wrapped herself in a cloak and gone outside to see what was to be seen, leaving Boggart, whom the Last Trump could not have disturbed, to sleep on.

The Bishop of Saint Albans was outside the door, watching a strange procession wending its way toward a turret stair that led down to the men's guest quarters.

Two men-at-arms, one of them Captain Bolt, were supporting a staggering Sir Nicholas Baicer while, in front of them, the knight's squire, Aubrey, was walking backward holding what looked like Marie's shoe in front of his master's nose as another man might tempt a dog into following him with a biscuit.

Adelia shut the bedroom door quietly behind her so that the ladies-in-waiting should not hear and turned to her lover. "Well?"

"It's young Aubrey's fault, he's supposed to measure how much Nicholas drinks at our feasts." Rowley was finding the occasion amusing.

"What has he done?"

It appeared that there was a fine line, only a cup or two of wine, to be drawn between a pleasantly tipsy Sir Nicholas and a Sir Nicholas who was overtaken by a lust that directed itself at feminine feet.

"Any woman," explained Rowley, still amused, "as long as she has such extremities on the end of her legs, is in danger of having a drink-sodden Sir Nicholas throwing himself at her boots and applying his tongue to their leather."

"And that's what happened to Marie?"

"So it seems. He must have outmaneuvered his squire. Last time it was one of the laundresses." He caught sight of Adelia's face. "No harm done. He'll snuggle down in bed with the maid's shoe and be off to sleep like a lamb. He won't remember in the morning."

"*No harm done*? The girl was frightened."

"Nonsense. It's one way of getting her boots clean. Now, then . . ." Rowley pulled Adelia toward him. ". . . since you're here . . ."

But if he intended an embrace, it was preempted by the Bishop of Winchester in his nightcap coming up the stairs to see what the fuss was about.

Rowley bowed to Adelia, said a polite "God's blessing on you, lady," and took himself and his fellow bishop off to their beds.

The male attitude toward Sir Nicholas's lapses pertained even among the ladies-in-waiting. Adelia, returning to the bedroom, heard Lady Petronilla lecturing her maid. "You must remember that all wellborn men have their eccentricities, Marie. We have to overlook them."

There was sleepy agreement from Lady Beatrix. "And, after all, Sir Nicholas's ancestors *did* fight alongside William the Conqueror in subduing the English."

Leaving a trail of well-licked feminine boots in their wake, no doubt. Adelia shook her head before laying it and the rest of herself alongside Lady Petronilla and going wonderingly back to sleep.

The next morning, apparently unaware of the night before, Sir Nicholas was his usual jovial self, whilst Aubrey the squire attended on Marie the maid with an apology, her missing shoe, and a silver piece from a supply of monies with which he'd been entrusted for such eventualities.

THE MONASTERIES AND PRIORIES they stayed at every night blended into one—the same welcome from the abbot/prior, the service, a feast, everybody taking care to show pleasure at entertaining their king's daughter. All of them were rich, mostly *very* rich; providing for so many people during such a stay could cost nearly as much as a year's income, though all of it would undoubtedly be passed on in extra tithes to their feudal underlings.

At first, while in Upper Normandy, the marriage cavalcade had kept to a disciplined and carefully planned procession. Outriders at the front, the princess's palanquin next, flanked by Sir Nicholas Baicer and Lord Ivo splendid in mail and helmets, alongside squires, bishops, and their chaplains plus a platoon of Captain Bolt's men, followed by more soldiers around the treasure-carrying mules with their stout iron boxes, then the higher servants, then the sumpter wagons, and, finally, the pilgrims.

But now, as day followed day without any untoward happenings, there was a relaxation. Pressing deeper into fine hunting country, more people, even some of the servants, gave way to the passion of the chase and followed either Lord Ivo or Sir Nicholas into the forests.

Captain Bolt might frown and forbid his men to follow them, but a general complaisance had overtaken the rest which, since the Bishop of Winchester smiled at it, he was powerless to halt.

Father Adalburt, a new convert, joined in the hunts on his *rouncey* but frequently got lost and, more than once, had to be searched for and kindly led back to the road.

Time and again, while Adelia itched with impatience, the entire cavalcade stopped in order to watch Princess Joanna fly her hawk and applaud its kill.

Inevitably, gradually, among the lesser servants, friendships were formed and enmities broke out, so that the procession thinned in some places and gained bulges in others, as if an otherwise smooth snake had swallowed, and was digesting, its lunch.

There was always a crowd surrounding the musicians, while the cart containing the master blacksmith and his equipment was left to travel alone, he being surly to every living thing except horses.

Bantering, flirting soldiers gathered around the laundresses' and maids' section. Even Captain Bolt permitted this as long as the patrols were kept up, the treasure carts guarded, and the rear protected. Most of his men were mercenaries, he said, and had to find feminine comfort where they could.

The chief laundress, however, a large woman with warts and an evangelical approach to religion—she affected to shrink back in holy indignation and mutter her prayers if Mansur was in the offing—swiped the men away and made sure of her charges' chastity by accompanying them into the woods during the stops for calls of nature.

An Englishwoman by the name of Brune, she'd been doing Eleanor's laundry for many years and had become a close friend of Joanna's nurse—a length of service and royal connection that gave her a good opinion of herself. "My girls shall keep their virginity for the good Lord's sake," she was heard to say unctuously to an approving Father Guy. "Like I kept mine."

"As if," Captain Bolt said, "anybody'd try to take it off her."

At night, Mansur and Adelia joined Dr. Arnulf in the princess's room to make the regular assessment of her health by checking the royal pulse and examining phials of the royal urine. By day, however, they rode farther down the line, away from the leading party, where Ward could trot along at their horses' heels without both him and Adelia attracting taunts from the ladies-in-waiting, nor the Arab having to endure the viciousness of the Saracen-hating chaplain, Father Guy.

Their new position at least made them popular with such of the rank and file who felt unwell or had sustained minor injuries and found Dr. Arnulf too lofty to attend to them.

"Cap'n Bolt said I was to come to the darkie doctor," James the wheelwright told Adelia as she splinted his crushed finger. "That other'n, he don't care for the poor. Bugger wanted a fee."

For Adelia the greatest happiness of being farther down the cavalcade was that, from time to time, Rowley could pause beside her as he rode up and down the line to see that all was well; precious, stolen moments for them both as he chatted ostensibly to Mansur in Arabic.

When he could spare the time, Locusta rode with them, apparently preferring their company to that of any other, and talking about Sicily.

So did Ulf. Other pilgrims were making friends among the royal servants and leaving the group to talk to them. Why shouldn't he?

So, too, when he wasn't hunting, did Father Adalburt, which was a surprise—and a not-unalloyed pleasure. The man was a fool. Because he spoke Latin and English, the latter being his native tongue, and was rarely in the company of those who couldn't, he showed astonishment when foreigners didn't understand him. He insisted on speaking to Mansur in a slow shout and being bewildered when he received no reply.

Every new thing amazed him. On passing a plantation of cork trees and requesting to know what they were, he refuted the answer with: "But there *are* no corks," as if expecting the branches to be laden with fully formed bottle tops.

"Why does the donkey not keep alongside his bishop?" Mansur asked, irritated. "Why does he plague us?"

Probably, Adelia thought, because the Bishop of Winchester was happy to get rid of him. Adalburt was amiable enough, his mouth always lolling in a smile, but how he had achieved his position was difficult to see.

"Because he's the bishop's bloody cousin, or something," Ulf, who'd done some research, said bitterly. "Been living as an anchorite for two years Scarfell Pike way, seemingly, and got a reputation for holiness. Told me he preached to the sheep. If he bored them as much as he does me, I'm sorry for 'em."

LOCUSTA AND HIS uncle had carefully chosen only accommodations capable of providing the enormous stabling and grazing necessary for the company and its horseflesh, good food, beds a-plenty without fleas—even baths. Establishments that didn't have the latter reckoned without Mesdames Beatrix, Petronilla, and Blanche. . . .

The Abbot of Redon, a somewhat smaller establishment than the retinue was used to, looked hopelessly into three beautiful, formidable faces. "But in this house, my daughters, we do not take baths except at Easter and Christmas, as advised by Saint Benedict—even then it is in the river."

The three looked for a withering moment toward the hapless Locusta. *No baths?*

He wrung his hands. "I'm sorry, I'm sorry, ladies. But to go on farther, or to have stopped earlier . . ."

The ladies didn't care about the difficulties of calculating a route.

"The river, though," Father Adalburt interposed brightly. "Is it not an example of God's bounty that He sent a river to flow past every great town that Man has built?"

The ladies didn't care about God's bounty, either. They turned back to the abbot.

"All very commendable, my lord," Lady Petronilla said, "but our princess is not Saint Benedict. She is a lady of the blood royal."

"From Aquitaine," Lady Beatrix pointed out. "And she has traveled through dust all day." She forbore to mention that, as well as dust, sweat was ruinous to robes that took a phalanx of embroideresses a year to adorn.

"Washing tubs will do," compromised Mistress Blanche. "My lord, you surely have washing tubs in your laundry?"

The poor man supposed that he had.

"Good," said Lady Petronilla. "Then please have all of them carried to our room. With lots of hot water."

Lady Beatrix patted the abbot's hand kindly: "We provide our own soap and towels."

In a steam-filled upper room—the abbot's was the only one large enough—Adelia watched the indistinct forms of maids come and go like ghostly water sprites as she rested her body in warm suds. It had been an unusually long journey of forty miles from their last stop to this.

From the dining room below rose the sound of tipsy men still at table singing a rousing chorus of the immemorial drinking song "*Gaudeamus igitur*." She could hear Rowley's voice among them. This was Calvados country; the abbey made it from its own apples and served it in place of ale, despite what the ascetic Saint Benedict would have said.

"Oh, dear," said Lady Beatrix through the scented vapor. "Sir Nicholas . . . Isn't Calvados very alcoholic?"

"Very," Blanche said. "We can only hope . . ."

Everybody in the room hoped with her.

From her tub in the middle of the mist, a wet princess changed the subject. "Are you sure God will not condemn us for too much bathing?" (The abbot had taken his revenge during his homily at supper by stressing the sin of vanity among women.)

"Definitely not, my lady," came Lady Petronilla's answer, stoutly. "Cleanliness is a godly attribute."

"So Mama says. But in his holiness Saint Thomas never bathed at all once he became Archbishop of Canterbury. They say he was crawling with lice when they undressed his dear body."

"That's saints," said Petronilla firmly. "It does not apply to ladies of gentle birth."

"But when we visited the shrine of the Blessed Sylvia, we were told that the only part of her she ever washed were her fingers."

"I'm sure she had her reasons, dear." This was Beatrix. "But the good Lord likes his queens to be *clean*." There was a soapy pause. "Along with their ladies-in-waiting."

Seated in her tub at the end of the row, Adelia grinned. These were acerbic women and no friends to her, but at this moment, with the ache of her limbs being soothed away, she blessed them. She had begun to see that, in their way, they were admirable, clustering protectively round their princess, jealous for her comfort—and their own, of course—entertaining her on the long, long marches with songs—each played a musical instrument—riddles and stories, always exquisitely turned out, their hair perfectly braided under circlets and floating veils, skin like silk on their slim figures, bodices low-cut to show alabaster cleavage.

Men who saw them floundered, later remembering a dream of beauty that would not come again.

It was, she supposed, what Rowley wanted for Allie. But what sort of existence was it? Was veneer enough? Only Petronilla could read, an exercise she confined to books of manners; all three were ignorant of history, except that of their ancestry, and none of them had any conception of life outside court. They talked dreamily of what noble husbands they could expect to be gifted to, as if their marriages were to be a lottery, which, presumably, they would be.

Adelia would have welcomed a peace pact in which to get to

know each of them better, but, regarding her as an intruder, they banded together so that their circle formed a fence against her in which their individuality was more or less lost.

Sighing, Adelia called through the scented steam for Boggart to bring her a towel, then winced as a crash indicated that an unguent bottle had been dislodged from the tub's edge—the girl was trying, bless her, but *trying*. "You can get into the water now, Boggart."

"Oh, yes, mistress. I'm getting used to that. And Ward's got powerful dirty today, I was wondering if I should take un in with me."

From among the vapors came a concerted chorus of "*Please*."

Dried and wrapped in one of Emma's cloaks, Adelia went out onto the landing, pausing in order to pick up her necklet with its cross from a table where the ladies had left their jewelry so that it should not get tarnished.

She couldn't find it.

Taking a flambeau from its holder on the wall, she held it over the table so that she could see better and searched again among the pile of glittering rings, brooches, and earrings belonging to the other women.

"Damn them," she said. "*Damn* them." The necklet was her only ornament, worn in remembrance of her childhood nurse, Margaret, who'd given her the original—a simple thing with a plain silver cross that she'd loved, but had put in the coffin of a murdered girl who'd greatly admired it, though, as soon as she could, she'd paid for another to be made exactly like the first.

To make sure, Adelia waited until a dripping Boggart and Ward emerged from the room of baths. "You didn't pick up my cross for any reason, did you, Boggart?"

"No, mistress."

"No, I didn't think you did. Damn them, those bitch . . . those blasted females have taken it to spite me."

Boggart considered. "Don't think as they can have, mistress. It was there when they all went in. I saw it. Ain't nobody left to come outside since."

In bed that night, Adelia lay awake for a while wondering who in the abbey was a thief, and why, out of all the jewelry on the table, he—or she—had stolen the one of least monetary value.

Well, with Allie waiting for her, time was of the essence and to make a fuss would only delay the morning's start while a search was made and people questioned, as well as make her even less popular than she was.

Yawning, she decided she would just have to employ another silversmith when she reached Sicily.

But the night was not over. . . .

This time the screams came from the gardens overlooked by the monastery's guesthouse windows.

This time they were terrible.

This time they were Boggart's.

There was a resentful mutter of "Sir Nicholas slipped his leash again" from one of the other women as Adelia ran for a cloak. Downstairs, she tugged back the bolts on the door and hurled herself into the garden.

In the middle of the lawn, Sir Nicholas's substantial and palpitating body was humped over Boggart's feet. His hands gripped her ankles so that moonlight threw the shadow of the girl's and man's figures onto the grass in the shape of a monstrous crochet, except for where a small dog tugged at the seat of the man's robe.

It would have been the scene of comedy if Boggart's mouth hadn't been contorted into a white O of horror and the screams pumping from it weren't those of a soul in remembered torment.

Adelia joined Ward in tugging at Sir Nicholas's robe—just as uselessly; the knight was fixed and oblivious. She tried kicking him. "Leave her alone, curse you," she yelled. "Curse you, you horrid old man, leave her *alone.*"

Later, she was to recall the sound of laughter coming from the guesthouse windows, but she knew then, and afterward, that this wasn't ridiculous; something terrible was happening.

She threw herself on the man and reached round his face for his eyes, digging her fingers into them. Even then, he shook his head like a bull so that her nails merely scraped the skin of his cheeks. But somebody was lifting her and Ward to one side while somebody else with more strength than she had was dragging the great bulk away from Boggart's feet and throwing it onto its back on the grass.

She had a glimpse of the knight's face, unrecognizably loose and vacant, before his squire and another man hefted him to his feet and carried him away.

Rowley was trying to comfort Boggart. "There, there, my dear. No need to be frightened; he has these turns, they don't mean anything. No harm done." She flinched away from him as he tried to touch her.

"Ask *her* if there's harm done," Adelia spat at him. She picked up the shivering Ward and put him in Boggart's arms. Then, with her hand on the girl's shoulder, she urged her toward a stone bench in the shadow of an arbor.

Rowley followed, at a loss. "Can I do anything?"

"No," Adelia told him. "We're going to sit here quietly for a while."

He sat with them, next to Adelia, while on the other side Boggart gasped at something they couldn't see. The girl was holding Ward so tightly that the tremors wracking her body were making him shake with her.

On the far side of the lawn, most of the shutters of the guesthouse were closing; entertainment over.

"Well, at least he left both her shoes this time," Rowley said, trying for lightness.

Adelia looked down at Boggart's shoes. She'd bought them for her in Caen, with another pair and some riding boots, to replace the hulking, hobnailed clogs—a man's, and far too big for her—that she'd been wearing in Southampton. The girl had clutched the new shoes as she was clutching Ward now, and for a long time couldn't be persuaded to wear them in case they were sullied. Eventually, Adelia had taken the clogs and thrown them away.

These were sullied now; the little ribbons that laced the sides had been mouthed so that they trailed limp and wet.

"Why does he do it?" Adelia asked. "What possible . . . *why*?"

"I don't know." Rowley paused. "She's been attacked before, hasn't she?"

"I think so."

"I'm sorry." He patted Adelia's hand and stood up. "She won't want me around, then."

"No."

For a moment, watching him walk reluctantly away, Adelia was overcome by her fortune in being loved by him. He was a man with failings, as all men had failings—as she was an imperfect woman—but his humanity concealed no clefts in which lay hidden monsters like that of Sir Nicholas; it went clean to the core.

We must both do better by Allie, she thought, *she needs the two of us. We must do it together.*

Boggart, staring straight ahead, began talking. "My fault," she was saying. "This un . . ." She clutched Ward harder. "His poor little belly were upset by summat so I reckoned to walk him. . . . My silly fault. I thought as he was a kindly gent'man. I smiled at him. Silly to make a fuss, no harm done, my fault . . ."

"Boggart," Adelia said. She put out a hand to the girl's face, to turn it toward hers. "You listen to me. *This was not your fault*. It's happened to others. Sir Nicholas is one of those men that has a demon caged inside him. Drink lets it loose. He attacked you, but it could have been anybody, any woman at all. It could have been me. You're no more at fault than . . . than a tree hit by lightning."

"Ain't I?"

"No."

"Tha's good, then." She sounded doubtful.

"Boggart. Something happened to you. Before this, I mean. Do you want to talk about it?"

"I'm all right, mistress. Really I am."

"No, you're not. It might help if you told me."

If Boggart was going to, the moment went. Somebody was approaching them from across the garden; Mistress Blanche was walking carefully, so as not to spill a mug in her hand.

She said: "I thought the child might need a pick-me-up. The kitchener gave me some milk. I've put some brandy in it."

Adelia had to untwine Boggart's hands from Ward's fur and, even then, hold the mug to her lips.

In her perfect enunciation, the lady-in-waiting said: "It's never nice, this sort of thing, but men are strange cattle. After all, he did her no harm. One just has to get over it."

Adelia looked up sharply, but the woman had taken thought and trouble for Boggart. There was humanity here, too; even fellow feeling.

"She's blaming herself, I suppose," Mistress Blanche said.

"Yes."

"One always does. Tell her not to."

It was an admission so unexpected and revealing, such an unbending, that Adelia instinctively put out her hand.

Mistress Blanche didn't take it; there were to be no all-women-together confessions. "I was concerned for the girl," she said. "And so should you be. She's getting cold."

Together, they got Boggart to her feet and took her back to the guesthouse.

FROM A WINDOW *Scarry has been watching them, laughing a little.*

He has been holding a silver necklet with a cross in his hand. Now he drops it carefully down a crack between two uneven floorboards.

WHEN ADELIA TOLD ROWLEY about the loss of her necklet, he was concerned. "I don't like you not to be wearing a cross."

"Why?"

"Every other woman has one; it singles you out."

Adelia shrugged. "I'm singled out already."

For a moment he looked into her eyes. "You are for me," he said.

When Ulf heard of the theft, he, too, became thoughtful.

"Funny that," he said. "Lord Ivo's squire told me as how somebody's been rummagin' in the luggage packs. Nothing taken, though."

"Why, do you think?"

"Lookin' for this, p'raps." Ulf patted the wooden cross poking out from his mule's saddlebag.

"That cannot be," Mansur said. "If a thief is after the sword, he would search for it in the treasure chests, not luggage."

"Would he, though, *would* he? Iffen he's clever, he'd reckon as how the king'd know them chests'd be the first to be raided in an attack and he'd reckon old Henry would've hidden you-know-what somewhere else."

Ulf's childhood had introduced him to the criminal mind, but this was too subtle for Adelia: "*If* it's the same thief and *if* he took my necklace instead of the ladies' diamonds, he's not as clever as all that."

Their conversation was interrupted by Admiral O'Donnell coming up on his magnificent bay, accompanied by Deniz on a donkey. When those two men weren't taking the rare opportunity, for seamen, of joining Sir Nicholas and Lord Ivo in a hunt, they spent a good deal of the time riding alongside Mansur.

Deniz said never a word, but his master persisted in asking the Arab about his native customs, telling stories of Ireland and seafaring to Adelia, and questioning Ulf about the Cambridgeshire fenlands. In fact, Ulf particularly seemed to intrigue him.

"Now isn't that the interesting young man," said O'Donnell, watching Ulf ride away to join his group. "A friend of yours?"

"As are all the pilgrims, I hope," Adelia returned.

"Not your usual pilgrim, though, wouldn't you say?"

"Is he not?" Adelia said, feigning boredom. "What's different about him?"

"Ah, well, I can't put me finger on it exactly . . . a certain lack of holy zeal, maybe. I'd say he lacks the sense of *mysterium tremendum* that most of them have, would you not agree?"

"I think he suspects Ulf of not being a real pilgrim," Adelia told Mansur grimly, after the Irishman had gone. "Why can't the blasted man leave us alone? I'm beginning to wonder if he's looking for Excalibur."

"It is for you that he joins us, I think," Mansur said.

"Nonsense, he's prying."

The Arab shrugged. "We have given nothing away."

But Adelia was left with the feeling that, somehow, they had.

"LUPUS, MEO CARO, *I have found Excalibur, I think. Henry gave it to his creature and she, with wily subterfuge, has it concealed,* arte perire sua. *The stinking cur that is always with her leaps on the youthful pilgrim with a rapture he shows to no one else except her Saracen and her maladroit maid. They are connected. Also, the boy is never without the rough cross he carries. Does it rattle if shaken, I wonder? I believe it does.*

Richard shall have it and make us rich as he promised. Let him create havoc with it, let him use it to kill his father, for that is what he secretly wishes. Our main purpose lies elsewhere.

PROGRESS SLOWED WHEN they joined the broad highway leading toward Aquitaine, for this was the main westerly route to the Pyrenees and the road was crowded with pilgrims on their way to, or coming back from, the great shrine of Saint James at Compostela.

Here was holy zeal a-plenty; the air thrummed with it as well as with a hundred different languages and the smell of unwashed bodies tinged by mugwort, a specific against weariness that most of the pilgrims had tucked into their hats or shoes. Those returning from Spain, limping from their long march, despite the mugwort, wore the apostle's token of a cockleshell and a look of exaltation. Villagers came out from their houses to beg their blessing or kiss the hands that had touched the sacred tomb.

The ones still on their way to Compostela were mostly rowdier, yelling hallelujahs, praising the Lord that their sins would soon be forgiven, some scourging themselves, some dancing, some clearly demented, some barefoot.

One tatterdemalion group surrounded Joanna's cart, shouting at her to come with them for the good of her soul. Captain Bolt's men would have dispersed them with the flat of their swords, but the princess showed her mettle by standing up and throwing coins into the crowd.

"I have made the pilgrimage, good people, and been blessed accordingly. Take these alms and may God speed you."

It was the ones pushing handcarts containing their sick relatives in the expectation that Saint James would cure them who concerned Adelia, and she went among them with her medical bag to try to treat them. In most cases she was waved away: "Thank you kindly, but Saint James'll mend us when we get to him."

"Leave them," Mansur advised. "There are too many of them."

There were, but she couldn't bear to abandon them, and he had to force her back on her horse or she would have been left behind.

At the next monastery, *Scarry watches his victim from a high window.*

"There she goes to the courtyard to subsume herself in the pilgrims' gangrenous flesh. And her lustful bishop with her, ostensibly to give comfort and alms, but in truth to be by her side.

"Yes, I hear you, beloved. We approach Aquitaine. It is time for the killing to begin."

TWO

Six

THE FIRST TWO KILLINGS appeared to be accidental—and one of them actually was.

The ladies of the party having retired to bed, the Abbot of Saint Benoît's was sitting late at table with his male guests, and offering them the opportunity to go after boar in an hour or two's time—boar hunting being best done at night when the male, most dangerous of quarries, leaves his sow and young ones in their lair to patrol the forest, snuffling his snout into the leaf mold and plowing the earth with his great tusks to sharpen them.

As Rowley explained to Adelia later, each man had feasted well but was not too drunk. Sir Nicholas had been watched carefully by his squire, who had seen to it that, when refilling his master's wine cup, there'd been a good measure of water in it.

The abbot was talking of the grandfather of all boars that had been ruining his sown fields through the winter, not to mention killing two peasants. A worthy adversary at the height of his powers, God love him, the abbot had said. To prove it, he had his huntsman bring to the table such of the brute's droppings as had been found so that the guests could assess them.

Also, the abbot went on, he owned a pack of boar hounds that were *sans pareil* and ready for the fray. He was sure the noble lords would wish to see them in action.

"You can imagine it, sweetheart," Rowley told Adelia, "nearly all the noble lords, and some not so noble, were on their feet in an instant, calling for their horses to be saddled, especially Lord Ivo and Sir Nicholas and, of course, the ubiquitous O'Donnell." Rowley's mouth went into the thin line it was beginning to adopt every time the Irishman was mentioned.

He went on: "I tried to restrain Father Adalburt because boar hunting is not for amateurs, but the idiot was squeaking with excitement and couldn't be persuaded. Locusta—poor lad, he doesn't get much chance to hunt what with having to act as route master all the time—he wanted to go. Even Father Guy was enthused and said he'd join in, at least to watch."

The Bishop of Winchester had declined on the grounds of being too old and tired. Rowley, reluctantly, had decided to accompany the hunt, mainly, he said, to keep his eye on the idiots.

IN THE LITTLE *stone lodge in the grounds of the Abbot of Saint Benoît's house, huntsmen are arming themselves. For this is where the good abbot keeps his spears, lances, crossbows, bolts, arrows and yew bows, his stabbing and gralloching knives.*

The men are excited and, as ever when boar is the quarry, a little nervous. Not so the hounds in the kennels next door; they are clamoring to be let out and do what they've been bred for.

Somebody chaffs Scarry for picking too slender a spear. "That'll never get through a tusker's hide."

Scarry gives a naïve smile. "Won't it?" But he hefts its weight and takes it all the same.

ADELIA WAS ATTENDING to sick pilgrims in the abbey courtyard as the hunt set off, its blare of trumpets and horns competing with the shouts of the whipper-in, the deep belling of the hounds and the rallying cries of riders.

She was in bed asleep when it returned but, like everyone else, was woken by the long note of a horn emerging from the forest sounding the mort, the salute to a dead quarry.

Except that this time it was not announcing the death of an animal . . .

It was raining. Monks, guests, and pilgrims gathered by the gates to watch the dripping hunt's return. A weeping abbot walked beside a hastily assembled travois on which lay two bodies.

The corpse of Sir Nicholas Baicer was taken immediately to the Lady Chapel. Lord Ivo, bleeding horribly, was carried to the abbot's room and laid on its bed.

The boar had indeed proved a worthy adversary; the dogs had found and bayed it; Lord Ivo and the abbot with their squires and huntsmen had dismounted ready for the kill.

But, though hounds were sinking their teeth into almost every part of it, the huge animal managed to charge and gore Lord Ivo in the groin, tossing him into the air, before the abbot's sword went deep into its eye.

"Only then," said the abbot, still crying, "did we notice that Sir Nicholas was not with us, indeed had not been with us when we found the beast. Being moonless, the forest was so dark that I fear many of our following missed their way. A search was instituted and at last we came upon Sir Nicholas, lifeless, being dragged by his horse, his poor foot still in its stirrup. Now God forgive me that this tragedy should come upon us . . . one fine knight injured unto death, another already gone to Paradise and my best boarhound with him. Surely, we are accursed."

With Mansur and Dr. Arnulf giving instruction, Adelia and the abbey's herbalist did what they could for Lord Ivo.

By general agreement, sphagnum moss was applied to his injuries to cleanse them and stem the blood. But, as Adelia could see, the tusks had gone in too far, his lordship was undoubtedly bleeding internally, and to stitch the wounds together would merely cause more agony without extending a life that was inevitably coming to its end.

She hurried from the room to fetch poppy juice from her pack and found Rowley waiting for her outside. "Is Ivo dying?"

"Yes. All we can do is to relieve the pain."

"How long?"

"I don't know." She was distressed.

"I'll go in. God have mercy on a good friend and a fine soldier."

When Adelia returned to the room, Rowley was holding Lord Ivo's hand while the Bishop of Winchester prayed as he readied the oils in his chrismatory box preparatory to giving the last rites. The abbot, still in hunting clothes, Father Guy, and Dr. Arnulf were discussing in low voices such of Saint Benoît's relics as could help forward Lord Ivo's soul to its immortal rest, while Mansur, apparently detached from the conversation, looked on with a concern unlike his usual impassivity.

Candles in their holders at the head and foot of the bed cast upward shadows that distorted the faces of the men standing up, turning their eye sockets into those of skulls.

Only the dying man's features were fully lit, and Adelia gritted her teeth at the thought of what agony he was in and with what courage he was bearing it. His eyes were shut, his lips compressed, but his hand gripped at Rowley's like a raptor's.

"Here, my lord," she said, passing the phial to Mansur.

Dr. Arnulf was on them in a second. "And what is that?"

"Poppy juice. Lord Mansur has prescribed it for the pain."

"*Poppy juice?*" This was Father Guy. "It is the devil's concoction. That dear man on the bed is being purified and redeemed by what he suffers. The agony of Christ endowed pain with his own touch of divinity. You, Arnulf, you are a clerk in minor orders as well as a doctor, you surely cannot agree to this. There are edicts from the Vatican. . . ."

"Indeed I cannot," Dr. Arnulf said firmly. "The poppy, *mandragora*, hemp seed, all are absent from my medicine chest."

Adelia stared at them, trying to understand what she was hearing. "That man is in torment. You can't, you *can't* deny him relief."

"Better torment of the body than the soul," Father Guy told her.

The abbot joined them, still smelling of the wide outdoors and the blood, Lord Ivo's blood, on the sleeves of his leather tunic. "My child, I have sent for the femur of Saint Stephen, the first martyr. We must pray that its application will aid this good knight through his martyrdom."

"Help me," Adelia said in Arabic.

Mansur acted. Snatching the phial from her hand, he showed it to Rowley, who looked toward Adelia. She nodded.

While the Arab held Lord Ivo's head up, Rowley administered the opiate: "Here, my dear friend."

While Father Guy raved that the noble lord had not yet made his confession, a furious Arnulf pulled Adelia out of the room.

"You chit," he hissed. "Do you and your master set yourselves up against the Holy Fathers, against practice as laid down by Blessed Mother Church?"

This was too much. She hissed back, "Since when would a true mother allow any son of hers to suffer as that poor man is suffering? Or any true doctor, either?"

"Do you question my authority?"

"Yes, I bloody well *do*." She stamped off down the corridor.

IT TOOK ALL DAY for Lord Ivo to die. Joanna and the ladies-in-waiting spent it in the abbey church, praying for the soul that had departed and the one that was about to depart.

Adelia spent it in her room. Twice more, Mansur came in to have the phial refilled. Lord Ivo had gained consciousness long enough to make his confession and receive the last rites from the Bishop of Winchester.

Dr. Arnulf and Father Guy, having washed their hands of the business, Mansur said, had left the sickroom.

"Good." But she grimaced. "We haven't made any friends today, you and I."

"Do we want friends such as those?"

"No. They call themselves Christians. When did Christ ever look on suffering without being moved to help it?"

"I do not think they are Christians, I think they are churchmen."

When he'd gone, she turned back to the window. It had begun to rain hard. She could see a river not far away, the heavy raindrops making discs in its surface. Under a dark gray sky, the forest beyond it appeared an indeterminate mass. It occurred to her that she knew the name of neither and felt the panic of an orphaned child taken away from everything it loved to be abandoned in a hostile landscape. The thought that Allie could be feeling the same bowed her down.

She longed for the comfort Gyltha would have given her. "*We been through worse nor this, bor*."

And so they had, but not apart.

It was dark when Mansur returned to say that Lord Ivo was dead. He handed her a monk's habit. "You are to put this on and join the bishop in the Lady Chapel."

"Why?"

"He thinks there was something strange about Sir Nicholas's death."

The awfulness of the day was suddenly released by the ridiculous. How typical of Rowley; not a beckoning to a lovers' tryst, but a command to waddle through a crowded abbey in disguise. To do what? Perform an autopsy?

She would go, of course. If she was caught, she could hardly be in worse odor with everybody than she was now. She would go because she was an iron filing drawn to that man's magnet. She would go because . . . well, because it was a silly thing to do, and silliness just now was a blessing.

She took her veil and circlet off her hair and pulled on the habit, putting its cowl over her head until the hem dangled over her eyes. "Do I look like a monk?"

"You do. A short one."

In fact, nobody noticed her. The abbey was in uproar: two important guests killed while under its aegis; people to be told, messages sent; funerals to be arranged; special services to be held; and, with it all, the holy hours to be kept. Monks scurried anxiously in from the rain and out again, cowls dripping, heads bent in an effort to keep their sandaled feet out of puddles. She could have made her way through them and been paid no attention if she'd been clashing two cymbals together as she went.

The Lady Chapel stood by itself, an adjunct of the abbey's church, and possibly its oldest building. The figure waiting for her was taller than its carved, chevroned porch.

"You took your time," it said. He twisted the handle ring and flung one of the door's leaves open with a crash.

Immediately, Adelia smelled incense, beeswax, and death. Inside the only light came from two tall candles on stanchions at the head and base of the catafalque where Sir Nicholas lay. Two monks knelt on either side.

The only sound in the silence was the ***plink-plink*** of rainwater seeping through a leak in the roof and into a bucket that was lost in the shadows.

Rowley said: "Thank you, brothers, you may leave. I'll watch over my friend for a while."

They were glad to go and rose at once. Rubbing their poor knees, they bowed to the corpse, the altar, then to the Bishop of Saint Albans before gliding out.

Rowley banged the door shut behind them and bolted it. "Now, then, come and look at this."

The body had been wrapped in a silk winding sheet. Usually, the face was left exposed, but not this time. Adelia might have been looking down on an Egyptian mummy.

Together and with difficulty—Sir Nicholas had been a heavy man—she and Rowley labored to unwind it from its cocoon.

When at last the corpse was exposed, she saw why the face had been covered; there was a jagged gap where one of the eyes should have been.

"What happened?"

"Young Aubrey found him first and began calling the 'Found.' Jesus, it was a fiasco, that hunt. Raining, dark as the Pit, too many men scattered among too many sodding trees, not knowing where one another was, me trying to round them up."

Rowley took off his cap to claw his fingers through his hair, and she saw that his face was pinched by tiredness and grief.

"Anyway," he said, "I heard Aubrey's horn and spurred toward it. The boy . . . he'd unhitched Nicholas's foot from its stirrup and put the body on the ground. He was crying over it. There was this great splinter in poor old Nicholas's eye, so we reckoned his horse had bolted and crashed him into a branch and that's what killed him."

"But you don't think so now?"

"Well . . . there was Ivo, Nicholas, no time to think anything. But when I was sitting by Ivo, trying to make sense of it all, it came to me that if it was the branch splinter that killed Nicholas, there should have been a lot of blood—and there wasn't. Dead men don't bleed; you taught me that."

"Something else killed him first?"

"That's what you're here for. And get on with it, they'll be bringing Ivo here soon."

Adelia pushed back her cowl. For a moment, as she always did, she knelt by the body, asking its forgiveness for her handling of it. The soul that had occupied it was absolved; the dead were sinless—also they were her business.

Whoever had done the laying out of the corpse had made a rushed job of washing it; there were green smears on the skin where the knight's clothes had been torn as he'd been dragged through grass. Stones and brambles had left long lacerations in the flesh.

"Give me more light."

Hot wax dripped onto unfolded layers of the winding sheet as Rowley picked up one of the stanchions and held it nearer. From behind her, in the darkness, came the regular, musical drip of water into its bucket.

"Hmmm."

"What?"

"This." Her fingers had found a flap of torn, corrugated skin on the upper left back and, beneath it, a hole. This was what had bled—and profusely; the negligent layers-out had left crusts of blood around it.

"Here." Adelia's fingers investigated deeper. "Something's embedded itself. I can feel wood."

She looked up. "Rowley, I think it's a spear shaft, very thin but, yes, I'm sure it's some sort of shaft, certainly a dart of some kind. It snapped off when he was dragged but this is what killed him; he was speared."

His voice shocked the quiet. "*Fucking poachers.*" His fingers went through his hair again, and he said more gently: "Jesus God, such an end for a man like this."

"What will you do?"

"Tell the abbot he's a bloody disgrace, letting poachers roam his purlieus shooting anything that moves." He went stamping around in the darkness, casting verbal damnation on villains who went out to kill other men's game, describing in detail the unpretty end of this one if Rowley Picot got hold of him.

Adelia heard the bucket kicked to Kingdom Come and go rolling across the tiles. She'd been hoping to wash her hands in its water.

She let him rave. There was something particularly terrible about death by mistake, and it was difficult to see what else this could be . . . darkness, rain; a peasant—hungry perhaps—concealed and waiting in the undergrowth, listening for the sound of animal movement; hearing the rush of something big; then the expert and very lucky throw of a homemade spear . . .

Nor was it uncommon. Her knowledge of English history was uncertain, but hadn't one of the Conqueror's sons, what was his name, been accidentally killed in similar circumstances? In the New Forest, that had been. Rufus, that was it. William Rufus. A king, no less.

When Rowley had quieted, she asked: "Do you want me to get the spearhead out? I'd have to go for my knives."

"No. Let's give him back his decency." He came back to help her.

When the last wrap was in place, she stayed on her knees awhile longer.

She looked up to find Rowley staring at her and was suddenly aware that her hair was tumbled about her shoulders and that she was beautiful, because she always was beautiful in his eyes.

"God help me, girl," he said, and his voice was raw, "but I'd tip this poor devil off his catafalque, throw you on it, and take you here and now. The hell with my immortal soul—and yours."

"I'd let you," she said.

But there wasn't time; even now they could hear feet sloshing through rain and voices chanting: ". . . *every tear from their eyes; Death will be no more* . . ."

Rowley had the door unbolted in an instant, and the procession came in, carrying Lord Ivo on its shoulders. ". . . *and crying and pain will be no more, for the first things have passed away.*"

Adelia covered her head and stood by the door to let the monks go by, then slipped away, unnoticed.

THE ABBOT HAD a bad time of it. While his bailiffs rounded up for questioning every man on his estates capable of throwing a well-aimed spear, he had to consult with the two bishops as to what should be done with the corpses. Sent home or buried *in situ*?

In the end, their hearts were cut out and placed in lead-lined caskets for their squires and servants to take back to the families. A messenger went galloping to Henry Plantagenet to inform him that he had lost two of his most trusted men.

The interment of the rest of the flesh was conducted in pouring rain in the Saint Benoît graveyard, where Princess Joanna wept for her knights.

As Sir Nicholas was lowered into his grave, Father Guy and Dr. Arnulf looked toward where Adelia was standing. The chaplain was heard to say: "I hope that female is happy now, for was she not the one who cursed this good man?"

WHEN THE PROCESSION finally set off again, now reduced by twenty or so servants, the absence of Lord Ivo and Sir Nicholas was palpable. There was a sense of unease, less laughter. For all Sir Nicholas's funny ways, he and Lord Ivo had radiated the stability and authority of their king and the lack made everyone else feel less safe.

The Bishop of Winchester was the most affected. He was noticeably more nervous than he had been; the Young King had failed the princess, and now here was tragedy come upon them. Echoing the words of his erstwhile host, he said: "*Surely, we are accursed*," and confided to his intimates that he was beginning to believe that God was displeased with their enterprise.

This was passed along the line, where ill-wishers like Father Guy, the princess's nurse, Edeva, and the head laundress, Brune, pointed out that of *course* God was displeased. Were they not sheltering in their company not only one of His avowed enemies, a Saracen, but his woman, who seemed to have the power to bring destruction on such men and animals who crossed her?

THE PROCESSION WAS now entering Aquitaine, the duchy named for its waters that had been Eleanor's and which, after her marriage, had been passed to Henry Plantagenet, and which, since her imprisonment, was under the governorship of their second son, Duke Richard.

The weather cleared so that the sun shone, as if it could do no less for the daughter of the land's beloved duchess.

Even the Bishop of Winchester cheered up. "We shall be safe now. The lionhearted duke meets us at Poitiers."

There would be no lack of knights with Richard escorting his sister to Sicily, he kept hundreds by him—not for the pretend war of tournaments, like his brother, but so that one day he could lead them to the real thing, crusade.

"Mad for it," Rowley said of him, grimacing; he was no enthusiast for crusading, nor for Richard himself. "But first he's got to pacify southern Aquitaine—and serve him right, he stirred it up in the first place. He thought its barons were being loyal to him when he led them against his father. In fact, of course, it was their chance to grab more land for themselves, and they see no reason to stop doing it now that Richard and Henry have come to terms."

"It looks peaceful enough," Adelia said, regarding the countryside with pleasure, "and so beautiful."

"Mistress, it is not beautiful in Limoges or Taillebourg or Gascony," said Locusta who, with Admiral O'Donnell and Deniz, had come alongside. "Duke Richard has subdued those at least and I saw what was left of them on my way through the country. We will avoid them as we go—what was done is not fit for ladies' eyes. *Bella, horrida bella.*"

"Savagery?" asked Rowley.

"Atrocity."

Rowley nodded. "He has that about him. His father believes in treating with rebels once he's defeated them—anything else is sowing dragon's teeth—but I doubt Richard sees the sense of it; the boy has the touch of the butcher in him."

"The lad's yet young," the O'Donnell said. "Didn't we all have the butcher in us when we were young? *Experto credite.*"

What butchery had the O'Donnell committed in his youth? Adelia wondered.

Rowley spurred his horse forward, away from the group; the admiral was not to his taste. Ulf didn't like the man either, but, as Locusta also rode off, Adelia was left with him.

"And where would the Lord Mansur be today?" he wanted to know.

"Occupied."

In fact, Mansur had stayed behind with Boggart at their last overnight stop in order to teach the girl how to wash, dry, iron, and fold clothes. This should have been the job of the laundresses, who were given special dispensation by Winchester's bishop to do their work on Sundays, the day when the column obeyed the Tenth Commandment to rest and stayed where it was. More and more often, however, Adelia's washing and Mansur's white robes were being returned to them still showing travel stains.

"Just carelessness," Adelia had said, to pacify Mansur, though she didn't think it was; Brune's hostility to the Arab and even herself was becoming increasingly blatant.

She'd added, hastily: "We won't say anything." The chief laundress was daunting and so, when he was roused, was Mansur; a quarrel between them would not be pretty.

But even in the past, when they'd traveled with Gyltha, Mansur had always done his own laundry; he was particular about it. Now, as *Lord* Mansur, he could not be seen attending to anything so menial, and was therefore making this attempt to transfer his skills to the slow-learning Boggart and taking it amiss that the chief laundress, whose duty it was, forced him to do it.

While Adelia was at the back of the line with the pilgrims, attending to a case of foot rot, he came cantering up to her, Boggart riding pillion with one of Adelia's cloaks under her arm.

Dismounting, Mansur took the cloak and shook it out in display. "It is still stained. I told the ugly bint to use fuller's earth on it. She has not."

"Oh, dear." Adelia put the pilgrim's boot back on with the instruction to keep the area between his toes clean and, above all, dry.

"I have reprimanded her."

"In English? Now this is a tincture of myrrh and marigold. No, you don't drink it, you apply it to the affected skin twice a day."

"I used sign language," Mansur told her.

"Oh, dear."

"It is time to complain of that fat camel to the bishop. She used sign language back. It was not polite."

"Oh, *dear*."

As they rode back up the line, Brune was waiting for them. She'd got down from her cart to stand in the middle of the road, red-faced, arms akimbo, with an expectant group of fellow servants round her.

"You, mistress," she shouted at Adelia. "Yes, you. I got a bone to pick with you." She turned dramatically to her audience while pointing at Adelia. "Know what she done? She only sends that big heathen to complain about her laundry, that's what she done. Babbling away in that squeak of his, he was, shakin' his black finger at me like I was dirt. Well, I ain't putting up with it, not from them as don't believe in our Lord Savior."

It went on and on, an outpouring of righteousness that Adelia, taken aback, could see had been in preparation for some time. Brune was enjoying it.

Adelia's friend Martin tried to intervene. "All right, missus, that's enough. . . ."

But the laundress was being carried away by her own oratory. Sweeping the groom aside, she raised her tirade's volume to make sure that the growing crowd could hear her. "I'm on the side of our dear Jesus, I am, my lord, and them as is spitting on his blessed cross in the Holy Land can do their own laundry, even if I'm martyred for it."

"What's this now?" Attracted by the rumpus, Admiral O'Donnell had come up unnoticed.

Brune turned to him. "I may be a common washerwoman, my lord, but Queen Eleanor used to say as my soul was as clean as my washing. 'You speak out for the Lord, good Brune,' she used to say. . . ."

"Ah, you're a fine doorful of a woman, Mistress Brune, but if it's a saying you want, I'll give you one of my old granny's back in Ireland: '*Spite never speaks well.*'"

With that he picked the laundress up like a sack and threw

her back in her cart. He dusted his hands and turned to the crowd: "And here's another one for ye: '*For what can be expected from a sow but a grunt?*'"

IN THE ENSUING *cheers and boos, for the head laundress is popular with some but not others, Scarry rides off, his head turned away to hide his gratitude for the fat plum that Lucifer has, again, dropped so lusciously into his palms.*

"Your God go with you, Mistress Brune. May you rest in peace."

Seven

ADELIA ALWAYS THOUGHT she would have got on well with Poitiers's first bishop despite the eight centuries that separated them. An independent thinker, most literate and forbearing of early saints, he'd had a wife and daughter—those being the days when the priesthood had been allowed to marry.

Also, she thought, anybody who, on converting to Christianity, had chosen the baptismal name of Hilarius must have been fun to meet.

As she rode close behind the princess's carriage, it was possible to believe that the city had never lost the good nature that Saint Hilarius, or Saint Hilaire as they called him now, had bequeathed it. Bells rang a welcome. The waving crowds lining the slopes of winding streets to see Joanna go past showed real joy at her return to her mother's people. She was their princess. From the overhanging windows, dried rose petals and affection came scattering down on the girl familiar to Poitiers since she was a baby.

They were to spend a week here and, desperate to hurry on to Sicily and get back though Adelia was, she couldn't but be glad of it. Humans and animals were becoming irritable with fatigue; they needed a rest.

As they emerged onto the plateau on which stood the heart of Poitiers, she heard Joanna give the appreciative moan of someone who'd come home. White stone towers and frontages were pinkish ochre in an evening sun that was turning the water of the encircling rivers some 130 feet below into calm, willow-draped coils of amethyst.

Adelia felt a pang for the exiled, imprisoned woman whose favorite seat this had been and who'd so indelibly set her mark on it. For who but Eleanor could have ordered the trees in the open spaces to still be so pretty in late autumn or set up playing fountains of nude figures that would have scandalized her first husband, the pious Louis? And, though the cathedral she and Henry had begun wasn't finished, its frontage was already a miracle of carving that told the Bible story, and it must have been Eleanor's influence that included in it a baby Jesus in what looked like his bath watched over by sheep.

Only a few miles away, in A.D. 732, Charles Martel, Duke of the Franks, had turned back the Islamic tide that was sweeping the Frankish kingdom and saved it from Moslem conquest—a turning point for Europe of which Poitiers was proud and which, Adelia feared, might cause Mansur's presence in the city to be regarded as an offense, especially among unsophisticates like the head laundress and Joanna's nurse, who would lose no time in broadcasting it.

Unlike the Young King, Richard Plantagenet hadn't rushed to meet his sister; he was not, as Adelia saw at a glance, an impulsive youth.

He stood at the doors of Eleanor's palace like a colossus, taller than and as splendid as Young Henry but weightier, both physically and mentally, and dressed in gold.

The brothers did not get on. They had combined in the revolt against their father, but when the three of them made peace and Henry II had ordered the elder to go and help Richard put down the Aquitanian rebels, the Young King had deserted the fight and gone off to take part in more tournaments.

Just looking at Richard now, Adelia knew that if it ever came to open war between them, the younger would win.

After he bowed to Joanna and kissed her hand, his deep voice rang over the courtyard: "Here is my beloved sister, princess of my blood. Who befriends her is my friend; who harms her shall feel the might of my fist."

Unnecessary, Adelia thought. *Who would harm that child?*

Joanna, however, gazed up at her brother in adoration as, with her fingertips on his, she was led into a hall as big and as impressive as any Adelia had ever seen.

The feast held in it that night also reflected Eleanor's taste—it certainly wouldn't have been Henry's.

Every course was elaborate; not a boar head without its tusks and an apple in its mouth, not a peacock without its fanned tail, nor an oyster without its faux pearl—yet the food was of a freshness suggesting that everything had been alive or growing yesterday in this richest of all countrysides. Youthful knights far outnumbered the women guests, which, again, would have suited Eleanor, who liked male admiration, especially from the young.

Her son did, too, it seemed. Though the women he knew well,

such as Lady Beatrix, Lady Petronilla, and Mistress Blanche, were being accorded the honor of sitting with him at the top table, as were the bishops of Winchester and Saint Albans, the handsome Locusta, whose lack of position and a title hardly merited it, was with them, and looking somewhat uncomfortable at being so singled out.

But then, Adelia thought, perhaps Richard wants to discuss with him the plans for the rest of their journey to Sicily.

Or was it that? When the duke addressed the ladies, which he did charmingly enough, his eyes were dull. When chaffing with his knights, or in conversation with Locusta, or accepting a dish from his kneeling page—a slim, beautiful lad—his whole face became refreshed.

Sitting in her unexalted place in the middle of one of the long tables below the dais, Adelia's glance met her lover's. She raised her eyebrows in interrogation.

He gave back the merest twitch of his head. *I think so.*

For a moment the intimacy of understanding between the two of them was so sweet she could think of nothing else. Again, she asked herself: *Why didn't I accept him when he offered? Fool, you fool, look at us now.*

She got herself under control and turned her mind back toward Aquitaine's princely duke. If she and Rowley were right, how dreadful for the young man. In the world's eyes, not just a sin but a crime; to be something nobody wanted him to be, not even himself. Perhaps, then, the frenetic need to save his soul and placate his disapproving God could only be assuaged by taking up His banner and killing His enemies.

His reception of Mansur had been as coldly courteous as it

had been to her but, presumably not daring to offend his father, he had at least given the Arab a place at the feast as high as Dr. Arnulf's.

On their way to their beds, Adelia heard Lady Petronilla say to the other ladies-in-waiting, "My dears, now we are *home.*"

IN THE CHILLY NIGHT, *two men are walking and talking in the garden that was once Eleanor of Aquitaine's. One of them has a massive shadow which sometimes blends into that of the other.*

"The sword is mine by right," he says. He keeps his voice low but it is deep with authority. "Who else am I but Arthur's heir? Who else will use it to defend our sweet and gracious Lord from His enemies?"

"I know where it is, and you shall have it by the time we reach Palermo, my lord," says the other shadow. "For, indeed, you are its rightful owner. Without you, Christendom will be cast into darkness and the Holy Places lost forever. Your father refuses to raise it in their defense."

"You will refer to him as the king." For all Richard's hatred of his father, anything that diminished Henry Plantagenet's royalty diminished his own.

"The king of course," says Scarry in apology. And then: "It is meet and right that you should have it, for if you could see the unworthiness of those to whom it has been entrusted, you would weep."

He pauses because there is a sob from beside him; Richard the Lionheart is *weeping. He cries easily; often he cries in church.*

After a considerate wait, Scarry goes on: "To take it is to rescue it from another thousand years of oblivion."

In the darkness, Scarry inclines his head a little, listening to the echo of his own words issue into the October air. That was rather fine; didn't sound like theft at all.

He resumes: "When the time comes . . ." It is a euphemism for the death of Henry II; both men know it. ". . . when the time comes it shall be as if it were rediscovered. And this hand . . ." Another pause as the lesser shadow blends into the first while Scarry plops a kiss on the royal palm. ". . . and this hand, this blessed, blessed hand, may then raise Excalibur that heretics everywhere shall flee in confusion at the sight of it, back to the Pit from which they were raised."

"Yes," Richard says. "Yes. It is meet and proper that this should be so. It is not demeaning that is done for the greater glory of God."

"It is not." There is a cough of some delicacy as Scarry slides from the divine to the financial. "And . . . er . . . there have been expenses."

"You will be paid as promised. On delivery. Now leave me."

Bowing, Scarry leaves and, looking back, sees that the colossus has fallen to its knees and its clasped hands are raised high in supplication for . . . what? Absolution? Removal of the thorn that so torments its poor flesh?

"You're praying to the wrong master, idiot," Scarry says quietly, and disappears into the blackness from which he has come.

EVEN THOUGH it was cold at night, these October days in Aquitaine were warm, and Joanna dived into her old haunts, a child again, scuffling through the autumn leaves as she played ball and blindman's buff with those of her own age, obviously as healthy as a ferret, leaving her doctors to their own devices.

There were creature comforts: enough bedrooms to give Adelia one of her own, to be shared only with Boggart and Ward—and, oh joy, it had a garderobe in it. There was a ladies' bathing place with a marbled, sunken bath twenty feet long. Every side table contained fruit and sweetmeats.

With it all, there was an alteration of sound. The Aquitanians amongst the wedding train had immediately reverted to their native tongue, the langue d'oc, so that the air of the palace echoed with it as if a breeze had wafted in from another, more exotic continent. It varied so much from the Norman French she was used to that Adelia, who soaked up languages like sand absorbs water, had difficulty with it at first but then, recalling her visits to the Occitan valleys of Italy, where the people spoke a patois version, was soon able to get her tongue round it and, when in church, to join the others in the Occitan version of the Paternoster—"*Paíre de Cèl, Paíre nòstre, sanctificat lo teu Nom*"—like a true Languedocienne.

However, the magic of the langue d'oc was not to be found in ecclesiastical chant but when it sang of love of woman. Draped over balustrades, leaning against statues, sighing, singing to their lutes and viols, were young nobles in whom Eleanor had inspired the tradition of courtly love. Any pretty noble lady would do; the thing was to adore her without hope of consummation.

Wherever they went, a flock of young men surrounded Lady Beatrix, Lady Petronilla, and Mistress Blanche like brightly colored birds around a spillage of corn.

Adelia, to her surprise, attracted a *trouvère* of her own, at least ten years younger than she was. She wondered if Sir Guillaume was too immature, too temporarily infatuated, or too stupid to realize that she was not of high birth and was in fact *persona non grata* amongst this newly arrived company or if, in this heady, enchanted place, nobody had bothered to tell him.

As she wandered the herb gardens, replenishing what stock from it she could, it was not unpleasant to be followed about by a youth who swore to the strum of a viol that he was wasting away for love of her.

Rowley didn't agree. He made a beeline for her. "And who's that popinjay when he's at home?"

Bless him, he can still be jealous. How satisfactory.

She said: "That's Sir Guillaume de Chantonnay. I think he sings rather well."

"Really? I've heard more tuneful corncrakes." He stalked off.

Practically the only person with whom Poitiers Palace did not agree was Father Guy. He was outraged by the palace's spiritual laxity in gambling. He loathed the singing that praised not God, but the female form. He saw damnation in the powder and paint, the low-cut dresses and trailing sleeves of the women—now ridiculously long—and in the short tunics that exposed the tightness of the hose over young men's buttocks.

He said so, volubly, and was further outraged that his fellow chaplain seemed delighted by all he saw. "Will you imperil your hope of Paradise?" he yelled at Father Adalburt when he caught him sitting up late with some of Richard's knights at a game of Hazard.

"But these worthy gentlemen *asked* me to join them," Adalburt bleated.

"Of course they did, you fool. You keep losing."

Adelia's only regret was that she now had no contact with Ulf. The pilgrims had been accommodated for the duration in a monastery just outside the city. However, it was nice to see more of Locusta, who, for now, could cease shuttling up and down between the voyagers and their nights' stay.

"You should try and rest more often," she told him. "You were beginning to look quite peaky."

Locusta grimaced. "It wasn't rest I was after." He looked to make sure he wasn't overheard. "To be honest, mistress, there's a lady in town whose acquaintance I was hoping to renew. She was very, um, *hospitable* to me when my uncle and I last passed through Poitiers, but the duke sees to it that I am kept in his company."

He looked round again. "Between you and me, practicing sword fights and tilting at the quintain all day is neither my idea of rest nor entertainment."

Smiling, Adelia sympathized. "Perhaps my Lord Mansur should claim you tomorrow to show him the town's pharmacists, and you could slip away."

"Mistress," Locusta said. "He would have my eternal gratitude."

But it was Adelia who was to slip away. . . .

The next day Captain Bolt took her to one side. "You'll be wanting somewhere to prepare your medicines and tinctures, mistress. There's a nice little house down on the River Clain would suit you."

"Thank you, Captain, but I don't need it." The palace's cook general had allowed her a space in one of his kitchens in return for her witch hazel potion to clear up his skin trouble.

"Yes, you do, mistress," Bolt insisted.

"No, I . . ." She saw his eyes. "Ah, perhaps I do."

It was a very small, somewhat crumbling house, very drafty and damp; its lower floor was essentially a boathouse and the blue-painted shutters to its upper rooms opened out onto a creaking, curlicued little balcony overlooking a quiet and deserted section of the river. At the back there was an outhouse that served as a kitchen.

To whom it belonged, Adelia never found out, but, for the purpose for which it was now intended, it was perfection—a boat could approach it unseen.

Nevertheless, it posed a quandary which, suddenly embarrassed and not explaining matters at all well, she raised with Mansur.

He went to the core of it immediately. "You wish to be alone there."

"Well, yes. In any case, as Lord Mansur you are too lofty to stay anywhere else except the palace, and for you and I to share such lowly accommodation would cause talk. But I don't like leaving you here by yourself. Duke Richard doesn't welcome you, for one thing, and, for another, you're not supposed to understand what anyone says."

But, it appeared, the former easygoing dukes of Aquitaine had been more tolerant of other races and beliefs than the present one was, and had brought back with them Arabs, even Jews, from the East who'd proved to be useful servants and had since become an accepted part of its palace's fabric, whether Richard liked it or not.

"There is a scholar in the library here, old Bahir," Mansur said. "He will keep me company, we shall play chess together. He translates Arabic texts so that the duke may learn more of Muhammad's faithful before he goes to kill them."

Captain Bolt had already been instructed to take care of her security. From among his men—a ragbag of nationalities that he'd formed into a cohesive force for Henry Plantagenet's sole use—one was deputed to assist Boggart in carrying Adelia's luggage and equipment down to the house and to act as sentry from a position in the boathouse.

"He's reliable, Rankin is, and not a talker," Bolt said, "that being just as well, for he's a Scot and most of the time nobody can't understand a word he utters."

Adelia doubted if anyone in the palace would be aware that she and her chaperone—Boggart—had left the palace; nearly all Eleanor's people had spent time with their queen in Poitiers at one point or another and were too busy carousing with old friends to notice the absence of a couple to whom they paid little attention anyway. Even if they did, the brewing of potions was a plausible excuse.

As she and Boggart set about cleaning their new premises—a process it needed badly—they heard a viol being struck up, immediately followed by a mellifluous voice from the direction of the riverbank.

I have seen my lady on her balcony
a-feeding minnows in the Clain,
kindly, considerately,
but me she feedeth with
far lighter sustenance.

"Blast that boy," Adelia said. She went out onto the balcony and tried to wave Sir Guillaume away.

He waved back.

Crossly, she returned to her work. "So much for privacy. Why doesn't he alert every bell ringer in town while he's about it."

"Sings lovely, though, don't he?" Boggart said.

"I suppose he does." She was disturbed; there had been somebody else out there; she'd glimpsed a tall, thin man staring at her balcony from across the river before he disappeared amongst the trees. It had looked, she couldn't be sure, but it had looked like the O'Donnell.

Sir Guillaume went on serenading.

For you, lady, three birds sing on every bough,
Yet, you care nothing for my song . . . (dompna pois de me no'chal . . .)

The refrain ended abruptly. There was a squawk and a splash.

While Boggart ran to investigate, Adelia confronted a figure that had appeared in the doorway. "What have you done to Sir Guillaume?"

"Pushed him in the bloody river. That'll dampen his ardor for him." At her look of concern, Rowley said: "He's all right, it's shallow here, he's just more wet than he was before. If that's possible."

Boggart peered in through the door, then led Ward away to join her in the outhouse.

Adelia said: "Poor Sir Guillaume."

"Poor me. Renting this hovel is costing me a fortune. Now get your clothes off."

She sighed. "Sir Guillaume puts it so much more nicely," she said and stopped her lover's mouth by kissing it before he could say what else Sir Guillaume could go and do.

The one bed in the one bedroom was dusty and made them sneeze, but sunshine on the river cast wobbling, fluid reflections on the ceiling so that they made love as if in a dream.

Now and then they found time to talk.

"I'm sorry for Richard," she said.

"I'd be sorrier if he were sympathetic to other people's sins. Seeing us now, he'd throw us into the Pit and think it another job well done for the Lord."

"I wonder how Allie is."

He sighed with her. "I do, too." Then: "I'll have to go back to my chaste bed for the nights. I've only got time to consort with loose women in the afternoons. Incidentally, Father Adalburt is giving the sermon in the cathedral tonight. Will you come?"

"I certainly shall."

Every now and then, the chaplains took turns to relieve the Bishop of Winchester of the duty of giving a sermon. Father Adalburt's turn came round more rarely because both Father Guy and the bishop found his sermons embarrassing. Everybody else flocked to them.

Not for the first time, Adelia wondered if the man could be as stupid as he looked, but it didn't stop her enjoying the entertainment he provided.

On this night, Father Adalburt surpassed himself. His subject was the miracle of holy relics. "While we have sojourned here in noble Poitou, I have taken the opportunity to visit Saint-Jean d'Angély wherein lies the sacred head of its patron, Saint John the Baptist."

He beamed at his congregation. "How can this come about, you may ask yourselves, for is not the head of that great prophet venerated in Antioch also? Thus I asked the prior of Saint-Jean d'Angély, how can this be? And thus he answered me, taking the dear skull in his hands: 'See you, O seeker after truth, that this is the head of Saint John when he was a young man; the skull at Antioch is his when he had grown into full maturity.'"

Adelia closed her eyes in bliss.

THERE WERE FOUR more days before journeying began again.

Though the two of them prayed for time like a couple condemned to the gallows, there were long hours when Rowley's duties called him away. Adelia spent them in the ramshackle outhouse with Boggart and Ward, pounding roots and seething herbs, waiting for him to come back.

It was during these occasions that a suspicion which had been growing in Adelia's mind for some time ripened into certainty.

She, like all the other women accompanying Joanna, had experienced difficulty while traveling in how to deal with the problem of menstrual cloths—circumstances that sometimes necessitated frequent changing on the road, a process to be carried out in secrecy since men, most of them with no knowledge at all of how the female body functioned, must be kept in ignorance of the fact that women bled every month. There had to be stratagems involving visits into woodland, covered pails filled with cold water for soaking, and a good deal of feminine cursing.

In all of these contrivances, however, Boggart had taken no part.

It could be put off no longer. "When's your baby due, Boggart?" Adelia asked, casually.

A bowl in which the maid had been pounding the flowers

and leaves of thyme to make an infusion for, ironically enough, Mistress Blanche's period pains, dropped to the floor and broke.

So, almost, did Boggart. "Mistress, oh mistress, you sure it's that? I wondered, I was so feared, I hoped it might be summat else and I was ill."

Adelia smiled. "I'm fairly sure it's a baby."

"Before God, I didn't mean it, what'm I going to do? Forgive me, mistress. Forgive me."

"Basil," Adelia said firmly. "Where did you put the basil tincture?" With one hand clasping the phial and a spoon, and another pushing Boggart before her, she took the girl into the house, sat her down, and made her swallow two spoonfuls of a concoction intended to lift the spirits, after which she herself took a place on the floor with her hands round her knees. "Now," she said. "Tell me about it."

There was nothing to forgive Boggart for. It was the old, old story of rape, or certainly coercion, by the lord of the manor—in this case Lord Kenilworth, to whose family Boggart had been sent as an orphaned child.

"He said I had to do it. Lie still, he said, and don't scream or I'd lose my place and he'd send me out onto the roads."

That, then, was why the girl had responded in such panic to Sir Nicholas's overtures to her shoes; any male sexual advance was, to her, a remembrance of rape.

She'd been too frightened to tell a soul, but had lost her place anyway because Lady Kenilworth, passing by the stable room and alerted by her lord's grunting, had looked in.

These things not only happened in the best households; they were expected. Lady Kenilworth, however, was in the vulnerable position of still being childless three years after her wedding and Lord Kenilworth was becoming impatient for a son.

Afraid for her marriage and that, *in extremis*, her husband might adopt a bastard as his heir, the woman had not only dismissed Boggart but made sure the girl wouldn't even be in the country if she gave birth to a child—hence an appeal to her sister-in-law, Lady Petronilla, the woman about to set out for Normandy.

Dear God, Adelia thought, into what depths female helplessness takes us. *I hoped it might be summat else and I was ill.* She wondered angrily what would have happened to Boggart if Petronilla hadn't given the girl to her unsuspecting self. Abandoned the child in a foreign field, friendless?

"When did it happen?" she asked. "When did he attack you?"

"Weren't just once," sobbed the poor Boggart, "but it begun Lady Day."

So the girl could have conceived any time from March, which might put her pregnancy into its seventh month, although the loose gowns she wore and the thinness of the rest of her body had concealed it until now.

Boggart went down on her knees, holding up her hands in supplication. "Don't send me away, mistress. Where'd I go? I can't make out what these furriners is saying."

Adelia stared at her. "Why would I do that?" She added, and it was true: "I like babies." In many ways, she regretted that she and Rowley hadn't had another child, awkward though it might have been. She patted her maid's hand. "We'll have this one together."

At which Boggart totally collapsed and had to be sat in a chair until she believed it and was coherent again.

AS IT TURNED OUT, Rowley and Adelia were granted only three days.

Late on the evening of the third, the soldier Rankin appeared at the door of the outhouse where Adelia and Boggart, having finished bottling cough mixture, were preparing for bed. "Ye'retaegotothapalacenoo," he said.

"Er?" Adelia was having difficulty with the man's Scottish accent.

Boggart, who was better at it, interpreted. "I think he wants us to go to the palace."

"Noo."

"Now," Boggart said.

With Ward at their heels, they reached the palace gates just before the guards closed them and were confronted by Captain Bolt carrying a lantern. He took Adelia's arm. "Trouble in the laundry, mistress, we better get down to it. Lord Mansur'll be needing you." He added: "M'lord bishop's already there."

He took them down to the undercroft, a huge, dark cavern in which pillars held up a vaulted ceiling over an enormous well and where laundresses had every sort of equipment to do their work.

Here, the princess's women had been able to catch up on the laundry that the sometimes primitive facilities of the various hostels they'd stayed at had denied them. (Brune had never let Locusta forget the monastery outside Alençon where the monks still used the river and cleaned their robes by beating them with stones.)

Sheets and clothing hanging from lines fastened from pillar

to pillar obscured the way, and Captain Bolt had to brush them aside as he led Adelia and Boggart toward a corner where more lanterns showed a gathering of people standing in a circle near one of the enormous iron washing vats set above its brazier. Ward pattered after them, then stopped and slunk away.

Rowley was there, so was Father Guy, Mansur, two of the palace guards, and one of Brune's young washerwomen, whose sobs were sending echoes hiccuping around the vault.

The head laundress, it appeared, would complain no longer.

"It was our turn to do the wash, the palace women'd done theirs," the girl was saying, "and we'd done ours and we'd gone up for the night and she saw us to bed like she does, then she come back down to see all was right for the morning wash, like she does . . . *did*, oh God have mercy on her poor soul."

"And?" Father Guy asked sharply.

"So when she didn't come up, I come down again to see why, and there she was with her poor head in the tub. Awful it was, master, awful."

Brune's body lay on the tiled floor, her soaked cap dislodged so that some of her hair dripped down an already dripping bodice. Her skirt was dry.

"Like this?" Rowley asked. He leaned over the edge of the vat, head down.

The girl nodded. She was clutching a scrubbing board to her chest like a shield. "I couldn't get her up, master. Tried and tried, I did, but she were too weighty, so I ran for help. And him there . . ." One of the guards nodded, ". . . he gets her up out of the tub but she were dead then, God have mercy, sweet Mary have mercy."

"Why is the vat full, child?" This was Father Guy, accusatory. "Do you not empty the water out at night?"

Apparently they did, then filled the vats again ready for the next day's wash. "Very particular 'bout that, she was. Saves time in the morning, see, all we has to do then is light the fires. Oh, God have mercy, master, she didn't . . . didn't mean to drown herself, did she? Say she won't go to hell, will she, master?" The girl collapsed under the thought of her chief eternally damned for the sin of suicide. Adelia went to comfort her.

Father Guy tapped his long fingers together as he considered. "I see no reason to assume such a thing; she was a God-fearing woman, one of the few amongst us, I fear. Was she in any way distressed today? No? Then cause of death is clear—an accident. Do you not agree, my lord?"

"So it seems," the Bishop of Saint Albans said. "What does the Lord Mansur think? He's the doctor."

Every eye looked toward Mansur, who spoke in Arabic. "What do you say?"

"I don't like it," Adelia said in the same tongue. There was a raw, red area on Brune's upper lip. She lapsed into Norman French for the benefit of the chaplain. "The lord doctor wishes to examine her."

Father Guy appealed to a higher authority. "Surely it is unnecessary for the Saracen to interfere, my lord bishop. It is obvious that this female had a turn, an apoplexy, *something*, as she bent over the tub, causing her to flop forward unconscious and drown. Let us inform the seneschal of the matter, *ratio decidendi.*"

Rowley made up his mind. "Get along and do it, then. And

while you're about it, Father, ready the palace priests for the poor dame's funeral."

"You . . ." Father Guy pointed at the guards, ". . . take her up."

"Not yet." Rowley's voice was sharp. "There's an examination to be made before we move her, and prayers to be said."

The chaplain hovered, casting venomous glances at Mansur, unwilling to leave a Christian corpse to a heretic. "Then let me fetch Doctor Arnulf."

"If you wish it, and if he's prepared to get himself out of bed, which I doubt. Now, Captain." Rowley turned to Bolt. "If you would escort this young lady to the buttery and see she's given some brandy. And you two"—this was to the guards—"bring a litter."

Before he went, Father Guy confronted Adelia. "I hear this poor woman quarreled with you recently, mistress."

"Does that matter now?"

"I hope it does not, mistress, I hope it does not."

Politely but firmly, Captain Bolt urged the chaplain toward the stairs to the hall, his other arm around the little laundress who went, still sobbing, still clutching the scrubbing board.

"Foul play?" Rowley asked when they'd gone.

"I'm not sure."

"Then *make* sure, and be quick about it."

Adelia wondered for a moment whether Boggart should leave, too, but, well, the girl was now part of the household and might as well be introduced to the work that it did.

"Prepare yourself, Boggart," she said. "I am going to try and find out exactly how this lady died."

She went down on her knees by the corpse. She paused to

make her supplication to the dead. *Forgive me and permit your poor flesh to tell me what your voice cannot.*

The jaw was showing early stages of rigor mortis. The red patch on the dead woman's upper lip had definitely been caused by friction.

Moving swiftly, Adelia began opening Brune's outer clothing, ignoring Boggart's horrified intake of breath.

There was deep bruising on both of the upper arms. "*Hmmm.*"

"Well?" Rowley asked with impatience.

He also was ignored.

Both eyes were shut—probably had been closed by one of the people who'd gathered around the corpse; there was nothing more naked than the staring eyes of the dead.

Adelia forced up one eyelid, then the other. She was remembering two corpses, that of an old man, the other a child, which had been brought at different times to her foster father for examination, both of them with an abrasion similar to Brune's on the upper lip—both unnatural deaths, as he had discovered.

Rowley and Mansur were talking quietly together, but she paid them no attention. Attempting to pull the woman's bodice down, she found it too tightly laced at the back. She looked up at Boggart. "Help me turn her over."

The maid shrank away. "Oh, mistress, it ain't right what you're doing."

Adelia, her nerves always frayed when her concentration on a corpse was interrupted, lost her temper. "Ain't right? It ain't right what's happened to this woman, and I need to find out why it did. She's heavy. *Help me turn her over.*"

Shocked—her mistress had never been cross with her before—Boggart did as she was told.

Parting the gray hair, Adelia found blood. After examining the wound, she undid the back of the bodice and pulled it open. Criss-crossed abrasions on the spine showed where the laces had been pressed into it. *Hmmm.* "Now we turn her over again," she said.

With the body once more faceup, and with Boggart still whimpering, Adelia exposed Brune's large white breasts. The chest was unmarked.

"In the name of God, hurry, will you?" Rowley was hissing. "They'll be coming for her soon. What's the verdict?"

Without haste, Adelia raised Brune's skirt and spread the legs. No, the vaginal area had been untouched.

Slowly, she sat back on her heels. "I'm fairly sure she didn't drown, Rowley. I'd like to dissect the lungs of course. . . ."

"Oh, yes, necropsy would go down *very* well," the bishop said between his teeth. "Of course you can't dissect her. In the name of God, just tell me what happened."

Adelia looked up. "I think she was smothered. Somebody hit her head from behind—Mansur, see if you can find a weapon—and then, when she staggered, pulled her down and knelt on her arms—see the bruising, there and there—while he held something over her mouth and nose, something rough . . . you see where it rubbed against the upper lip?"

"This?" Mansur had found a coarse towel on the floor. One of the pegs that had held it up remained on the washing line, the other was still attached, as if the cloth had been snatched down.

"Quite likely. And there is blood in her eyes, typical of asphyxiation."

"Murder, then," Rowley said.

There was a squeak from Boggart.

"I'm afraid so."

"Must have been a strong fellow, she's a large lady."

"He hit her on the head first with something heavy and sharp, perhaps a sword pommel, something like that, and weakened her. . . ." Adelia looked up at Mansur, who shook his head; he'd found no weapon. "But, yes, he was strong—I doubt a woman could have done it. She struggled, poor thing, hence the mark on her lip where the cloth rubbed against it."

She closed her eyes, imagining the scene, the frantic turning of the head, the poor, thrashing legs . . . "And then he lifted her up to prop her over the tub with her head in the water, hoping we would think she'd tipped forward from a sudden apoplexy and drowned."

"Damn," Rowley said with force. "Well, put her clothes straight."

"But the sheriff, somebody in authority, must see these injuries first. What's the procedure in Aquitaine?"

"The procedure is that this woman appears exactly as we found her. So *do* it."

She didn't understand why he was cross, nor why he and Mansur were looking at each other as if they knew something she didn't. However, it wasn't decent that the corpse should lie there exposed as it was; presumably the sheriff, a coroner, whoever it might be, could do the examination when it came to laying it out.

Between them, Adelia and Boggart made Brune respectable again.

The guards returned with a litter, lifted the corpse, and took it away with the bishop's cloak laid over it.

Rowley didn't go with them. Instead, he took Adelia's chin in his hand and looked into her eyes. "She drowned, sweetheart. Brune drowned."

"What are you talking about?"

"Is there any indication as to who killed her?"

Helplessly, Adelia looked around. Apart from the towel the killer had dropped, nothing; wet footprints were all around the vat, but so many of them as to be useless. "No . . . somebody . . . a man most probably. We must start inquiries."

"And how many men do you suppose are in this palace?"

Now she was becoming angry; he was frightening her. "More than have access to this undercroft. There can only be a few allowed down here."

"You think so? Did you notice the steps down to this place? Entrance tucked away, virtually deserted at this time of night? Anybody, not just servants, could sneak down here."

"Someone might have seen him, Rowley. We must ask."

"*No, we mustn't.*" He took her by the shoulders and shook her. "Do you know how long that would take? What it would entail?"

She was bewildered. "It doesn't matter. I don't want a delay, either, but there's a killer loose. . . ."

"There isn't. Is *not*. This is a case of drowning pure and simple, an accident."

He stiffened; the sound of voices was coming from the stairs beyond the curtains of washing; officialdom was arriving. "Quick, get her out of here, Mansur. Explain it to her. I'll stay. Go with them, Boggart."

Boggart and a still-bemused Adelia were dragged away to a dark corner and made to stand behind a sheet. Several people were blundering through the forest of washing toward Rowley and the lanterns. She heard the deep voice of the seneschal and then Lady Beatrix's as the lady-in-waiting passed her: "*Oh, I* agree, *absolutely frightful. Drowning herself, so careless of the woman. Joanna will be inconvenienced, there was nobody like Brune for getting stains out of embroidery. . . .*"

And Lady Petronilla: "*What* is *that smell?*"

Adelia, who feared they'd scented Ward crouching at her feet, held her breath, but the ladies went past without seeing her. "*Oh, my lord bishop, there you are. Is this where it happened? How terribly, terribly ghoulish.*"

"We go," Mansur whispered.

They went. Rowley had been right; the stairs led to a deserted passageway.

Nobody was in Eleanor's garden either, and it was there that Adelia refused to go any farther. "Are you going to alert the authorities or am I?"

Gently, Mansur steered her to a bench and sat on it beside her. Boggart crouched nearby, holding on to Ward for comfort and looking nervously around at the bushes for murderers.

The Arab's voice was a bat's squeak in the darkness. "She insulted you. They will say you had her killed. Or made her kill herself."

Adelia's mouth fell open. "What are you *talking* about? I wasn't here. The guards saw me come in. Captain Bolt . . ."

Mansur went on as if she hadn't spoken. "That you wished her dead, perhaps inspired her or someone else to see it done." He took her hand. "We are strange to them, you and I. There has been misfortune on this journey; the Bishop of Winchester talks of little else. I can listen because they think I do not understand them and I hear disquiet. Three times now you have been angry, first with the horse Juno . . ."

"I wasn't angry with her. . . ."

"And then with the Sir Nicholas . . ."

"I wasn't . . ."

"More recently with Brune."

"She was angry with *me*."

"And all three have died in circumstances that are odd. A horse eats poison, a knight is shot while hunting, a woman is drowned."

"They can't think I killed any one of them. Each time I was somewhere else."

"You did not have to be there. You engineered it. Or I did. The horse, the knight, both were murdered. If this time, Brune's death is deemed an accident, they may regard the fact that she offended us as a coincidence, but the Bishop Rowley does not want attention drawn to her killing. It will be bad enough as it is; there will be talk, superstition."

"That's nonsense. Why would we want her dead? For what reason?"

"Why would anyone want her dead? And therein lies the reason. Publicly, she offended only us."

She was following his remote, high voice as if through a fog, unable to see which direction its meaning came from. "And how are we supposed to have made someone kill her for us? Or have her put her head in the tub from a distance?"

"Witchcraft." It was said mildly, as the Arab said all things mildly but, for Adelia, it was a blast of putrefaction into the night air. It felled her so that she put her arms over her head to shield herself just as the little laundress had held the scrubbing board between her and evil.

Witchcraft. Always, *always*, since she'd left Salerno, where they knew what she was, and what she did, and appreciated her for it, superstition had attached itself to her heels so that the skill she'd been granted to benefit mankind must be hidden by stratagems so wearying that she was sick of them.

But there was one thing it could not do. She brought her arms down and sat up.

"It doesn't matter," she said. "Somebody killed Brune, they took away her life, her *life*, Mansur. Her body cried it out to me, her soul cries it. I cannot, I *will not* allow murder to be ignored."

"She was not a nice woman," Mansur said stolidly.

"She was murdered. She was alive. The span God allotted to her has been taken away. Whether she was nice or not has nothing to do with it."

"They will think that anyone who crosses us is cursed."

"*She was murdered*." Adelia got up. "I'm going to see the seneschal and tell him what happened."

Mansur didn't move. "No." It was said quietly.

Adelia turned round to stare. "You can't stop me."

"I shall say that you are mistaken. The woman drowned by accident. I am the doctor, Rowley is the bishop. We will speak against you."

The betrayal took her breath away; this man had looked after and defended her all her life, he'd never refuted her. He would do that? Rowley would do it? She could stand on the highest tower in the palace to shout "Murder" and be deemed insane because Rowley and Mansur, the only authority she had, would deny it?

By submitting to the superstition that others would lay against her door, these two men, *her* two men, had joined themselves to the great enemy, killing everything that was rational, allowing fallacy to win. It *had* won. Without them, her testimony would be the mere squawk of a madwoman and result in nothing but hubris.

She felt a terrible grief, for Brune, for the science of reason that always lost to unreason.

Mansur, knowing her, said: "It is for my sake, too. A Saracen is always a witch. If Gyltha were here, she would say the same."

She couldn't bear his presence anymore and went away from him to weep and rage in the shadows, circling the garden like a lost soul.

Still on his bench, Mansur had begun talking in English to Boggart, talking endlessly, it seemed, explaining the fact of himself and her mistress, what they did, what they had done, and why.

The sound meant no more to Adelia than the stridulation of a cricket. She kept on walking. She had never felt lonelier.

After a while, a hand touched her sleeve. "Let's go up, mistress, you need your sleep."

"Do *you* think I'm a witch, Boggart?"

"Well . . ." Boggart's eyes were still swiveling from the information about Adelia's history and profession that Mansur had given her, and she was incapable of being less than honest. "Maybe, mistress, but I reckon as you're a white one."

It was too late to go to the house by the river; the palace gates were shut for the night. Unnoticed, the two women returned to the great hall and the stairs that led to the ladies' apartments.

In the gloom, squires and servants were setting out the pallet mattresses in the niches of the walls where they slept. By the light of a single flambeau stuck in a bracket in the center of the floor, a group of thirty or more knights and courtiers were drinking and playing dice.

As Adelia reached the top of the staircase and started toward her room, one of the players let out a whoop at a lucky roll. "*Mirabile dictu*," he cried.

Adelia stopped still. They were the very words screamed with the very exultation in the very voice she'd once heard in a forest between Glastonbury and Wells when two of its outlaws, capering and dressed in leaves, had threatened to rape and tear her apart. Excalibur had killed one—no, *she* had killed one.

The other?

Boggart was at her side, concerned. "What is it, mistress?"

No, it couldn't be. Captain Bolt and his men had subsequently cleared the forest, quartering every man jack in it and hanging the pieces from its trees.

"What *is* it, mistress?"

"I thought . . . A man called Scarry . . ." She pulled herself together. "But it wasn't him, he's dead."

Eight

AT FIRST, it was a subdued train that left Poitiers to set out once more on its journey. For Joanna, her ladies-in-waiting, her knights, bishops, and servants, it was expulsion from the Garden of Eden, even though Richard and his knights were to accompany them the rest of the way to Sicily.

For Adelia, it was the most dreadful thing she had ever done. She wasn't leaving Paradise; she was deserting the dead. At Brune's funeral, everybody else had watched a coffin lowered into the palace's graveyard; Adelia had seen only a woman being murdered over and over again; she'd cowered at the laundress's shriek of "Betrayer" dinning into her ears. It overrode the voices of Mansur and Rowley when they tried to talk to her so that she barely heard them, or wanted to.

Nor had she noticed the looks, some frightened, some accusatory, directed at her and Mansur as they were left to stand by themselves at the funeral service.

But as, under a crystalline sky, the procession began following the Vienne, loveliest of rivers, gradually the general mood lifted. Otters slid into the waters, making V-shaped ripples as they swam. Herons stood still, elongated sculptures, waiting for the moment to spear an unsuspecting, sinuous trout. Overhead, squadrons of cranes flew south to their winter quarters, oblivious of the long train of people and animals lumbering along below them.

Not that *lumber* was the appropriate word. Duke Richard kept a brisk pace, and, on such a fine, dry day, the princess and ladies-in-waiting had abandoned their palanquin for horseback in order to ride with him, surrounded by a bright crowd of his knights with harness bells jingling, their songs, shouts, and laughter sending affronted, cawing rooks scattering from elms into the air.

Even the Bishop of Winchester was seen to smile as he bumped along on a horse too big for him.

Adelia, still cross with them, did not want to talk to the only two people, Mansur and Rowley, who would have talked to her.

As usual, Sir Guillaume had urged his horse toward hers and was singing at her:

I am with my beautiful beneath the flowers,
until our sentry from the tower cries: "Lovers, get up!"
for I clearly see the sunrise and the day.

"Oh, shut up," she told him and rode down the procession to ride alongside Ulf, a Gyltha substitute, the only person apart from God to whom she could unburden herself.

He wasn't sympathetic. "They was right," he said of Mansur and Rowley.

"In the name of Heaven, boy, how were they right? They

caused me to sin against everything I believe in; they cut out my tongue. They made me fail in my duty to the dead."

Ulf was unshaken. "Seems to me your duty's to the king and his daughter, see her safe. That's what you took on, ain't it?"

"I could have seen Joanna safe and still done what I ought."

"No, you bloody couldn't. There's mutterings already. You got to be careful. Iffen you'd done your duty by that old besom, you'd've got more attention to yourself than you have already." He frowned; he, like Mansur, heard things that Adelia didn't. "You're feared by some parties. There's them as'd like to see you left behind, or worse. There's some as is even blaming you for Young Henry not comin' with us. Ain't that right, Boggart?"

He was speaking English, and Boggart, from her mule, replied: "I'm afeared it is, mistress. There's them as think you got *powers*."

"*Somebody's* got powers," Ulf said. "I reckon as *somebody* round here's got it in for you. Somebody poisoned that bloody horse deliberate, somebody done old Brune deliberate, all to make you look bad." He had a sudden idea: "Here, suppose that's why old Sir Nicholas got speared?"

"For God's sake," Adelia said wearily. "You're being stupid."

"I ain't so sure. You got a particular enemy amongst this lot? You done anyone wrong lately?"

"I deserted Brune."

The three rode together in silence for a while, the two mules occasionally having to be restrained from taking a bite out of Adelia's palomino palfrey, a little horse of gold-dusted hide with flaxen mane and tail, as if they resented its beauty. Rowley had secretly bought it for her at Poitiers and, in memory of their time there in a dusty bed, had called it Sneeze.

The name had made Adelia laugh. Still did, despite herself. And it *was* a lovely day. And Ulf, with his truculence, *did* so remind her of his grandmother, even to the slight, downy dark hair that had begun to show on his upper lip.

Cheered, she changed the subject. "I never told you how I found Excalibur, did I?"

"Ain't seen you since."

So she told him about the discovery of a little cave on Glastonbury Tor, the skeleton within it, and the unprepossessing weapon with its dull patina that her daughter had fished out of the cave's pool. Of how she'd given it to Emma's Roetger and how, when he'd cleaned it, they'd found the name *Arturus* set into its fuller. Of how Roetger, dear man, had given it back to her and, eventually, she had given it to Henry the king.

But, inevitably, under Ulf's questioning, the story—she shouldn't have started on it—led on to the darkness of a forest glade, and what had happened there.

"And all you and Mansur and Rowley are doing," she finished, "is making me imagine vain things. The night before last I even thought I heard Scarry shouting out at a dice table, so you've got to stop . . ."

But Ulf had dug his heels into his mule's side and was riding off toward the front of the column, the wooden cross bumping wildly on his saddle as he went.

Minutes later, two horses were beside hers, one bearing the Bishop of Saint Albans, the other Captain Bolt. Rowley was angry: "You heard Scarry's voice and didn't tell me?"

"I imagined a voice that *sounded* like Scarry's," Adelia told him. "Stop all this fuss."

"And did you go to look, see if it *was* him?"

"Please, not that again. I don't believe he was in Somerset and I *certainly* don't believe he's here. How could an outlaw insinuate himself into . . ."

Rowley turned to Bolt. "Did you hang *all* the cutthroats in that bloody forest, captain?"

"Thought as we did," Bolt said. "Many as we could lay our hands on."

"You see?" The bishop leaned over to take the reins of Adelia's horse and halt it. "Will and Alf were probably right; Scarry could have escaped. What did he look like, this dice player?"

"I've no idea, I didn't bother to go and see."

"What did *Scarry* look like?"

"I don't know that, either," she shouted back. "He was . . . he and Wolf were out of a nightmare . . . dressed in leaves . . . it was dark . . . their faces were painted."

"Think."

She was reluctant. Shaking her head, she said: "Educated, I suppose, he spoke Latin." The lament as the man had taken his dead lover in his arms rang in her brain once more: "*Come back, my Lupus. Te amo! Te amo!*"

Rowley nodded. "Educated. What else? What age? What height?"

"I don't know. *I don't know*." The two men had been creatures emerging from a different age, as tall as trees. "This is silly, Rowley, he can't be here. How could he be here?"

"Think, will you?"

She tried. "Well . . . oh yes, he was dark. I remember his arms, black hair . . . but that may just have been shadow."

"Dark," Rowley said bitterly. "Very helpful." Nevertheless, he and Bolt and Ulf began listing the black-haired men in the company. Father Guy, Father Adalburt, knights, squires, servants who were swarthy, Captain Bolt's men, Bolt himself, Rankin the Scot, young Locusta, the O'Donnell . . . it went on and on.

"And any one of them could have been at that dice game," Rowley pointed out. "It's an eclectic group."

"Oh, go away," Adelia told him. It was difficult enough believing that Scarry was the one who'd been after her in Somerset; impossible to think that a painted outlaw could have joined Joanna's company and pursued her across the Channel, however good his Latin.

She refused to dwell on it.

FROM HALF A MILE down the column, it was possible to see that something was wrong, causing Adelia and Mansur to urge their horses into a canter that took them to its head, where Joanna and her principals were gathered about a figure that overtopped them all.

Duke Richard was in gleaming mail; under his arm he held a helmet encircled by a gold ducal coronet. His face was set, exalted, and he was paying no attention to a distracted Captain Bolt and Bishop of Winchester.

Rowley detached himself from the group to approach Mansur and Adelia. "Richard's leaving us," he said bitterly, in Arabic.

"Where's he going?"

"To war."

"He can't do that."

"Actually, I think he has to. There's a galloper just come with news. Angoulême is in revolt; the duke can't allow that, though if you ask me it's his fault the bloody place revolted in the first place."

Angoulême. Angoulême. From what Adelia could remember of Locusta's map, the county was due south of them. "We have to go back? Oh God, Rowley, how long will a war hold us up?"

"We're skirting round it. We can't afford to lose more time, and the duke's convinced he can defeat Vulgrin of Angoulême within days. He's called for reinforcements."

"And can he defeat him?"

"Oh, yes. He's no favorite of mine, Richard, but he's a superb general. If I were Count Vulgrin, I'd start running now."

Adelia looked toward Joanna. "Poor love," she said.

"Poor Locusta, he's near tears. We'll be departing from his precious route; he'll have to arrange a new one, which, where we're going, won't be easy."

But Adelia's sympathy was for a princess deserted by one brother and now another.

Joanna, however, appeared concerned but not alarmed.

She's used to it, Adelia thought. The girl's young life had been spent watching her parents put down rebellion somewhere or another in their empire; she had seen her mother and brothers rise up against her father. Her world was sown with Hydra's teeth; for her, revolt and battle were the natural order of things. *And so they are, except in England and Sicily*.

The knights and their squires were leaving immediately. An extempore service was held in a grove beneath the high, gaunt branches of a chestnut tree to bless and speed their war.

A troubled Bishop of Winchester stumbled in his office, but Duke Richard showed no sign of restlessness as his impatient father would have done; he drank in the prayers, praise, and blessings. God's goodwill meant much to him.

As over two hundred throats said a last "Amen" that rumbled through the forest, he rose to his feet and strode over to Joanna, who was still kneeling. "I leave you in the care of the good Captain Bolt and the Lord's keeping, royal sister. Our enemy shall be cast down, and you and I shall be reunited at Saint Gilles, if not before. May the saints look kindly down on us."

He drew his sword and raised it high. "For Jesus."

"For Jesus," echoed his men.

He's magnificent, Adelia thought, *but his element is battle. God preserve us from him.*

A knight in full mail rode up to her, his helmet with its nosepiece making his face unrecognizable from all the others around them. But the voice was familiar even though, for once, the lyrics it sang were ugly.

Maces and swords, helms of different hue,
Shields riven and shattered in the fight,
The steeds of dead and wounded run aimless o'er the field,
Men great and small tumbled into the ditches,
Dead with pennoned stumps of lances in their ribs. . . .

Links of his hauberk hissed as Sir Guillaume dismounted, took off his helmet, and tucked it under his arm. "I go to war, lady, but I leave my heart in your keeping. I beg a remembrance from you to be buried with me, should I die."

Oh, you young idiot. Adelia's heart went out to him; his face shone with excitement. That he could be one of those in a ditch with a broken lance through his ribs wasn't in his mind. He saw only glory—and a fortune. By taking hostages and loot, an untried knight could make himself rich in battle. If he survived.

"Ah, lady, your gentle woman's heart quails at the thought of war, as it should, yet how else may I be worthy of you but by showing my prowess in conflict? The neighing of mettlesome chargers, the clash of steel, the cry of battle . . . a remembrance, I beg."

She gave him the last of Emma's kerchiefs that she kept tucked in her belt—the others had gone for bandages. "God keep you, Sir Guillaume," she said, and meant it; he was *so* young.

She watched him hiss happily away to join his fellow knights, tying the fine linen around his arm as he went.

TO AVOID RIDING into conflict, they turned southwest into what was, as far as poor Locusta was concerned, unscouted territory, a wilder countryside of more steeply wooded hills, deeper, faster-flowing rivers.

It was also lonelier.

Captain Bolt didn't like it and redoubled his outriders. "Suppose that Anglim fella ain't being chased eastwards. Suppose he doubles back. The princess'd make a fine hostage, let alone the treasure chests, and I ain't got enough men to hold off an army."

His nervousness transferred itself down the line. Cooks rode with roasting spits in their hands, laundresses grasped washing sticks, the morose blacksmith held a fearsome hammer. Archers had their bows across their saddles, quivers ready on their backs, and Captain Bolt clustered more of his men around the princess's palanquin and the treasure chests.

Ulf worried about the content of his cross and added a spear to his equipment from one of the armory mules. "Any bugger who tries to get you-know-what off of me is going to get what-for."

"I think it was more in danger when we were with Richard," Adelia assured him.

"Crusade?"

She nodded. There wasn't a land on the continent that didn't have its own version of the Arthurian legend; flourishing Excalibur, most powerful of mythical weapons, would endow Richard with a symbol of leadership over the different nationalities of Christian knights gathered in the Holy Land almost as potent as the Cross in the fight against the pure black Al-Uqaab flag of Muhammad.

Ulf spat. "Well, he ain't getting it and nobody else, neither. The king and Prior Geoffrey said as I was to take it to Sicily, and to Sicily it's bloody well goin'."

Locusta did his best, riding ahead, searching for a hospice in a countryside without signposts, sometimes finding one, sometimes not.

Twice, they had to spend the night in the open under the pavilions and tents they carried with them, making little towns of canvas, their fires and lanterns the only glimmer in the darkness, listening to the hoot of owls and the bark of foxes.

Villages were few, tiny, and invariably perched high away from the road, which was as empty as if the few occupants of the land had seen what must still appear a formidable procession coming and had shut themselves away, like flowers curling up at the approach of night.

For good reason. With the prospect of having to feed the company themselves, the train's sumpters fell like wolves on such sheep as they saw, requisitioning them in the name of King Henry and carrying them off to be roasted.

Luckily, the weather blessed them; by day they rode under skies of clear, forget-me-not blue. There were still hazelnuts and late blackberries in the hedges, and men and women stopped to gather them as they passed before hurrying back to the procession, unnerved by a quiet in which only birds twittered.

They were now in the Massif Centrale. Riders had to dismount, and mule drivers bellowed obscenities in order to encourage their animals up ever-steeper hills and then rein them in down the other side.

It took time. *It took time*. Sometimes they made barely ten miles a day between stops. Adelia, nearly sobbing at the delays, thought constantly of Allie.

I don't want to be here, I want to be with you.

AT THE RIVER LOT, they looked for the ferry that would take them over it. Except that there was no ferry.

"What do you mean burned?" Locusta raved at the ferryman standing by what had once been a landing stage.

"I *mean* as Lord Angoulême set fire to it," the man said wearily. "Three days ago that was. So as to stop the duke chasin' him over the river. No bloody thought for my living, neither of 'em."

"Where can we find other boats?"

"Ain't any. Lord Angoulême burned them an' all."

So much was obvious; a great river that should have been dotted with waterborne traffic was empty to a sky that smelled of ash.

"Then, what are we to do?"

The ferryman didn't care; his employment was gone and so was his livelihood until a new ferry could be constructed—"always supposin' the buggers don't come back and burn that."

He spat and pointed his thumb downriver. "Lord Richard went thataway. You better go east to find another crossing; ain't been any fighting in that direction, far as I know. Make for Figères. Biggest town round here, Figères."

"How far is it?"

"Two days' ride." He gave them directions.

"At least we'll be going east," Locusta said to the Bishop of Saint Albans, as they rode back to rejoin the procession. "We've been going too far west."

"I know, but we daren't risk taking the princess into a war."

"Another night in the open," Locusta groaned. "And no baths. My lord, I'd be eternally grateful if you would break the news to the ladies-in-waiting."

"That's your job," Rowley told him. "I'm not that brave."

THE ROUTE TO Figères meant taking a wide traverse through the mountains. Thus they came across the hilly little village of Sept-Glane. . . .

It was a tiny hamlet, hardly worth razing to the ground, but its lord was Vulgrin of Angoulême, so Duke Richard, in passing, had made an example of it.

Nothing was left of cottages and cultivation except cinders. On its terraced pastures, dead animals were beginning to balloon. Its men had been taken away—for what purpose was unknown. Weeping women and children scrabbled for tubers in the blackened earth of their fields.

Rowley ordered a halt so that food and money could be distributed but he knew, as the victims knew, that Sept-Glane was dead.

IT WAS EARLY the next day, after another night under canvas, that Ulf, who'd been riding alongside Adelia, suddenly thrust his cross at her, got down from his mule, and ran toward a neighboring wood, clutching his stomach and vomiting.

Handing over the cross to Mansur, she dismounted and chased after him. The youth was squatting when she found him. "Get away," he groaned. "I'm dying."

She hurried back to her horse for her medicine bag, passing other men and women running toward the trees on the same errand as Ulf.

By midafternoon the procession had been forced to halt as more and more of its people succumbed.

"You've got to find somewhere we can use as a hospital," Adelia told Locusta. "And quickly."

"Around *here*?" The mountains on all sides, covered in the soft shrub that the natives called *garrigue*, were empty even of sheep.

Adelia pointed to a track that climbed to their right, eventually losing itself in distant trees from which issued a thin spiral of smoke. "Up there?"

She watched him put his horse at the hill, and then joined the emergency conference of bishops, doctors, chaplains, the Irishman, and Captain Bolt that had gathered in the middle of the stony road they'd been following.

Dr. Arnulf was shrill: "It is the plague. The princess must be got away immediately."

There was a squeak of alarm from Father Adalburt. "Plague?"

But Adelia had been asking questions amongst the servants, both sick and well. Yesterday, it appeared, their ale had run dry and, while charity was being distributed in Sept-Glane's fields, they had filled up a cask with water for themselves from one of Sept-Glane's wells.

"My Lord Mansur doesn't think it's the plague," Adelia said, carefully. And explained, "Only those who drank the water are sick."

There was a moment's silence. Then: "Dear God," Rowley said. "Richard poisoned Sept-Glane's wells."

"I'm afraid . . . Lord Mansur is afraid that he must have done."

It was the standard practice of lords to deprive the enemy of fresh water during a war, an atrocity that visited more suffering on innocent villages caught up in it.

"It is the plague," Dr. Arnulf insisted. "I shall accompany the princess and her household to Figères. I shall administer my specific against contagion to her. . . ."

The Bishop of Winchester fell to his knees: "God, God, how have we offended thee that Thou sendest this misfortune upon us?"

"How many of our people are ill?" Rowley wanted to know.

"Thirty-four," Adelia said, "but Lord Mansur believes there will be no more. The rest of us drank from different ale casks." (The elite had its own and better brew.) "If we hadn't, if we'd drunk the water, all of us would be showing signs of the flux by now. Luckily, the princess has been unaffected."

"We cannot take that risk," Dr. Arnulf said, hurriedly. "I must accompany her to safety."

"Let him go, Rowley," Adelia said swiftly in Arabic. "He'll just be a hindrance."

"You're going with him, I can tell you that much."

An expression that Gyltha and Mansur knew well settled on Adelia's face, making it squarer and heavier, a this-far-and-no-farther look. "*I am staying with my patients.*" Every word emphasized; she had failed in her duty to Brune, she wasn't deserting again.

Her lover recognized defeat.

Locusta joined them, gasping from haste and with a young woman riding pillion behind him. "Nuns up there . . . Two of them. This lady is Sister Aelith, she says. . . . There's an unused cowshed. . . ." He helped her dismount.

Sister Aelith bobbed to the company, shrinking back slightly at the sight of Mansur—Languedoc's occupation by the Moslem army one thousand years before had left a folk memory in which the word *Saracen* was still synonymous with *ruin.*

"He's a doctor," Locusta told her impatiently. "Tell them, tell them what you told me."

Sister Aelith bobbed again. "My mother says she is sorry to hear of your trouble and offers our old cowshed for those who are ill—she is cleaning it now."

"Anything, Rowley. We must get these people where I can treat them."

Decisions were made, swiftly—the condition of the sick was becoming more and more pitiable and dangerous.

The princess, her retinue, treasure carts, and every healthy servant were ordered to go on to Figères.

Dr. Arnulf couldn't get them away fast enough.

Rowley was to help in getting the invalids to the cowshed and then maintain liaison between them and Figères for as long as the illness lasted. Locusta was sent ahead to warn the town of the princess's coming.

To everybody's surprise—and Adelia's distaste—O'Donnell said he, too, would stay. "For sure Lord Mansur'll be needing another pair of manly hands. He'll get two, for Deniz will be with me."

The sick were urged up the track to what was to be their hospital—a transfer subject to pitiable stops that left an unsavory trail behind them.

Against a slope stood a typical Angoulême cowshed, with a half wall on one side that left it open to the air. Redundancy had tumbled one end to the ground, though the rest looked sturdy enough. Outside was a dew pond.

By the time Adelia and her patients arrived, the hard-baked earth floor had been swept and a woman, clad in black like the younger nun, was busily stuffing straw into sacks to make palliasses.

She came forward. She was a small, upright woman whose astute dark eyes, though she was not old, shone out of the deeply creased face of one who had been too much out in the sun, like winkles set in ribbed sand.

Rowley bowed to her and explained who they were and their situation. "May we know to whom we are indebted, Mother . . . ?"

"Sister," she told him. Her voice was unexpectedly deep and had the heartiness of a vocal slap on the back. "We are all brothers and sisters in this world. I am Sister Ermengarde. This is my daughter, Aelith. You need help? Splendid, you have found it. We are itinerants but, by the Mercy, we are settled here for a while. Since we keep no cows, this shed is at your disposal. Also, I have sent word to nearby villages to requisition every chamber pot they have."

Thank the Lord, a practical woman. But even in her relief, for a second it flashed across Adelia's mind that there was something strange about the two nuns. To judge from their black robes, they were Benedictines, but they wore no scapulas and their veils were merely scarves tied round their heads like those of peasant women.

Presumably they had chosen the religious life but hadn't yet been officially incorporated into an order by their bishop. Peculiar, though, that they were itinerant; nuns usually stayed where they were put.

There was something else odd about them, something missing. . . . Dammit, what did it matter? They were godsent.

The immediate concern was to get the patients cleaned of their vomit and bloody diarrhea; they'd need swabbing down and their clothes burned before they took to their clean palliasses, a process that necessitated a privacy separating the men from the women; in Adelia's experience, embarrassment weakened a patient's chance of recovery.

"Blankets," she said, "and plenty of them. My lord bishop, if you would ride after the baggage train and bring some back . . ."

Rowley was off in an instant.

". . . and fires. Admiral, if you and Master Deniz could start collecting wood." She bowed to the elder nun. "Sister, I speak for my Lord Mansur who is the doctor among us . . ." and expounded her needs.

Within minutes, Sister Ermengarde had fetched what sheets and blankets she had and buckets of water were being lugged down from the well of the hidden convent higher up the hill.

Captain Bolt caught at Adelia's arm. "Me and my men have got to go with the princess and the treasure, mistress; they're ill enough protected as it is . . ."

"Of course you do, of course you do."

". . . but I'm sore concerned at leaving you without a guard."

She smiled at him and pointed around her at a landscape in which nothing moved but hawks circling the sky. "Who's going to hurt us?"

"True enough. Nobody ain't even likely to know you're here. Still, I ain't comfortable in my mind. This ain't nice country; got something nasty in its bones, I reckon."

"We'll be all right, Captain."

He nodded. "God bless you, and God deliver my Scotsman." Rankin, too, was among the patients, one of the sickest.

"I'll do my best."

He kissed her hand. "You allus do."

Rowley, also, was agitated at leaving her, but with the Bishop of Winchester near a state of collapse at this latest manifestation of God's displeasure, he was the only capable Church official left to the princess. "Somehow, I've got to find out where Richard is. And find out where *we* are. And send back to Poitiers in case it's had any messages for us from King Henry."

"Go," Adelia told him. "There's nothing you can do here, in any case. I have enough men."

He looked, frowning, toward the O'Donnell, who had already got fires going. "That's what worries me."

At the back of the shed, shivering male patients were washed down by Mansur and Sister Ermengarde—nuns being accepted as sexless—while in front of it a similar service was performed for the equally shivering women by Adelia and Sister Aelith, then the patients were put to regain warmth by the fires.

"You keep away, Boggart." Adelia wasn't having her maid and the baby subject to possible contagion.

Inside, the O'Donnell, having sent Deniz to unpack their mule, had slung up a ship's sail from the cowshed's rafters to act as a partition and was collecting the timbers that had fallen from the ruined end in order to replace them.

Catching Adelia's look, he swept off his cap. "Lady, I'm a sailor and an Irishman, I can do anything."

"Tormentil," Adelia said, turning to Sister Ermengarde. "We're going to need tormentil and lots of it."

Armed with trowels and baskets, the two of them, accompanied by Boggart and Ward, began digging like badgers in a nearby meadow for the rhizomes of a yellow-petaled herb which, when shredded, powdered, and mixed with water, would provide the only astringent likely to act against dysentery.

"It is what I myself would have recommended," Sister

Ermengarde said. "And you have some opium for the worst cases? Splendid, splendid."

Opium. For a moment, Adelia stared at this Christian and then shook her warmly by the hand.

THE FERRYMAN'S DESCRIPTION of Figères as a town had been an exaggeration. Or perhaps the man hadn't traveled much. It had a tiny priory, a granary and a water mill, some crumbling, corkscrew streets, and an equally crumbling, empty château above the river, and these, since they lay on the southernmost tip of Aquitaine and therefore constituted part of the lands of the King of England, had now been commandeered in his name. The Bishop of Saint Albans and Captain Bolt were in agreement that they would not take Princess Joanna farther until they could make contact with Duke Richard and be apprised of his situation. Their party, due to the absence of the sick, now numbered less than ninety people, too few to venture into disputed territory.

With this in mind, messengers were sent north, to Périgueux, to Poitiers, to civilization generally.

All that could be done now was wait. The princess and her retinue were installed, though uncomfortably, in the château with the treasure chests, while Captain Bolt's men, in tents, made a ring of canvas and steel around them.

The Bishop of Winchester and his chaplains and servants had to snuggle down in a priory whose prior and one monk eked out a living from the soil. Poor Prior James looked on as the royal sumpters examined its granary and barns, filled with the summer's corn and hay, and pronounced them able to feed the procession's horseflesh for at least a fortnight.

For the first time in weeks, the work of administering to the princess and her train could be pursued in one place, so that Joanna and her nobles might pleasure themselves at leisure. She and her ladies cast their hawks upward at the myriad migrating geese flying overhead; the men went hunting or fishing in the Lot's rich currents.

With all this to-ing and fro-ing, it was possible for an individual to go missing for a day or more without comment. . . .

SCARRY? HE ALSO *has sent a message, a secret message carried by a well-bribed servant. A wonderful calm has descended on him as he sees the map of events that his Master has unrolled at his feet.*

"Cathars," he says. "O Great Being, thou hast provided Cathars for our purpose. They have been foretold, for who but You would have connived to put them in my way—and hers? It was Your hand that guided mine when I took her cross."

For Scarry, though he has not traveled this remote area, knows its flavor. He knows that the Cathar heresy has begun creeping through it like tendrils of flame ready to burn it up and that the Church is afraid of its scorching.

He also knows, for they once met at a convocation at Canterbury, a Vatican-trained prelate who now, if Scarry's memory is correct, serves the Bishopric of Aveyron, a diocese less than fifty miles away.

Scarry is not acquainted with the Bishop of Aveyron but he knows that man's flavor, too, and it tastes much to Scarry's liking. He is sure—for has it not been prearranged?—that his message to Father Gerhardt and his bishop will be received and acted upon with the enthusiasm belonging to all frightened, cruel, and self-serving men.

As for Excalibur, that lesser matter, it is as good as in Duke Richard's hand already.

UP THE HILL, in the kitchen of the nun's convent—little more than a cottage of milky gold stone surrounded by a large vegetable garden—young Sister Aelith and Boggart pounded rhizomes until their fingers bled. The dog Ward, having waited to be given food, had to go hunting for his own.

Down the hill ran a wooden gutter, constructed by the O'Donnell and Deniz, bringing clean, cold water from a mountain stream.

Inside, the cowshed hospital echoed with cries. Dust-moted beams of light coming through its ramshackle roof fell on thirty-four prostrate men and women squirming in agony. Bunches of lavender, peppermint, thyme, and rue hung from every available nail, and others were tucked into the nurses' robes. Reed fans were needed to cool the fevered patients, all of whom had to be kept clean as well as being given constant drinks of tormentil infusion.

Filled chamber pots were hurried away, washed, and brought back in an endless, exhausting chain.

Nurses fought for their patients' lives; patients fought for their own—some harder than others.

The little laundress who had come across Brune's body died quickly, as if the shock of that discovery had weakened her will.

She was followed by the morose blacksmith who, of all the men—and men made up the majority of the sick—found the humiliation and powerlessness of his illness too much to bear.

Ulf, whose physical and mental constitution had been strengthened by his upbringing in the food-rich, dogged-minded fenlands of Cambridgeshire, bared his teeth like a tiger at the grim reaper hovering over him.

It was especially the older men with a background of poverty, like the Scotsman Rankin before he'd become a mercenary under Captain Bolt, whose spirits wavered under the onslaught.

"Canna," he said as Adelia, with one arm under his neck and the other holding a beaker to his lips, tried to force him to drink.

"Yes, you can." She was learning to understand his speech. "And you're going to. What will Captain Bolt do without you? What will I?"

At first, the sight of Mansur's head with its kaffiyeh bent over them caused some sufferers to panic, but eventually his imperturbable calm soothed them and they clung to him in their pain. The Irishman, on the other hand, told jokes to the sick as he tended them and, though they grated on Adelia's ear, they seemed to enchant both patients and nuns to the good of both.

It was a tug of war, and the strain for those pulling against Death on behalf of their patients tired them to the last fiber. Adelia and Sister Ermengarde rarely left the cowshed but took alternate rests on a hay bale when they dropped.

Rowley and a servant came every day from Figères, to bring bread and clean linen and so that those desperate to unburden themselves of their sins could do so to a bishop in case they went to their God unshriven.

Jacques the harness maker and Pepé, one of the cooks, died and were buried in graves that O'Donnell and Deniz hacked into the limestone of the hillside, but by the fifth day those who were going to survive were recovering, including Rankin.

TWO MEN ARE *meeting by night at a quiet crossroads halfway between Figères and the town of Aveyron. Their horses are tethered to a fallen walnut tree while they walk and talk, keeping their voices low even here, where there are only owls and foxes to hear them.*

"All this can be delivered," Scarry says, "for the Bishop of Saint Albans is Henry of England's representative and he has been summoned to negotiate between all parties. What secret decisions are made amongst them I shall know of."

Scarry is selling power, for knowledge of what goes on at the innermost conferences of the great is above rubies to those with ambition. And Scarry's price is cheap, as he makes clear but insists on—fifty gold coins and the mere ruination of one particular soul.

"Unless that is done, your master can go whistle for news that will advantage him," he says, pleasantly.

Father Gerhardt is aware that his master does not like whistling, nor will pass up an opportunity that may well prove golden, as well as delivering an old enemy into his hands.

"It shall be done," Father Gerhardt tells Scarry. "And now, where is the bitch?"

Scarry tells him. Father Gerhardt's bitch is not Scarry's bitch. But since a burning always makes good entertainment, he will attend that of them both.

ROWLEY AND LOCUSTA brought visitors with them; Lady Petronilla and Mistress Blanche had come on behalf of Princess Joanna to inquire after the patients' health.

Adelia looked up from spooning vegetable broth into the groom Martin's mouth, to see what looked like two ravishing butterflies settling their wings outside the cowshed door—well outside.

Lady Petronilla stayed there, enumerating to the O'Donnell the gift of goodies the princess had sent. "Some girdle bread, fig and raisin custards—the Figères monks are *masters* of custards—oh, and some lavender oil to put on poorly heads."

Damn, Adelia thought, *I was hoping for some meat.*

Blanche, however, ventured into the cowshed, a clove pomander held close to her elegant nose.

"There's no plague here," Adelia told her sharply.

"It's not a rose garden, either," Blanche said equally sharply.

It wasn't, but it was clean and tidy. The rows of palliasses were now on boards with legs that kept them off the ground; there were fresh straw pillows for the patients to rest their heads on. Mangers that erstwhile cows had fed from were now lined with grasses and filled with dried herbs.

She resumed spooning broth into Martin's mouth while the lady-in-waiting strolled along the beds, asking benign royal questions: "How long have you been a mule driver, my man. Really?" "I've seen you before, haven't I? Hadwisa, of course. We'll soon have you better, Hadwisa."

She lingered, watching Adelia. "How many of our people have you lost?"

"We've *saved* thirty out of thirty-four, thank you very much."

But it appeared that Mistress Blanche had not meant to be critical. "When the flux attacked one of my father's castles, half the sufferers died."

"Ah," Adelia said, still put out. "I suppose he didn't have a witch and a Saracen looking after them."

Surprisingly, Mistress Blanche smiled. "Perhaps it would have been better if he had."

Well, well, a compliment.

Adelia said: "The true saints are the two nuns who took us in. I would introduce you, but they're returning some of the chamber pots we borrowed."

"How tasteful. The princess shall be visiting you tomorrow, she can thank them then."

When the two women had gone, attended by Locusta, Adelia waited until the bishop and his flock had finished their prayers, then asked him to bring strong beef broth with him tomorrow: "We haven't been able to give the patients meat since we came; the sisters are vegetarians."

Rowley nodded. "I was afraid they were."

"Why? What's wrong with that?"

"Come for a walk."

Followed by Ward, they strolled down the hill together, Adelia glancing anxiously back in case one of her patients suffered a mishap in her absence. The sun was chilly. They sat down under the bare branches of a lonely fig tree.

Rowley took her hand. "Sweetheart, at last we're in touch with the outside world. Our messenger met up with King Henry at Périgord. I'm being sent away. I've got to go ahead. The trouble with Angoulême has stirred up the southern lords. . . ."

He was leaving her. That was all she heard before the old, old misery took her in its jaws. He was going. Even such snatched moments as they'd had together were to be taken away.

He went on talking, explaining the region's constantly shifting and bloody history. "We're approaching the southernmost boundary of Henry's empire," he told her. "From here on we'll be in dragon country."

He spoke of the dragon lords who took any opportunity to ride to war and invade their neighbor, of alliances kept and broken, of counts, viscounts, princes, Alfonso of Aragon, Roger of Carcassonne, Raymond of Toulouse, D'Albi . . . the names drifted up into the branches above her, translating themselves into rapine and corpses.

"So there it is," he said. "I have to make sure Joanna has safe conduct through to Saint Gilles. There's to be an attempt at a peace conference at Carcassonne. . . ."

"When are you going?" she asked.

"Tomorrow. And . . ." His fists clenched. "I won't be coming back."

"*Not coming back?*"

He reached into his robe and brought out a parchment from which dangled a heavy red seal. "Read this."

She began reading: "*To our best beloved Rowley, Bishop of Saint Albans, greetings in the Lord from Henry, King of the English, Lord of Normandy and Aquitaine* . . ." She skimmed through the titles; they could take forever. "*Know that we have need of your esteemed service in Lombardy. . . .*"

She handed it back. "Just tell me."

It was politics. It was to do with Emperor Barbarossa and the Lombardians, with popes, anti-popes, staying on good terms with some, undermining others.

She stopped listening. Henry. The king. Always his king. Above God, above everything: Henry Plantagenet.

"You do see, sweetheart," he said desperately, "Henry can't afford trouble in Northern Italy. Diplomacy and guile are necessary." He looked at her and became angry. "*Peace*, mistress. Stopping people dying. I've got to go."

"I know."

In silence, they watched a robin hopping incautiously near their feet in a search for worms.

"Will we meet in Sicily?" she asked eventually.

"No. I'll be there for the wedding, I hope, but tomorrow you're going straight back to England, you and Mansur. I've arranged with Captain Bolt . . ."

She sat up, making the robin flutter away. "I am *not*. You know I want to go, but Henry entrusted Joanna's health to me. . . ."

"Yes, you bloody well are. There's somebody in her household means you harm, and I'm not just talking about Father Guy. You go tomorrow."

He could answer the call of *his* duty, but *hers* was of no account. By God, she'd been right not to marry him; he'd have stifled her.

He said: "And the sooner you get away from those women back there, the better."

"I'll have you know, those two nuns are better Christians than . . ."

"They're not nuns," he said. "They're Cathars."

Cathars.

She stopped shouting at him. *Cathars*. Another word that carried disturbance with it. A name hardly heard in England, nor in Sicily for that matter, but it brought a response of unease from somewhere in her memory. "Cathars? Aren't they heretics?"

"Yes, they damn well are. I'd no idea their heresy had spread so far north. Of course they don't eat meat; it's forbidden them. Didn't you notice neither of those women wears a cross? Which reminds me, I meant to replace yours—this is dangerous territory to be without one. There's bishops around here would as soon put a Cathar on the fire as kindling." He leaned back and regarded her without enthusiasm. "They'd throw *you*, if they saw you now. What the hell are you wearing?"

"Aelith lent Boggart and me some of their robes. One felt the cowshed was not the place for Emma's satins. Rowley, we've been trying to save lives. Ermengarde, Aelith, they're *good* women; they've worked like mules. If Christianity isn't about tending the sick, what is it about?"

"It's not about Cathars calling us the Church of Satan, and refusing to pay their bloody tithes because they say we're all corrupted by riches."

A diamond flash of the bishop's seal ring on his finger as he gestured made Adelia's lips twitch; he saw it and tucked his hands into the folds of his excellent robe, like a boy whose fingers had been raiding a jam pot.

"Well . . ." he said. "Well, the point is . . . the point *is* that, now it's turned out not to be the plague, Joanna, like a good little princess, has decided to come and pay a royal visit to her faithful servants. When she does, she'll bring Winchester with her to give his blessing to the sick and *he'll* bring the chaplains. For Christ's sake, imagine what Father Guy will do when he realizes that you and the others have been sojourning with a couple of heretics who reject the Trinity. . . . God's eyes, Adelia, they believe in reincarnation. *Reincarnation* . . . I ask you."

She got to her feet; the last thing she must do was bring trouble on two women who'd been so kind. "Tell Joanna she needn't visit. Most of the patients should be ready to travel this afternoon if you send us some carts. The Irishman can go with them. I'll come along with the rest tomorrow."

"And then set out for England?" he insisted. When she hesitated, he said: "I've spoken to Mansur. He agrees."

In which case he'd manacled her, just as he had at Poitiers. Without Mansur she had no standing. "Damn you," she said.

"Good." He took up the letter again; he had the look he wore when he was about to disarm her. "So now, I'll read you Henry's postscript. "*And to my daughter's lady Arabic speaker, her king's greetings. She is to know that a certain child at Sarum progresses well under the care of the queen and a dragon of the name of Gyltha with whom she is acquainted.*"

"Oh." Adelia sat down. "Oh. She's well. They're both well."

"Less than a month ago." He was pleased with himself. "Henry's messengers travel fast."

She began pummeling him in her joy. "You couldn't have read that first, could you? To hell with Barbarossa and Lombards and popes, the most important thing in it was about our daughter."

He caught her hands and imprisoned them in his. "You'll miss me until I get back to England," he said.

"No, I won't."

"You will. You adore me."

And the trouble was that she would, and did.

CARTS WERE SENT, and by evening the cowshed hospital was cleared of all patients except Ulf and Rankin who, Adelia felt, could do with another night's rest.

She went down to the road to watch the little procession wind its way toward the mountains that hid Figères. In the light of the torches they carried, she could see hands that she'd held when they were suffering waving to her. She waved back and saw the O'Donnell sweep off his cap in salute.

The Irishman had been curiously reluctant to go. "I'm not happy we should be leaving you behind, mistress. Master Ulf's been telling me there's a mysterious killer been stalking you like a fox after a chicken."

"Has he indeed?" She'd have a word with Ulf. "The fox exists more in that lad's imagination than real life. But we'll be leaving ourselves tomorrow. And I understand that you're needed at Figères right away."

"So my lord Saint Albans tells me."

"Then you must go." (From the first, Rowley had looked with a jaundiced eye on what he called the admiral's wish to soothe the fevered brow of Adelia's patients. "*Wants you to soothe his fevered prick, more like,*" he'd said.)

If the summons to Figères was Rowley's ruse to prevent the

O'Donnell spending one more night in her company, she was relieved by it; helpful as he'd been, the Irishman still made her feel uncomfortable; his eyes were too long, and they watched her too much.

"Will you not at least keep Deniz by you?" he'd asked.

"No." She'd been sharper than she meant to be. "I have Mansur and Ulf and Rankin." Then, because in truth she didn't know what she'd have done without him and his Turk, she said: "We are eternally grateful to you both."

He spread his hands. "*Ipsa quidem pretium virtus sibi*, mistress. Virtue is its own reward."

He wasn't cast down by her refusal; he went off singing. Even when the carts had disappeared into the twilight, she could still hear his voice:

But they couldn't keep time on the cold earthen floor
So to humor the music, they danced on the door.

Walking back up the track, she stopped at the cowshed to make sure that Ulf and Rankin were warm enough by the fire that Mansur had built for them, then went on up to the nuns' cottage.

In telling her about Cathar belief, Rowley had expected her to be as indignant as he was. He was, in his way, a very orthodox Catholic, which, she supposed, a bishop had to be.

She'd found the Cathar faith strange, certainly, but then she found some of the precepts held by the established Church to be as strange. The Trinity, for example; she'd never been able to get her mind to encompass that precept. It was in the Cathars' favor that they rejected it.

To Cathars, it appeared, the material world was the devil's creation. The soul had to be liberated from it by living a pure life so that, when the body died, it could be returned to the light of Heaven which was its proper destination.

Since God wouldn't have sent his son to live bodily amongst evil, Christ had been a spirit and, therefore, could not have suffered crucifixion—hence their refusal to recognize or wear the cross.

"And they recognize women priests as well as male," Rowley'd said, shaking his head. "*Parfaits*, they call them. *Perfect*, God give me strength."

"Tut-tut," she'd said. "Women priests. Enough to make the angels weep."

"Enough to make *me* weep. And take that look off your face."

Reaching the cottage now, she saw that Sister Ermengarde was speaking to someone who was only a shape in the orchard, so she sat down on a bench by the front door to wait for her.

Boggart was sitting in the open doorway, using the light from the room behind her to practice stitching, using a threaded bone needle on a scrap of cloth given her by Ermengarde, who'd been horrified to learn that the girl couldn't sew.

"The bishop's making plans to send you, me, and Mansur home tomorrow," Adelia told her. "Will you be glad to see England again?"

Boggart's response was immediate. "*He* won't get me again, will he?"

Who? Oh, poor child, the rapist. "No, he damn well won't. If nothing else, we're under the protection of the king now. If that man so much as looks in your direction, which he won't, Henry will cut off his whatsits and fry them with parsley."

"'At's good," Boggart said in relief. "Been a rare thing, though, ain't it, traveling with royalty an' seeing all these wonders? Still, it'll be nice to meet up with your Allie."

"Yes, yes it will."

From up here it was possible to see a faded violet flush behind the western mountains still left by the sun's departure, but it was cold and she was glad of her cloak.

Ermengarde joined her on the bench. "That was a friend of ours come to warn us. Aelith and I must leave this place tomorrow. The word is that the Church is hunting for us. Splendid. It means we've frightened the devils. Of course, you and yours are welcome to stay on here as long as you like."

"I know we are." Adelia put out her hand to touch Ermengarde's. "But we're ready to go now. I'm leaving for England myself tomorrow. I'm sorry you have trouble."

It was as if the two women knew each other well, but, actually, it was almost the first time they'd been able to sit together and converse about something other than their patients.

From behind them in the cottage came the sibilant, feminine sounds of sweeping and scurrying as Aelith, now free from the hours of nursing, got ready to leave it.

Like the stars, the full scent of the late autumn night was emerging. Ward, with his head on Adelia's foot, and a nearby tethered goat added their own flavor to it.

"We *expect* nothing but trouble from a world created by Satan, nor from that Roman Church of wolves," Ermengarde said.

The large voice of the little woman boomed its heresy into a dusk speckled with flittering bats.

Adelia flinched. *If they should hear her*. There was nobody to hear; yet the feeling persisted that somewhere out there, in the mountains, the vast monolith of the Church was listening. "*This ain't nice country*," Captain Bolt had said, "*got something nasty in its bones*."

"Where will you go?" she asked.

"North. We've done well here. Adelia, you should see us in dispute with priests in the town squares—it is splendid; their blasphemy and corruption are shown up for what they are. Now we must go north to tell the people of the true faith, of the divine spark that is trapped in their mortal bodies until it should be reunited with Heaven."

The true faith, thought Adelia. They all claimed it: Christian, Roman, Greek Orthodox, Jew, Moslem, Cathar, every one of them assured that the right way to worship God belonged only to them.

Now it was Ermengarde's hand that reached out to Adelia's. "The flame burns strongly in you, my child. I see it. How splendid it would be if you joined us, to become a *parfait*."

Adelia coughed. Rowley had said that to become a "perfect," she would not only have to abandon meat and live a life of poverty, she would have to become chaste.

"Too difficult?" asked Sister Ermengarde.

If this woman had seen her and Rowley saying good-bye to each other under the fig tree, she wouldn't ask. "I'm afraid I love a man."

"More than God?"

"Yes."

Ermengarde sighed in pity. "Once Aelith was born, my husband and I found that our love had turned to the spiritual. He, too, is a *parfait* now." She became brisk again. "Well, you must just make sure you starve yourself of the sins of the flesh on your deathbed. We call it the *endura*. Without it you will be condemned to be born again in another human body, or even as an animal, until your soul is pure enough to enter Heaven. That is why we abstain from meat in our meals—you never know who you'll be eating."

Adelia laughed. "I'm going to miss you, Ermengarde."

"And I you . . . Doctor."

"Oh, dear. Has it been that obvious?"

"It is in everything you do. '*Neither do men light a candle and put it under a bushel.*' So the Sermon on the Mount instructs us. Jesus used the word *men* in the sense of all humanity, of course, for men and women are equal in the sight of God." Sister Ermengarde harrumphed. "Catch the Pope in Rome agreeing to *that*."

Ward growled. He'd stood up, his fur raised in a ridge along his back. His snout was pointing down the hill to where the flames of the fire outside the cowshed seemed to have multiplied and were streaming back and forth, occasionally disappearing and appearing, as if from a rush of activity. A lot of shouting started up down there.

"What is it?"

Adelia got to her feet and squinted down the hill. Against the light of the fires, she could just make out the shapes of men wearing helmets. *Oh, God, Richard's war has spread to here.*

Whoever the men were, they were coming up the hill. Now

she could hear what they were shouting: "Heretics," they yelled. And, "Burn."

For a second, Ermengarde was still. "They've come for us." Then she whipped around, shouting. "Aelith. Out the back. Run, I'll hold them off."

She gave Adelia a push before grabbing at Boggart's hand in an effort to raise her up. "Run, both of you. *Run.*"

Unwieldy from pregnancy, Boggart was struggling to rise. As Adelia went to help her, the men closed in; she was enveloped in a smell of sweat and iron. Even in her terror, she knew it was the Cathars they'd come for, not her, and that Aelith, at least, must get away.

Ermengarde had slammed the cottage door shut and was shrieking and struggling to keep it closed. Adelia joined her where she clung onto the latch. "Leave her alone, leave her *alone.*"

She felt her collarbone break as one of the men tried to wrench her away, but she still held on.

The two women gave Aelith just enough time to clamber out of the back window and escape into the woods. But they couldn't save themselves—or Boggart.

Nine

BOTH COWSHED AND COTTAGE were put to the flame. "Like you fucking Cathars when we get where we're going," the leader of their captors assured them.

"We are not Cathars," Adelia told him, struggling for calm, aware that she and Boggart had their hair bound up like any Cathar women and were wearing the black robes Aelith had lent them.

If she was distancing herself from Ermengarde, she was sorry, but so be it; she was only telling the truth, and there were the others to think of.

She said: "We are the servants of King Henry Plantagenet, and he'll be mightily displeased if we're harmed."

"You're fucking Cathars, that's what you are," he'd said, and spat. "And where we're going ain't Plantagenet land."

At that point there'd been no sign of Mansur nor Ulf nor Rankin, and she was in terror in case they'd been killed. Then some more men came up the hill, and from their midst she heard the multilingual oaths of Mansur's Arabic, Rankin's Gaelic, and the good fenland English of Ulf—the latter cursing his captors and demanding in God's name that his wooden cross be returned to him.

The captives' hands were bound with ropes, each of which was tied to a saddle of a captor's mule.

It was difficult to tell how many soldiers there had been during the assault because their leader immediately sent some of them off to pursue Aelith. Of the seven who were left when the others rode away, the torchlight showed rough country faces and tunics bearing what looked like an ecclesiastical blazon. They addressed their leader, who, like them, spoke with a strong Occitan accent, as Arnaud.

Adelia asked again and again where they were to be taken and why, but received no more reply than did Ulf's threats that Henry II would spill their captors' guts when they got there—the men didn't understand them anyway.

Arnaud gave a signal, the ropes around the prisoners' hands tightened as the mules moved forward, and the march began.

The mountains were too rough even for mules to go at anything except walking pace, but every pull on the rope sent pain through Adelia's broken collarbone. Also, she'd lost a shoe in the struggle and her right foot was being pierced by thorns.

An occasional reassuring whiff told her that Ward was sticking, unnoticed, to her heels. Yet who was there to follow the scent? Rowley had gone to Carcassonne.

"Are we going to Carcassonne?" she asked.

Nobody answered her; Arnaud had ordered silence.

Betrayed. Somebody had told the authorities where Ermengarde and Aelith were staying. It could have been anybody, a peasant looking for reward, a Cathar hater. And he or she had entangled the rest of them in the betrayal.

Whoever the mercenaries were, they knew these mountains well; they followed wide tracks mostly, but now and then diverged from them so that the prisoners' legs were torn by prickly brush that sent up the smell of thyme and fennel as they went.

The sound of hoofbeats announced the arrival of the men who'd gone hunting the escapee. "Lost her," Arnaud was told. Ermengarde uttered a shout of triumph and was hit across the mouth for it.

Progress became harder when the mercenaries threw away their spent torches and proceeded by moonlight.

Through it all, and despite more punches because she wouldn't keep quiet, Ermengarde sent up long and confident Cathar prayers.

Adelia's eyes were on Boggart, tied to the mule beside hers. When the going became too rough and the girl fell, Adelia shouted at its rider: "Damn you, mind that lady, she's expecting a baby." To her surprise, the man dismounted and heaved Boggart onto the mule in his stead. Arnaud, who was in the lead, didn't notice.

It was impossible to calculate in which direction they were going or even to keep track of time; everything reduced to the necessity not to stumble, to stay on one's feet, not to surrender to thirst and fear.

When would it be day? When would this stop?

Suddenly Arnaud shouted that he was going ahead "to tell 'em we're coming" and kicked his mule into a trot to disappear down a wide track into the darkness. After he'd gone, the man who'd shown care for Boggart proved his humanity once more by ordering a halt so that the captives could be given a drink. The water was warm and stale and the leather on the flasks it came in smelled foul but, oh, it was beautiful.

The march began again.

At last the mountains ahead became jagged shapes against a dim reflection of a dawn still down over the horizon. They funneled down on three sides of what was, so much as could be seen of it, a sizable town.

Figères? No. Rowley had said that Figères was little more than a village.

A hope reared that it was Carcassonne, one of Languedoc's major cities, where Rowley was going. And yet she'd had the idea that Carcassonne was built on a plain.

She heard Ermengarde say, "Aveyron," as if something had been extinguished in her, and one of the men laughed.

It was just waking up as they reached its outskirts. A woman emerging from one of the houses to empty a chamber pot shouted at her family to come and see. Shutters were flung back; questions, dogs, and children accompanied the prisoners up a winding, cobbled track toward a square formed by buildings of considerable size. Adelia glimpsed a tall tower and cupolas like graceful saucepan lids outlined against the rising sun.

Up and up into a square, where Boggart was lifted from her mule and the ropes binding the prisoners' hands were replaced by manacles. They were ushered into a magnificent, arcaded hall, where a line of liveried servants carrying food dishes into a room on the right paused to stare at the prisoners and were commanded to be about their business by a tap from the staff of a heavily robed steward. A line of people in a gallery above their heads goggled down at them.

In the middle of the hall, a man in the cassock of a priest sat at a table, a scribe beside him. There was an oath and a scuffle and, looking back, Adelia saw that one of the riders had taken Ward by the scruff of his neck and thrown him outside the doors that were then closed against him.

Ermengarde had recovered her courage. Pushed in front of the table, she addressed the priest politely in Latin: "*Ave,* Gerhardt," and then, louder, in Occitan: "*Ara roda l'abelha.*" ("That bee is buzzing round again.")

There was a laugh, quickly suppressed, that caused an echo making it impossible to tell where it had come from.

"*Father* Gerhardt to you, bitch," the priest said in Latin.

"My father is in heaven. Are we to dispute again? Splendid."

Father Gerhardt addressed his scribe. "Ermengarde of Montauban, a self-confessed Cathar. Write it down." He raised his head. "Or have you repented, woman?"

"I repent of nothing."

"You are charged with preaching heresy throughout this region in defiance of the edicts issued by His Holiness Pope Alexander the Third. The punishment is death by burning."

"I do not recognize such edicts, nor your Satanic Pope. I have preached only true Christianity."

"We have the statements of witnesses." Father Gerhardt pointed at a roll on his table.

"Splendid."

Stop it, stop it, Adelia wanted to shout at her. The statement of an ignorant man as he'd set fire to Ermengarde's cottage—*Like you fucking Cathars*—she'd taken to be the threat of a bully; now it was being translated into something else. Here, they were enclosed in the efficiency of a powerful machine, in front of them was a man about serious business, a stone-faced man whose eyes—the only mobile thing about him—had flames in them.

They can't, she thought. *Not us. Henry's anger would be terrible—don't they know that? They* must *know.*

But around her were the indifferent mountains of a landscape where the Plantagenet writ did not run. She'd wandered into somebody else's story, not hers. It was a mistake, she was going to die by mistake. She willed Ermengarde to cower, plead, whisper repentance, instead of shouting for her own execution—and theirs.

One by one they were made to stand before their inquisitor and told to give their names, place of birth, and occupation.

Their explanations were cut short: "You are Cathars, you were found consorting with Cathars."

For all that she was shaking, Adelia tried for indignation when her turn came. "It is disgraceful that we are treated like this. Who are you? Where is this place?"

"You are in the palace of the Bishop of Aveyron." The priest had the thin, protuberant features of a dog and an expression that suggested he would be better for going muzzled.

"Then inform your bishop that we are under the protection of the Bishop of Winchester, who is with Princess Joanna at Figères, and the Bishop of Saint Albans of England, whom you can find at Carcassonne. We are servants of Henry Plantagenet, and we have been traveling with his daughter until . . ."

"You are Cathars, you were found consorting with Cathars." It was a mantra.

Mansur's questioning was briefest of all: Who he was or what he was doing in Languedoc was of no interest—his color and robes were those of a self-confessed, if different, heretic; he could burn with the rest.

WHEN HE'D FINISHED his interrogation, Father Gerhardt took up his papers, left the hall for the palace's dining room, and passed through it to the breakfast room, where a table winked with crystal glass and gold plate.

Above, a flat ceiling glowed with Bible scenes painted by a master; below, the morning robe of the man at the table was no less inspired with autumn color and the skill of embroideresses.

The Bishop of Aveyron, a plump man with clever eyes, took one more honeyed fig, wiped his fingers on the linen napkin tucked into his neck, and looked up. "So the information was exact?"

"In every detail, my lord. I doubt we'd have found her hideout without it. Unfortunately, she managed to delay the men's entry long enough for the daughter to escape. I've ordered a hunt for her."

His bishop waved a hand in dismissal. "Do we care about the daughter? Ermengarde is the one we wanted."

"And now we have her."

For a moment these two very different men shared the same searing memory—a black-clad woman standing in the town square making fools of them both: "*Leave me alone, old men. Abandon either your luxury or your preaching.*"

The townspeople had laughed at them. *Them.*

"Also," said Father Gerhardt, "we have written proof against her. Our men searched the hovel before setting fire to it. There was a gospel written in the langue d'oc."

The bishop shook his head sadly: "Gerhardt, Gerhardt, is there no end to Cathar evil? Where *should* we poor Latinate clergy be if the common herd were able to listen to the holy word in their own language?" He stretched out his hand to take one of the soft, white rolls nestling in a basket that his steward had just put in front of him. "You and I would have to go begging our bread."

Gerhardt was put out; he never knew when his bishop was joking.

"A joke," the bishop explained, seeing him puzzled. That was the trouble with priests who brought their zeal straight from the Vatican, no humor.

"Yes, my lord. And the foreigners captured with Ermengarde? Our bargain with the informant was to ensure that they suffer the same punishment, but I have to tell you"—Gerhardt said this with reluctance—"they persist in their story that they are all servants of Henry Plantagenet."

"And *they* are? Tell me again."

Father Gerhardt consulted his list. "A youth purporting to be a pilgrim—the cross he carried was of interest to our informant, if you remember, and as it was of no account our men let him have it. A female servant who is pregnant . . ."

The bishop stopped using his butter knife in order to wave it. "Pregnancy does not absolve her. Root and branch, Gerhardt, root and branch. Remember that."

"Yes, my lord. Then there is a mercenary speaking a language nobody can understand. Also a Saracen, and a woman who interprets for him." Gerhardt looked up. "She is the woman our informant is eager to have destroyed—if the others die with her, so be it. Surely no Christian king would inflict wharf rats like that on his daughter?"

The bishop shrugged. "I wouldn't put it past this one from what I've heard, not Henry. Yes, I have no doubt they are who they say they are."

Father Gerhardt was taken aback, not so much by fact, but that his bishop was making no bones about it. "Yet do we need to worry about his opinion?" he asked. "A priest killer?"

"Ah, but a priest killer who's done penance for Becket and been accepted back into the fold." The bishop poured himself another glass of wine while he considered. "I wonder. Can we afford to offend the King of England?"

"If we don't, we lose a spy who can take us into the center of the king's web. Moreover"—a flash of Father Gerhardt's canines showed his happiness at imparting a nugget he'd been hugging—"my lord, I can tell you that the Bishop of Winchester and others in the princess's party complain that the Saracen and his woman are witches. They say the two have brought bad luck on them. They would not be unhappy to lose them."

"Witches, eh?" The bishop liked that.

"Yes, my lord. Apparently, the Saracen's woman has fed a love potion to the other bishop, Rowley of Saint Albans, so that he lusts after her and will hear no word against her."

"I thought she was supposed to be plain."

"She is, my lord, which only emphasizes the strength of her magic."

"A Jezebel," mused the bishop. "'*And Jezebel was cast down, and the dogs did eat her, and no more of her was found than the skull, and the feet, and the palms of her hands.*' A gratifying image, I've always found. So wholesale, don't you think?"

"Indeed, my lord." Gerhardt refused to be diverted. "Nor does this harlot wear a cross. Both she and the maid are dressed as Cathars. In any case, they've spent time with Ermengarde and so will have been infected."

The bishop smiled. He was fond of the principle of *post hoc ergo propter hoc*. So useful.

Father Gerhardt raised flailing arms in appeal to Heaven. "When, O Lord, *when* wilt thou grant us full crusade against this cancer?"

When indeed, the bishop thought. Increasingly severe anti-Cathar edicts had been issued by the Vatican for over thirty years without, so far, calling for a crusade against the heretics. Yet crusade was the only option, as the bishop knew; the infection was becoming a plague.

A new order was needed. A man to raise the Holy Cross against the Cathars in the teeth of the Pope, begin God's righteous slaughter.

Lying in his bed at night, the Bishop of Aveyron sweated into his silk sheets. If it was successful it would take him high, perhaps to the throne of Rome itself. Failure . . . ?

Tapping his teeth, the bishop looked up at the depiction of the Garden of Eden on his ceiling. He was particularly fond of it; the artist had let himself go as far as Eve's naked body was concerned. "This informant, we're certain of him, are we?" he asked.

"A valuable man, my lord. As I said, he is privy to what passes between the English bishops and their king; he will be in Sicily when Saint Albans arrives after negotiating with Barbarossa and the Lombards. What are a witch and a ragbag of nonentities to set against that?"

But the Bishop of Aveyron's careful mind had made itself up; he hadn't got where he was today by being rash.

"Nevertheless, we must be sure. The Plantagenet is soft toward heretics, yet his arm is long and on the end of it there is a hammer. There is no need to anger him at this stage. Feelers, Gerhardt, we shall put out feelers; nothing too definite on either side. All we need to know from the princess's officials is: If we have found some heretics wandering in the hills and consequently disposed of them, shall they be missed? Will that fit the situation?"

"From what I gather, the answer will be no, my lord."

"I gather that, too. But hold off until we get it. As for our 'perfect,' you may proceed as planned." He smiled again; this time his priest knew he wasn't joking. "Bring the town in to witness it."

"Where do you want the prisoners lodged, my lord? The dungeons?"

The bishop tapped his teeth. "No, let them have a view of what they may expect. Clear out the tower room and put them up there for now. Set trustworthy guards, mind. Sometimes I think the contagion has infected my own palace."

When Gerhardt had gone, his lord poured himself another glass of the vintage from his vineyard near Carcassonne and sipped it while he engineered a new vision of Ermengarde, his black-clad tauntress, this time tied to a stake with faggots laid around her feet.

He saw himself thrusting a torch into the wood like a penis into her parts and sighed because, alas, that pleasure must be left to the executioner. One day, though, yes, yes, one day, the flames he'd light would consume them all . . . men, women, and children.

This really was most excellent wine.

AND SCARRY? *He's been very busy.*

As he promised, he led the heretic hunters to the cowshed. He saw Mansur, Rankin, and Ulf go down fighting. He watched the capture of the women up the hill. Then he began looking for something. He found it—lying in one of the mangers where Ulf had left it. A rough wooden cross.

Now, back at Figères, he is levering out some of the nails that hold together a rough-looking cross. He is doing it quietly, so that no sound escapes from the spartan monk's cell in which he is lodged.

He takes off the crosspiece and applies an eye to the resultant space. What he sees, packed carefully in horsehair, is a sword pommel gleaming with amethysts. Incautiously, he neighs with satisfaction.

There is a call from the cell next door: "Are you unwell, brother? I heard you cry out."

"I am well, brother, I thank you. I was carried away by the glory of my God."

"Amen to that. Good night, brother."

In reinserting the nails by hammering them with his fist so as to make no more noise, he tears his hands, a fact that he only notices because he can smell the blood.

He doesn't feel pain much anymore, does Scarry. On the other hand, his sense of smell has become excellent, returning him to his days in the forest with Wolf, when they could sniff their quarry through all other conflicting scents, hunt it down, play with it before they killed, and then dance in its split paunch, animal or human.

He puts his bloody hand up to his nose, just to make sure it is there.

With luck and opportunity, he should soon be savoring the odor of a woman's burning flesh.

ADELIA HAD HER FOOT in Boggart's lap and was hoping very hard that it hadn't become infected by the thorns the girl was teasing out of it.

Ulf was pacing up and down, up and down, getting on everybody's nerves. "There was some other bugger in the cowshed when they got us. He was looking for something while the bastards were tyin' us up. I reckon it was my cross."

"We know," Mansur said wearily. "The one comfort is that he will be unaware of what's inside it."

Ulf turned on him. "*But he did*. I keep telling you, he asked for it particular. He *knew*. And he wasn't one of them who took us over the mountains, he disappeared once they'd got us down."

"Didn't you recognize his voice?"

"No, kept his bloody cloak over his bloody mouth, didn't he."

"Leave it, laddie," Rankin told him. "There's nae thing we can do about it. For now, let's save our breath to cool our *parritch*."

What *parritch* was, Adelia had no idea, but she was grateful to him; the Scotsman was proving as firm a rock as Mansur.

A grizzled man with a face like a battered turnip. The march over the hills must have been hard for him who'd been so ill, harder for him than Ulf, who had youth on his side. All the way, he'd muttered strange and incomprehensible oaths to himself and his eyes under their curled, upsweeping gray brows suggested that, if his hands were free, his captors would be dispossessed of certain limbs, but, and this was strangely comforting to Adelia, he showed lack of surprise at the situation in which he found himself. Maybe life in the Scottish Highlands combining with that as one of King Henry's mercenaries had weathered him against anything it could come up with.

When, just now, she'd felt obliged to apologize for it, he'd patted her hand and said: "Aye well, as we say back hame, a misty morning may yet become a guid clear day."

Ulf continued to chafe and pace. "There was something about him. Never saw his face, but the way he moved . . . I swear I'd seen the cut of him before. Jesus Christ, where *was* it?"

It was a rhetorical question and one he'd put so many times that nobody bothered with it. He gave up and turned his attention to the turret room's two unglazed windows. "Both big enough for us all to get out, despite the mullions," he said, "iffen we had some rope."

They didn't have any rope, and one window overlooked the square some dizzying hundred feet below, while the drop from the other one was at least fifty feet onto some palace roofs.

Now he was looking out at the square and adding a commentary to the sound of hammering and sawing that the others could hear perfectly well.

"Building a bloody dais," he said bitterly. "That's so the nobs won't miss anything, I suppose. Gawd, they're putting canvas over the top, 'case the bastards get rained on. Why'n't they hang out some bloody bunting while they're about it?"

The boy was torturing himself—and them—for losing Excalibur. Adelia waited until Boggart had bound her foot with a piece of cloth torn from her petticoat, and then hopped over to where he was standing. She put her arm round his shoulders. "We're all tired, let's get some sleep."

"Only one stake so far," he said.

She looked out with him; the stake stood in the center of the square, commanding it like a maypole. The piles of wood around its base formed a platform. Five other stakes were stacked ominously against one of the walls.

"Not us, then," Ulf said. "Not yet."

"It won't be. We told them who we were. They'll have sent word to Princess Joanna or Rowley—I told them he was at Carcassonne. The name of King Henry must carry some weight, even here."

"Where've they put Ermengarde?"

"I don't know." The Cathar had been taken away immediately after questioning.

"What treacherous bastard gave away where she was?"

Adelia didn't know that either.

"I liked her," Ulf said.

"We all did." *We're talking of her in the past*, she thought.

"You reckon as Aelith got away?"

"I think so. Dear God, I hope so."

"What'd them women do to earn this? Apart from acting like Christians?"

"I don't know."

Eventually, Ulf was persuaded to lie down with the others on the floor.

It was cold up here. The five of them hadn't even been provided with straw, let alone beds. There'd been no food, nor drink, either. The one convenience was a bucket that had been thrown in after them.

However, after that long and terrible march, the imperative was sleep; Mansur, Rankin, and Boggart were already succumbing to it. Watching Ulf's dour young face relax, Adelia, agonized, thought of his grandmother and what she would say if she saw him now. And Boggart with the new life inside her . . . And Allie, always Allie. *Are you asleep, little one? Don't miss me. Be happy*.

How had they all come to this?

Ever prepared to assume guilt, Adelia went over the circumstances that had led them here . . . back, back to accepting Henry Plantagenet's commission in the first place . . . but she *hadn't* accepted it, he'd forced her into it . . . back to the education and foster parents who had made her into a person ill-starred and at odds with everything the world demanded of womanhood . . . back to being born at all into such a world.

Boggart's ministrations had eased her foot, but Adelia's shoulder was hurting.

She untied the cord from about her waist and made it into a sling in which to rest her arm. Then, wrapping her cloak around her against the cold, she shuffled to find a comfortable position on the boards of the floor, and lay down, using Boggart's now-ample rump as a pillow. . . .

She was in a classroom back in the Salerno medical school and a high, pedantic voice from someone she couldn't see was lecturing on the subject of burning at the stake.

"Better for the victim if the wood is piled high up to his or her armpits, thus providing a quick death from the inhalation of smoke. . . ."

It was a relief to be woken up by the grind of a turning key in the lock of the door. The only light in the room was from the star-sprinkled sky outside the window. Two of the men who'd dragged them over the mountains came in. One had a spear at the ready; the other—he was the one who'd been kind to Boggart and given them water—carried a tray on which were five bowls, some stale rye bread, and a container of surprisingly good lamb stew.

"Ask 'em when they're going to let us go, the bastards," Ulf told Adelia.

She repeated the question, without its embellishment.

"Only way you're getting out is in flames," the spear carrier said.

But the kindly one said: "When we gets word."

"What's your name?" Adelia asked him.

"Don't tell 'em, Raymond," the spear carrier said. "Ah, *shit*."

After the guards were gone, there was discussion in the darkness about what Raymond's "*when we gets word*" meant.

"It means they've sent to get confirmation of who we are," Adelia said firmly. "Or they're contacting Rowley. We'll be out of here in no time."

Appetite satisfied, still tired, the prisoners settled down to sleep again.

"*If, on the other hand,*" the dream lecturer persisted, "*the faggots are merely laid at the victim's feet, he or she will suffer maximum pain until he or she dies of shock and blood loss. . . .*"

"No." Adelia sat up. The lecturer's voice had been her own. Digging her nails into her palms so that she shouldn't hear it again, she stayed awake for the rest of the night.

IN THE MORNING, their hands were tied and their feet put into irons before they were led down the turret's winding staircase and into the open air, where gray clouds were being blown fast across the sky.

Men-at-arms stood at each entrance to the square; townspeople were being ushered into it by others who made sure that dogs and goats did not wander in with them. Some of them had baskets on their arms as if they'd been interrupted in their marketing.

The prisoners were led to the dais and made to clamber up on it so that they could both see and be seen, though the men and women funneling in only glanced at them briefly, then looked away, almost without interest, almost as if tied and manacled beings were the usual people in the usual place.

Boggart was on one side of Mansur, Adelia on the other with Rankin next to her and Ulf next to him. Behind them was scaffolding where the frontage of an ancient church was being rebuilt with stonework that was already a marvel of carving.

Ahead and higher than the church stood the bishop's palace, modern and pristine, with glazed windows in rounded arches, and the sculptures of its portal telling the story of Jesus's life.

It was a beautiful square. With a stake at its center.

Adelia thought she could hear Ward barking somewhere and wondered where he could get food and if he would find water.

She wondered whether Allie was being allowed to fly her

kestrel; she wondered if little Sister Aelith had got away; she wondered where Rowley was now.

Her mind kept to these things, away from the here and now, which was a charade that would end with the stake and its woodpile remaining untouched and everybody being sent home. Human beings did not burn one another, not in these times; it was a threat from another age always held over the heads of heretics, Jews, witches, and other nonconformers but never actually performed now, *not now, dear Lord, not now*.

The abnormality of everything rushed at her, causing panic. Beyond these roofs and turrets was a pitiless landscape that was too high and too jagged. This square was full of people who were nothing to her, as she was less than nothing to them.

No, she told herself, *it won't happen*. Those churchmen over there on the bedraped dais opposite were commanded not to shed blood. Ergo, they wouldn't, *couldn't* let it shrivel in burning flesh. And the stake with its platform of bundled wood was there, *there*, in the center, and she wouldn't witness it because it wasn't happening . . . and she could hear Ward's bark again and she would die if somebody didn't help him and keep him and Allie from being lonely which, of course, somebody would because there was kindness in this world, there had to be kindness or there was neither health nor purpose in it. . . .

The press of townspeople was now so large that the prisoners could look down on the caps of the men and the intricate weave of the women's wide straw hats just below them. There was none of the excitement with which crowds so often attended an execution; these people were sullen. Cathars or not, they didn't want this.

A woman below Adelia spoke to the one next to her. "Ermengarde." It was as if the word said everything that was to be said.

"I know," her neighbor said.

"How'll she bear the pain?"

"Let us pray God will take it on Himself."

There was a clash of spears; men-at-arms were saluting the Bishop of Aveyron as he came out of his palace, wonderful in cope and miter. He had a dais of his own and was assisted onto it.

Adelia closed her eyes as he began speaking. It was a fine voice, rich in tone and sorrow, and the moment Adelia heard it she knew Ermengarde was going to die today.

"My dear friends, you are assembled here as good people and good Christians to witness what must be done for the sake of all our souls. . . ."

There was a sudden yell of "Persecution"—a man's shout, brave and clear. Immediately, there was a tramp of boots as men-at-arms parted the crowd to try and find its owner. *God bless him*, Adelia thought, *whoever he is. We are never quite alone*.

"Persecution?" queried the lovely voice. "But not every persecution is blameworthy; rather it is reasonable for us to persecute heretics, just as Christ physically persecuted those whom He drove out of the Temple. To kill wicked men and women in order to save their souls for the sake of correction and justice is to serve God. And so we must do today."

More tramping boots; they were bringing Ermengarde into the square. A phalanx of monks began chanting.

Adelia opened her eyes. The Cathar looked so small. She was bareheaded and the wind whipped her gray hair around her face. She was uttering her own battle cry, *bless her, oh, bless her*. It rose above the wind and the chanting monks: "'Beware the false prophets who come to you in the guise of lambs wherein lurk voracious wolves.' So says the gospel of Matthew. Their God is of the Old Testament, ignorant, cruel, bloodthirsty, and unjust. . . ."

There was a crack, and she was silenced.

A murmur like a breeze ruffling corn ran through the crowd, and the bishop shouted over it: "You hear, good people? This woman's blasphemy is proved out of her own throat."

Adelia forced herself to keep looking; to hide one's face from courage like this was to betray it; she was a witness.

Tiny and dowdy against the tapestry of the clergy, surrounded by men-at-arms, Ermengarde strode on bare feet toward the stake like a bride on her wedding day. She was led by a priest walking backward and holding a jeweled cross in front of her. There was blood on her mouth.

Boggart began to pant. Ulf and Rankin were swearing.

Adelia looked across at the churchmen, amazed. *Are you blind? Don't you see the bare feet, the simplicity, the loneliness? This is the Via Dolorosa.*

Ermengarde was lifted onto her platform and tied to its stake. They were standing her on the pyre, not within it. One of her feet dislodged a faggot and a man-at-arms took time to replace it neatly.

The chanting came louder. A bible was offered but Ermengarde turned her face away from it, one side of her damaged mouth moving in prayer.

A man in a hood that covered his face came forward holding a lit torch. He looked at the bishop, who nodded and dipped his plump, steepled hands.

There was a *whoomph*; they'd poured oil on the wood.

Adelia pushed her face into Mansur's sleeve. She heard the crackle of flames and spitting wood that she'd heard a thousand times in comfortable kitchens where fire cooked meat on a spit. Her remorseless anatomist's brain followed the sequence of burning feet, calves, thighs, hands, torso, and no death, no death until the conflagration reached the breath of the mouth and extinguished it.

Nor did God take the pain upon Himself. Long before the end, Ermengarde was screaming.

Ten

PERHAPS, HAVING SHOWN his five prisoners the end that awaited them, the Bishop of Aveyron was now concerned in case they dislodged the mullions on their turret windows and threw themselves out. Perhaps he felt the morality of a bishop demanded that he should not keep men and women confined together. Whatever the reason, a few hours after Ermengarde's ashes were chucked onto a midden, Adelia, Boggart, Rankin, Mansur, and Ulf were transferred from the palace's highest point to its lowest and then separated, male from female.

With their feet free but hands still tied, they were led down the circular stairs of the turret, across the great hall and the stares of its people, to where another staircase skewered itself deep into the earth, past an underground guardroom and down again, to a blind tunnel of a dungeon and the row of cells lining its walls.

Every push, every jerk on Adelia's arms stabbed at her damaged shoulder—the cord she'd made into a sling had been tossed away by the guard who'd tied her hands. She hardly noticed it; the pain was inconsequential compared to the agony she'd witnessed.

Their hands finally released, she and Boggart were pushed into one cell, Rankin, Ulf, and Mansur into that next door, and the keys turned on them.

If they'd wanted to, they could have conversed by putting their faces to the small barred apertures in the doors and shouting to one another, but they didn't. None of them had spoken since they'd been taken from the square.

Slumped on the stone floor, holding tightly to Boggart's hand, Adelia knew that she should break the silence, say something to put heart into them all, but was incapable of doing it. She was unraveled; the only thread holding to sanity was the thought that Rowley would come for them. But even when he did, none of them would ever be free of a scar that flames and screams had branded on their memory—*we have seen a human being burned alive.* Like the others, she was past anger, past prayer; she was reduced to an enervating astonishment at the hideousness Man was capable of—and even that flickered only occasionally in a stupor ending in helpless sleep.

Rowley didn't come for them that day. Nor the next.

FATHER GERHARDT RODE to Figères, taking with him greetings, perfume, wine, foie gras wrapped in fig leaves, and cheeses of the region from the Bishop of Aveyron to the King of England's illustrious daughter.

Since the hour was too late to disturb the princess up at the château, the Bishop of Winchester, Father Guy, Father Adalburt, and Dr. Arnulf received him—with embarrassment—in the priory's little refectory, where they had been sitting late at supper. (The prior had gone to bed; he had weeds to hoe in the morning.)

"I fear you find us benighted, Father," the bishop told him. "As you see, we have been dogged by misfortune on this leg of our journey. I am ashamed that we cannot receive you with better state."

"Not at all, not at all." Father Gerhardt pretended not to notice the spade somebody had left standing in a corner, nor the remains of a plain, bucolic meal still on the table, nor that the man standing behind the Bishop of Winchester's chair was the only servant in a room lit not by good beeswax candles but tapers made of rushes.

Nevertheless, notice them he did; Scarry's information was proving exact so far.

Accepting a glass of wine, Father Gerhardt studied faces.

He looked briefly into the eyes of Father Adalburt, who smiled foolishly back at him; he saw that Winchester's bishop was a tired old man; and that the two who would be his allies were Father Guy and Dr. Arnulf. Yes, just as he'd been told.

"My lord, I bring a letter from my lord of Aveyron." He bowed and handed it over. "And now, with your permission, I would be grateful for a night's bed—it has been a long ride."

("Give them the letter, then leave them alone to read it," his bishop had told him. "They will betray more easily if they are not watched by an outsider.")

That set the cat among the pigeons. A bed? Oh, Lord, a bed. The good bishop was already doubling up in his with the prior, while the two chaplains and Dr. Arnulf were sharing the only other.

"Perhaps Captain Bolt can provide one," Father Guy suggested. He addressed the servant sharply: "Peter, escort the good Father up to the château. And then come back and clear this table of its detritus, it is a disgrace."

When the door had closed, he picked up the letter. "Shall I read this to you, my lord?"

"Read away. My old eyes fail me in this light."

"*From the Bishop of Aveyron to his brother in the Lord, Bishop of Winchester, a heartfelt and respectful welcome. This poor region is honored by the presence of a noble princess and her religious advisers whose reputation for holiness and wisdom has come before them. . . .*"

"How kind," said the Bishop of Winchester, wiping his eyes, "Isn't that kind of Aveyron."

More than half the scroll was taken up with compliments, an invitation to grace Aveyron palace, more compliments.

The Bishop of Winchester's head began to nod. Father Adalburt started chalking notes for a sermon on his slate.

Not until the end did the letter reach its nub. . . .

"*My lord, you will know, in your wisdom, that the foul heresy of Catharism has been spreading throughout this country, and that some of us fight its contagion that it may not infect all Christendom. Accordingly, I must bring to your lordship's attention that, in this great struggle, the Lord has allowed to fall into my hand five such heretics found wandering the hills. . . .*"

Father Guy's voice paused for a moment, then he read on.

"*Normally, it would be the work of a moment to mete the punishment inflicted on all who preach false doctrine on these wretches—two women in Cathar dress and three men—were it not that they make some claim to be connected with Princess Joanna's court. I assume this to be the impudence expected of those who spread evil falsehood, yet I feel obliged to bring the matter to your lordship's attention. Should you, my dear brother, as I expect, refute this claim, I shall act as I act against all who threaten blessed Mother Church. I await your word to be returned by the hand of my good and faithful chaplain, Father Gerhardt.*

"In the meantime, that God pour His blessing on you is the dearest wish of your servant, Philippe of Aveyron."

("They will know, as I know, that these are their people," Aveyron had said. "But if I am to satisfy our informant, while at the same time avoid bringing the Plantagenet's wrath on my head, it is they who, like Pontius Pilate, must wash their hands and permit the execution. And I want it in writing.")

Father Guy's hands took care in rolling up the scroll, his eyes avoiding those of Dr. Arnulf sitting very upright in his chair.

Something, some *thing*, a fetid eagerness, came into the little room, deepening its shadows; it hung in the dusty rafters out of sight, watchful, timorous, obscene.

THE CELLS STANK and were dark, containing only a bucket. There were no windows; the faintest gleam touched the tunnel outside where it filtered thinly round the circular stair from the torches in the guardroom above.

They were beetles in blackness; they crouched beneath the weight of the palace's mountainous boot in case it descended and crushed them. What if there was a fire? Who would care if insects locked in at the bottom of the pile couldn't get out?

The only thing that stopped Adelia becoming a whirling, screaming ball of panic was Boggart, who, she knew, had to be in the same state yet was fighting it because she was. They were like two playing cards propping each other up; if one went so would the other. Presumably, to judge from their silence, the three other prisoners were doing the same.

Yet there were noises; the tunnel had its own creaks and whimpers. Ulf broke the silence: "Anybody else down here?" But the shout sent up diminishing, skipping reverberations of "anybody else . . . anybody else . . ." like answers from the dead, and he didn't do it again. Certainly, no living voice replied.

Food was presaged by the sound of clanking. Each of the two guards who came to feed them had a chatelaine chained to his belt such as were usually worn by ladies to attach useful feminine things like scissors, thimble and needle cases, keys to store cupboards, etc. The guards had only keys, massive keys.

The women's door was unlocked first. One of the guards shoved in a tray while the other stood back, spear at the ready to repel any rushed escape. The door was locked again. Adelia and Boggart heard the procedure repeated next door, then listened to the rattle of keys as the guards climbed the stairs to their post.

Darkness.

"CATHARS? WHY WOULD Cathars be connected with the princess?" The Bishop of Winchester was having trouble catching up.

"They are not, of course," said Father Guy, soothingly. "It is their ploy to escape punishment. As my lord Aveyron says, all heretics are liars. These are nothing to do with us."

"It is strange, though," the bishop continued. "Is it possible . . .

could it be that . . . how many of our people stayed behind in that nuns' hospital at the last?"

"Oooh," Dr. Arnulf said casually. "Seven? Eight?"

"Not five, then?"

"And remember, my lord," pointed out Father Guy, "the Bishop of Saint Albans said before he left for Carcassonne that he would be sending the Saracen and his female back to England. It is safe to assume that they have already gone."

"Taking the others with them, one supposes," Dr. Arnulf said.

"Also, they would be taking the direct route back to England; they cannot have wandered so far off it as to encroach on Aveyron territory."

"Nor would they be dressed as Cathars."

The chaplain and doctor were topping each other, and doing it well, though they avoided each other's eyes like secret lovers. Father Adalburt watched them, smiling his vacant smile.

The Saracen, thought the Bishop of Winchester wearily. The Saracen and his woman—what was her name? They had blighted with ill luck a journey already hard enough for an old man; he was dreading its recommencement. "I wish the Bishop of Saint Albans were here," he said. "He would know, but, alas, we shan't have his company now until we reach Sicily."

Father Guy in no way regretted my lord of Saint Albans's absence. "My lord, why should we concern ourselves over a faraway group of unbelievers?"

Dr. Arnulf didn't regret it, either. "Totally unnecessary."

They kept quiet while their bishop mused. He was roused by the return of Peter, who began clearing the table; like most of the servants, the man was wearing the Plantagenet leopards on his tunic.

Plantagenet. The word jolted the bishop out of his reverie. Troublesome and unlucky as the Saracen and his woman had proved to be, King Henry had stressed their importance. Perhaps all pains should be taken to ensure that they were safe—the king's toes, if stepped on, could deliver a devastating kick.

"Should we not send someone back to Aveyron . . . to see if there has been some unfortunate mistake . . . ensure that the bishop's prisoners do not include our people?"

Father Guy put out a hand to quell a hiss from Dr. Arnulf. "My lord, if I may say so, that would be an error reflecting badly on yourself. It would indicate to this foreign bishop that you have allowed Princess Joanna's train to be riddled with heretics, or why else should you even inquire for these?"

"Oh, dear, yes. No, we mustn't do that."

"I don't see why your lordship is even troubling yourself with the matter," Dr. Arnulf said. "The bishop's prisoners are dressed as Cathars, therefore they must *be* Cathars."

The old man sighed. "Very well, then, I suppose we must send a letter to Aveyron tomorrow disclaiming any knowledge of these people."

Doctor and chaplain took in a breath and then dispelled it.

The thing that Aveyron's letter had brought into the room's shadows grew in size, vibrating slightly.

Father Guy said swiftly: "Allow me to pen it, my lord. Best it were done right away. If you will retire, I'll bring the letter to your room for your signature."

"Thank you, my son." My lord of Winchester raised himself

from his chair, making gratefully for his bed, a tired man made more tired by the uneasy feeling that something had got away from him.

As the door closed behind him, Father Guy's eyes at last met those of Dr. Arnulf.

The doctor nodded. "Write the letter, then," he said.

OUTSIDE ONE OF the tents surrounding the château, Admiral O'Donnell was playing chess with Locusta by the light of a fire.

"Ah, Peter," he called as the servant passed him. "Who's our visitor? The one with a look that would perish the Danes?"

"Brought a message from the Bishop of Aveyron, my lord."

"Did he, now?" The Irishman moved his queen. "And what was the letter about?"

Peter told him.

"Cathars," said the O'Donnell, nodding. "Bad cess to 'em."

"Checkmate." Locusta grinned. "You're off your game tonight, my lord."

"To you the glory." He stretched and yawned. "And me for me bed. Good night, gentlemen."

SINCE LIFE, even in despair, had to be lived, the prisoners made the best of it.

They established their own routine. Every morning—if it *was* morning—they took turns to press their faces to the doors' bars and talk to one another. This was harder on Adelia and Boggart than the men since, to reach the aperture, both women had to stand on tiptoe, a stance that couldn't be maintained for too long.

Then, at Adelia's insistence, they all took exercise by walking twenty times round the walls of the cells. These were of stone and extensive, something their occupants were forced to establish by pace and feel. Rankin, during one of his conversations with Adelia through their door bars, shouted: "For what wud a man o' God want wi' sic space for his paiks, lessen he's a black-avised, messan-dog o' a limmer?"

Which, interpreted, was a good question. Had the bishops of Aveyron who'd built this place so distrusted their flock that they envisaged incarcerating the hundreds these cells could hold? Was the present incumbent expecting to fill them with Cathars?

In the afternoon—if it was afternoon—they kept up their spirits by singing or reciting, each taking it in turn to stand near the door so that his or her voice could reach the others. In the case of Adelia this was a penance, for her as well as everybody else; she had the singing voice of an off-key crow and restricted herself to chanting nursery rhymes her childhood English nurse had taught her in Sicily.

Ulf's voice was little better so he chose to recount tales of Hereward the Wake and the fight that fenland hero had put up against William the Conqueror. Mansur's high, clear treble sent songs of the Tigris-Euphrates marshland into which he'd been born ringing down the tunnel. Boggart sang pretty ballads she'd picked up from market-place minstrels. Rankin, in a tuneful and deep bass, rendered incomprehensible but heart-stirring airs from the Highlands and bewailed the fact that he hadn't his peeps with which he could have kept up their spirits even further.

"Er, 'peeps'?"

"Bagpipes," came the gloomy explanation in Ulf's voice. "We been spared them at least."

This was their defiance: no hymns, never hymns; in this place they would not give voice to the God worshipped by the Bishop of Aveyron.

But they became more and more tired; their scraps of food were leftovers from the palace kitchens and, always supposing the cook hadn't spat in them, were of good quality but too meager to be sustaining. Adelia, her shoulder aching badly, berated the guards on behalf of Boggart who, as she pointed out, should be eating for two, but the rations weren't increased so she went without herself.

And still Rowley didn't come for them.

Eventually, they stopped singing; emaciation does not lend itself to song. Mostly they sat quietly. Even Adelia had given up pointing out that the length of their incarceration proved that Aveyron was waiting for word from Figères before he took any action—there had been time for it to come many times over.

It was Ulf, next door, who tired her even more. His youth gave him the energy to be furious at what, he had now contrived to believe, was treachery to Adelia, not Ermengarde, a theory he kept putting forward to her through the bars of his cell.

"They was after you," he insisted.

"They were after Ermengarde," she said wearily. "They just happened to capture us with her and thought we were Cathars."

"Oh, I grant you the bastards were after Ermengarde, but who told them where she was *knowing* we were with her and they'd take us for Cathars? Eh? Tell me that. She and Aelith had been refugin' in that cottage for months, why did the bastards come for her when *we* were there? Eh? Too much of a coincidence if you ask me."

There was a simpler explanation and Adelia had pressed her face closer to the bars of her door so that she could voice it quietly because it was too awful to be spoken out loud.

"Ulf, it was *us*. Rowley and Locusta were riding back and forth to the cowshed every day. Two well-dressed men like that—they were bound to attract the attention of people on the road. They made somebody curious; perhaps he crept up the hill to find out where they were going, saw the Cathar women, spread the word. God forgive us, it was *us*. We led Aveyron's men to her. . . ." She couldn't finish.

But Ulf equated their misfortune to others that had marred Adelia's progress on the journey: the death of the horse that had thrown her, the murder of Brune who had railed against her. "I tell you, some bugger was out to bring you down. *You*, not her."

Hunger and her aching collarbone brought on a terrible irritation. "Well, they've done it, haven't they?" she shouted. "And all of you with me." She heard her voice rippling along the tunnel, carrying defeat with it, and tried to make amends: "But Rowley will come, I know it."

She no longer knew it, and after that she gave up saying so.

THE RATTLE OF KEYS coming down the steps from the guardroom brought the prisoners' bodies to attention and slaver to their mouths, but bewilderment to their minds. Had another twenty-four hours gone by? It wasn't time for their meal yet.

Though light came into the tunnel, their doors remained locked. Hauling herself up so that she could look through the bars, Adelia saw Father Gerhardt standing outside Mansur, Ulf, and Rankin's cell. There was a scroll in his hands, and his teeth were showing in the glare of torchlight held for him by one of the guards. "Can all of you hear me?"

Nobody answered; they could hear him.

He began reading. *"Hereby is notification from our good and saintly Bishop of Aveyron that the five Cathars in his custody have been found guilty of the most foul sin of heresy. Whereof it has been witnessed that they did congregate in a hut in the hills to perform wicked acts, the devil manifesting himself to them in the shape of a black dog, the Cathars prostrating themselves before it and performing lewd dances. . . ."*

There was uproar from the men's cell; Mansur was shouting in Arabic, Rankin in Gaelic. Above them both rose Ulf's voice: "Witnessed? Who witnessed that? Give us his name, you bastard."

". . . after which each applied his and her lips to the creature's rear end in a kiss and did begin copulating with one another . . ."

"Dog?" asked Boggart, trying to hear. "Only dog we got was Ward."

Adelia shook her head. Inevitably a dog. Or a goat. Sometimes a cat or toad. And always the *osculum infame*, the obscene kiss. It was the age-old accusation made against Jews, supposed witches, heretics; never varying except in small detail. God, how tired she was.

Ulf was continuing to demand the name of their accuser. "You bastard, we ain't even had a trial."

Stop it, she thought. *Darling boy, save your breath. We're not under Henry Plantagenet's justice now. No trial here, no defense, just sentence.*

Father Gerhardt went steadily on, his rising staccato drowning Ulf's shouts like a hammer. *"In accord with which acts, it has been agreed that such wickedness has proved these heretics barred from the mercy of Christ and that their bodies must suffer the penalty of burning that their souls might appear before God's great Judgment Seat in some part purified of their great sins. The sentence to be carried out at twelve noon tomorrow."*

The priest rolled up the scroll and signaled to the guards to light him back to the steps.

Ulf's voice became a scream. "In the name o' God, send to Carcassonne, ask the Bishop of Saint Albans. We ain't Cathars, he'll tell you."

"Your bishop is no longer at Carcassonne; he has gone down into Italy."

"Send to Figères, then."

The priest paused and turned. His smile, if it was a smile, widened. "We *have* sent," he said, "*and* received a reply. They don't know you."

Adelia let go of the bars and slid down to the floor. A small hand felt for hers in the darkness. There was a whisper. "Burn us? They going to *burn* us?"

She was dumb.

"Cut me," Boggart said urgently. "You got to cut me."

Adelia held her close. "Shhh."

"Get the baby out. Don't let 'em burn my baby. Cut my belly open, get the baby out. Pull it. You can do that."

"Sweetheart, I can't. *I can't*. Almighty God help us, I can't do anything."

"IT IS DONE, *Wolf, my love. The long plan, all our wiles and stratagems have borne their fruit. She'll die screaming. And, yes, we shall be there, you and I. We will creep away to watch her burn, sniff the smell of roasting pig, see her pork form a rich crackling before she crumbles to cinders.* Quae vide, *my Lupus. See what I have achieved in your name and be proud of me."*

BOGGART WAS QUIET NOW. They were all quiet. Adelia's cell was full of Allie and music. She watched her child dance, the little hands waving.

The notes became discordant, changing into the rattle of keys.

God, they're here. Allie. Not yet, not yet. Jesus, I'm so afraid.

They were opening the men's door. A kerfuffle—*bless them, they won't go without a fight. Me, too. I'll run on their spears. God be with me in this, the hour of my death.*

She was so deaf and blind with terror that she didn't hear her own cell door opening, nor see the light as it shone on where she crouched, clutching Boggart in her arms.

And then Mansur was in front of her, holding out his hand. *Yes, my dear, I'll go with you. Just stay close, promise to stay close.*

Ulf and Rankin, they were all there. And, behind them, somebody else, telling her something . . . about *shoes?*

"Take them off," he was saying. "Tuck them in your belt. Is the woman sensible? And the Boggart's. Quiet as mice, now."

She'd heard the voice before, seen the man; couldn't put a name to him. But now here was Ulf's face, alight and eager. "Come on, missus, ups-a-daisy." He leaned down and snatched off her shoe, the only one she had.

They were out in the tunnel, following a torch held by the strangely familiar man.

Up the stairs to the guardroom, where a figure in Aveyron uniform was lying on the floor—his throat cut.

The man put the torch he was holding into a wall sconce and left it there, so that its light shone wetly on the blood of the guard he'd killed.

Up again, into the palace hall. Darkish, lit by a single flambeau; bodies lying in the shadows of the niches. Dead, too?

No, asleep. Servants. She could hear snores. It was night, then. The floor seemed to spread for miles, like a lake, before it reached the outer doors leading to the square; impossible to cross without waking the sleepers.

She was gathering herself now, terror replaced by another comprising wild fear and hope as their bare feet hurried soundlessly over the tiles, following the man . . . *it was the Irishman*. The O'Donnell was helping them escape. Rowley had sent him to get them out of here.

But he *wasn't* getting them out. Instead of heading for the main doors, the man was taking them toward the entrance to the tower in which they'd first been imprisoned. Its door was open. He stood beside it, waving them to start the ascent ahead of him. *We've been up there*, she thought. *There's no way out that way. I don't trust him, I don't trust him.*

She could hardly stand and argue; one of the sleeping bodies against the nearer wall was muttering and stirring. Mansur, Ulf, and Rankin were already at the foot of the tower steps, looking back to make sure she and Boggart were following. Quickly pushing Boggart into the turret, Adelia went in after her, the Irishman at her back. As he closed the door behind them, its hinges squeaked—and her nerves with them, so that she stood still, frozen, waiting for discovery. Instead she got a shove and a hissed: "Mother of God, will you *move*?"

With the door shut, they were in blackness. Up, then, up the winding thread of steps, feeling their way, up past doors leading to store cupboards, some of them open, others shut, none of them apparently occupied. Adelia gave a fractious whisper over her shoulder: "Why are we going up, not *out*?"

"This *is* out. Get on."

It cost her, it cost all the prisoners, weak as they were, to keep climbing. Sobbing for breath, Boggart was beginning to lumber and Adelia had to reach up until, with her one good arm, she located the girl's backside and she could push.

An unencumbered moon shone into the top room; better still, night air came in through the windows smelling of fields and distance; their laboring lungs sucked it in.

Boggart sank down on the floor, exhausted, but the Irishman pulled her to her feet. "Not yet, missus. Now we go down."

The mullion of the window overlooking the rear roofs of the palace had ropes tied round it in complicated knotting; a grappling hook by which they'd been thrown up in order to catch round it was on the floor.

"Who goes first?" the O'Donnell said. "Easy as kiss-me-hand and the good Deniz down there ready to catch you."

He looked toward Adelia. She shook her head at him; if it *was* as easy as kiss-me-hand, then Boggart must have the first chance of escape. But the maid shrank back, frightened, and Adelia wasn't going without her. Probably, she thought, I'm not going at all, not with this bloody shoulder.

"I'll go," came Ulf's voice.

Was that Ulf, that stick of a boy with hollow eyes and cheeks? Was the bearded scarecrow Rankin?

The others watched as the Irishman put a loop round the boy's left foot and made sure his hands were firmly grasping another length of rope. "I'll ease you down, lad. Just keep hold." He leaned out of the window and, cupping his own hands, hooted like an owl.

There was an answering hoot from far below. "Off you go now, as my old granny said when she kicked the peddler over the cliff."

Leaning out, Adelia saw the moonlight touching Ulf's tow-colored hair and the white of his knuckles around the rope as he went down with the O'Donnell above paying it out, using the mullion as a fulcrum. The black depth below rushed up at her so that she flinched back before forcing herself to lean out again.

Ulf had stopped, he was stuck; he was struggling with a shadowy figure.

"They've got him."

"Who has?" The O'Donnell stuck his head through the window. "No, that's Deniz. Your boy's just made the first of the descents, that's all."

There were *two*? Yes, of course, this was the window at the back of the turret, but after the roofs below it lay another drop of at least fifty feet. Again, Adelia felt the helpless irritation of hunger and fear. This was overelaborate and dangerous; Boggart wouldn't be able to do it; she didn't think *she* could. "Why couldn't we go out through the doors?"

O'Donnell raised an eyebrow. "Well now, I don't think the guards outside would've liked it. They'll not be as sleepy as the lad downstairs."

Whom he'd killed.

Outside an owl hooted.

"He's down," the Irishman said, pulling the rope back up. "Next."

Rankin went, breathing hard. After an age, the owl hooted again.

Mansur was next; he didn't want to go before the women, but Boggart was panicking and Adelia wouldn't leave her. As the Arab clambered out into the moonlight, Adelia saw that his robe was filthy, he who'd always been immaculate.

We stink, she thought, all of us. Except him. From what could be seen in the moonlight, O'Donnell looked neat and contained; he was insouciant, as if unloading cargo from one of his boats, whistling quietly to himself when he took the strain, his muscles stretched against his shirt which, she knew, was splashed at the front with the blood of the guard downstairs.

Mansur's descent seemed to take longer than Rankin's, which had taken longer than Ulf's. Over the noise of her own breathing, Adelia listened desperately for an outbreak of shouts from outside or from the base of the turret when it was discovered that their cells were empty. . . . They *couldn't* be so lucky; this was a big palace, heavily populated. . . .

"Now, then, ladies."

"I can't," Boggart said. "The baby . . ."

"Just the thing for him," the Irishman told her firmly. "Dandling in the air? He'll love it. Come on now."

Between them, he and Adelia persuaded Boggart to put her foot in the loop. Getting her squeezed through the window's frame and its mullion was more difficult—Adelia gritted her teeth at the thought of what the constriction might be doing to the fetus in that extended belly—but at last the girl was out. Her agonized face went down into the darkness.

When the owl hoot came, O'Donnell hauled in the rope again. "Come on, missus."

Adelia gritted her teeth. "My collarbone is broken."

"Which side?" There was no sympathy.

"The right."

"Hold on with your left hand, then."

Her foot was put into a loop, an extra swath of rope wound around her body and tied with another complicated knot.

"Don't look down," the Irishman said. "Keep your eyes on me."

She didn't; she looked firmly at the stones that went sliding just beyond her nose.

Actually, with her good hand clinging onto the rope, her left foot braced against her own weight, and her right pushing herself away from the turret wall, the descent wasn't as horrendous as she'd thought.

When at last her feet touched tiles, she was enveloped in a strong smell of sweat as the waiting Turkish squire released her from the harness and put his little hands to his mouth to give a final hoot. Her rope went snaking upward.

She was on a flat roof of some building. At last she saw what they were about; on this side the turret towered over a building that formed part of the palace's rear wall and the wall gave onto wasteland that, in turn, gave way to a hill.

Above her, the O'Donnell slid down easily with the grappling hook under his arm. He gave it to Deniz and shook his head at the rope still dangling from the window. "It's a sad thing to leave all that fine hemp. Ah, well, maybe the good bishop'll hang himself with it."

Taking her left arm, he hurried her over the roof to where a rope ladder was tied to a stanchion. "Can you manage, missus?"

She didn't know if she could; there'd be fifty feet or more to go. Peeping over the edge, she could see only blackness.

As she hesitated, he got onto the rope ladder himself, curving his body outward so that it could form a cradle for her own. "Manage now?"

"Yes."

It was still difficult; the ladder swung outward and from side to side and she could only hold on with her left hand, but with the fear of falling negated by the Irishman's arms forming a protective circle, she managed it. Deniz slid down after them in one movement.

They were outside the palace—*out*. In the shadow of its retaining wall what seemed to be a large company was shifting about nervously: two horses, two hounds, the laden mule that had always carried O'Donnell's equipment, Mansur, Boggart, Rankin, Ulf—and the recumbent body of a man.

Instinctively, Adelia bent over it. O'Donnell nudged her with his boot. "Sentry. Leave him." He looked toward the others and spoke in Arabic. "Get 'em mounted, Deniz." Turning back, he handed Adelia the shoe she'd lost outside Ermengarde's cottage. "You'll be needing this."

From somewhere in the depths of the palace, an alarm bell began clanging. The empty cells had been discovered.

Already, the darkness of the fields ahead of them was beginning to lighten. Deniz and the O'Donnell were shoving Boggart onto one of the horses, Mansur was commanding her to move. "'Delia, *now*."

Unable to help herself, Adelia touched the recumbent sentry's neck. He was dead. As her hand withdrew, something squirmed toward her and licked it.

It was Ward.

She gathered him up, hugging his thin, dirty body to her own, before she was dragged away and, still clutching her dog, was thrown up on the horse carrying Boggart. Ulf scrambled up behind her. Rankin and Mansur were already on the other mount.

Then they were off, hounds, horses, mule, the O'Donnell and Deniz loping beside them with reins in their hands.

Not fast enough, she thought. The bare hill ahead was brightening by the second; they would be as obvious on it as a cluster of running deer, but not as speedy. She heard the Irishman puffing at Deniz: "They'll . . . look to the square first. Minute or two . . . before they think of the tower."

A minute or two. A minute or two to cover acres of open ground. Not enough. She could hear shouting coming from the palace, orders being given, the bell clanging and clanging.

They were reaching the top of the hill, disturbed larks rising up, fluttering and twittering as if to warn Aveyron that the heretics were loose. Were over it. Into trees. No slowing down. *Lord, dear Lord, forgive my sins. Don't let us burn, don't let us burn. Have mercy on us.*

They snaked through woods, they splashed along streams to throw off the scenting hounds yelping in the distance behind them; they jolted up gradients of scree that gave way with loud rattling beneath cantering hooves and the running men's feet. No stopping, no stopping. Except once when, under the shelter of a mountain's overhang, they watched a file of mounted men on the skyline encouraging their dogs to search, O'Donnell and Deniz with their hands clasped round the muzzles of their own two hounds to stop answering yelps.

Off again, under a bleak sun that stared accusingly down at them, into the shade. No stopping, no stopping, up and down a landscape that reared around them to make progress more difficult. On until, whether they died in flames or not, they must stop, but were forbidden by the Irishman's insistent: "Not yet. We're not away yet."

"We must," Adelia whispered. "The baby." God knew if that child could bear any more of this—certainly Boggart couldn't; the girl was only semiconscious.

"Not yet. We're not away yet."

Thirst. A scrabble in a mountain stream to scoop water into their mouths and let the horses and mule nuzzle it. Off again, bumping, holding on, O'Donnell and Deniz tirelessly dragging at horses that began to stumble.

Darkness, chill. The sound of dripping water. A cave. They were all inside. A stop—please God the last.

"This'll do," the O'Donnell said.

IT WAS A WONDERFUL CAVE, once the escapees were fit enough to appreciate it—a process that took time, rest, food, and plenty of water from the clear, cold lake that lay within it.

The floor was of blackish earth embedded with big, round pebbles, and, though the entrance to it was narrow, the walls rose to something near cathedral height so that voices were returned in an echo that recalled to Adelia the tunnel outside their cells.

"A land of caves, the Languedoc," the O'Donnell told them, "as riddled with holes as a weeviled cheese."

But how, she wondered, *had he known about this one?* There was little opportunity to ask him; as they recovered, Mansur, Rankin, and Ulf were full of questions. . . .

"Well now, that five Cathars were claiming to have acquaintance with Princess Joanna struck me as strange when Peter—you remember Peter who usually served us when we dined? When he told me about Aveyron's letter, I wanted to make sure it wasn't the five of you, unlike some who didn't care. I left word at Figères that I was going ahead to Saint Gilles to arrange shipping. Instead, Deniz and me went to the cowshed to find it burned down, and the Ermengarde's cottage with it. Well, a nod is as good as a wink to a blind man, my old granny used to say."

"But how did you find us?"

"It was the odiferous mongrel," the O'Donnell said. "What we did find, lying near the cottage, was one of her ladyship's shoes. A good deal of time we'd have wasted but for that. *Her* scent would have faded after all this time but that dog's could survive a sea gale, and his head was forever on her feet. I gave the shoe to my hounds to sniff, and right enough, didn't it lead us straight over the mountains? And there was our little stinker whining to get in through the Aveyron palace gates. Thank him nicely, now."

Adelia rubbed her cheek against the head of the dog in her arms. The mongrel had been much wasted by his vigil outside the palace, barely able to walk—he'd had to be put up on the mule amongst its packages during the escape. Though he was recovering now that he was being regularly fed, his mistress could hardly bear to let him go; as both of them were almost as filthy as each other, she could indulge in petting him as he deserved.

However, it was the Irishman the rest of them thanked with every grateful protestation they could think of. He and Deniz had scouted the palace, made their plan, used their rope craft—"Never venture forth without plenty of rope and a good mule to carry it"—to get in, and out.

"But how did you know *where* in the palace we were?" Ulf asked.

Affecting to preen, the man put his thumbs under his shirt collar. "We put up at an inn, Deniz and me, two innocent pilgrims on their way to the shrine at Rocamadour, and careless with their money. "*Isn't this the grandest town with the grandest palace you've ever seen, Deniz?*" "*Sure and it is, master—I wonder what it's like inside?*"

He put his hands down. "We didn't need even that stratagem. The town was still talking about Ermengarde, God rest her soul, and anticipating the burnings to come—without much enthusiasm, I may say. Not a popular man, Bishop of Aveyron. There was much discussion about whether you were in his cells—they're not popular, either, I can tell you—or in the tower. By the time it had finished, we knew every mouse hole in the place."

Who are you? Adelia wondered. The fleeting reference to Ermengarde and burning had been made easily and it was as if his account of their rescue might have been a mere exploit carried out on a whim. Yet to do what he had done argued a ferocity of purpose to free them, which their previous acquaintance hardly merited. He had saved their lives at considerable risk to his own.

She asked what was, to her, *the* question: "Was it the Bishop of Saint Albans who sent you after us? Where is he?"

"In Italy, lady." O'Donnell's long eyes slid toward her. "Went straight on to Lombardy, as ordered by King Henry. He'll be joining up with us in Palermo, when he's spared."

Ulf said: "So he doesn't even know . . . ?"

"About your abduction? No. Still thinking you're on your way to England. And nobody likely to tell him different"—the eyes slid again—"though I'm sure, if they had, the dear man would have been posthaste over here to box Aveyron's ears for him and get you out."

Ulf was asking why the Bishop of Winchester hadn't done it, why they'd been abandoned. . . . Something like that; Adelia had stopped listening.

She got up and wandered over to the lake at the rear of the cave, took off her shoes—one of them was worn through now; both of them disgusting—to walk into its shallow, icy water.

The king, first and foremost. Never her. *I could have died.* This hideous resentment might be unfair—Rowley hadn't even known of her danger—but she felt it, God, she felt it.

I could have died—and that I didn't, nor the others, has been due to a virtual stranger.

She stood still so long that the ripples she'd brought to the surface of the water became still and, dim though the light was, reflected her image in it.

A mess was what she saw; hair like a bramble bush—what had happened to the scarf Ermengarde had lent her?—and beneath it a face distorted with dirt and despair.

"Cheer up, now." The Irishman stood at the edge of the lake, watching her. "We'll have you to Palermo in a wink."

Not Palermo. I want to go home to Allie. Her eyes still on the water, she said: "I don't know why you did what you did, but I thank you. For all of us, from the depths of my heart, I thank you."

He turned away. "You'll be needing a new pair of shoes," he said.

WOLF IS BARKING *inside Scarry's head. "How did they escape? Where did she go?"*

"I don't know, I don't know. Stop it, my love, you're hurting me."

It's the worms; they twist and squirm through holes in his brain so that he can't think for pain.

"You promised."

"Cathars must have rescued her."

"Find her. Destroy her. I am you and you are me, forever. Homo homini lupus*."*

"I shall, I shall. Will you give me peace, when I do?"

"Oh, yes, then we shall both have peace."

But the worms keep up their squiggling, for all that Scarry can do in trying to take his head off and let them out.

DENIZ MADE HER SHOES. The burden his mule carried was a cornucopia from which the little Turk produced a huge needle, oiled thread, canvas, and a piece of leather.

While he was at work, the ex-prisoners did their best to become clean.

With the men standing dutifully outside the cave entrance, eyes averted, the two women stripped and used the lake as a washtub for themselves and their clothes. Adelia tried to persuade Boggart to immerse herself completely, as she was doing, but the girl stayed on the edge with Ward, laving herself and pleading her pregnancy. "Be a shock to the baby, missus."

Perhaps she was right; the water was *very* cold, but, to Adelia, its bite was almost baptismal, taking away stain not only from her body but, in part, from her soul.

Whatever it was, she emerged tingling with a new determination. *I'm alive and, God dammit, I'll stay alive. I'm going to get back to Allie.*

The mule's pack did not include soap, so laundering was less successful; even scrubbed and dried in the sun, the ex-prisoners' clothes were poor excuses for garments. The O'Donnell's sash, which he gave to Adelia to make a sling for her arm, looked positively resplendent against the rest of her once she was dressed.

He also produced an old cloak and hood so that Mansur's

ruin of a headdress—which the Arab insisted on still wearing—would be covered.

"So much the better for those who see us," he said, when they were all inspected. "Tagrag pilgrims trying to find their way to Compostela and not so much as a cross in their pockets to keep the devil from dancing, as my old granny used to say."

He wouldn't let them stay in the cave longer than two days. "For if I'm aware of this one, maybe so are our pursuers."

How *was* he aware of this one? Ulf, who'd spent a lot of time deep in conversation with O'Donnell and to whom Adelia posed the question, grinned and said: "He's in the smuggling business, missus, ain't you got that yet? There's more goes into these caves than escaped prisoners."

A man of diverse activities, then—fleet owner, transporter of crusaders, smuggler, killer, savior . . . He bewildered Adelia. Despite what she owed him, she still found herself uncomfortable in his company. The others didn't; to them he was an angel only lacking the wings.

Mansur, who knew her too well, said softly: "He had to quiet those guards, 'Delia. There was no other way than by a knife."

"I know," she said. "I just wish . . ."

She was leaving too many dead behind her.

Ulf inquired of the Irishman the details of what had taken place at Figères and, after listening, came storming over to where Adelia was resting.

"Did you hear that? Hear *that*? They denied us. Bloody Judas Iscariots, the lot of 'em. Sent a message to Aveyron saying we was none of theirs. *None of theirs.*" He was almost dancing with rage.

"*Now* will you believe me? There's someone doing dirty work somewhere."

"They should have made sure, I suppose, but it's understandable. They assumed Mansur and Boggart and I were on our way back to England. They couldn't have expected . . ."

"Understandable? They near as a button got us all burned—*and* it was deliberate."

"No," she said firmly, "whatever it was, it wasn't deliberate."

The boy's shoulders sagged. He gave a despairing glance in the direction of the others and left her alone.

On the second night they set off again, going by moonlight. Adelia would have preferred them to be able to rest up longer—for Boggart's sake, if not her own—but O'Donnell insisted that Aveyron's men might be searching every cave in the area.

"Our good bishop'll not be lightly robbed of his human torches. He's mounting a crusade all his own—setting an example to the Pope."

"Where are we going?"

"A long way. A village I know, not too far from the coast."

Though they weren't being dragged this time, and could take turns riding, the going was as heavy as it had been when tied to their captors' ropes. The moonlight deceived them into taking false steps and the mountains became steeper.

Until she got used to them, Adelia found Deniz's shoes difficult to walk in. Whilst the miracles of invention—a shaped sole of leather to which sailcloth was stitched and then tied up round the ankle so that her feet looked like two perambulating plum puddings—were serving her well, they were less than supple.

By day, they stayed under the cover of trees somewhere near a stream. Mansur, Ulf, and Rankin took turns keeping watch, while the Irishman, Deniz, and the hounds went hunting, and the women gathered wood and searched for late herbs with which to flavor a game stew. After this, they slept the sun down from the sky before starting afresh.

Eventually, the O'Donnell decided they were beyond Aveyron's reach and could start traveling by day. "Time I ventured into civilization and got us more horses."

"Civilization." Adelia savored the word. "I can get us some new clothes." And then remembered she had no money; her purse had been in Ermengarde's cottage, along with her medical pack.

"I'm going alone," he said. "Quicker. As for clothes, I'll see what I can do, though I doubt the country market I've in mind will provide much in the way of fashion."

"Thank you," she said tersely. She'd never been dependent on a man, even on Rowley, and she hated that she was dependent on this one who had done so much for her already.

He rode off the next morning, taking the other mount with him, and didn't come back until evening, riding a shaggy black pony with six others like it on a leading rein behind him. "Mérens stock," he said of them, "nothing stronger for mountain going." He'd also bought sacks of oats for horse feed, two shapeless, heavy woolen smocks for Adelia and Boggart—"all I could find"—and some equally thick cloaks, as shaggy as the ponies, for all of them. "We'll be needing these. It's going to be cold."

It was. During the day they were kept warm by their cloaks and the steam rising from their laboring ponies, but by evening it was near to freezing. At least they were at liberty now to build roaring fires at night, for there was nobody to see them.

Adelia had not believed that there could be such a vast stretch of uninhabited country. Occasionally, in the distance, they spotted a shepherd and heard the tiny wail of a flute as he piped to his flock, but that was all.

The landscape became dramatic, plunging into deserted, isolated valleys before rearing toward the sky in chaotic formations of crags that grew out of the close-fitting grass that covered them like the top of a man's bald head emerging from a fringe of hair. There were tarns, still little lakes trapped in a mountain scoop that reflected clouds and sky and circling eagles.

There was no stopping, except to let the ponies graze, and no roads, though it seemed as if they followed some track that now and then revealed itself in worn, close-set stones, and Adelia wondered if some ancient people had built themselves a way that led to the coast.

They became hardened, surprisingly fit, even Ward. Rankin especially was a man reborn, whistling and singing songs from the Highlands of which this country reminded him. "It suits me well," he'd say. "Ay, it suits me well. A drap of *usquebaugh* and I'd call the king my uncle."

"Some rotgut they drink in Scotland, so he says," Ulf explained to Adelia. "Made from peat water, Gawd help us."

Adelia's worry was for Boggart who, when it was time to rest the ponies by dismounting and leading them, had developed the slight waddle of a woman in late pregnancy.

The Irishman noticed it. "When's the baby due?" he asked when the two of them were walking together alongside Ulf.

"I don't know, she doesn't know, either. Could be this month, could be next." Adelia realized she'd lost track of time. "What's the date?"

He pushed back his cap and ran his fingers through his hair, calculating. "Must be Saint Cecilia's Day as near as dammit."

Nearly the end of November. And going south, farther and farther away from Allie. She panicked: "Why can't we use a decent, fast road? Why do we have to stick to these bloody mountains?"

He shrugged. "For one thing, your ladyship, there's only one road round here and that leads to Toulouse, which, I may tell you, we're bypassing because if Princess Joanna's procession has left Figères, which it will have by now, that's where it will be passing through and I've no wish to bump into it. For another, where we're going is *in* the mountains, and the track we're on is as quick a way to get to it as any."

"What does it *matter* if we bump into the others? Why can't we rejoin the procession?"

"Acause," Ulf intervened, patiently, "you got an enemy in the undergrowth and until he's flushed out we ain't taking no more risks, are we, Admiral?"

"He's right, lady," O'Donnell said. "There's been too many nasty coincidences, so Master Ulf's been telling me, and a good run is better than a bad stand, as my old granny used to say. In the name of God, what are you *doing*, woman . . . ?"

Adelia had fallen over again. "Lying down with my face in the grass," she hissed. "What are *you* doing?"

She saw a flash of his white teeth as he extended a hand to help her up, but suddenly she'd had enough. She was lost in this limbo on top of the world; they were all lost; they would wander it forever, die in it.

Hammering her fists on the ground, she gave way to a temper tantrum. "I don't know where we are. I don't know where we're going. I don't want to be here. I hate this bloody country, it's cruel and I *hate* it. I hate everything. I want my daughter, oh God, what am I *doing* in this place? *I want to go home.*"

It was Mansur who lifted her up and led her away. He sat her on a rock, knelt down, wiping her face with his sleeve, and chastising her. "You are rude to him. None of us want to be here, yet we are in the merciful hand of Allah who sent this man to us. Without him, we would have followed Ermengarde to the fire."

She leaned forward so that she could bury her face in the rough, strong-smelling wool of his cloak. "I want to go home, Mansur."

"I know." He let her cry herself out, patting and soothing her like she patted and soothed Ward when he was frightened.

At last she raised her head. Over the Arab's shoulder, she could see Rankin staring at the sky as if it was of absorbing interest. Deniz had taken feeding bags from the mule's pack so that the ponies could have some oats. The O'Donnell was watching him, chewing on a piece of grass.

Boggart and Ulf were staring after her in alarm, and she thought how good they were; apart from Ulf's lament for Excalibur, there'd been no whining from either of them. They made her ashamed.

Still sniveling, she said: "I'm sorry."

He patted her again. "If you break, we all break."

Wearily, she kissed him and stood up. "I'm not broken, just a bit creased."

She walked over to the O'Donnell. "I'm sorry," she said. "It won't happen again."

He took the piece of grass out of his mouth. "I'll get you home," he said quietly, "but first I fulfill my obligation to Henry and his daughter, for that's my duty."

"I understand."

"Now here's the plan. I lodge the five of you in this village I know whilst Deniz and I go on to Saint Gilles. My ships are there, but my captains'll not sail without I tell them to."

She nodded.

He went on: "If Joanna's arrived, I launch her and her party off to Palermo. If she's not there yet, I give my captains their sailing orders for when she *does* come. Either way, I'll be back for you. How'll that be?"

The sky was all at once brighter; somewhere a chaffinch was trilling as it did in England; the world had righted itself.

She smiled at him. "I am ashamed," she said.

"No need." Abruptly, he got up and went to help Deniz with the ponies.

"Ain't he a marvel, missus?" Boggart whispered.

"Yes," Adelia said, and meant it. Suddenly she grinned. "But if he mentions his old granny again I'm going to kill him."

Eleven

THE CASTLE OF CARONNE gave the impression that a dragon had landed on a jagged mountaintop, had fancied its effect against the limitless sky, furled its wings, and turned to stone. Then, as if the dragon could afford it protection, a village had snuggled itself into the forest just below, forming a horseshoe of houses edged with fields so steep that the sheep and goats grazing on them appeared lopsided. At the very bottom was a little church.

Away in the long way distance but still visible were the Pyrenees, the snow-topped range of mountains over which lay Spain.

"That's where we're going?" Adelia asked the O'Donnell. "That castle?"

"That's where we're going. You'll be safe there. Even Cathars are safe there."

She nodded. A stronghold. But it had become embedded in her that Cathars were safe nowhere, and this prominence was visible for miles. She saw the all-encompassing eye of the Cathar-hating Church swiveling toward it, marking it, watching its victims as they crawled up to it—and wrinkling in a foreboding wink.

Perhaps it was strongly defended.

It didn't help that they arrived at dawn, reminding the five ex-prisoners of their entry into Aveyron; the village's cocks crowing, shutters opening, people calling to one another to come out and see.

But this time the calls turned to welcome. "Don Patricio. Look, it's Don Patricio." Children, shouting the name, ran ahead as the Irishman, waving to his admirers, led his little cavalcade up the main street, and up again over chasm-crossing bridges, through mossy, crumbling archways until they reached half-open doors and the dim interior of the castle's hall.

"It's Don Patricio. Don Patricio."

In response to the children's noise, a woman whose bare breasts were concealed only by her long and beautiful dark hair came out of an upper room to lean over a balcony and smile at the Irishman. "Is it you, Patrick? Where's my silk?"

"Not this trip, my lady. Where's your husband?"

From the language both were using—an individualistic and just understandable version of Occitan—Adelia realized that they were amongst Catalans, who populated both sides of the Pyrenees as well as the mountains themselves. These were a people who regarded themselves as a separate nation from the French, Spanish, or Plantagenet kingdoms—disliking the French most of all.

"Dead last Michaelmas, alas," the woman said.

Widowhood didn't seem to be overburdening her with

grief—a young man was emerging from the room behind her, hastily buttoning himself into a priest's cassock.

O'Donnell called: "Come down, then, Fabrisse. I have some refugees for you."

While she went back to fetch some covering, the priest sidled quickly down the stairs, his hand flicking embarrassed blessings toward the newcomers before he disappeared through the entrance.

The woman came down in a more leisurely fashion, making the most of it, her superb legs showing through the gap of the cloak she'd wrapped herself in.

"Ladies and gentlemen, I present to you the Countess of Caronne," said O'Donnell.

"The *Dowager* Countess," she corrected. "And any friends of Don Patricio's are welcome here. You'll forgive the count himself not making an appearance. At the moment he's asleep in his cradle."

She had a lovely, dangerous face; high cheekbones; dark, slanted, amused eyes that studied each of her ragged guests while the introductions were made, raising her eyebrows at the unprepossessing dog they had brought with them, taking in Boggart's pregnancy with approval, dwelling particularly on Adelia.

"You have luggage?" she asked and was told they had not. "Then we must see what we can do in the way of clothes—they will have to be of hemp, unfortunately, this man"—she bared little white teeth at the Irishman in a snarl—"having neglected to bring what I ordered. But breakfast first." She let out a screech. "*Thomassia.*"

There was an answering screech from somewhere to the left. "*What?*"

"Breakfast for seven, two of them to be taken up to the solar . . ." Her eyelashes fluttered at the O'Donnell. ". . . where you can tell me all about it."

They're lovers, Adelia thought, and felt a curious sense of relief, though she wasn't sure why. Adding the title of "philanderer" to the man's many facets placed him for her; putting him in a category that was recognizable, an adventurer with, quite probably, a woman in every port—this sort of woman; lovely, careless with her favors.

I can be easy with him now.

Breakfast was generous: goat's cheese, goat's milk, ham, sausage, smoked trout, fresh bread fetched from the village with a strong olive oil to dip it into, herb-flavored wine, some preserved figs that had been picked from a tree that rambled around and into the kitchen's window slit, all of it served by Thomassia, a stubby young woman, whose nonstop instructions in a Catalan patois made her sound bad-tempered but which, from the way in which she kept nudging her guests' arms toward their wooden plates, seemed to be urges to keep them eating. Ward, a type of dog she'd not seen before—who had?—made her laugh and was thrown scraps until he could eat no more.

Thomassia was especially solicitous toward Mansur, frequently extending her hand to him. "*S endeví—ina, s endeví—ina, el contacontes*."

"What does the bint want of me?"

"I think," Adelia said. "I *think* she's asking you to tell her fortune."

Mansur was offended. "I am no cup reader."

"*I'll* tell the lassie her fortune." Rankin leaned over the table to grab Thomassia's hand. Even while cramming food into his mouth, he hadn't taken his eyes off her. "Tell her she's a wee angel, so she is, and all this feast lacks is parritch. Tell her she's destined for a fine husband."

Adelia did her best. "What's parritch?" she muttered at Ulf.

"A mess of cracked oats. He made me eat some once. Never again."

Finally replete, they were returned to the hall and saw what, because they'd been so grateful for its immediate protection, they'd missed at first—a poverty that had not been reflected in their meal. The furniture was sparse and worn, some of it battered. The stones of the floor showed grass growing through cracks. Other cracks in the walls had either been roughly repaired or not repaired at all, letting in long bars of sunlight.

It occurred to them that the stables they'd passed on their way in had been empty, nor had there been any sign of servants other than Thomassia.

Hardly what was to be expected of a comital palace.

Adelia remembered Henry Plantagenet's contempt for countries which, as this one did here, maintained a system of partible inheritance, by which land and property were divided equally between heirs.

In England, under Henry II, Norman law insisted instead on primogeniture, whereby the eldest legitimate son inherited everything. "Primogeniture forces younger brothers to go out and work for their bloody living," the king had told her. "It leaves estates intact, keeps a proper aristocratic structure, it means a lord *is* a lord." He'd added what was of more importance to him: "And he's easier to tax."

Dividing property, subdividing it for the next generation, then for the next *ad infinitum,* meant, he'd said, "that some poor sod ends up with a title, a few fields, and not so much as a clout to wipe his arse on."

Presumably, the baby Count of Caronne asleep in his cradle upstairs was such a one.

So we're vulnerable, Adelia thought, because these mountain people in their poverty are vulnerable.

There could be no protection for the Cathars here, not even the Catholics who tolerated them; no true asylum here from the rich, omnipotent enemy that surrounded them. They might think themselves secure, but Adelia knew they were not.

IN THE ROOM UPSTAIRS, where the arms of Caronne were carved into one of its thick stone walls, the Countess of Caronne sat on her rumpled bed, listening, her eyes watching the O'Donnell where he stood at the window looking out over its colossal view as he told his tale.

When he'd finished, she said: "That was a risk you took rescuing her, Patrick."

He didn't turn round. "That was a risk I took rescuing them *all*."

"Her."

He gave a grunt that was half a laugh. "So obvious?"

"To me, yes."

He slammed his fist on a sill two feet thick. "Why? Will you tell me that? Why? Of all the women . . . she's nothing to look at, stubborn as a Munster heifer, and all she can see is her *fokking* bishop."

The countess shrugged her white shoulders. "It happens. Not to me, Blessed Mother be thanked, but it happens."

"I never thought it." He went and sat beside her on the bed. "Look after her for me, Fabrisse. Deniz and I will have to leave tomorrow."

"I will."

He gave her a kiss. "She's a useful doctor, should you be ill. There's thirty of Joanna's household wouldn't be alive today if she hadn't dragged them back from their coffins. And a smile on her to light up the sun."

"I said I will look after her."

"I am sorry about your husband."

She shrugged, sliding a patched work shift over her magnificent body. "He was old."

"Will you marry again?"

"I may have to; it depends who offers."

"Meanwhile . . ."

"Meanwhile."

They smiled at each other. As she leaned down to search for her clogs, he tweaked her backside for old times' sake. "You're still the most beautiful woman I ever saw," he said

"I know." She gave him a push to the door. "Silk," she reminded him. "The price has just gone up; it must be *orfrois*, with spun silver in the weft. And a jointed knight puppet for Raymond when he's older, and a cloak for Thomassia, English wool is preferable, and a new skillet, and we have run out of cumin . . ."

Still enumerating, she accompanied him down the stairs, his arm round her shoulders.

BY THE TIME Adelia had finished milking her third goat of the morning, Thomassia and the Dowager Countess had done ten each.

A cold wind was blowing through the goat pens—a wind of some sort was always blowing up here—but, wrapped in her cloak, she had been warmed by the activity. She sat back on her haunches, her shoulder aching only slightly—it was getting better. So, she thought, was her prowess at milking. The other two women had been surprised when she'd approached the first set of goat teats with a scientific interest that had turned out in practice to be totally inept.

"You've never milked *anything?*"

"It wasn't on my school's curriculum."

That she had attended a school, let alone a medical school, also amazed them; the countess could sign her name; Thomassia wasn't able even to do that.

Adelia would have kept her education from them, but it appeared that the talkative Irishman had made it known. She became worried that they might broadcast it. "I've had to learn that, outside Sicily, the terms *female doctor* and *witch* are synonymous."

"No, no," Fabrisse said easily. "Nobody will betray you. We have no truck with authority here."

Caronne, it appeared, was a stopping place on a secret route to the Catalans in the Pyrenees, receiving and passing on visitors whom the Church would not only have abhorred, but imprisoned—or worse. Adelia and her friends were merely part of a succession of smugglers, Cathar perfects, wandering Moslem soothsayers, and other oddities to whom Caronne had provided refuge; its own position being too anomalous for betrayal. When the Bishop of Carcassonne's tax gatherer rode up the mountain on his tithe-collecting visit—he was expected any day, so a lookout had been posted—there would be a rush of villagers herding as many of their taxable sheep and as much of their grain into the deep recesses of the forest as possible, hoping that their absence wouldn't arouse his suspicion that too few herds and sacks remained.

This, despite the fact that not handing over the bishop's portion would, according to the Church, send their souls to hell.

Neither did Fabrisse, a Catholic devoted to the Virgin Mary, see any reason to believe in the rightness of the men who ruled her faith and distorted its precepts. Many of her friends in the village were Cathars and, though she deplored the fact that her own Church was everywhere in the region losing ground to Catharism, she would no more have betrayed them than she would have thrown her beloved baby son over her castle ramparts. All were locked together into a united front of shared poverty.

"The count used to say he owed nothing to a tax inspector who rode up here on a fine horse with a retinue of inspectors more richly dressed than he was. Jesus told us to render unto Caesar that which is Caesar's, but he did not anticipate that His own Church would itself become Caesar."

It was a view that suffused the entire village. When Adelia

and Fabrisse were passing through its square one evening on their way to take a fennel chest rub to the countess's elderly Cathar friend, Na Roqua, Adelia heard the gathering of men sitting under the shade of an elm tree discussing the *carnelages* tax which would soon be due.

"Why *should* we have to pay over so many of our lambs to the bishop?" one of them asked; obviously an annual and rhetorical question.

"Don't let's pay anything," another voice said. "Let's kill the bishop instead."

Listening to the rueful laughter, Fabrisse said to Adelia: "You hear? You are safe here. You must not fear."

She's so easy, God protect her. But I saw Ermengarde burn; she didn't. She's right, though, I must stop being frightened, I'm tired of being frightened.

Even so, she couldn't help asking whether the village priest would keep silent. "Won't he tell his bishop about us, about you, the Cathars?"

"*Him?*" The Dowager Countess's perfect eyebrows rose in a comic arch. The priest's carnal sins ensured both his silence and collaboration, his services to Caronne's lonely women not being restricted to the masses he performed in church.

Adelia was becoming very fond of the Dowager Countess; indeed, had never met anyone quite like her. There was a high honesty to her that prevented Adelia categorizing her as a loose woman; it was all one with the woman's disregard for the rules men made.

She made no bones about the fact that, husbandless just now, she had physical needs; why not cater to them? She took the young priest from the little church to her bed rather as other people took a hot brick on which to warm their feet. (Adelia wondered if, when Fabrisse went to confession, he absolved her of a sin they had committed together.)

"Besides," Fabrisse went on, "you are the Irishman's friends, and therefore honored guests. Your safety is of utmost importance to us."

"You all trust him that much?" Adelia couldn't help asking.

"Of course. Don't *you*?"

"Yes, yes, I do. It's just that . . . he risked his life for us, and I still don't see why he should have."

Fabrisse's eyes rested on her face for a moment. "Don't you?" she said again. "Then, in that, I cannot help you."

IN CARONNE, EVERYBODY, noble or peasant, worked with his hands. Fabrisse might be the countess, but she didn't find it demeaning to fetch water from her well in jars balanced on her head as the other women did, nor chop her own firewood, nor do her own laundry in the stream below the castle. She and Thomassia were mistress and servant but both joined in the gathering on Na Roqua's roof balcony of an evening with several of the other village women to spin or comb one another's hair with a nit comb—a sign of friendship—whilst they gossiped.

Adelia gathered that the women had a rougher time of it than their menfolk, working just as hard for less reward, any objection being overridden or even met with the occasional blow. They didn't complain of it, being used to it, but it was apparent that they flowered once they were widowed—and mostly Caronne women lived longer than the men.

Na Roqua, Fabrisse's friend, for instance, and her neighbor, Na Lizier, had set up their own businesses since their husbands died and now ruled their sons and grandchildren like the matriarchs they had both become.

BY DAY, BOGGART and Adelia helped Fabrisse and Thomassia with their chores and began the endless preparations for Christmas, which, whether their views coincided on the birth of Jesus or not, Cathars and Catholics celebrated at a feast for the whole village in the castle hall.

Mansur, Ulf, and Rankin spent their time assisting the village shepherds with their flocks—a purely male occupation—or used their skills to try to mend some of the castle's dilapidation.

Taking part in these things restored to the ex-prisoners a good deal of what the Bishop of Aveyron had taken away. Rankin, especially, was most at home. "Like the Highlands wi'out the bloody rain" was how he described it, though it was beginning to be apparent that, for him, part of Caronne's attraction lay in his growing friendship with Thomassia.

We're being absorbed, Adelia thought. *This marvelous, peculiar place is taking us into its heart.* She was taking it into hers, but there was no sign of the O'Donnell coming to take the five of them away, and at any time the snow might come, to cut them off from the outside world.

At night, thinking of Allie, she wondered how long this idyll would last, or how long she wanted it to.

ON CHRISTMAS EVE MORNING, the women were preparing for the next day's feast in a kitchen festooned with the hanging corpses of hens, ducks, and geese waiting to be put on their spits, when Mansur appeared in the doorway. "There is trouble in the village."

Adelia dropped the hand mill with which she'd been grinding chestnuts for the *torte aux marrons*, Caronne's version of Christmas pudding.

Her eyes met Boggart's in the same terror. *They've come for us.* Then, with Thomassia, Fabrisse, her baby son tied to her back, and Ward at their heels, they pelted outside and heard the screaming coming from down the mountain.

Not again, God, please not again.

It sounded like slaughter. It wasn't; when they got there, it was Na Roqua standing on the flat roof of her house, yelling at Na Lizier, who was standing on hers and shrieking back insults across the narrow alley that divided their two houses.

Just two women quarreling. Thank you, Lord, thank you.

A crowd had collected to watch so that Fabrisse had to elbow her way through it. "Sancta Maria, what is happening here?"

"Stand back," Na Roqua screeched at her. "Don't go into that alley. Just see what lies within it."

The thin morning sun hadn't yet reached the passageway and Fabrisse had to peer to see what her old friend was pointing at. Adelia peered with her and managed to make out the body of a large male goat lying on the baked earth with its head twisted at an unnatural angle.

"She has killed him," howled Na Roqua. "The jealous bitch enticed him onto her roof and threw him off."

"I wouldn't entice him into hell," Na Lizier screamed back. "*Which* is where he belongs. I never touched the brute."

"Oh yes you did. Look, look, there are no hoofprints in the alley. Did he fall into it from the sky, then? You pushed him."

"No, I didn't."

"Blessed Mother," Fabrisse whispered. "It's Auguste."

Adelia had already encountered Auguste—there was a goat-toothed tear in the sleeve of her new hemp gown to prove it. The ram was Na Roqua's pride and joy, but a pest to everybody else, roaming at will, eating whatever it could reach, and trying to copulate with anything that had a corresponding hole. (It was no coincidence that Auguste was the Christian name of the Bishop of Carcassonne.) That he hadn't come to a sticky end before this was because the village was even more frightened of Na Roqua than it was of the goat.

It did *look* like murder. Na Roqua was right, there appeared to be no hoofprints in the alley; Auguste certainly hadn't wandered into it. Adelia tried to keep her face straight. "Such a relief," she whispered back. "I thought it was something dreadful."

There was no amusement on the countess's face; it was pale. "This *is* dreadful. Not only will it ruin Christmas, it will start a feud that could last for years."

"A *goat*?"

"These are my people, 'Delia. I know them and I tell you that a rift between the Roquas and the Liziers . . ."

It had already begun. Amongst the onlookers, a Lizier grandson had made an unfavorable comment on Na Roqua and was being berated for it by one of her sons.

"You must do something," Fabrisse said.

"Me?"

"Yes, yes. You are the famous doctor. Ulf says you solve mysteries, solve this one."

With narrowed eyes, Adelia glared toward the edge of the crowd where Ulf stood with Mansur, Rankin, and Ward, all of them watching the growing row with interest.

"*And solve it so that nobody is to blame,*" Fabrisse hissed. She stepped forward and raised her voice to a pitch that cut through an increasing pandemonium. "Listen to me. *Listen* to me."

There was immediate quiet; the Dowager Countess might dress in tatters but she was Caronne's authority.

Holding Adelia's sleeve and displaying her like a landed fish, she shouted: "Here is someone who can solve this puzzle. This lady is a mistress of the art of death. Don Patricio told me. He said that the dead speak to her."

More silence. At last, one of the Roqua sons said: "You mean, Auguste will tell her what happened?"

"Yes," said Fabrisse.

"For God's sake . . ." Adelia muttered.

"I don't care," Fabrisse muttered back.

"But I don't *know* about goats."

"I don't care. It is why the Virgin sent you to us."

That was why, was it? It was ridiculous; Na Roqua and her family were Cathars; Na Lizier and hers, Catholic. Two faiths could live side by side without quarreling, while the death of a damned goat could start a vendetta. Yet Fabrisse, who knew these people better than she did, was truly concerned that it would.

Oh, Lord, what to do? I suppose I owe it to this woman, to this village, to keep the peace. Somehow.

But a *goat?*

However, Adelia was Adelia; if there was a truth to find, she had to find it, no matter what came later. Death was her business. For the first time in a long time, she must practice her profession.

Breaking away from Fabrisse's retaining arm, she strode toward Na Roqua's house and opened its low door, to be afflicted by a strong stink of goat—when Auguste had not been pursuing his wanderings, he'd shared accommodation with his mistress.

The windows were shuttered against the cold, as they were in all Caronne's houses, so that, when they were at home, its people lived in a semi-darkness lit only by a fire.

Adelia examined the lintel of the front door, then opened the shutters in order to look at the floor of the room into which it led. She climbed the stairs, studying each step as she went. Into the upper room, then up again to the roof, where the gaze of Na Roqua and the crowd below fell upon her with embarrassing expectation.

She returned downstairs, this time into what was usually the kitchen but here had been transformed into a place from which Na Roqua, having no use for a kitchen thanks to being supplied with food by her daughters-in-law, ran her wool-carding trade.

One side of the room was packed with sheep's wool and smelled strongly of its lanolin, although, sniffing hard, Adelia caught another whiff of goat. A set of shelves held a carding wheel and combs, a few of which had fallen on the floor.

She spent so long considering the place that, when she finally emerged outside, the crowd was getting restless. "Auguste can't tell her much in there," somebody pointed out, to a growl of agreement.

"For sweet Mary, it's the *animal* you're supposed to be examining," Fabrisse told her quietly, and then, shouting to the crowd: "Be quiet. She is listening to Auguste, she follows his last steps."

Adelia ignored them all. She crossed the entrance to the alley to go next door into Na Lizier's house.

Impossible to tell anything from the front doorstep, too many feet had passed over it. The stairs, though—only Na Lizier had climbed them today to judge from the thick shape of her boots in their dust. No, oh dear, here were the smaller prints of a hoofed animal.

Na Lizier had lied.

But, ah, *this* was interesting; the hoofprints showed signs of dragging the higher up the stairs they went, occasionally overlaid by the tread of shoes. By the time they reached the roof, they had been obliterated as if badly swept by a duster. Had Na Lizier poisoned or tried to strangle poor Auguste and the goat had hauled himself up to the roof to get away from her? Or to sniff fresh air?

Hmm.

Emerging into daylight once more, Adelia gave a clear order: "Take the body to the castle. There I will listen to what Auguste has to say."

She felt a fool and a fraud, but for her own satisfaction she was going to perform an autopsy on the damned goat—*though God knows how I'll find anything.* And she'd need privacy for it; Na Roqua was unlikely to regard the butchery of her pet as "listening." Also, the castle hall possessed a large stone table.

It might have been the funeral of a hero. Under the stern eye of Na Roqua, Auguste was laid reverently on a blanket and four Roqua men, taking a corner each, carried him shoulder-high up the tiers of the village street, the Lizier family reluctantly following behind.

In the hall, Adelia turned to Ulf, Rankin, and Mansur. "Light some candles and get these people out of here. You stay, I may need you."

Na Roqua wanted to stay, too, but was persuaded by Fabrisse that the mystery to be performed could only be attended by those who were in tune with the soul of the corpse.

"But I have always been in tune with Auguste," Na Roqua complained.

"Has he spoken to you since he died? No. He will only talk to a mistress of the art of death. In private."

"*You're* staying," Na Roqua pointed out.

"It's my damned castle. Now go."

Thomassia was sent out with the old woman to console her during the wait.

Once candles had been lit and the doors shut, Rankin and Ulf heaved the body onto the table while Boggart was sent to the kitchen to find the sharpest knife it had.

Tentatively, Adelia felt Auguste's neck and then the rest of him. Rigor mortis hadn't set in yet, which meant, always supposing rigor obeyed the same law in goats as in humans, the beast hadn't been dead long.

Anyway, since according to Na Roqua he'd been alive when she went to bed, whatever had happened to him had taken place at some time during the night.

It would be interesting to see whether the fall had killed him or he'd been dead before he hit the alley. She was beginning to suspect the latter.

The three men were entertaining themselves with making up reasons for the goat's demise that would satisfy Na Roqua and not implicate Na Lizier.

"A massive eagle picked him up and let him fall into the alley."

"A self-respecting eagle wouldn't touch him. No, he farted himself up into the air and dropped in."

Adelia ignored them. She took the knife from Boggart, wondering where to start.

Ulf grinned. "Goats, eh? How the mighty are fallen."

"Shut up," she told him. "Your chatter got me into this. Now, then, you men each take a leg . . . that's right, and turn him onto his back."

With Rankin holding up the goat's extensive and flea-ridden beard, she began the incision at a point just below the chin.

She hadn't even got as far as the wattle when she found out how Auguste had died. Something had blocked his throat.

Drawing the object out, she put it on the table near a candle.

"What in hell is that?"

"I don't know, it looks like sheep's wool." She used the knife to stir the mass apart. There was chewed wood in it, and some nail-like pins.

"Na Lizier *did* kill him, then," Mansur said. "She choked the brute."

"*Hmm.*" Adelia put the knife down and began pacing, fitting together what she had learned from inspecting the two houses with this latest discovery.

"Well?" Fabrisse demanded at last. "What do we tell those two old women that won't start a war?"

Adelia made up her mind. "The truth. They are both to blame."

Once the incision had been neatly sewn up and the beard combed down over it, Na Roqua, Na Lizier, and the rest of the village were allowed into the hall.

"Auguste tells me that what happened was this," Adelia said clearly. "You, Na Roqua, left the door to your carding room open last night. . . ."

"No, I didn't," Na Roqua shouted. "I never do."

"You did last night, so Auguste says."

The old woman sulked. "Well, I may have done."

"And Auguste found his way in and began eating your sheep's wool. . . ."

"That wouldn't kill him," a Roqua son pointed out. "Auguste could eat anything."

"He also ate at least one of the carding combs," Adelia continued firmly. "Its pointed pins stuck the ball of wool into his throat so that he couldn't swallow it. In his distress he found his way out into the night air and then he stumbled into Na Lizier's house—your door wasn't on the latch, was it?"

Na Lizier shrugged. Nobody in Caronne bothered to secure their doors—who was there to secure them against?

"Again, gasping for air, he made his way up the stairs to the roof. The exertion drove the comb's pins more firmly into his poor throat, blocking it up with the wool, so that, by the time he gained the roof, he was dying. Auguste tells me that Na Lizier found him there dead when she got up this morning and, frightened that

Na Roqua would suspect her of murdering him—*as you did*, Na Roqua—pitched his body into the alley. He doesn't blame you for that, Na Lizier, any more than he blames you, Na Roqua, for carelessly leaving the carding room door open. He wishes you both to be the friends you always were."

Some of it was speculation, but some of it deduction; it was the best she could do.

There was silence in the hall, except for an onset of grizzling from the Count of Caronne, still tied to his mother's back and wanting his next feed.

The suspense was awful.

Na Roqua's walking stick rapped on the stone floor as she made her way over to where Na Lizier stood. "I am sorry," she said.

"And I am sorry."

The two old women embraced.

Under the wave of cheering, Fabrisse put her arm around Adelia. "Our savior," she said.

Auguste was picked up once more by the Roqua sons and taken away for honorable burial.

Following them out, Na Roqua paused to stare into Adelia's face. "Did Auguste happen to tell you whose body his soul will inhabit now?"

"Er, no. I'm afraid he didn't."

Na Roqua sighed. "You should have asked him."

Solving the riddle of Auguste's death had been an incident of little moment compared to other investigations Adelia had successfully pursued, but for the health of Caronne it had been important, and at the Christmas Eve feast that night, she was the heroine.

Grateful Roqua and Lizier men presented her and the other ex-prisoners with beautifully wrought sheepskin coats; she had to raise her beaker and drink in reply to the dozens of toasts that were made to her; a wreath of bay leaves was put on her head; and, finally, after three hours of eating, and leaning somewhat heavily on Mansur's arm—the Arab, banned by his religion from alcohol, being the only sober person around—was put on a chair on a platform in the bailey to watch the village dance around the enormous bonfire that Ulf and Rankin had built for the purpose.

It wasn't possible for the visitors to join in; the tapping, leaping steps of the dancers—men revolving around the fire, women and children forming little prancing rings of their own on the edges—were too complicated for the uninitiated to join in.

Music was being provided by panpipes, but all of a sudden there was a blast of sound as Prades, the local blacksmith, blew down a pipe he was holding into a fearsome-looking contraption that looked like nothing so much as an enormous pig's bladder with some of its tubes still attached. The resultant wail was so loud that it could have been heard ten miles away. Adelia found herself flinching. *They'll hear. They'll come.* She pulled herself together. *This sound belongs to these mountains; why should anyone come?*

"Oh, bloody hell," Ulf said. "It's the bagpipes."

Rankin, who'd been lolling on the platform, drunkenly nuzzling Thomassia's cheek, was all at once on his feet. "D'ye ken that? By all that's holy, it's the peeps. The *peeps*. I've come home."

He aimed himself toward Prades like a thirsty man toward a fountain, clutching at the man's arm, begging.

"He's not, is he?" Ulf moaned. "Yes, he bloody is. He's going to get himself some peeps. We're doomed."

And for the first time in a long time, Adelia laughed.

THE SNOW THAT Adelia dreaded might stop the O'Donnell coming for them did not arrive, but neither did the O'Donnell. Instead a Cathar perfect arrived to spread his faith in the village.

"Oh, God," Adelia said, when she heard. "He'll put you in danger." The "you" was becoming as important to her as the "us."

"Will you stop it?" Fabrisse said wearily. "We have posted lookouts for strangers. Brother Pierre is known to us, a good man. He is at Na Roqua's if you want to go and hear him."

Adelia consulted the others.

"We should go," Mansur said. "He may have news of Sister Aelith." The thought of the hunted, motherless girl disturbed them all.

They didn't see the perfect, not that day; they were precluded by the number of bodies crammed into Na Roqua's house, and by those sitting outside it, listening to Brother Pierre's voice issuing through the windows. He was reading from the Cathar bible in the Catalan patois the villagers could understand, speaking Christ's words in their own language rather than in the Latin spouted by the priests.

Adelia knew by now that, if Caronne's villagers were illiterate, they were at least masters of debate, especially on theological matters, and that questions and answers would extend deep into the night.

Leaving the others to listen, she walked back to the castle, followed by Ward, and braved the cold wind for a while on its bridge to look toward the ice-capped peaks of the Pyrenees.

They were a climate gauge; they played Grandmother's Footsteps; sometimes, as now, their clarity augured a fine day; when they jumped forward, so near that they seemed only a mile or so away, they foretold bad weather. She had come to love them, imagining them as a refuge where misfits like herself could live free on those tree-crammed, bear-haunted, wildlife-infested slopes. *I could settle there*, she thought. *Allie and Gyltha and Mansur and Boggart and Ulf and I, we could be safe. Henry Plantagenet couldn't find me and send me on any more missions ever again.*

A voice in her head asked: *And Rowley?*

Suddenly she wanted him very, very badly. *He can come, too*.

There was a nudge on her ankles; Ward was getting cold. She patted his head, and they went together into the castle.

"Were *you* never tempted to become a Cathar?" Adelia asked of Fabrisse, who was putting the Count of Caronne into his cradle.

"No." Fabrisse bent down to kiss the count's cheek. "When this one was born, he was ill, so ill. We didn't think we would save him. That *parfait* back there, he came to me and said I shouldn't feed my child, to allow him to suffer the Cathar *endura* and let him die. He would administer the *consolamentum*, he said, so as to ensure that little Raymond would be an angel of God in Heaven. But I would not do it. How could I withhold my milk from my own flesh and blood? We fought for him, Thomassia and I, and he lived."

It was in accord with what Sister Ermengarde had said. Adelia shook her head in amazement at the way every established religion she knew of, even this one, tried to pervert simple, human love out of its natural course.

HALFWAY THROUGH THE next morning, little Bérenger Pons, who'd been sitting, shivering, in the church's high window, watching the track that led eventually to Carcassonne, snatched up the handbell that lay beside him and began clanging it even as he scrambled down his ladder. Still ringing, he ran up the village street, shouting at the top of his squeaky voice: "The *bayle*. The *bayle* is coming."

Immediately, women emerged from their houses and hurried to the communal barn that stored the grain sacks. Men dropped what they were doing in the fields and ran to the sheep pens. Na Roqua came out of her doorway, pulling with her the Cathar perfect who'd spent the night in her downstairs room. As if he were a horse, she gave him a slap on his rump to set him galloping toward the castle.

In the castle itself, Fabrisse pushed the priest out of her bed and rushed out to look down on young Bérenger as he arrived in the hall still gasping his message. "How long before he gets here?"

"Thirty paternosters, maybe thirty-two." Having no clocks, Caronne people didn't reckon time in minutes.

"Good boy. *Thomassia*." She rushed to raise the rest of her household. "Quick, quick. The bishop's tax inspector is coming. Follow Thomassia."

Scrambling into their clothes as they went, Adelia, Boggart, Mansur, Rankin, and Ulf made their way down to the hall, Fabrisse's priest with them.

Thomassia was already there, heading out of the entrance, waving her arms to spur the fugitives into a run. There was a momentary constriction at the end of the bridge as they were joined by the Cathar perfect while the Christian priest, still buttoning himself up, pushed past him to gallop down the hill toward his church. Then they were on a path that wound round the back of the castle and headed down toward the forest. On other tracks, they could see shepherds urging their flocks in the same direction, their huge white-coated Pyrenean dogs snapping at the animals' heels to make them go faster.

Adelia picked Ward up—the shepherd dogs terrified him—and kept running. Ulf, Rankin, and Mansur brought up the rear, helping a lumbering Boggart to keep going.

The forest enfolded them, but Thomassia, holding her chest with the effort, kept on, eventually veering away from the track to wade through dead bracken until she came to a full stop facing an outcrop of rock draped with overhanging ivy. She pulled the thick fronds aside to reveal a cave and ushered them in. "Stay."

Backing out, she arranged the ivy so that it recovered the entrance.

In the dimness, the deep voice of the Cathar perfect said: "She will return to the castle, brushing out our tracks as she goes. A good woman, Thomassia."

Of them all, he was the least out of breath; he'd run with an easy lope, thin brown legs showing beneath the robe he'd tucked up into his belt. Stooping to try and get rid of the stitch in her side, Adelia gasped: "I suppose you're used to this."

"It has not been unknown." He sounded amused. He gave a bow.

Adelia introduced herself and the others.

"What's them people who live in caves. Troglodytes. That's what we're becoming," Ulf grumbled. "Bloody troglodytes. Well, I suppose it gives us a day off work."

It was a point and, like the peasants they were turning into, he and Rankin, Mansur, and Boggart used the time to doze.

Adelia, the only one with reasonable Catalan at her command, felt that she should be entertaining the perfect with conversation, but kept quiet, hoping the man wouldn't raise a matter she dreaded.

He did. "You were at Aveyron with Ermengarde when she died," he said.

"Yes."

He surprised her. "I saw you. I was there also, a witness, hidden in the crowd. I sent up prayers for her soul, not that she needed them, the good, good woman. And I prayed for you and yours. I rejoice in your escape."

Adelia said shortly: "You were brave to be there." She changed the subject. "Have you any news of Sister Aelith?"

"We have sent her into the Pyrenees until she has recovered her courage to come back and resume her mission."

"I hope she doesn't."

"She will. She is her mother's daughter. She, too, was at Aveyron."

"Oh, my God, tell me she wasn't watching."

"No. She stayed in one of our friends' houses near the palace gates, but she wished to be in the vicinity, as close to her mother as possible."

Adelia nodded. She could understand that.

Brother Pierre continued to talk.

"I'm sorry." Adelia roused herself from thoughts of the girl's agony. "I didn't catch that."

"I said there was another one of Princess Joanna's party there; Aelith saw him when he was going through the palace gates. Another witness to pray for Ermengarde, perhaps."

"I beg your pardon?"

"Someone she had seen with you, when you and the people who were sick arrived at her and Ermengarde's cottage in the hills. I think that was what she said."

"No," Adelia said, "there wouldn't have been anyone else we knew."

"Oh, yes," Brother Pierre said. "Aelith recognized him."

Adelia felt the blood drain from around her mouth. Somebody they knew had watched Ermengarde burn. Somebody had seen them in chains—and had not reported back, *had done nothing about it*.

"What . . . ?" She couldn't get the words out. She tried again: "What did he look like?"

"Who?" The perfect had reverted to other matters.

"The man Aelith saw. What did he look like?"

Brother Pierre shrugged. "She did not say."

But she'd recognized him as one of their own.

Clutching her head, Adelia tried to reconstruct the events of the day when the dysentery had struck. Ulf had been taken ill on the road, others had started to fall, Locusta had gone looking for somewhere to take them. . . .

He'd come back with Sister Aelith, yes, that's right; she remembered him and the little Cathar coming down the hill, the offer of the cowshed as a hospital. And then . . . what happened then? There'd been a discussion, Dr. Arnulf saying it was the plague. . . . Who else had been there in the road that Aelith had seen?

The perfect was becoming concerned for her: "Are you unwell, my child?"

Adelia got up and ran to where Ulf was sleeping. She shook him. "Who else was there?"

"Eh?"

"On the road, that day . . . the dysentery . . . when we first met Aelith . . . who *else* was there?"

"What're you talking about?"

Adelia told him.

Ulf took in a deep breath of satisfaction. "What did I say? Didn't I say there's been a snake in the grass all along?"

"But who *is* it?" She shook him. "Who was there that morning?"

The others were awake now.

"She wouldn't have seen Joanna or the other ladies, they were ahead," Mansur said.

"No, this was a man."

Boggart chimed in. "There was Bishop Rowley . . ."

"We can discount him."

". . . Captain Bolt."

"It wasn't him. Who else? Bishop of Winchester, of course, but he's unlikely. . . ."

"Admiral O'Donnell."

"Yes."

"That pesky doctor . . ."

"Arnulf, yes. Go on."

"Them two chaplains, the silly one and the other. Never liked either of 'em."

"Might it have been one of our patients?" Mansur suggested. "There were plenty of them."

"God help us," Adelia said, "I don't know. *I don't know*."

"It was Scarry," Ulf said. "Been him all along. Ain't he clever? Murderin' and poisoning everybody's mind against you so that they was glad to abandon you to Aveyron, and us, too."

She gave a moan and stumbled away from them. She felt ill.

She knew that she'd been afraid, *and had been all along*, to believe that a malignant being was after her; it put her at the center of everything, a protagonist in a Greek tragedy pursued by a revenging Fury.

It's not me, it's not me.

But it *was* her, she could see it now; she, and only she, had been the reason why so many had died in the pursuit. Blundering, stupid, deliberately blind, she might as well have been a Medea leaving the bodies of slaughtered children behind her.

Somebody had wanted to destroy her, had inflicted the persona of "witch" upon her so that the people she'd traveled with had been prepared to let her and four beloved people suffer at Aveyron.

Facing it now was like being slammed against a wall. *I can't think about it*.

But this was where avoidance stopped. *You have to think about it*.

After a while she sat down and began to consider in the only way she was capable of—as a doctor diagnosing a sickness by its symptoms and history.

When had it begun? The horse, oh yes, the horse. It had been poisoned.

What next? Brune, poor Brune. No, first there had been Sir Nicholas, whom she'd cursed and who'd been killed because of it.

The death of a horse, the theft of her cross, the murder of two innocent people, betrayal to the Cathar-hunting Aveyron and its result—*not that, not that, but of* course *that*—another murder, a woman dying in flames. Oh, God, she had led him to Ermengarde.

All this engineered by a mind so careful, so skilled in its cunning, so disordered that Adelia's reasoning brain couldn't encompass all that it had done, let alone *why* it had done it. Only that it was insane.

And then she thought: *But it didn't begin in Normandy.* . . .

It had started in England, in that faraway happiness on Emma's estate with Allie, with sane men and women and a football match. The poison had been there.

And then she thought again: *But it didn't begin there, either.* . . .

Its beginning, for her, was in a Somerset forest, where two outlaws had pranced out from the trees; green-and-black, fantastical pagan bodies that had rustled with the leaves they wore, and she had killed one to save her own life and that of the men she was with, and earned the lasting hatred of the other.

The dimness of this cave with its filtered light was not unlike that of the glade where Wolf had skewered himself and Scarry had keened for him in Latin.

And this is where he has brought me; all the way from there to here.

She heard a light snoring; the perfect had gone to sleep. The three men were talking quietly. . . .

"It was Scarry, I tell you. Been him all along. Only enemy she's ever made."

"What about the black-avised buzzard who stole the cross off us in the cowshed, was *that* Scarry?"

"Don't bloody know what Scarry looks like, do I. Never saw the bugger."

Excalibur. Another theft, not of a life this time, but of something Henry had entrusted to her, as he'd entrusted his daughter. Scarry had taken both so that she had failed in the one thing she prided herself on—her duty.

Mansur was kneeling in front of her. "I know you," he said. "It has not been your fault."

"No." She raised her head, and her voice made everybody jump. "The BASTARD."

AT THIS MOMENT, *Scarry, too, raises his head as if a bugle call from far away had suddenly cleared it of its worms. Into the holes they have made has come knowledge.*

"I know where she will be," he says to Wolf.

"Where?"

"Palermo. She will come to Palermo."

"How do you know?"

"Because that was the assignment Henry gave her, to look after his daughter. I read her mind now, Wolf of mine; she is a dutiful woman, she will not want to fail her king."

"And we will kill her there?"

"Yes, my dear." Scarry's smile is almost sane. "As the armies of Octavian and Mark Antony met on the battlefield of Philippi, so we shall meet her at Palermo."

THE TAX INSPECTOR WENT, expressing strong dissatisfaction with the paucity of tithes he and his men were taking back to their bishop.

Young Master Pons, once more situated in the window of Caronne's church, had watched them wend their way down the mountain, his bell beside him in case the thieving bastards should turn around and come back.

They did not; they disappeared as the sun was lifting from the cold earth beneath their horses' feet.

It was the next day when he saw another figure leading a string of mules coming out of that same mist. His hand reached for the bell, and then drew it back.

He slid down the ladder and danced hopefully around the visitor—sometimes this man carried sweetmeats in his pack.

Together, they went up toward the castle.

Adelia was already in the kitchen so that she could use it before Thomassia came in to prepare breakfast for them all, boiling into a thick paste the gel dripping from the leaves of aloe vera that she'd cut into a basin. One of the Lizier sons had whispered in embarrassment to Mansur that he was suffering from "an itch" without defining in what area it was plaguing him. Mansur had passed on the message and Adelia, hoping that it was merely a genital rash and nothing worse, was compounding a soothing ointment for it.

"Time we go, lady," a voice told her.

Adelia straightened her back. The goblin shape of the little Turk, Deniz, was standing in the doorway. She looked for the Irishman behind him, but Deniz shook his head. "Admiral at Saint Gilles still. We meet him later. You all come now. Pack. Quick."

Although there wasn't much for them to pack, the farewell to Caronne took time; it was difficult to express sufficiently their indebtedness and gratitude to so many people, and painful to leave them.

"We needn't say good-bye yet," Fabrisse said. "I'm coming with you as far as Salses. I hold a small château by knight's fee off Raymond of Toulouse down there—or, rather, my lord of Caronne does. Deniz tells me the O'Donnell has procured my silk in Saint Gilles and his ship will deliver it to Salses before he sets off for Italy. Na Roqua's daughter-in-law will wet-nurse my lord until my return. In fact, we'll take a couple of the Roqua men with us to carry back some salt, our supply is low."

There was one very hard parting. . . . Adelia saw the grief of it in two faces.

Rankin was the last to join them. As he came slowly down the stairs, bagpipes under his arm, she faced him. "You're not coming with us," she said.

"What ye jabbering, woman? Indeed I am."

"No. You're going to stay here and marry Thomassia."

A light came into the Scotsman's eyes. "I'll not deny . . . but it'll never be said of Rankin of the Highlands he was a dairty deserter."

"It's not desertion." She'd brought enough trouble on him. "You have been a rock to us. We love you, but we'll be safe now and Thomassia needs you. This is where you belong."

"Ay, she's said she's willin', the canty wee girl, and I've become rare fond of this clachan, but . . ."

Adelia kissed him. "There you are, then."

Standing on the ramparts of the castle with Thomassia beside him holding the Count of Caronne, he played a wailing lament on his pipes to the little party as it went trickling down the mountainside like a tear on a giant's cheek.

THREE

Twelve

"WHAT IS IT?"

"There's a light out at sea. Flashing."

Adelia got out of bed and joined Fabrisse at the slit window in the upper room of the Château de Salses's keep where it looked out on the Mediterranean. "Must be from a ship," she said helpfully.

"Of course from a ship," Fabrisse said. "The question is, whose?"

It could be the O'Donnell, who so far hadn't turned up. It could be friendly smugglers. It could be a less friendly force ready to invade the Count of Toulouse's territory. It could be decidedly hostile pirates intent on pillage and rape.

If it was either of the last two, the Château de Salses was not equipped to hold them off. In fact, Adelia thought, it couldn't have held off a couple of determined winkle pickers.

The Château de Salses, originally a fortress, was even more dilapidated than the Château de Caronne. Beautiful from a distance, Adelia had to grant it that. As she and the others had ridden down the hills toward it on that first day, it had looked like a large crenellated pink cake against the chill blue water lapping its seaward wall.

On closer inspection, defensive walls of the same dusty pink sandstone crumbled into the moat around them, bridges sagged, while a weedy bailey contained a tall keep/watchtower with an unsafe interior circling staircase, and some reed-thatched stables and working quarters.

"I can't afford to keep it up," Fabrisse had said cheerfully, if obviously, "even though it provides most of my income. We're nearly on the border of Spain here and out of the way, so it's useful for smuggling, though not enough." Feeling she hadn't done it justice, she added: "But at some point B.C., Hannibal brought his army through here on his way to Italy."

Perhaps the elephants trampled it, Adelia thought. There didn't seem to have been much renovation since.

"They're signaling," she said now, watching the light appear and disappear at erratic intervals.

"Question is, who to?" One never knew who skulked in the lonely hills behind them.

Leaving Boggart to sleep on, they lit a taper, wrapped themselves in cloaks, and went cautiously down the staircase, trying to avoid its missing steps, to the bailey.

Deniz, who'd been keeping watch, was in muttered conversation with Johan on the seawall.

And that was another thing; at the Château de Salses there had been no sign of the knight whose service in war to Count Raymond of Toulouse, when called on, was the fee Fabrisse should pay for holding the castle. (Knowing Fabrisse, Adelia suspected that she gave her rent to Count Raymond in other ways.)

What it had instead was a flock of goats, and an elderly man with shrewd eyes and a clutch of grandsons whom Fabrisse had introduced as "my bookkeeper, Johan"—a euphemism, as it turned out, for the manager of her smuggling trade.

"Who is it, Deniz?" Fabrisse called softly.

"She the *Saint Patrick*."

The O'Donnell's flagship. That was a relief. It was also a summons they had all been awaiting for some days.

"I shall be losing you tomorrow," Fabrisse told Adelia sadly. "He'll have made arrangements to send you all back to England."

"No," Adelia said. "We're going with him to Palermo."

Ever since she'd been surprised by the terrible indignation that had come over her in the cave at Caronne, she had regained certainty.

How dare he, how dare he, I won't HAVE it. She'd been hired by Henry Plantagenet to do a job; so far Scarry had made her fail in her obligation, but she would see it through to its end if he killed her for it—or she killed him, which she was now perfectly prepared to do.

"Oh-ho," said Fabrisse, looking at her. "We have stopped being frightened."

"No, but I have stopped running."

Oddly enough, it had been overhearing Rankin call her pursuer "the black-avised buzzard" that had raised her spirit. She'd forever cherish the phrase for taking the demonic out of her demon. It had turned hooves into human feet. Whether she could unmask and disable the buzzard, she didn't know, but *by God*, she would try. After all, madmen had their own vulnerability.

She and the others had gone over and over their time with

Joanna for any clues to Scarry's identity; who'd had the opportunity; who'd been where and when to do what he'd been able to do. As Ulf had said: "Who was it in that company kept buggering off?"

Practically everybody on what had turned out to be an erratic and rambling journey, that was the trouble.

Well, who had a mind that could influence other people's into making Adelia seem a curse they were glad to offload onto a bonfire?

Who indeed?

They had scoured their impressions and memories until they could practically work out Scarry's shoe size, but putting a face to him eluded them.

Eventually . . . "Ain't got no further, have we?" Ulf had said, in defeat.

But Adelia, looking out over the Mediterranean, with Fabrisse beside her, was aware that they had. Scarry was like the light she could see flickering out at sea, a promise that he was somewhere in the darkness with the sword he had stolen. How she knew it, she wasn't sure, but she knew for certain that he was going to Palermo, that she would meet him there—and defeat him.

She heard Deniz's voice come down to them from the seawall. "Somebody rowing ashore."

"*Now?*"

It was an overcast, moonless night, and at this point the land petered out into minuscule islands like scattered, tufty sponges that provided a better, almost unnavigable, defense against nighttime seaborne invasion than the castle walls.

"Signal 'stand by and show light.'" Deniz came down from the walkway. "He brings goods."

"Patricio, Don Patricio. My silk, hurrah." Fabrisse hurried off to prepare food for her visitor.

Adelia waited while Deniz lit a lantern and flashed a signal to the invisible vessel out at sea, then accompanied him through the castle postern to the beach beyond.

Behind them, they could hear Johan calling for his eldest grandson to come and help prepare the mules that would carry the landed contraband into the keep, but on this side the only sound was the waves soughing softly against the shore. Adelia hadn't stopped to put on her shoes, and the sand was cold against her feet. The ship had ceased signaling now, leaving Deniz's lantern a solitary gleam in the blackness.

"It's not just the countess's silk, is it?" Adelia asked Deniz. She'd seen his face in the lamplight.

The Turk shook his head. "He signals 'trouble.'"

Adelia ran back the way she'd come in order to rouse Mansur and Ulf and put on her shoes. *Trouble*. God dammit, was there ever anything else?

It was a chilly wait; the northern Mediterranean could be very cold in winter. The men warmed their hands at the lanterns they'd brought. Adelia stamped about in an effort to keep warm and tried to work out the date. It would be what . . . early January?

More than four months since she'd said good-bye to Allie. If the O'Donnell's arrival this night meant another delay, she'd . . . she'd kill somebody.

Fabrisse turned up with another lantern.

Ulf looked up; his young ears had heard something. Another second, and they'd all caught the creak of oars straining in rowlocks. Deniz waded out into the water, holding his light high.

Mansur and Ulf went to help him drag the rowing boat in. When they came back, they were supporting someone between them . . . a woman. . . .

"*Blanche*?" Adelia shook her head to get her eyes in working order. "Mistress Blanche?"

The lady-in-waiting fell on her. "You've got to help her. Mother of God, she's so ill. Help her. She's dying."

"Who?"

But now the O'Donnell was coming ashore, squelching through the water.

He was carrying something in his arms.

It wasn't Fabrisse's silk, it was Princess Joanna, and he was echoing Blanche. "Help her," he said to Adelia. "I think she's dying."

THERE WAS A scramble to clear the bottom room of the keep and lay Joanna on the table at which soldiers had dined in the days when the room had been a guardhouse. Lanterns were hung.

Joanna was feverish and barely conscious. Her right knee kept rising toward her abdomen. It was a struggle to undress her because Mistress Blanche held on to Adelia like a drowning woman to a raft, begging her to save the child. "Use witchcraft," she kept saying. "I know you can, everybody knows it. You saved those people from the flux, it was you, I saw you. Save her.

I don't care how, but save her." Eventually, she had to be forcibly restrained by Ulf and taken outside.

Adelia began her examination, barely listening to the O'Donnell telling the others what had happened.

"She was taken ill almost as soon as we got her on board at Saint Gilles," he was saying. "Doctor Arnulf diagnosed acute indigestion, he's been treating her with seethed toad, powdered unicorn, cramp rings, various talismans, and I don't know what else. The good Bishop of Winchester's been reciting Psalm 91 over her *ad infinitum*. And her only becoming sicker and sicker."

He broke off as Adelia abruptly left the room and headed across the bailey to where Blanche sat on a straw bale, her head in her hands, with Ulf awkwardly patting her shoulder.

The lady-in-waiting looked up at Adelia's approach. "Can you help her? Can you make her well?"

"Has she been constipated?" Adelia asked.

Ulf growled with embarrassment, but it was a measure of Mistress Blanche's desperation that, after a second's hesitation, she nodded.

"Nausea? Vomiting?"

Blanche nodded again.

"Hmm."

Adelia went back to the keep.

The O'Donnell was still talking: ". . . frantic she was. It's my opinion, Blanche is the only one of those three women who cares more for Joanna than for herself, Lord bless her. When I suggested to them we sail to Salses, where her ladyship here was *in situ*, the other two set up a caterwauling about what'd the king do to them if he learned they'd delivered his daughter to a witch and a Saracen, what'd Sicily do, what'd dear Doctor Arnulf do. I told them, I said, dear Doctor Arnulf's doing damn all except kill her quicker. . . ."

On the table, Adelia pressed gently on the lower right quadrant of the girl's abdomen and then quickly removed her hand. There was a moan. The right knee flexed again.

"So we kidnapped her, Blanche and I. Left the other ladies asleep, had my lads lower the dinghy with Joanna in it, and here we are, and may God save us all from perdition."

"So brave to dare it." This was Fabrisse. "'Delia, isn't he *brave*?"

Adelia didn't hear her. The muscles she'd pressed had been rigid.

"And Duke Richard?" Mansur was asking.

"He doesn't know. He'd already left for Sicily aboard my *Nostre Dame.* The royalty don't travel together in case of accidents." O'Donnell broke off again and looked toward Adelia, who'd left the table and was sitting on a chair, much as Blanche had done, with her head in her hands.

He strode over to her: "She's dying, isn't she?"

"I think so."

"Can you save her?"

Adelia shook her head. "Even if I could have, and that's very doubtful, I've no equipment. It was at Ermengarde's."

"Now, then." He went away, calling for Deniz: "What did you do with that damned contraption I brought?"

When he came back, he was carrying a wrought-leather, silver-bound case. "Will this do? I, er . . . liberated it from Arnulf's cabin while the good doctor was sleeping."

Inside, calfskin pockets held flasks, a well-thumbed urine chart, greasy ointment pots, tweezers, a rusty wound-cauterizing tool, a mallet, presumably for rendering difficult patients unconscious, pliers for pulling teeth, also rusty . . .

Adelia threw the instruments on the floor as she delved for the pots and flasks, opening them, sniffing, discarding. The tenth pot held what she'd been looking for—and had dreaded. So did one of the larger flasks. It appeared that, for all his pious protestations. Dr. Arnulf kept anesthetics among his medicaments.

There were no knives—apparently Arnulf obeyed the papal edict of 1163, which had banned the shedding of blood.

"No knives," she said, and was ashamed of the relief in her voice.

"For what do you need knives?" the Irishman asked. "I've a fine dagger, if that's of use."

"Knives?" asked Fabrisse. "If it's knives you want, Johan's the man; he travels to Leucate every week. There are some of his fellow Jews there, and he does their slaughtering. He's a, what's it called . . . a crocket?"

"A *shochet*?" Adelia raised her head. "He's a *shochet*?"

"I believe so. Anyway, he has a fine collection of knives, very sharp, very clean; he's particular about them."

"Yes," Adelia said slowly. "Yes, he would be."

It was why Jews often stayed healthier than their neighbors, and so were accused of poisoning Christian wells when plague broke out. Adelia's foster father, Dr. Gershom, a nonpracticing Jew himself, put it down to the religion's command that ritual slaughtering equipment must be be kept honed and clean. It was his contention that the stale, stinking, bloody filth on the knives of Gentile butchers helped to putrefy their meat.

God, dear God, every excuse she had for doing nothing was being taken away from her.

She closed her eyes and went over her diagnosis again. Pain in the abdomen's lower right quadrant, the flexing knee, rigid muscles. Classic symptoms, her foster father had told her. On the corpse of a child he'd shown her what lay beneath those muscles—the large intestine with a small, wormlike pouch emerging from the bottom of it.

Neither Gershom, nor Gordinus the African, her tutor at the Salerno School, had been able to explain its function. Gordinus had referred to it as "the vermiform addimentum." Gershom called it "an appendix to the cecum of no damned use whatever except to become diseased."

And Joanna's appendix was diseased.

I need air. Adelia got up and went out into the bailey, puffing hard. Dawn was breaking, the clouds had cleared, and, with her dog wheezing behind her, she climbed the steps of the seawall into the light of a freezing, breathless day.

To her right the two Roqua sons were filling sacks from the glaring white squares of the Salses salt pans. Beyond them, naked vines stood in neat rows ready, when in season, to produce Salses wine, a substance so rough it could clean armor.

But it was the sea Adelia looked at; blue and gold in the rising sun, tranquil, its touch on the shore like the regular breathing of a child, its only ornament the distant *St. Patrick*, O'Donnell's ship, riding quietly at anchor while, on board, its passengers seethed, some with worry for their princess, Dr. Arnulf with resentment, and none of them able to do anything about it unless they swam the couple of miles to the shore.

Adelia would have given anything to change places with them. "Father, help me," she said, and it wasn't just God she prayed to but the Jew who had brought her up and had faced what she was facing now.

The responsibility was crushing her. "Father, help me. The only time I've used a knife these last months was on a goat—and that was dead."

A cry came from behind her as Mistress Blanche scurried up the seawall steps, followed by the O'Donnell. "Why are you standing there? Why aren't you *doing* something?"

"Because what I have to do may kill her anyway," Adelia said, her eyes still on the sea.

She took a deep breath and turned to face them. "I cannot magic her well, I wish I could. I am merely a doctor. You see, there is an organ in our bodies . . . here." She pressed her hand against the right side of her stomach. "Sometimes it goes bad. . . ." She wondered if she should go into the subject of suppuration and fecal matter, and decided against it. "I believe it has done so in the princess's case and must be removed."

"Removed, how?"

"Well, by making an incision above the affected area and taking the bad piece out." *Dear God, if it were only that simple.*

"With scissors? Like cutting cloth?" Blanche's knowledge of incisions extended only to dressmaking.

"Yes, except that we use a knife."

If Blanche's face had been wild before, it was ghastly now. "You make a hole? In the skin?"

"Yes. It is sewn up afterward. . . ."

"But it will scar her, won't it?"

"I'm afraid so, yes. . . ." She was going to go on and assure the poor woman that her princess would feel no pain, that there had been preparations of poppy in Dr. Arnulf's bag. . . .

This, however, was not the lady-in-waiting's concern. "You can't." She made a rush for the steps as if to go down to Joanna and protect her, but the Irishman stopped her. "Now, now, Blanche. Listen to the nice ladyship."

Blanche thrashed at him. "Don't you see? *He'll reject her*. Dear Mother of God, he'll reject her."

"I don't understand." Adelia really didn't. "The princess is very ill. There is a remote chance that by doing this I can save her life."

Blanche put her hand over her mouth and began rocking.

The O'Donnell took Adelia's arm and led her farther along the wall. With the sun on it, his face was lined and the eyes she'd distrusted were infinitely tired. "That poor lady is between Scylla and Charybdis, mistress," he said, quietly. "On the one hand, she's desperate for her mistress to live. On the other, if the princess survives this procedure . . . *Will* she?"

"I don't know."

He nodded. "If she lives, she'll be imperfect, d'ye see? Scarred by an unholy operation. Damaged goods, you might say. King William could reject her, might even have the right to reject her, I don't know. And how would our good Henry take that humiliation? A spurned daughter? Wars have started for less."

Adelia saw. This wasn't just a sick patient they were discussing, it was a bargain between kings and countries. The girl lying on the table in the keep was of international importance. If she died from the operation, and most likely she might, Adelia herself would be accused of killing her. If Joanna survived—as two of Dr. Gershom's patients *had* survived—her surgeon would be equally culpable of—what was it this man had said?—damaging the goods, *royal* goods. Either way, the political ramifications would engulf not only all of them, but a continent.

From the first, she had known that any operation was a sin against the teachings of the Church, subject to rigorous penalty—all surgery was that; it was an accepted hazard for those who possessed the skill and were compassionate enough to use it to save a patient's life. That the School of Medicine was known to permit it put it at risk from the Church.

But this, *this* intervention could not be hidden; Joanna's body was a present from the King of England to the King of Sicily; when its wrapping was taken off in the bridal bed, its blemish would be discovered, the jewel found imperfect, deliberately spoiled by what was, in the eyes of the Church and, undoubtedly, a royal Christian husband, an act of the grossest impiety.

Adelia thought of all this, of the far-reaching consequences, and knew that in the end, *it didn't make any difference*.

She looked up at the Irishman. "It doesn't make any difference," she said. "It can't. A doctor's duty is only to the patient. Joanna is dying. Because there's just a chance of saving her, I have to take it."

"What *are* the chances?"

"Well, it's been done. My tutor performed the operation once, on an old man, but the patient died; it was too late, the organ had burst and spread poison. My father . . . I was assisting when he saved two by it, both children." It was strange, she thought, how the condition so often affected the very young. "I also assisted when three others died—it's such a horrible risk."

"But you know how?"

Tears were making her eyes blink. "O'Donnell, I don't want to do this, I don't want to, but I've got to. I can't just let her die."

"Yes," he said gently. "It's the reason I love you."

He watched her face and gently reached out with his finger to raise her dropped jaw. "Did you not know? Ah, well, it's no matter."

No matter? *No matter*? He had stupefied her. All she could find to say was: "*Why*?"

It made him smile. "Now, then, if I knew that, we'd have the answer to why the sun comes up and goes down."

She would have done anything then, *anything*, to help the pain of this wonderful man to whom she owed everything, anything not to hurt him. But the one thing he wanted of her, she was incapable of giving him.

"I didn't know," she whispered. "I'm so sorry. So sorry."

"No need. But it had to be said. Go along now, and get ready."

THE OPERATING TABLE, Gershom said, was an altar on which the surgeon laid his supplication to God and, like all altars, it had to be pristine. Just as he who was to be dubbed a knight the next day took a bath before his night's vigil in church, so must the supplicant surgeon and his offering be cleansed in the sight of God so that, if the surgeon's prayers were accepted, God would return that offering to health.

Now Adelia became tigerish. Everybody was put to work. The suffering princess was removed from the keep's table and laid on a couch while Ulf and the O'Donnell dragged the table itself out into the open air—there'd be more light there—and made to scrub it as it had never been scrubbed before. Johan's knives gleamed well enough, but they were nevertheless once again put into boiling water, as were the needles and silk thread from the sewing basket that Mistress Blanche, for all her panic, had brought with her from the ship, along with her face powder, rouge, and scents.

Everything, everything must be holy.

As Adelia lowered a basket of the wool swabs she would need into the vat's bubbling water, Mansur touched her arm. "You know you are mad? You should leave the girl be, she is in the hands of Allah."

"No, she's in mine. Oh, God, Mansur, I'm so frightened."

He sighed. "Well, well, they can only hang us once. What did the gladiators say in the arena? 'We who are about to die . . .'?"

She wasn't listening to him. "Is Fabrisse scrubbing our clothes?" She must be washed of her sins, of the guilt of Brune's death, of Ermengarde's. She had to be pure for this, all things had to be pure.

The Arab nodded. "Scrubbing hard. We shall be in clean robes." He allowed himself a smile. "But they may be wet."

It was in the middle of all this that a cry came from the top room of the tower. Fabrisse went up to see about it and returned, grimacing. "Boggart's waters have broken," she said. "The baby's coming."

"Not now, oh, not now."

"Now."

Adelia took in a deep breath. "You'll have to see to it. Take one of the *shochet*'s knives. And you . . ." She turned on Mistress Blanche, whose worry, so far, had kept her from being of use. "You go and help."

"But I . . ."

"*Help, I said.*" Adelia bit her lip and lowered her voice. This was, after all, a brave and loving woman. "Blanche, my dear, you had the courage to bring Joanna to me, now you must leave her in my hands."

FOR OVER AN HOUR, Ulf and Johan with his collection of grandsons had been squatting in the bailey, well away from the table in its center, like people watching a sacred, terrible rite from a distance—as they were.

Despite a bright sun, it was bitterly cold. Mansur, who leaned over the table, the long fingers of his left hand holding the cut edges of flesh apart, swabbing with his right, shivered in his damp clothes. O'Donnell, standing next to a smaller table, on which implements and flasks lay on a cloth, also shivered—despite the fire in the brazier next to him.

A fresh blanket had been tucked around the head, arms, and legs of Joanna in her laudanum sleep, but the flesh of her bare white stomach was goose-pimpled, except for the gaping slash down it.

From the top bedroom of the keep, where Boggart's contractions were coming hard and fast, deep, loud, involuntary huffs from her lungs groaned round the bailey like the blasts of a horn.

Adelia was aware of none of it, not noise, not the passing of time, not people, not fear, not even the humanity of the body on which she operated. She was battling with the enemy, a plump, yellowish, glistening, red-veined vermiform tube proving difficult for her tweezers to tease away from the rest of the gut. It hadn't yet perforated, thank God. But it was taking too long.

At last she had it. Still holding the tweezers in place, she gestured for O'Donnell to pass her a knife, and cut.

"Cauterizing iron. Quick."

There was a hiss. The body on the table jumped and Mansur, in response to Adelia's brief look, held the laudanum sponge to Joanna's nose.

The worm was thrown into a bucket.

Now the sewing up. "Needle." She was passed the curved steel needle from Blanche's sewing kit and knotted the sutures.

"Brandy." The wound had alcohol squeezed over it and was covered with lint.

Adelia took a swig of brandy herself and then sat down on the ground, staring into space, still clutching the bottle.

She only looked up as Fabrisse came out of the keep with a lustily bawling baby in her arms.

Joanna was breathing, but the battle for her life would continue and was now mostly in the hands of God. Adelia had done her best; it remained to be seen whether it was good enough.

FOR A WHILE it looked as if the Lord had given and the Lord was taking away. Donnell, as the new baby boy was called, thrived while Joanna went into a delirium and Adelia into panic.

The Irishman rowed out to his anchored ship to tell those aboard that it was still touch-and-go for the princess, but that "Lord Mansur's ministrations" were doing her good.

He refused their demands to take them ashore and ordered his crew to keep all passengers on board, where water, wine, and food would be rowed out to them.

There was to be no mention of an operation; if Joanna died, it must be assumed that she had succumbed to the illness that had been the reason for her abduction in the first place—some small protection for Mansur and Adelia, who would be blamed by Arnulf and the others for the princess's death in any case, but might possibly save them from their almost certain execution were it known that death had been caused by the child's body being cut open.

Even Henry II's fondness for Adelia would not outlive that.

Blanche, however, was unlikely to keep silent. She struggled between Scylla and Charybdis, the two monstrous, crushing rocks between which she had placed herself. Her grief and self-condemnation were heaped on Adelia's head as the two of them kept their vigil beside Joanna's bed. Sometimes it was: "You have killed her." At other times: "Better I had let her die than bring her to you."

Even when Joanna's fever began to abate, the outpourings continued—though always where the girl couldn't hear them: "What is she now? Dear Mary, Mother of God, you have ruined her."

The scar was undoubtedly terrible; Adelia was no needlewoman; on the seventh day, when she took out the stitches, it remained a violent, puckered obscenity on otherwise pearl-colored young flesh.

Adelia said nothing in her own defense. She was too humbled. For her, the scar represented only the amazing endurance of the human body, the quick healing of young flesh, and a loving God who had forgiven the temerity of the one who'd inflicted it by granting a miracle.

THOUGH THE O'DONNELL was impatient to begin the long sail down the coast of Italy, Adelia insisted that Joanna recuperate for another week after the removal of the stitches. The child did well, though when, on the third day—the tenth after the operation—she was allowed to begin walks around the bailey, Mistress Blanche pointed out angrily that the princess did so with a certain stiffness.

More days, then, to help the muscles recover, days to discover what a nice child she was. Without the enterprise of Eleanor, and with none of Henry's command, she had a gentle charm all her own. An intimacy grew between them all that allowed the princess to discard royal aloofness and be lighthearted in their company. Ulf told her bloodcurdling stories of Hereward the Wake, which delighted her, even though most of that fenland gentleman's exploits had been directed against her great-great-grandfather, William the Conqueror. There were more bloodcurdling pirate tales from O'Donnell, while Mansur, for whom she'd developed a great regard, improved her chess.

She was captivated by Boggart's baby and the curl of his fingers round hers. She wanted to know if giving birth hurt—"Mama said it didn't much"—and Boggart tactfully said: "No more'n is natural."

But it was Adelia who most intrigued her. Like all practicing physicians, Dr. Arnulf had taught the princess that medicine was an occult secret to which he alone held the key; that it should be a science which even a woman could practice was a concept she found difficult to comprehend.

"But if God ordained that I should die, wasn't it a sin to go against Him?"

"Why should God make an ordinance against knowledge? It is *there*, a resource that only He could have put into the world for us to use. Deliberate ignorance is the sin. Obviously He did not mean you to die. Mistress Blanche knew that."

"It was a miracle, then?"

Oh, dear. She didn't want the child to believe she was a saint. "In the sense that Nature is a miracle. Nature has secrets that God wishes us to learn. If He didn't, a swordsmith wouldn't know how to forge steel, nor an herbalist how to extract the health-giving properties of plants. I am not a witch nor a miracle worker, just a mechanic, no more, no less, trained by a school that believes in discovering what things God has created in order to relieve His people's suffering. Like all mechanisms, your operation could have gone wrong; that it didn't is a privilege for which I send up prayers of gratitude every day."

Joanna smiled. "So do I." She became royal. "My father will ever be in your debt; so will my husband."

Husband. She was still only eleven years old—there had been a birthday celebrated at Saint Gilles.

They became friends. Every night, when her wound was being checked, she wanted to hear about Adelia's upbringing, which she thought exotic. She especially liked tales of Allie. "Mama loves animals, too; they should get on well." She was suddenly wistful: "What fun to be Allie."

Adelia wanted to spirit her off so much just then that, on impulse, she said: "We could always ask the O'Donnell to sail us into the blue . . . run away."

"And be a pirate?" Joanna was amused. "How funny that would be. Why should I run away?"

"Well . . . just suppose you don't like Sicily."

"But I *shall* like it. It's my duty, I shall be queen of it."

Adelia never mentioned the subject again. If there was steel in Joanna's gentle soul, it was stamped with the word *duty*; it could not occur to her that she was ill used or, if it did, she'd suppressed the idea. What she *was* aware of was the diplomacy involved; her father had arranged a most excellent marriage to a king, as he had arranged her sisters'. It was her destiny; she had no other.

WHEN ADELIA JUDGED her patient fit enough to leave the Château de Salses, and before they were rowed out to the *St. Patrick*, the O'Donnell lectured her and her companions "*privatim et seriatim*," as he said, on the necessity for watchfulness.

"We don't know which damned vessel Scarry's on, if he's on any," he said. "We had to divide the household between three crafts. Most of the servants along with the horses are in my biggest cog, *The Trinité,* which set out at the same time as the *Nostre Dame* that's got Richard aboard. Scarry could be on either, but he *could* be skulking aboard the *Saint Patrick,* in which case I'll be too busy keeping an eye on wind and weather to see what he's up to.

For all any of us know, we're taking our goose into the fox's lair, as my old granny used to say."

He looked straight at Adelia. "You be afraid, now. Fear keeps you on the *qui vive*."

There was no sentiment in the way he said it, no fond glance; he could have been talking about a breakable piece of cargo that needed careful stowing in his ship's hold. His declaration of love might never have been made, but it placed a burden on her, as it does on those who cannot love in return.

If it hadn't been that she'd met Rowley first, she could have loved this man, she thought. Bold, confident, amused and amusing, and, hidden beneath it all, an infinite kindness.

But as he'd said, one had as little control over one's heart as over the rise and fall of the sun—and she'd given hers to somebody else.

She had kept faith with him and told nobody about what he'd said, not even Fabrisse, though, she realized now, the woman had known all along.

Dear God, but she would miss Fabrisse, who had become her twin. When it was time for the two of them to say good-bye, they clung to each other, rendered almost inarticulate by a parting that would inevitably be permanent.

At last Adelia tore herself away. "I owe you so much. . . . I can't . . ."

"Don't." Fabrisse wiped away tears. "To me, you have been . . . I will never find . . ."

"Fabrisse, take care, take *care*."

"You are the one . . . *you* take care."

Yet, as the hopeful, yelping seagulls following their boat dotted Adelia's view of the diminishing figure waving energetically from the castle seawall, it seemed to Adelia that the woman in greatest danger was not herself, but the one who defied the Church by her loving shelter of Cathars. For a second, a bonfire flared in Adelia's mind, and the person amidst its flames was not Ermengarde, but the Dowager Countess of Caronne.

ON BOARD THE *ST. PATRICK,* Captain Bolt had been chafing badly at the absence of a princess he'd been ordered to protect and spat hard words at the O'Donnell for taking her away. Pleased as he was to see Adelia, his anger made him unapproachable and it wasn't until a day or two later, when he'd calmed down somewhat, that she could tell him of Rankin's defection.

That didn't please him, either. "Happy, is he? He's no right to be happy, bloody deserter."

In fact, the reception to Adelia and the others was cold. The only welcome was to the princess. Even this, though made to appear ecstatic, was overdone, for underlying it was resentment that she had been content to recuperate among magicians and foreigners rather than insist on being returned to her own dear household.

Joanna's nurse's reception was the most honest: "You naughty little widdershin, you. Why'n't you take me along? What they been a-doing to you, so pale as you are. Still and all, my honeypot, you're alive and that's a mercy o' God."

Blanche's greeting from her two fellow ladies-in-waiting was chilly; she had broken ranks, not consulted, preferred a Saracen and a witch to the orthodoxy of Queen Eleanor's own choice of physician.

What they would say if and when they saw the scar on Joanna's abdomen, Adelia didn't like to think.

The Bishop of Winchester lectured Blanche and the O'Donnell for their temerity in kidnapping the princess. In view of Joanna's good spirits, his chiding was unheated, but it was noticeable that he did not include the names of Mansur and Adelia in his prayers of thanksgiving for his charge's safe return.

Father Guy took their reappearance hard and refused to speak to them.

Dr. Arnulf tried squirming his way back into royal favor. An unfortunate episode, but one he was prepared to overlook; however, had the dear princess stayed under his supervision, she would not be so pallid nor show that slight stiffness when she walked.

Joanna was having none of it. She owed her life to Adelia and knew it, though she upheld the fiction that it was to Lord Mansur to whom her recovery should be attributed. Both had to be treated with honor in her presence. Mistress Adelia was even promoted to sharing the royal cabin—and, yes, the dog with her. (Ward, like her new friend, Ulf, made Joanna laugh.)

The fact of the scar seemed to concern the princess not at all. Perhaps she thought it would never be seen; nudity was *infra dig* for noblewomen; they usually wore a light shift even in the bath. Adelia was afraid that the girl didn't realize she would have to strip naked in front of her husband, or even if she was fully aware of the sexual side of marriage.

And when would that be imposed on her? What sort of man was William of Sicily?

When the nurse Edeva, in a rare burst of confidence, confessed to Adelia that she had never seen "my lambkin so blithe as aboard this here ship," Adelia hoped that this time spent on board the *St. Patrick* wouldn't turn out to be the most carefree of Joanna's life.

It was a cold voyage but one made under a clear sky. The O'Donnell took advantage of a bitter northerly wind and crammed on all sail, sending *St. Patrick* bowling along at a rate which was fast but which, now that Joanna and the others had gained their sea legs, upset nobody's stomach. For Adelia, there was a reassuring sense of freedom that convinced her Scarry was not on board.

She spent what time she could on the quarterdeck with Mansur and Ulf, watching Italy go by and wondering whether the traffic on the coast roads that she could see in the distance included one particular rider heading for Sicily.

After two days, her captain took pity on her. "If it's Saint Albans you're looking for, he'll be long farther south by now."

"If he hasn't been held up in Lombardy," she added uncomfortably.

"Ah, now, a little thing like international relations shouldn't stop him from keeping an appointment with you in Palermo." The Irishman's mouth twisted. "It wouldn't stop me."

Adelia winced. She said quickly: "Will we catch up with Duke Richard?"

"Overtake him, at this rate. *Nostre Dame*'s not got the speed of *Saint Patrick*. The *Dame*'s a lumberer, and she needs to set in for forage and water from time to time, so I had to allocate Locusta to her captain for his advice on the friendliest ports."

Somebody else was missing from *St. Patrick*'s complement. "It was an odd thing," the O'Donnell said, "but embarking at Saint Gilles, our good chaplain, Father Adalburt, who is not the idiot he looks, was taken by a sudden determination to sail on *Nostre Dame* with Duke Richard. Now why would the man desert his princess and bishop like that, d'ye think?"

Adelia shrugged. "I suppose Richard's religious views accord more closely with his own."

"'F you ask me," Ulf cut in, gloomily, "he reckons he's got better prospects under the duke. He can go crusadin' with him. He'll probably end up Bishop of Jerusalem."

"God help the Holy Places," O'Donnell said, and Adelia laughed.

The Irishman had a thought and turned to Ulf. "A wooden cross, was it?" He used his hands. "So big by so big?"

"Yes." Ulf had never left off bewailing the taking of his cross; not just because he was afraid to face Henry II and tell him he'd lost it—though he was—but because he was tortured by the thought of great Arthur's Excalibur in dirty hands.

"Well, I'll tell you," O'Donnell said, "I've not remembered until now, but I saw a wooden cross being taken aboard *Nostre Dame* at Saint Gilles. I remarked it because it was so rough a thing, not at all like the jeweled crucifixes that went on with it."

Ulf's hands clenched. "Who was carrying it?"

The Irishman shrugged. "One of the crew, I think."

Ulf looked at Adelia. "Scarry. I told you, I *told* you, that was Scarry in the cowshed."

"Dear God. I'm sorry, my dear, so sorry."

"What're *you* sorry for? You said Richard'd want it and now he's got it, that murdering bastard's sold it to him."

The *St. Patrick* yawed slightly and the O'Donnell went aft to shout at his tillerman to keep his eye on the wind.

"What're we going to do?" Ulf demanded.

"I don't know. Nothing we can do." Except despair at the perfidy of men in their lust for power.

EVERYBODY WAS ON DECK to stare at Vesuvius on the evening that they sailed past the Bay of Naples. The volcano looked flat-topped and disappointingly undistinguished.

Father Guy took the opportunity for an extempore sermon, explaining that the eruption that Pliny the Younger described had been God's punishment on Pompeii's and Herculaneum's citizens for their wickedness in not being Christians. "Just as our Lord destroyed the Cities of the Plains."

Joanna interrupted him. "Mistress Adelia was found on the slopes of Vesuvius, weren't you, 'Delia?"

"I was."

"How romantic," Lady Petronilla said, acidly. "Like baby Moses in his basket. Only drier."

"So if we miss Sicily and sail into Egypt, we've got somebody to lead us out of it," said Lady Beatrix.

It was getting chilly. Everybody except Adelia and the watchful Mansur deserted the quarterdeck for the warmth of the lower deck.

We'll be passing Salerno soon. Past the two best people in the world. I don't even know if they're still alive. Dear Lord, let them be alive so that, perhaps, on the way back, I may see them again.

A hand touched her shoulder, making her jump.

It was Blanche. "We're only days from Sicily. What are we going to do? Mother of God, what are we going to *do*?"

"I don't know," Adelia told her. "But I was just thinking about my foster father. Some years ago, he was called to Palermo to attend on King William. He's a great doctor, you see."

"William?"

"My foster father."

"And he cured the king? What of?"

"I didn't ask. He wouldn't have told me, a patient's complaint is confidential."

Blanche was stuttering with hope. "Perhaps . . . perhaps he took a worm thing out of William as well. Do you think the king's got a scar like Joanna's?"

"I have no idea. Probably not."

"Your father might have influence with the king, he could plead with him for Joanna's sake."

Adelia was irritated. "Why should anyone plead for her? William's lucky—he's getting a sweet-tempered bride instead of a dead one."

But Blanche had seen a life raft in what she was certain would be the wreckage of Joanna's marriage. Within minutes, she was begging the O'Donnell to put the *St. Patrick* into Salerno and haul Dr. Gershom aboard.

Impatient though he was with any further delay, the Irishman agreed, mainly because of Adelia's joy at the thought of seeing her parents so soon.

It was not to be. As the *St. Patrick* rounded Punta Campanella, the wind of a typical Mediterranean storm veered them helplessly westward. By the time it released its grip and returned to its former direction, *St. Patrick*'s position was due north of Sicily and the ship could only make a straight run to the port of Cefalù.

It was there that Princess Joanna asked for the assurance that Adelia would put off the return to England long enough to see her married. "Promise me. Promise."

"I promise."

IN THE DARK *hold of the* Nostre Dame, *an exchange is made between Scarry and Duke Richard's secretary; a rough wooden cross for a purse of gold.*

But the duke is not as pleased as he should be and summons Scarry to him. "They say you are ill."

"No, my lord. It is merely that being at sea does not agree with me. I am well enough." And indeed Scarry does feel better than he did, though every now and then, when he is alone, he unscrews his head in order to relieve it.

"They say you talk to yourself."

"Not to myself, my lord, I pray to my God."

For, truly, he does pray to Satan. And, to Wolf, he has to give constant reassurance: "She will be in Sicily. There she was ordered, and there she shall die."

Sometimes Wolf believes him and sometimes he doesn't, which is when their arguments attract attention.

"It is good to talk to the Almighty," the duke said. "But see to yourself, you are covered in grime. I have no use for the deranged."

Scarry, who has moments of wonderful clarity, knows in that moment that Richard has forgotten the service that he, Scarry, who is now expendable, has rendered him. Scarry knows that the duke believes the sword has been willed miraculously to him, as if God's arm has pierced the clouds with it and put it into his hand to be used for God's almighty purpose.

"Who does that bastard talk to?" Wolf wants to know as the duke walks away.

"The wrong deity," Scarry tells him.

Thirteen

ADELIA, MANSUR, ULF, and Boggart, carrying her baby, stood hidden amongst the crowd on the road to Palermo's gates to see Joanna ride up to the capital of her new kingdom to be received by her bridegroom and rank upon rank of Sicilian ambassadors and clergy in peacock robes.

She was accompanied by Richard, whose height made her look even smaller than she was. Ulf peered for Excalibur, but whatever sword was in Richard's bejeweled scabbard, it wasn't King Arthur's.

For once, everybody's eye was on the princess, not her brother. The ladies-in-waiting had dressed her in pearl-encrusted gold, a diadem encircled the long fair hair, her head was held high on its little neck, and she was smiling.

Watching her go past, Adelia could have cried; so brave, so tiny. As Ulf said—with tears in his own eyes—"These bastards better be good to her."

It looked as if they would be; the people standing twelve deep along Joanna's route shouted huzzahs and blessings to their new queen, scattering bay leaves for her white palfrey's gilded hooves to tread on.

Ahead of her went the trumpeters, all shining, flag-bedecked silver. Behind rode Petronilla and Beatrix, pretty and laughing, and Blanche, also pretty, but with the strain showing; then the Bishop of Winchester and the chaplains.

Then the O'Donnell in Arabic robe and face-enfolding white headdress, the traditional garb for an admiral of Sicily, an honor that had been given him for his services to the country.

Then gleaming knights with spears, their horses with scalloped scarlet reins and saddles, and behind them Captain Bolt, his men in Plantagenet uniform with the brass-bound treasure chests.

England was doing its princess proud.

Then they'd gone. A curve in the road to the gates, and the press of people, denied Adelia the view of Sicily's king and whether the reception committee contained the Bishop of Saint Albans.

If Rowley *had* arrived on the island, the O'Donnell had promised to contact him to say that she had, too, and was well. Which was good of the Irishman, though he took no pleasure in it.

"Where will you be staying? Out of sight, I hope."

"My foster father has a house he keeps for his visits to Palermo. In the Jewish Quarter by the Harat al-Yahud." It was a joy to say it. "We'll stay there until the wedding."

"Make sure you do."

He'd arranged for Adelia, Boggart, Mansur, and Ulf to disembark from the *St. Patrick*, with Deniz accompanying them to act as go-between, before anyone else. "And see you're veiled if you venture out."

As they gained the teeming streets of Palermo, their ears were deafened by the noise of four different languages—all of them official—being screamed at once; their eyeballs were assaulted by clashes of violent color; their nostrils shriveled under an onslaught of every kind of stink mixing with every kind of perfume; they had to dodge peddlers trying to sell them sugared almonds and ribbons, and prostitutes of both sexes wanting to sell something else. They had to get out of the way of trains of mules and donkeys carrying spices from the East or building materials from the North, resist the call of traders from their shops in the arched walkways, make sure that the purses the O'Donnell had provided them with weren't cut from their belts. . . .

For Adelia, it was magical. "Look, look. See that ruined temple? It's Greek. My father said that Archimedes taught there when he wasn't in Syracuse. . . . And that building's the Exchange, and down there's the Street of the Scent-makers—just sniff. . . . And the mill over there, can you see it? That's where they make paper. . . . Stop a minute, I must buy some *cassata*, you'll love it, Boggart. It's an Arab cake; Mansur calls it *Qas'at*. . . . And *sciarbat*—Lord, I hope old Abdalla still sells it—he makes it from fruit chilled by mountain snow. . . ."

She was a child again, on a visit with her parents to a sanctuary of marvels. She'd thought then that every capital city must be like this one; now she knew that Palermo was the most brilliant, prosperous metropolis in the world, unique.

Even so, she was entering the past through a different gate; she was Odysseus succumbing to the song of the Sirens, not returning to Ithaca. This could truly be home only if Allie and Gyltha were to join her and Mansur in it.

The Arab, like a man long parched of water, disappeared to say his prayers in the first mosque vouchsafed to him since he and Adelia had set off for England.

As they waited for him, Boggart, clutching Donnell, saw her first camel train: "What-a mercy is them things? Lord bless me that I should see hillocks on the move."

But, marvel though they did, it was the sheer heterogeneity of the city that soothed the souls of the four former prisoners of Aveyron, who'd seen what intolerance could do.

Sometimes, savoring the moment, they stopped to watch those who would be mortal enemies elsewhere walking together in reasoned argument; they saw a fellow with a cross on his tunic—thus showing that he was on his way to the Levant to kill Saracens—bemusedly asking for directions from an Arab; a skullcapped Jew chatting with a tonsured monk; the high hat of a Greek Orthodox priest wobbling at a joke told him by a Norman knight.

"It hasn't changed," Adelia said happily.

"It has," Mansur told her. "There are more Christian churches and fewer mosques. Fewer synagogues, also."

She hadn't noticed until now, but he was right; the ringing from the bell towers was louder than she remembered it, louder than the calls from muezzin.

To Ulf and Boggart, however, the mixture was astonishing. "I thought King Henry was liberal," Ulf said. "Look how good he treats his Jews, but this . . . How'd this happen?"

"The Normans," Adelia told him. "The Normans happened."

And hardheaded, cutthroat adventurers they'd been.

Of genius.

Led by a couple of land-hungry brothers, the Hautevilles, they'd hacked both Sicily and Southern Italy into submission, taking it from Arab domination. They'd then promoted Arabs to be their advisers, along with every other intelligent race that could be of use to them. Dissension cost money and men to put down, *ergo* the Hautevilles ensured that there were no second-class citizens in their new realm to cause trouble. Thus, out of it, they'd made a kingdom that outshone any other, just as Sirius put all other stars in the night sky to shame.

"Mind you," Adelia pointed out, "it's a volatile mixture." Sicilians were prone to flashes of extreme violence in family vendettas. The occasional minister might get himself assassinated, not because of his race or faith but because he'd made himself unpopular. "And there are back alleys where it's not safe to go at night—nor in daytime, for that matter."

Let it only change for the better, Lord. Let it live forever.

At last they reached the Harat al-Yahud, a great gateless arch—for what did the Jews here need to be gated against?—with the Star of David carved boldly into its stone.

Adelia found herself trembling; beyond it lay another of Sicily's many worlds, *her* world; a different smell, henna blossom and caraway seeds, all the spices of the Song of Solomon; children playing catch amongst black-hatted men with ringlets poring over chess tables, matchmakers bargaining as they drank kosher wine, the drone of the Shemoneh Esreh prayer issuing from the synagogues.

And kindness; as the child of a revered visiting doctor, she'd had blessings showered on her, not to mention sticky *abricotines* and *barfi badam* from every sweetmeat seller she'd passed.

She clutched Mansur's arm as they turned in to a street of tightly terraced houses. "They might be here, they might. They could have come for the wedding." She turned to Deniz and pointed: "That's the house we'll be staying in."

The Turk was in a hurry to get back to the admiral, so he left them.

But the door that always stood open to patients, whether they could pay or not, when Dr. Gershom and Dr. Lucia were in town was closed, so were the shutters.

With tenderness Adelia put out her hand to touch the mezuzah in its little barred niche in the doorpost. "They're not here." She could have wept.

There was a shriek from next door. "Adelia Aguilar. Is it you, little one?" She was enveloped in plump arms and a smell of cooking. "Shalom, my child, you are a blessing on my old eyes. But so thin, what have they done to you, those English?"

Here at least was comfort. "Shalom, Berichiyah. It is lovely to see you. How is Abrahe?" She made the introductions. "This is Berichiyah uxor Abrahe de la Roxela, an old, old friend. She keeps the key to our house and is good enough to look after it in my parents' absence."

Berichiyah dressed little differently from Sicily's other respectable women—here, as everywhere else, Jews mainly adopted the wear of the country they lived in. The chinstrap of a stiff linen toque encircled the ample wrinkles of her face; the crease of an enormous bosom was apparent above the bodice of a stiff gown, its skirt pinned up above a petticoat, but nobody could have taken her for anything other than Jewish, and she would have been offended if they had.

"Aren't they here, Berichiyah?"

"They wrote they might be coming, but maybe, maybe not."

There was something chilling in the "maybes" that caused Adelia to ask sharply: "They're not ill?"

"No, no, not ill. In their last letter, both well." Berichiyah changed the subject. "Wait now, while I let you in. How long are you here? I hope long enough for me to put flesh on your bones."

She disappeared and came back with a key. "Go in, go in. Everything is clean, the beds are aired. I will fetch Rebekah's cot for the baby, her Juceff has grown out of it. Ten grandchildren have we got now, Adelia. Six boys, four girls. And a great-grandson—our Benjamin married the ax maker's daughter last year. . . ."

They were swept into a dark, shining interior that smelled of beeswax and astringent herbs.

"Is Abrahe well?" Adelia asked.

"Not well, my dear, not well at all. Now he has the gout, poor man, and even your father can do nothing for it."

Berichiyah's husband had enthusiastically embraced ill health for years, teaching his wife to read so that she could run the date-importing business that he'd inherited from his father, leaving her, while doing it, to provide for and bring up their many children whilst maintaining the fiction, as she did, that he was still head, if the ailing head, of the household.

"Exhausted, the lot of you. You will want to be quiet tonight, so I will bring you some stewed kid and tzimmes, enough for all. You remember my tzimmes, Adelia? But tomorrow night you eat with us."

That happiness, however, was denied them.

STILL WEARING THE sheepskin coats from Caronne, they went out the next morning to purchase badly needed clothes. Adelia took them to the market square in La Kalsa, the working-class area of Palermo, where Mansur could find new robes and headdresses and she and Boggart and Ulf outfit themselves as well as buy clouts and a new shawl for young Donnell—and do it cheaply.

Borrowing from the O'Donnell had worried her but he'd said: "Rest easy now, I'll charge it to King Henry."

"Oh, he'll like that."

It was while Boggart was poring over a stall carrying a selection of bright secondhand skirts that Adelia, holding Donnell, became transfixed by the booth next door. Four marionettes were being manipulated by people unseen behind the backcloth of a tiny stage. Palermo was famous for its marionettes; her parents had bought her one when she was a child, a wooden, painted little knight that she'd ruined by operating on it.

Here was another knight, presumably the epic hero Roland of Roncesvalles energetically clashing swords with a frightening-looking Moor. What caught Adelia's eye, though, were not the humanoid puppets, but a comic mule and camel chasing each other round the left-hand side of the stage, legs kicking, their mouths opening to bite and shutting again.

Allie would love them.

Whether she could afford more of the Irishman's money to buy both for her daughter was the problem.

"One though, eh, Donnell?" she asked the baby, whose

eyes were fixated on the bouncing puppets. "The camel? The mule?"

That was when somebody pushed something between Donnell's shawl and her hand.

Automatically feeling to see if the purse at her belt was still there, she whipped round to see the back of a dowdy-looking man disappearing quickly into the crowd.

"What is it, missus?"

It was a piece of paper—a substance still virtually unknown in England—sealed with two drops of unstamped sealing wax.

"To Mistress Adelia from her friend, Blanche of Poitiers, greetings," she read out. *"Be at the Sign of Jerusalem in the Street of Silversmiths within the hour."*

The script was looped and cursive. "I didn't think Blanche could write," Adelia said.

"She can't," Ulf said immediately. "That's Scarry, that is. Lurin' you to your death, that's what he's doing."

Ulf was suspicious of all males who looked at them sideways and kept his hand constantly on the hilt of his sword—another gift from the O'Donnell.

"He wouldn't have found us this quickly. I'd better go; Joanna may need me."

"At a bloody tavern?"

"You do not go without me," Mansur said.

"Nor me."

"Nor me."

Adelia looked at Boggart. "We can hardly take the baby."

"Well, I ain't leaving him, and I ain't leaving you." She added: "And we ain't leaving Ward on his own here, neither."

Ah, well . . .

The Sign of Jerusalem stood, or rather leaned, end-on to the silversmiths' street down an alley deserted except for a vulture energetically pecking at the carcass of a dead cat. It didn't look like a tavern, more a shack due for demolition; the crusader cross on its sign was barely visible under peeling paint, and its shutters were barred up.

Mansur's hand went to the dagger at his belt. Ulf drew his sword. "Don't reckon this place gets much custom," he said.

Ward made a halfhearted attempt to scare off the vulture but gave up when it ignored him.

The man who opened the door to Mansur's rap wasn't a landlord either, to judge from his tabard, which was embroidered with two golden lions bringing down two golden camels, the arms of Sicily's kings ever since their conquest of the Moslems.

He stood well back to bow them in. "Mistress Adelia?"

"Yes."

He picked up a lit lantern from a dusty table and opened his other hand to show Adelia a ring.

She nodded and turned to the others. "It's Blanche's."

"And who are you?" Ulf wanted to know.

"I am your guide. Be good enough to follow me." The man spoke Norman French with a Sicilian accent. He indicated an open trapdoor with a short flight of steps leading downward into darkness.

"We ain't going nowhere less'n we know where," Ulf told him.

"Really? It was understood that Mistress Adelia has an enemy and it were better her whereabouts were not known. Follow me, please."

The steps were slippery. Ulf, still carrying his sword, went first, followed by Mansur, to whom Adelia passed down Baby Donnell before giving a hand to Boggart. They had to wait while Ward made an ungainly descent.

"Exciting this, ain't it, missus?" Boggart said nervously.

The bravest of the brave, that girl. Adelia could only pray she wasn't leading her into more trouble; this passage might be out of *One Thousand and One Nights*, but it could lead to a sultan angry at being given a damaged bride.

It was a long tunnel that led eventually to steps up into a garden and a grilled gate in a wall guarded by fearsome, turbaned, baggy-trousered guards with scimitars.

Mistress Blanche was waiting for them, trembling with nerves. "He says he'll see you, 'Delia. I haven't told him, only that you saved her life. He remembers your father well. If you explain, tell him, then, perhaps . . ."

"Explain?"

Blanche grabbed Adelia's neck with two hands as if she would shake it. Instead, she hissed into her ear. "The scar, woman, the *scar*. Persuade him, beg him, tell him how lovely she really is."

"She *is* lovely."

"In our eyes, but he's expecting perfection." She fell back, crossing herself. "I can't bear her to be rejected. Mary, Mother of God, let him understand."

The guide was gesturing to them to hurry. Blanche, it appeared, was going no farther. In that case, Adelia decided, neither were Boggart and the baby; whatever was coming, they must have no part in it. "Look after Boggart and Donnell for me," she said. "And the dog."

Blanche nodded and wrung Adelia's hand as if sending her to war, then turned away, dabbing her eyes.

At a nod from the guide, the guards opened the gate and they were in a pillared walkway running beside a little tiled square, like an atrium, with a fountain playing in it.

Into a great and gilded chamber. More terrifying but obliging guards, more chambers, until the last—largest and most gilded of all—from which, even through the door, they could hear the noise, like a thousand birds twittering at once in a giant aviary.

Adelia's eyes met Mansur's. She knew what was beyond the door; the kings of Sicily might be Normans, but they had adopted—and obviously still kept—this most Arab of customs.

The door was opened. Inside was an enormous room full of women, some of them elderly, most of them young and olive-skinned, all beautiful and all in billowing silk, for though the night outside the filigree bars on the windows was cold, these were tropical birds and were kept warm by fifty or more chased lamps and braziers.

Some lay on divans, but most were playing games or dancing or wheeling in acrobatics. Their guide stopped; he was going no farther. He put out an arm to halt Ulf, whose mouth had sagged open as he looked in. "Not you," he said.

Mansur patted Ulf on the head. "This is a harem," he said, "and you are a whole man. Enter, and these guards will have to kill you."

Ulf was drooling. "Be bloody worth it," he said.

He was left behind, and the doors closed on him as Mansur and Adelia stepped in.

The room stilled for a moment at the sight of Mansur, as did the chatter, but then the kaleidoscope came to life again, reassured by the presence of one who'd been instantly identified as another eunuch.

In one corner of the room, some of the young women were working at silk looms; it looked an incongruous activity amongst all this recreation, though the owners of the slim hands shuttling back and forth seemed happily engrossed in what they were doing.

A tall eunuch, who'd been strumming a long-necked lute, put the instrument down and came toward them, touching his forehead and breast. "*As-salaam aleikum.*"

"*Wa aleikum salaam,*" returned Mansur.

The man relapsed into perfect Norman French. "Lord, Lady, I am Sabir, most humbly at your service. And now, Gracious Ones, if you would be good enough to follow me . . ." He gestured to one of the harem's older women. "Rashidah shall chaperone the Lady Adelia."

Adelia had begun to wonder whether the king was going to receive them in the chamber to which selected ladies from the harem were summoned for his sexual pleasure, but the room they entered had no samite drapes, no couches, no erotic pictures. A magnificent, claw-footed desk stood in its center. Books and scrolls lined three of the walls, and a superb tapestry depicting hunters in full cry through a forest in which peacocks wandered covered the fourth.

This was the office of a Norman king, not an Arabian sultan.

But it wasn't a king sitting behind the desk; it was a frog. The hood of a burnous framed features with the smooth, greenish pallor of an amphibian. Either the princess's kiss to her king had reversed the fairy story, or this was not the king.

The man stood up, showing that he was squat. He salaamed, gesturing for them to take the two chairs on the opposite side of the desk, and greeted them in Norman French that had a lisp to it.

"May I present myself? I am Jibril, emir secretary to the *Musta'iz,* the Gracious One, who will join us in a minute. Lord Mansur, you honor us. As for the Lady Adelia, you have been much missed from this kingdom. The King of England's gain was our loss; it was with deep regret that seven years ago I signed the permission to send you to him, knowing we were losing a most accomplished doctor and that our esteemed Doctor Gershom would be losing a daughter."

He bowed. His eyes were the only things about him that weren't froglike. They directed themselves from beneath the pouched skin like skewers.

Adelia bowed back. *It was you, was it?*

"May I hope that your return to us is permanent?"

"I'm afraid not. I have to go back, I have left my child behind." She had a sudden fear that they weren't going to let her leave.

But Jibril said: "So we understand. May you be happily and safely reunited with her."

"Thank you." *They have spies everywhere*, she thought, *they even know Allie's sex*. Still, she'd almost forgotten the relief of being in a country where a female doctor was not an abhorrence.

"We fear the journey from England has been a difficult one. We learn from the Lord O'Donnell that you have been pursued by a malevolence that wishes you harm. The Glorious One wishes me to tell you that, should he be discovered here in Palermo, that being shall be hunted down and killed like the dog he is."

"Thank you, but I don't think that's what this meeting is about, is it? You want to discuss the Princess Joanna." *Let's get it over with.*

Jibril's lips made a horizontal stretch; presumably he was smiling. "You have adopted English directness, lady. Allow me to do the same. The Lady Blanche tells us the princess was taken ill as she boarded ship at Saint Gilles and that drastic measures had to be taken by you to save her life. Would you be good enough to inform us of what they were?"

She took a deep breath. "I was forced to operate." She went into the explanation of the appendix, its putrefaction, etc.

"The procedure has left a scar, of course. Lady Blanche worries that it may displease the king but I am certain that, as a man of sense, he would prefer a scarred bride to a dead one. I can assure you that it makes no difference to the princess's beauty or disposition, which is of the sweetest."

The secretary's lips stretched wider. "Already, so much is obvious. We are all charmed by this jewel of England. The scarring is of no moment if it saved the dear one's life; a diamond with a flaw can be more beautiful than one without. That is not our concern. . . ."

It isn't? Thank God, thank God. Then what are you worried about?

"What we would wish to know is whether this operation has had any other ill effect? On her future and that of her marriage?"

It was Mansur who caught on. He said in English: "He wants to know if Joanna can still have children."

Adelia blew an "oh" of relief. Was that it? Of *course* that was it. She and Blanche had been worrying over the wrong cause. Scarred or not, Joanna's function was to give William sons. An heir was vital if Sicily was to remain in the hands of the Hautevilles. Childlessness in a king was not just a personal tragedy, it meant the sweeping away of his entire administration; possibly civil war as differing claimants jostled to take his throne.

"I assure you, my lord, that as far as I know, Joanna is capable of having as many babies as God and the king give her."

The little skewers that were Jibril's eyes had become mercilessly sharp, like his voice: "And that is the truth?"

"The woman is incapable of speaking anything else," Mansur told him.

"The cecum is nowhere near the womb," Adelia said. "I can draw you a diagram, if you like."

For the first time the secretary's smile was genuine. "Spare me that. And forgive me." He was a different man. "We need a son and heir, you see. We are surrounded by enemies who will take Sicily over the brink if there is no succession."

"*Aha.*" Here was an opportunity.

Adelia said: "My lord, the King of England entrusted us with bringing King William a gift; next to his daughter it is the greatest he could bestow. To be used against a mutual enemy, he said. He's sent him Excalibur."

Excalibur. The beacon of light that sprang into every eye at the mention of the name was lit even in this Arab's. The Normans had brought the story of Arthur with them when they came, and it had taken root; there was a strong Sicilian legend that Arthur roamed Mount Etna.

Jibril leaned forward; he knew the sword's value to whoever owned it. For the first time, he was abrupt. "Where is it?"

If Richard had it, and Adelia was almost certain that he did—Henry had as good as warned her—then now was the time to betray him. Though carefully.

She explained how the sword had been hidden in a cross and given to Ulf to carry. "It was lost when my companions and I . . . fell into some difficulty that separated us from Princess Joanna and her company for a while, but we have a hope that Duke Richard may have found it. It—or certainly the cross that contained it—was seen being carried aboard the *Nostre Dame*, just before she set sail from Saint Gilles."

She looked into Jibril's eyes and knew they saw everything; this man would have spies scattered through every country in the known world; was probably more aware than she was of Richard's ambition.

"If Duke Richard has taken it into his keeping," she went on, "it may be that he wishes to give it to King William himself and, I am sure, will present it when he feels the moment has come."

"I am sure he will," Jibril said.

That was enough; the word was out. Subtly, it would be made known to Richard that William was aware of Henry's intention to give him the sword and had every expectation of receiving it.

She could do no more.

"'*To be used against a mutual enemy*.' That is King Henry's message?"

"Yes, my lord."

"Which one, I wonder; we have so many." But Jibril was a happier man. "Name your reward, my dears."

The reward was to have the advantage of being direct. "About the babies, my lord. The princess is not ready for them yet."

"My dear Lady Adelia." It was said with reproach. "Is our Gracious One a barbarian? He is not. Princess Joanna shall enjoy her childhood until such time as . . . ah, here he is now."

A man came into the room. He was as beautiful as his palace and, despite the long, fair hair of his Viking ancestors, almost as eastern. Slippers of engraved red leather ending in a point were visible under his tasseled burnous of soft wool. He trailed servants, scent, and Oriental courtesy, touching his forehead and breast in a salaam as they were introduced to him. It was disconcerting to hear him speak in Norman French and invoke the Virgin rather than Allah as he expressed his gratitude for "this pure pearl of England whose life and safety is so dear to me and for whom I am eternally in your debt."

He gave a look toward Jibril, who nodded—*business concluded satisfactorily*—and then he was gently chiding them. "But why were you not with my princess when she arrived? You, who have done so much for her, should have been in the royal train. Where are you staying? No, you are to lodge at the Ziza during your time here; you and your household are my honored guests. Mansur, my friend, do you hunt? Lady Adelia, I was in debt to your esteemed father, and now to you. . . . And how is my cousin of England?"

He was young, twenty-four, twenty-five perhaps, and, to judge from his charm, let alone his harem, experienced with women—as a nation expected its king to be, while at the same time expecting perfect fidelity from its queen. But there was none of the forcefulness nor sign of the overweening intelligence possessed by his future father-in-law. Henry Plantagenet wouldn't have left the questioning of Joanna's fertility to a secretary; important decisions were his alone.

With trepidation, Adelia suspected laziness. Undoubtedly Joanna would fall dutifully in love with him. It would probably be a happy marriage from that point of view, but whether William had the energy and acumen and kingship to maintain the balance on which his realm depended she was less sure.

The room became full of servants bringing sherbet, cakes, and two little velvet cushions with leather cases on them. The Lord Mansur stood up to be invested with the Order of the Lion, the Lady Adelia to have a gold cross hung around her neck. Both received heavy purses that chinked.

"Accept this from our grateful hands. We hear that yours were taken from you."

"Thank you, my lord, thank you." *Where* do *they get their information?* She fingered the cross, bending her head so that she could see it properly, and swallowed. It was studded with diamonds, enough to keep her and Allie in comfort for the rest of their lives.

When William had gone, Jibril said: "And now, dear lady, there are covered carts waiting outside to take you and your household to the Ziza Palace. In return for the princess's life, it is the Gracious One's obligation and ours to safeguard your own, therefore the transfer will be done in secrecy. Nobody but ourselves shall know where you are."

It wasn't a request, it was a command. The king was in Adelia's debt; honor demanded that nothing should happen to her until it had been repaid.

Le roi le veult, she thought.

The Ziza, one of the palaces that ringed Palermo like a necklace, was rumored to be the loveliest of them all. Her father and mother had once taken her to stare at the great Arabic inscription round its entrance arch: *This is the earthly paradise that opens to the view; this king is the Musta'iz; this palace is the Ziza* (noble place).

Well, a little bit of luxury wouldn't come amiss for once.

"That would be very nice," she said.

LATER THAT DAY, in a room of the Palazzo Reale, two men were having a discussion. A beautiful room, one of many designed for valued guests; a curved and painted ceiling met the arches of the walls in a frieze of sculptured marble fruit while, in the resultant niches, real pomegranates and oranges were piled in boat-shaped porphyry dishes on silver-topped tables. In case the guest should be cold—for though Palermo weather begins to warm in February, it was still chilly—bowls of scented oil burned in the braziers.

The discussion—it was taking place in English—was less civilized.

In fact, the room might have been a ring in which two fighting dogs strained against their leashes in order to tear out each other's throat.

"And where is she now?" The Bishop of Saint Albans didn't like the tale he'd been told of what had happened to his woman since he'd last seen her, and he didn't like the man who'd told it—a man who didn't like him either.

"I don't know." The lightness with which Admiral O'Donnell

said it, and the ease with which he lolled on a brocaded ottoman while saying it, was an affront in itself.

"Of course you bloody know."

"Indeed, I do not. We parted at the boat. I came on with the princess; she went off—apparently, her family owns a house in the Jewish Quarter. But she's gone from there, the others with her, and the neighbors don't know where."

In fact, he had a good idea that she was in the safekeeping of Jibril, who'd questioned both himself and Blanche closely on the happenings during the princess's journey, and shown a great interest in Adelia's whereabouts. Yes, he was pretty sure the woman was somewhere in one of the royal palaces, in safety, thank God, but damned if he'd say so to this bishop who'd done nothing to ensure it. Let him sweat.

"Why in hell didn't you bring her here?"

"Well now . . ." If it was possible to lounge with even more annoying elegance, the Irishman did it. "I decided that rejoining a royal household where somebody wants her death was not perhaps the finest move she could make."

Did you, you bastard, Rowley thought, *and what gave you the right to decide what she should do and shouldn't?* And then he thought: *Saving her damned life, I suppose.*

Well, he could still regain the high ground. "I've found him," he said.

"Scarry?"

That's jolted the bugger. "Come over here."

The Irishman approached an exquisite three-legged table covered with papers and scrolls. "How did you do that, now?"

"Look at this." Rowley picked up one of the scrolls. In his

triumph, he'd lost aggression. "We had to submit a list of the names of Joanna's household to the majordomo here at the palace, everybody traveling with her and requiring accommodation." He batted his fist against the side of his head. "God Almighty, I don't know why I didn't think of the names before . . . it's there as plain as bloody day."

The bell for Vespers could be heard ringing close by from the nearby San Giovanni degli Eremeti, which, with its vermilion cupolas, looked more mosque than church. Rowley ignored it.

It was a long scroll. It held not only names, but the person's occupation and place of origin.

Rowley pointed. "There."

The Irishman studied the name. "*Him*? It's never him, surely. Jesus, he was . . . That doesn't necessarily mean he'd be called Scarry."

"I know. But Scarry's a nickname—his outlaw name, and the odds are it was adapted from this. It surprised me, too, but there's no other on that list would lead to it—I've studied them all. And when you come to think about it, he's the only one with the opportunity."

"But he's . . . I never even considered . . . Where is he now?"

"Nobody knows. Disappeared since the *Nostre Dame* landed. Which clinches the matter. Apparently, he was becoming more and more odd every day."

"*Odd*? I can think of more fitting terms. So he's roaming the city somewhere?"

"I presume so. I've got men out looking for him—and her. In the name of God, why did you let her loose?"

O'Donnell fingered his chin. "Well now, she's promised

Joanna she'd see her married, so she'll be in the cathedral for the wedding the day after tomorrow. She's a woman who keeps her word . . ."

"*I know that.*"

". . . but I'll find her before then." He got up and began moving toward the door.

Rowley stopped him. "*I'll* find her. She's *my* woman, O'Donnell."

There was a smile of apparent surprise. "Is she now? Is she? And you a bishop." The smile went. "Should have taken more fokking care of her, then, shouldn't you?"

ULF REACHED FOR a honeyed date, a delicacy he'd not encountered before but found to his taste. "What's funny about that? I don't *need* any more silk. Go home dressed like this, and the lads'll throw me in a pond for a clothes horse."

"You look very nice," Adelia said. They all did. Her own bliaut fitted like a skin at bosom and waist while its sleeves and skirt trailed in wafts of exquisite silver-green. "Though perhaps violet was a mistake with your complexion."

"I like violet."

Mansur pursued the matter. "So the majordomo asked you if you wanted a silk worker sent up to your room, and you said no."

"I'm not saying it ain't a nice room, but I don't want it cluttered with looms and such, do I."

"It's a euphemism," Mansur told him.

"Didn't want it cluttered with euphemisms neither." Then it dawned. "You mean . . . ? Hell and sulfur. *And I said no.*"

"Quite right, too," Adelia said. "Think of the poor girl."

"She might have liked him in violet," said Mansur.

Adelia put her arms behind her head and listened to a bird singing on an almond tree branch that was beginning to bud.

She remembered Homer: *I was driven thence by foul winds for a space of nine days upon the sea, but on the tenth day we reached the land of the Lotus-eater.*

Boggart, cradling Donnell after his evening feed, came back from her regular, self-imposed tour of the gardens that she made "so's he can sniff all them lovely scents up his little nose."

She, too, was elegant. Like Adelia's, her hair was encased in a pearl caul. Admittedly, things still tended to fall over when she passed them by, but clumsiness disappeared when she had Donnell in her arms; there never was a mother so attentive.

Adelia sat up and took the baby from her so that she could snuggle with him among the cushions and feel the down of his head against her cheek. He smelled of fresh air and milk. "No lotuses for you," she told him, "not until you've got teeth."

"Ain't tried lotuses," Boggart said. "They as nice as couscous?"

Even Ward had a silver collar round his neck. Since he'd played his part in the rescue from Aveyron, the Ziza's Moslem servants had been told to quash their antipathy to dogs as unclean beasts. At first, he'd been offered a home in the only canine residence the palace contained, the royal kennels, but since its hunting pack of salukis had terrified him, he'd been allowed to rejoin Adelia and the others as one more honored guest.

His mistress had asked if she might send a message to the Bishop of Saint Albans to tell him where she was, but Jibril's command that her whereabouts be kept a secret from everybody was obeyed to the letter, and her request had been ignored—courteously, but ignored.

Rowley had arrived in Palermo, they'd told her that much. Yes, my lord bishop was also aware of her presence in Sicily, but it was better, since spies were everywhere, that there be no contact between the Ziza and the outside world.

Well, she'd said to herself, *I shall see him at the wedding.* And an unworthy thought had followed that one: *It won't do him any harm to wait until then.*

It was unfair on Rowley and, perhaps, the O'Donnell, who had taken such care of her, but she had no energy for men and the emotion they engendered. Indeed, it hadn't been until she was installed in the luxury of the Ziza that she'd realized that she and the others were tired to the bone.

It was enough, it was deep sensual pleasure, to be waited upon like pashas, to take a soak in a heated pool big enough to swim in, to be massaged, oiled, perfumed, to have beautiful clothes laid out for their choice, to have cooks vying to tempt their appetites with dishes that took the palate to succulent heaven.

All this in an edifice built for Norman kings by Arab craftsmen so that they wandered through an eye-bewildering, senses-enchanting, fountain-murmuring zigzag of stalactite and honeycombed ceilings and dazzling mosaics amidst living, pacing peacocks.

It suited the four of them to be by themselves, to banter and remember another time of friends and contentment in Caronne. Each knew that the others woke up sweating from nightmares of screams and flames. In Adelia's dreams a murdered laundress came time and again to point a shaking, accusing finger, but though they shared these memories they didn't speak of them, trying to make themselves well in an earthly paradise and each other's beloved company.

To be guarded by the scimitar-bearing men who stood at every entrance was, for the time being at least, not irksome but a source of comfort. Adelia convinced herself that, whoever he was, Scarry had died, or given up and gone away, to bother her no more.

If she could have had Allie and her parents with her, it would have been as near Heaven as she could reach.

In one of the poorer areas of Palermo, a landlord and his wife are discussing the man to whom they have just rented a space in the attic of their shambling lodging house.

"His money's good," Ettore points out. For rooms are at a premium with the forthcoming wedding attracting so many people into the city, but the fact that the stranger hadn't quibbled at being charged a gold tari for what even Ettore can't claim to be luxurious accommodation has taken the landlord aback.

"Did you look at his eyes?" Agata crosses herself. "Made me go all gooseflesh. And not a word out of him. Don't you leave me alone with that creature."

Her husband, too, has been perturbed by his new, silent guest, but a gold tari is a gold tari. "His money's good," he says again.

"Another present, Rafiq?"

The majordomo's hands were cupped as if he offered the gift of a sip of water. "From the Gracious One, lady. I was to say that it arrived by boat this morning. It is in the Court of the Fountain, if you would follow me. It is for the Lord Mansur also."

Mansur, Adelia saw, kept his hand on the dagger in his sash as they went; even here, he was never as relaxed as she was, always scanning the walls to the gardens as if Scarry might leap over them with a knife in his teeth.

It had been an overcast day, and the court was made chilly by the water spurting from the stone lion's head in the wall where two people, a man and a woman, stood under one of the palm trees, watching the stream's twirling progress along the conduit in the tiled floor.

They turned.

The man had a close-shaven beard and humorous eyes. He was slightly shorter than the elegant woman with him.

They were a couple that had once come across a bawling, abandoned baby girl on the slopes of Mount Vesuvius during an exploration. Childless themselves, they had taken the baby home and, in raising it, had given it the profit of their affection and exceptional intelligence. On finding, as she grew up, that their foster daughter had a mind to match and even outrank their own, they had enrolled her in the School of Medicine at Salerno at which they were both professors.

Adelia stumbled toward them to take them in her arms. In laying her face against theirs, she felt the same tears of gratitude on their cheeks that were falling down hers.

EVEN WHEN DINNER was finished, the explanations were not, and the company, sitting cross-legged on its cushions, remained round the table long after the dishes had been cleared away.

"But this is terrible," Dr. Gershom said, not for the first time. "Who is this monster? Such a thing to happen to our darling."

"We must remain calm," Dr. Lucia told him—it was her mantra. "Jibril will find the madman and have him put away."

"He had better. She doesn't leave my sight until he is." He looked at his wife: "And I *am* calm, woman."

"No, you're not. Only when dealing with your patients. They will live longer than you do, old man."

It was an old, old exchange that, to Ulf and Boggart, taken aback, sounded like the beginning of an argument.

Adelia and Mansur caught each other's eye and smiled. No change here, then. This ill-assorted couple bantered, sometimes insulted each other, to a degree that concerned strangers, especially those who, like most Sicilian husbands and wives, used elaborate courtesy to one another in public, whatever they might do in private. Those who knew them well, however, recognized the disguise of a devotion so deep that each had preferred ostracism from their families, one Roman Catholic, the other Jewish, rather than not marrying.

It had never occurred to Adelia that her foster parents' arguments were anything other than freedom of expression, nor that the roots of the tree sheltering her while she was growing up could ever be shaken.

"And Henry Plantagenet to tear a mother away from her child?" asked Dr. Gershom. "Is that *royal*? The deepest-dyed ruffian would hesitate. I need to see my granddaughter."

"We shall see her if we go to England."

Adelia caught her breath. "You might come to England? When? Why didn't you tell me?"

Dr. Lucia said: "Some time ago, that deepest-dyed ruffian of your father's sent us a most courteous letter, praising you, Adelia, and saying that if we should wish to visit England, he would be delighted to have us under his protection."

"*Henry* did?" Adelia was amazed.

Gershom sniffed. "Every now and then one of his fancy couriers has called in at Salerno on his way to Palermo with a letter to tell us how you get on. Your mother thinks that's courtesy. I say it's no more than our due for taking our daughter from us and keeping her away. His invitation is a puff, a sop to keep us happy."

"Oh, no," Adelia said, still surprised, but with certainty. "No, it isn't. If he's offered you a place in England, he truly wants you there."

The Plantagenet did nothing out of sensitivity. She wondered why he had done it at all; she hadn't thought he'd even been aware of her parents' existence. But he was a canny monarch with a network of information like no other, and two more of the world's most gifted doctors would be of considerable use to his kingdom.

What amazed her was that they should be considering it; she'd thought them too deeply founded into Southern Appenine rock to be dislodged.

Staring at her mother, Adelia saw what, in the misty happiness of seeing her again, she had missed—a dent on the woman's cheekbone.

She leaned over to touch it, gently. "How did that happen? Has Father been beating you again?"

"I should have," Gershom said bitterly. "If ever a stubborn, obstinate maypole of a woman deserved knocking down, it is that woman there. Didn't I tell her not to go visiting her Salerno patients without Halim to guard her? Did she listen? Mansur, my old friend, where were you? You'd have seen them off." His face changed. "They stoned her."

"Stoned her . . . *Who did?*"

Unperturbed, Dr. Lucia said: "Oh, it was a monk. In the Via Mercanti. I think he was a brother from the San Mateo monastery. An inept thrower, in any case; his other stones missed."

"Dear God. But *why?*"

"Presumably because I am married to the Jew you are pleased to call a father."

"It is true," Gershom said. "The next day the amiable fellow arrived with reinforcements and broke all our front shutters, which, on the whole, was preferable to stoning your mother, though not so good economically. Wood is expensive. We complained to Bishop Jerome, but nothing was done; there was no prosecution."

"*Why?*"

"Child, your parents are an affront to God. A Jew, a Catholic, living together? Insupportable. Enough to make angels weep and disturb the Heavens." Gershom sighed. "Even your aunt Felicia has found it necessary to leave us and retire to the Convent of San Giorgio."

Felicia? And this was the woman who'd kept the household in Salerno running with the ease of oiled wheels so that her younger, medically gifted sister could concentrate on her profession.

"Well, well," Lucia said. "She was getting old. Maybe we had become too much for her."

"No," Gershom said. "She was frightened." He took his daughter's hand in his. "Things have changed, little one. Simeon and his Arab wife have been driven out, so has our excellent Greek chemist—you remember Hypatos who was so ill-advised as to marry a Catholic girl?"

"Nobody *used* to mind—well, they minded but it was tolerated. . . ."

"But you are remembering the days when the Christian Church here overlooked mixed marriages. It no longer does. William is being pressured to replace his nonbelieving advisers with those of the Latin faith. Even Jibril has to pretend that he is a Christian convert when he's in public—he told me so himself when we arrived."

"I know it," Mansur said. "Did I not say that there were fewer mosques than there were?"

Aveyron.

Adelia got up and opened the door into the garden so that she could breathe. *Not here, oh God, not here.*

They had stoned her mother, stoned her, in *Salerno,* which had been a boiling pot producing the greatest social, political, and scientific advances the world had ever seen. She'd thought that its steam would spread throughout every land to be sniffed appreciatively by men and women with the wit to envisage a future in which there was no racial or religious conflict.

Don't let the sun set on it.

But the sun *was* setting. A huge semicircle of orange was

turning the gardens into amber as it sank. Far off, she could hear the summonses to evening prayer coming from minarets, muezzins, and campaniles. In town, the white robes of Arabs, Norman tunics, monks' habits, and Jewish cloaks would be brushing past each other on their way to the mosques, synagogues, and churches of their various faiths.

But Mansur was right; what had once been musically discordant concordance was now dominated by bells for Latin vespers.

Not Aveyron. Not here.

Gershom joined her. He put an arm round her shoulders. "It is grief for me to tell you, my child, but you would not be allowed to study in Salerno's school now."

Adelia turned to stare at him. "No *women?*"

"No women. No autopsy, either. Occasionally old Patricio sneaks the corpse of a destitute to me, but . . ." His hands went up toward the sky. "How can we mend the human body if we do not know how it works?"

They stood together, watching the great semicircle turn to gold and diminish into a final, lustrous arc before it disappeared entirely and left them in the dark.

IN THE ATTIC *of Signor Ettore's lodging house, Scarry is seated on the truckle bed with its stinking mattress. He stares, unmoving, at the plaster peeling on the wall.*

His landlady is right about his eyes; they are beautiful in their way, clearly defined slit pupils set in very white whites and totally without emotion—a wolf's eyes.

Fourteen

IN ALL ITS HISTORY, Palermo had not seen such splendor as attended the wedding of its lord to the King of England's daughter. The city was so lit by lanterns and flambeaux that the blaze brightened a dull sky and turned vivid the crowding, exulting press that made its streets almost impassable.

In the cathedral itself, the packed congregation might have been enclosed in a jewel of flashing and infinite color.

Like all the other ladies of privilege crushed into a roped-off area of the nave, Adelia was veiled. Two centuries of Arab rule had left a legacy of Islam that respectable Sicilian women, whatever their religion, had yet to discard.

Boggart and Dr. Lucia, also veiled, were seated in a compartment high up in the southern clerestory—a Christian imposition on what had once been Palermo's greatest mosque—behind a filigree screen that had a shutter which, should young Donnell start to cry for his next feed, could shut out the noise from the rest of the congregation.

Mansur, who, with Ulf and Dr. Gershom, was lost somewhere on the other side amongst the vast male congregation, had become alarmed again now that they were leaving the protection of the Ziza and had forbidden the women to attend unless they wore the anonymous veil.

"The Scarry may be in the cathedral. He knows your faces, but we do not know his."

Dr. Gershom hadn't wanted her to come at all, but Adelia had promised to see Joanna married and would do no other.

The argument had gone on for some time; they were to be carried to the cathedral in palanquins, like potentates. When Mansur, whose height made this form of conveyance too uncomfortable for him, had said he would walk beside them, there was an immediate outcry; it was obvious to everybody that his actual purpose was to scan the people they passed in case Scarry was among them ready to attack. For the Arab, the assassin had gained superhuman qualities.

"You great gawk," Ulf had said, "if he is in the crowd, he'll recognize you. Might as soon stride along ringing a bell and shoutin', 'Make way for the Lady Adelia.'"

"I shall not do that," Mansur said. "I, too, will go veiled." It was not unreasonable; many Arabs, especially the most orthodox of their faith, wore the *tagelmust*, the strip of cloth covering the lower part of the face.

"Let him," Adelia had said at last. "At least, it'll keep the dust out of his nose."

There had been dust in plenty, but no Scarry. Looking through the curtains of her palanquin at Mansur striding beside her like a watchful Tuareg, Adelia had been reminded that they were leaving Eden's Garden to return to the world of suspicion and fear.

But while, for Mansur, her parents, and Ulf, the immediate

threat was Scarry, she was more concerned by a wider and greater menace which, here in the cathedral, was being reinforced—the wedding had been taken over by the Latin Church; she saw few Jewish rabbis among the congregation, fewer Greek clergy, while Mansur was among only a select number of Moslems wearing Islamic robes.

Yes, it was a Christian ceremony and had to be. *But it's not representative of what Sicily stands for*, she thought. It begged the question as to why William had allowed a coercion that his father and grandfather would not have stood for.

The king worried her. She'd seen nothing of him since that one meeting and hadn't expected to, but Mansur brought back gossip from his fellow eunuchs at the Ziza that was not encouraging.

"They say he spends too much time in the harem."

"He's popular with the people," she'd said defensively.

"Because he has beauty and charm. Because the country is in a time of peace, but he does nothing to maintain it and they are afraid. He is weak, they say. The Norman feudal lords are creeping into power in his government and bringing their Church in their wake."

And then Mansur had surprised her. He added: "*Our* king would have kicked their backsides for them."

Our king.

"Dear God," she'd said, after a moment. "Mansur, we've become *English*."

Now, here in the cathedral, she let her eye follow a march of slender, Saracen pillars eastward, past the high altar to the presbyterium, up the apsidal wall with its prophets, saints, and cherubim to the great mosaic that presided over them all.

Where Christ God looked back at her.

At least, if the face wasn't God's it was surely Man's at his best and highest-achieving. In tiny tiles, some Byzantine genius had captured strength, love, and tenderness to give life to the Pantocrator he worshipped—and was right to worship, for here was a Ruler of All who could embrace man, woman, and child with a compassion that discounted color of skin or faith.

Adelia looked into the dark, pouched eyes that looked back into hers. *Don't let them change you, don't let them.*

There was a swirl of trumpets, and she had to turn away as the crowd in the nave parted to give passage to the procession of princes, archbishops, bishops, and ambassadors making its way toward the choir.

There was only one for her.

Rowley looked uncomfortable, as he always did when he was in full regalia; the miter had never suited him.

She loved him all over again, had never stopped loving him. Only a grubby and unworthy fit of pique, she realized, had stopped her going to him the minute she arrived in Palermo. In seeing him now, she no longer cared that his duties had taken him away so that she'd been left to the protection of another man. There *was* no other man; never would be.

Dare I wave at him? Ooh-hoo, sweetheart, I'm here.

Hardly. The moment had passed in any case; the sumptuously robed men processing the nave now were lesser bishops and clergy from other countries.

One of them, the Bishop of Aveyron.

Adelia put her hand to her mouth to stop a moan. The

monster was here, invited, accepted, a symptom of gangrene, which, if the princes of the world did not cut it out, would infect the earth. And there, going past now, was the other ghoul, Father Gerhardt—and Father Guy with him, chatting, as if contagions were multiplying and joining up.

She looked toward the face of the Pantocrator. *Don't let them, don't let them.*

A choir had begun singing an epithalamium, announcing the arrival of the bride.

Adelia had to crane her neck to see the smallest figure in the cathedral come walking slowly up the aisle, accompanied by her brother.

Across his outstretched palms, Duke Richard carried a glittering sword, ready to lay it on the marriage altar. Excalibur had finally reached the destination for which it was meant.

Adelia thought of the Glastonbury cave where it had been found and in which the quiet bones of its original owner still rested undisturbed. She stood on tiptoe to look for Ulf—this was his moment as well as hers—but she couldn't see him.

Beside her brother, her hand on his arm, Joanna looked like an exquisite, trailing forget-me-not. They'd dressed her in the same lovely blue as the Pantocrator's cloak. There were flowers and diamonds in her hair.

But she was tiny, so tiny. Adelia wanted to snatch her up and run.

What would they do to her, these wolves in their cassocks and copes? What inept bloodletters would they call in to attend to her if she fell ill again?

The ignorant are trying to set science back a thousand years. They may succeed. Nor can I be your doctor anymore, little one; they wouldn't let me. In any case, there is another child who needs me, and I must go home.

Home, she thought. *This isn't home. Home is Gyltha and Allie and Rowley and a rainy little island ruled by a bad-tempered king who looks forward, not back. I shall go home.*

But first there was a marriage ceremony to be performed.

WHERE *IN HELL IS SHE?* The Bishop of Saint Albans, crammed like a celery stick between the two pumpkins that were the Bishop of Winchester on one side and the papal legate on the other, ran his eyes over the nave's congregation, trying to locate his woman. Or, if not Adelia, then the thing that was out to harm her.

In the last three days, he'd enlisted keen-eyed, sharp-witted Palermo-born Sicilians to try and find its hiding place. He'd spent his own nights in this city asking questions, hunting. Nothing. The snake had slithered into the undergrowth so that it could rise and strike when the opportunity came.

He's here, somewhere in this packed, bloody cathedral, because she's *here, and he knows she is.*

Rowley's eyes went back to the women's section. There were two hundred or more females in there. Why did they all have to look the same? Apart from the fact that some were wider or thinner, taller or shorter than others, their bloody veils rendered them indistinguishable bottle tops.

Are you one of them, damn you? Which one?

And what the hell am I doing here, bobbing up and down like an over-

dressed cork, praying for this, for that, and not giving a tinker's curse for any of it because it is nothing—dear God, not even God—if I lose her.

IN ANOTHER PART of the cathedral, an Irishman used his height to peer over surrounding heads in order to find the only one that mattered to him. He was angry at himself, and her; of all the women he'd known throughout the seven seas—most of them intimately—he was flummoxed by why he'd been cursed with this one.

I am a Colossus, did you know that? I stride the oceans, I can forward wars and I can hinder them. Mermaids fawn on me. Women beautiful as the dawn wait on me; whores and saints and some that are both. And in the middle, like wrecking rock, there's you.

She wasn't beautiful, he'd seen camels more graceful than her as she stumped along, glaring at fokking plants in case they'd be of use to her fokking patients. And never a look in his direction; the only smile on her for that fokking useless bishop, lighting up the world with it.

Why would I die for that one? Because, O'Donnell, you poor bastard, the moment you saw her, her dimensions fitted exactly into the empty space in your misbegotten soul, and there's damn all you can do about it.

BETTER PLACED THAN *all of them to have a view of the congregation below, another pair of eyes looks down from behind one of the artful pillars of the cathedral's northern clerestory.*

The monkish usher, who'd asked the eyes' owner what he wanted up there and tried to impede him reaching it, lies on the steps of the concealed staircase with gushing holes where his own eyes had been.

The thing that had once possessed an identity of its own, and is now a dead man called Wolf, gives a red-tongued yawn. There is no need for him to concern himself; she will be revealed to him, just as the path that has led him to this place has been cleared for every step he's taken against her in the last 1,000 miles.

He lets drops of the usher's blood drip from his knife onto the floor, then peers into the congregation below. It is merely a matter of waiting. She will be shown to him.

IN THE ZIZA PALACE, Ward had been fed and watered—at arm's length—by the servant Rafiq, and then shut in the Lady Adelia's bedroom until she should return.

For a while the dog slept, then began snuffling at the door which, when it opened to allow a servant to come in with a duster and horsetail polish, he slithered out of, unseen. He was good at slithering, an art that he'd perfected at the Ziza, where dog-hating servants tended to give him a surreptitious kick if they saw him.

Until he came to the entrance hall, he went unnoticed. Its great doors were open to allow fresh air through the hall's tunnel vaulting and into the rest of the palace, though guarded by the scimitared sentries, men who, in Ward's experience, were harder kickers than most.

He made a dash for it and, hearing the shouts behind him, skirted the pool outside at a speed that left him panting as he gained the slope to the busy streets. There the stinks were delicious. Flattening and weaving to avoid the boots of passersby, Ward enjoyed them, forgetting Adelia and adding his own contribution.

But now, ah, here was a scent he recognized; it wasn't Adelia's but one equally familiar and pleasing. The dog began the arduous job of detecting it from a thousand others so that he could trace it; sniffing, occasionally making a false cast, but finding it again, following the route that Mansur had taken to the cathedral.

THE BISHOP OF WINCHESTER was making the most of his allotted part in the wedding by droning Latin supplications at a length that matched the other Latin drones preceding his.

The mass of bodies in the cathedral was producing a heat that had encouraged an usher to open its doors in the hope that fresh air might dispel the sleep overcoming most of the congregation.

In fact, the only invigorating part of the ceremony so far had been when Duke Richard revealed the provenance of the sword he carried. He'd lacked grace in doing it but, adapting the words from the Book of Samuel with which the priest Ahimelech had given the sword of Goliath to David, he'd handed Henry of England's gift to William and mumbled: "*Ecce hic gladius Arturi regis.* Behold, great king, I give you Excalibur."

The woman next to Adelia had grabbed at her with hennaed fingers: "Excalibur. Did he say *Excalibur*?"

"Yes."

"Arthur is here, then. Arthur has come to us." It was a susurration on every breath so that, for a moment, the very saints in their plaques seemed to whisper a name that would make Sicily invulnerable.

Again, Adelia had looked for Ulf but, again, couldn't see him.

After that, the ceremony once more degenerated into ordeal

by boredom, and Adelia wondered how Joanna and William were surviving it on their knees, knowing, God help them both, that it was to be succeeded by another immediately afterward when they moved to the palace's shimmering Palatine Chapel for Joanna's coronation.

Adelia's eyelids drooped and, being so tightly wedged between other women, she was able to doze standing up.

She woke up when a clear voice said: "In the name of the Father, the Son, and the Holy Spirit, take and wear this ring as a sign of my love and faithfulness."

They were exchanging rings. Joanna was married.

Hopefully, Adelia looked to her left where the side door led to the cathedral's cloister. Only a moment ago, it seemed, the afternoon winter had been shining through it; now it was diminishing into twilight. The day was nearly over.

Not the ceremony, however; the congregation wasn't to be released yet; not until Joanna and William had signed a register of their marriage.

She felt a jab in the ribs from the lady next to her, whose temper, despite the joy of Excalibur, had not been improved by heat or overcrowding. "Is that you? Kindly control yourself."

Adelia, equally irritable, denied any lapse in good manners. But there was undoubtedly a sudden and awful smell. She looked down at her shoes to see that they were being rolled on by Ward in his pleasure at having discovered them. "I'm afraid it's my dog."

"Then get rid of it before we all faint."

Adelia managed to reach down and gather Ward up. The chance of reaching the side door through her packed neighbors seemed remote, but, though they tutted and exclaimed behind their veils, a waft of Ward sent the ladies stepping back on one another's feet in their eagerness to clear an exit for him.

"You," Adelia said, when she'd gained the cloister, "what am I going to do with you?"

She pulled one of her long silk sleeves out of her cloak and knotted its end round the dog's collar. If he wasn't to infect the cathedral again, she would have to wait until the service inside was over and the others could rejoin her, which might well be another half hour or longer.

The sky had turned gray at the onset of evening, with occasional gusts of wind that blew dust along the cloister; it would be a cold wait.

It was then that she thought of the marionettes at the stall in La Kalsa's piazza. She could now afford both the mule *and* the camel, probably the fighting men as well, though Allie would be less interested in them than the animals. This empty time was as good a moment to buy them as any; tomorrow might be taken up with other matters, seeing Rowley, going home, perhaps.

Well, damned if she'd return to England without a present for her daughter. And La Kalsa wasn't far away; she could be there and back in no time. . . .

THE SUDDEN DISTURBANCE among the female guests had drawn attention to a woman leaving the cathedral with a horrible-looking dog in her arms.

On the men's side of the nave, Mansur began struggling through impeding bodies to reach her, his flailing arms making a passage for Ulf and Dr. Gershom behind him.

Up in the clerestory, behind their filigree screen, Dr. Lucia and Boggart, with Donnell in her arms, started up and headed for the stairs.

The Irishman hadn't seen Adelia go, but, alarmed by Mansur's sudden movement, he began making his own way out.

From his higher position in the choir, the Bishop of Saint Albans saw all this, and something more—the shadow of a figure with a knife in its hand slipping along the clerestory.

I'll never get to the side door in time.

Go the front way and the hell with everything.

Rowley charged out of his stall and began running, stripping off his cope as he went. He sent his miter spinning onto the altar steps, his jeweled crook of office still bouncing and clattering on the stones of the nave for some seconds after he'd disappeared out of the cathedral's great front door, leaving a shocked and staring congregation behind him.

THE MARIONETTE-MAKER, a fat and elderly bearded Greek, was being difficult. "Signora, the knights, yes, I have plenty of those, but of the beasts I have only the two my sons are manipulating this moment. They are a draw, a favorite with children, I cannot let those last two go until I have made more."

It was a ploy, of course. The damned man was going to put up the price; he'd seen her standing outside his booth before she came in, slavering over the dancing, kicking camel and mule; seen, too, that she was richly dressed, despite the unlovely dog to which her dangling sleeve was attached.

The booth was basically a long, thin canvas tent and smelled of paint and wood shavings. At this end, directly behind the stage, the backsides of two younger men waggled as they leaned over its little proscenium arch, expertly working the strings of the puppets for the benefit of the openmouthed children and adults outside who watched them. At the other end, the tent's flaps were pulled up to let in light on a long bench on which lay half-finished figures amidst a complexity of struts and string.

Signor Feodor had sat her down when she'd entered, offered her a glass of sherbet, and got ready for the bargaining without which no sale in La Kalsa was complete.

She sipped her drink: "How much, Signor?"

"For the knights, a gold tari. For the animals, two."

"*Each?*"

He spread his hands. "What would you, Signora? The articulation to make them kick and bite is complex. Also, as I say, I am reluctant to let them go."

It was a ridiculous price. Normally, she'd have pretended to walk out of the shop, and he'd have called her back with a lower offer, and she'd have pretended to leave again, and he'd have called her back . . . but it would take time that she didn't have—while he did.

"Three tari for the lot," she said.

"You would ruin me, Signora? Five."

"Four."

"Four and a half, and I am a fool to myself."

"Done," she said. "Wrap them up."

She'd surprised him; he'd have gone down to three and a half. He was on his feet in a second, tapping the son pulling the animals' strings on his rump. "We have a sale, Eneas."

Because she'd overpaid, much grateful attention was given to parceling the puppets. She would be traveling far with them? Then they must be encased in wool to prevent damage. And the lucky recipient? A girl? Allow us to include a box of Greek delight for her. . . .

Ward was pulling at her sleeve and making the noise in his throat that indicated he'd smelled something or somebody he knew and liked. Still sitting with the glass in her hand, Adelia turned her head to peer through the narrow gaps in the calico ribbons that hung over the booth's entrance to keep out flies.

The piazza was beginning to celebrate its king's wedding; flares were being lit, merchants were redoubling their efforts to sell plaster-cast depictions of a crowned bride and groom, drink stalls were doing a roaring trade, and, in the square's center, a dais was being put together for a band to accompany the night's dancing.

"Who've you seen, you silly dog?"

Then she saw who it was because his was the only figure in the piazza that was totally still. A man she knew was standing on the far side of the piazza under a fan-shaped palm tree, looking toward the booth, where the two remaining marionettes were still jouncing.

He and she had traveled the same one thousand miles—much of it together.

"Poor thing, he's ill" was her first thought; his hair, which was capless, had been allowed to grow bushy, his robe was worn ragged, while his face had the fixity of suffering.

Adelia got up to go and greet him. As she did it, the wind gusted, swaying the fronds of the man's palm tree, raising his hair, and sending shade and light flickering over him as, once, they had flickered over a wild figure in the glade of a Somerset forest, striping his face as it had been striped then.

The eyes gleamed when the light caught them, then went dark; they weren't staring at the marionettes; it was the booth's curtain strips. When the same gust of wind that had revealed him blew them aside to reveal her, he smiled. She saw his teeth. And the knife in his hand.

She couldn't move.

"There, Signora. Signora?"

The string handle of a heavy parcel was being slipped over the untrammeled wrist of her left arm. Still she didn't move.

All this way, destroying as he went, unsuspected. He'd killed. He'd smiled and killed . . . who? She was unable to remember, only that they were dead. Now it was her turn.

A group of people moved, chattering, across the square, blanking him out for a moment. When they'd gone, the space beneath the palm tree was empty.

She began to move backward slowly, pulling Ward with her, the parcel weighing on her other arm as it groped for any obstruction behind her. It was a shrinking away, not so much through terror for herself—though she was terrified—as through a dreadful revulsion. That thing out there was disordered, no longer human, more a giant poisonous insect unable to control itself; its antennae had discovered her and its fangs would sink into her whether or not there were people around to watch.

"*Get away. Get away.*" She didn't know if she said it to the creature or herself.

"Signora?"

She kept backing off until she bumped into the marionette table. Then she turned and began running for the opening at the rear of the tent, Ward galloping beside her.

She was in an alley. Turn left, yes—if she turned left and left again she would be farther down the piazza. The antennae would wave and not locate her. Run. She'd run with everything she had, regain the cathedral and be safe.

She swung left, but there was no other turning to the left, only another alley going to the right. She took it. Again, no left turn.

She ran, doubled back, took a narrow cut between some houses where crumbling balconies overhead formed a roof that gave an echo to her running footsteps—and, she thought in her panic, somebody else's.

There was no one around. Everybody had gone to the main streets to join in the celebrations. The noise of music and singing faded into quiet as Adelia became lost in the labyrinth that was the oldest and poorest part of La Kalsa. . . .

ROWLEY HURLED HIMSELF through the streets, shoving people out of the way, yelling for anybody who'd seen a lady and a dog. A garishly dressed woman held out her arms to him. "A lady and a dog," he shouted at her. She laughed, and he pushed her off.

A beggar obstructed him and Rowley knocked him flying before he realized the man had nodded. He went back and hauled the wretch to his feet. "A woman and a dog."

"Dressed pretty, was she? Her headed that way, sir. Have pity on an old crusader, sir." With one hand, the beggar pointed toward La Kalsa's piazza and extended the other for money.

He didn't get any.

Running, Rowley entered the piazza. It was full of men, women, and children dancing. Shouting for Adelia, he broke through prancing circles of dancers that merely reformed behind him.

Jesus Christ, where was she? What the hell had she come here for? If it *was* her.

He began looking into shop fronts. "A lady and a dog? Has she been here?"

And then, because God was good, a fat fellow standing outside a marionette booth beckoned him over. "The lady with the dog?"

"Was she here?"

"Such a nice lady, the dog . . . well. Bought my best creations . . . for her daughter, she said. I have others, sir, if you . . ."

Rowley shook him. "*Where did she go?*"

"Out the back, sir, I don't know why. She was running. . . ."

So was Rowley, through the long tent, into the alley, shouting her name. Running, Jesus, she'd been *running*. He felt for his sword and remembered that he was a bishop—had been—and bishops didn't wear swords, not in a cathedral at least.

Just as well; if he found her, he'd kill her with it. "Where are you, damn you?"

The alleys turned and twisted; he turned and twisted with them.

He saw a tattered shrub in a pot indicating that the hovel it stood outside of served ale. He'd seen it before, minutes ago, same hovel, same fucking shrub. He was going in circles.

Stopping, he could hear other voices shouting her name; he thought one of them was Mansur's high treble.

And someone else, nearer, was calling his. "My lord bishop. Bishop Rowley. Bishop Ro-ow-leee."

Father Guy. Father Guy had run after him.

Almighty God, they were looking for him; *him*, the bishop who'd gone insane. He'd shamed the English Church in front of a thousand Sicilians; he was their responsibility; they couldn't let him scamper the streets yelling for a woman. They'd take him back and shut him up somewhere because, whatever he was, he'd always belong to the Church.

The chaplain had people with him, was coming nearer, talking. "He must be found, proctor, you understand? I want all your men out."

A deep voice: "We'll find him, Father."

The bastards'll hold me up.

He backed into a doorway and stood still as death.

Nearer now. "Lost his wits, poor fellow. Ugh, these stinking by-ways." It was Dr. Arnulf.

When they'd passed, he dodged down a narrow cut-through to get away from them and found himself in a dilapidated square with a horse trough in its middle. His eye caught a movement on the far side, the flick of a cloak's edge as its owner disappeared around a corner. He ran after it and leaped on a hurrying figure, bringing it to the ground.

It swore as he turned it over. It was Ulf.

"Have you seen her?"

"No. Thought I heard the bloody dog bark, though."

"Which way?"

"*This* way."

They hared off together, but there were a thousand dogs

loose in the city and—"*Sod it*"—Ulf's boots slid in a deposit left by one of them, sending him sprawling.

Rowley ran on. Ahead was a cross street with a flambeau guttering in its bracket at a corner of the intersection.

And there she was. He saw her as if in a bright frame. She was standing on tiptoe with her back to him, trying to read a street name by the light of the expiring flambeau. The dog was at her feet.

He heard Ulf coming up behind him, cursing. To his left, at the top of the street, a tall man in white robes was hurrying down it. Mansur.

Another figure was coming up on his right out of the darkness.

Hearing him swear, she turned around and came toward him, smiling. He went forward and took her in his arms, still cursing her for the fright she'd given him.

The miserable light from the flambeau glinted on an upraised blade over her shoulder.

He swung her round so that the blade went into his own back, once, twice, before the killer was pulled away and Ulf pinioned the arms while Mansur drew the curved dagger from his sash and cut Locusta's throat with it.

THEY DRAGGED ROWLEY into the vestibule of a shabby tenement. Adelia never let go of him, crawling beside him with one arm under his back so that it was raised above the dirty floor, the blood from it pouring over the crook of her elbow.

Knowledge deserted her; she didn't know what to do.

Help me, I don't know what to do. But her mouth was too frozen to say the words, and she looked up into the faces of Mansur, Ulf . . . and recognized neither of them.

"Get away, woman. Let a proper doctor see to him." Another face, mouth puffing from exertion. Arnulf's hands were on her shoulders, trying to pull her off, so she sank her teeth into his wrist to stop him.

He fell back. "She's bitten me, the bitch has bitten me."

A calm voice said: "Adelia." It was Dr. Gershom's.

"Yes?"

"Let me look, child. We'll see what the damage is."

"Yes, Father." Sense came back to her; she had help; she was a doctor again. She said: "Somebody bring a light."

Light came.

Calling for quiet, Dr. Gershom tore open the front of Rowley's shirt and pressed an ear against his chest to listen for any sucking sound. He heard none. "Not the lung, I think," he told her.

"I'm frightened it's the liver."

"Let's see."

Rowley was heaved onto his side, and they ripped away the back of his shirt to see what lay underneath.

Two wounds, both gaping, both deep. Downward and sideways strokes had gone into the heavy musculature of the back between the posterior axillary lines.

"I don't know," Dr. Gershom said. "I don't know. Maybe . . ." He avoided looking at his daughter. She was bunching the folds of her skirt around her fists to press them into the wounds—the blood immediately soaked into the silk until it dripped.

Gershom knew, as she knew, that even if no major organ had

been touched, part of Rowley's clothing had most likely gone in with the passage of the knife and would turn the area round it putrid if it wasn't got out.

"I need my equipment," he said. "We'll get him to my house . . . operate . . . something to carry him on."

Mansur moved to the stairs and ripped out two of its risers with the ease of a man pulling up grass.

"No." For a dying man, the voice was clear. "They'll find me. Take me home. Adelia? Are you there?"

"I'm here, dearest."

"Who, my son? Who will find you?" Dr. Gershom asked.

Adelia knew. *They*. The "they" who would claim her lover for their own, who'd absorb their bishop back into the organism that was blanketing the world, the "they" who would take this man away from her for the last time and give him to the torture of their doctors.

She looked up and around. So many people in this dirty place. How had they all come here? Had they flown?

There were those she loved: her father, her mother—tearing her own petticoat into strips for bandages—an agonized Ulf and Boggart with her baby, Mansur, tight-lipped, efficiently making a stretcher. . . . And the O'Donnell, the O'Donnell had come. . . .

Behind them, the enemy; Dr. Arnulf, Father Guy, outraged and giving orders to a large man in clerical robes. "Fetch help, Master Proctor. It is not seemly for a bishop to die here. Bring assistance. He must be taken to the cathedral, relics, the last rites. . . ."

"*You shan't have him.*" In this unreality, it was all she knew.

"The woman is a witch and must be arrested. . . ."

Now the O'Donnell had the chaplain by the throat and was shaking him like a bundle of straw. "You touch her, you bastard . . ."

But the proctor had gone. They'd be here soon to take him. They'd taken Ermengarde.

There was a bloodied bundle half in, half out of the vestibule's entrance where somebody had kicked it out of the way. Its throat was severed. Her eyes passed over it, had no interest in it; the insect had done its damage and now was squashed; she felt nothing for it. Only Rowley mattered.

"*Adelia?*"

Her mother was pushing her gently. "Let me take over now, little one." Dr. Lucia was holding clean, folded pieces of petticoat to stanch the wounds, other strips were bandages. "He needs to be able to see you."

Relinquishing a post she would have given to nobody else, she lifted her dripping hands from her lover's back and moved so that her mother's instantly replaced them.

She went to kneel on the other side of Rowley and put her face close to his, touched it.

"Is it you?"

"It's me. Don't talk. We're going to make you well."

He smiled and shut his eyes. "Take me home, sweetheart," he said again. "England . . . with you. They mustn't have me again."

"They won't." He wasn't theirs, he was hers.

"Sweetheart?"

"I'm here, Rowley. Stay still, we'll have you out of here in a trice."

"Get me home. Get me to England."

"I will."

But Arnulf and Guy were here. Others would come. They'd follow the trail of a man carried through the streets on a stretcher, like the killer had trailed her. Only a matter of time . . . Time. It was ebbing away . . . like Rowley's life.

She said: "We're taking you to my father's house first, dearest. We can mend you there."

"Better be . . . bloody quick about it."

He put her back in time and space. If he could swear, he could live.

She looked for the face of the Irishman. "My father and I are going to save him," she said; she was quite clear about it. "But then I want you to take us home, before the Church can find us. Sail us home, O'Donnell. All of us. To England."

Father Guy's back interrupted her view; he was facing the O'Donnell. "Admiral, I forbid it. This man is a lord of the Holy Church. I have men coming. . . ."

There was a smack and he fell. Ulf had punched him. The O'Donnell picked him up and threw him into the street. "And you, too," he said to Arnulf. "Before I kill you."

They went, stumbling, shouting for reinforcements.

Mansur and Dr. Gershom were lifting Rowley onto the stretcher, carefully, carefully, putting him on his side so that Dr. Lucia's hands could keep stanching the wounds.

Adelia's eyes never left the O'Donnell's. "We're going to mend him," she said, "then you must sail us home. The land route . . . too hard on him. A calm voyage while he gets better. Please, I beg you."

He stared back at her. The man was dying; she had his blood

on her face. And did she know what she was asking? How long a voyage? Through the Pillars of Hercules with their sudden storms? Running from fokking Barbary pirates? Beating up the bloody coast of Portugal until the Gulf Stream took them north?

But he would. She'd never love him, but he would. He'd still the seas for her.

"I'll take you," he said. "All of you."

He watched her turn to her lover. "My lord O'Donnell's taking us home, Rowley."

"That's right. . . ." The voice was getting weaker. "I'll live if you take me home."

"Is that a bargain?"

A slight nod.

"It'd better be," she told him.

Mansur and Ulf lifted the stretcher, Dr. Lucia and Adelia on either side of it, Adelia still holding Rowley's hand, the dog at her heels. Dr. Gershom. Boggart stooping, with her child in her arms, to pick up a package that contained marionettes. Behind them the O'Donnell.

On their way out, they stepped over the corpse of the man known as Locusta, who'd once been William of Scaresdale, and who'd at last found peace in the filth of a Palermo street.

And left it there.

Author's Notes

ADELIA AGUILAR, my fictional mistress of the art of death, came about because in twelfth-century Salerno, then part of the Kingdom of Sicily, there really was a great School of Medicine, which not only permitted the practice of autopsy, but also took women students. We know this because of an extant treatise on women's medicine, known as the Trotula, which was written by a female professor.

Sicily was then the most liberal, forward-thinking realm in all Christendom, treating its Arabs, Greeks, Jews, and Normans as equal citizens, something that occurred nowhere else. (Two fine books on the subject are *The Normans in the South* and *The Kingdom in the Sun* by John Julius Norwich.)

The school disappeared in the thirteenth century, probably under pressure from the Church of Rome, which regarded the science of autopsy *and* women doctors as anathema.

PRINCESS JOANNA'S JOURNEY from England to Palermo to marry King William of Sicily at the age of ten is another historical event.

We know most of her route. We know that she was accompanied at certain points by two of her brothers—Henry, the Young King, and Richard, later the Lionheart. We know that it was interrupted at one point when she had to be taken ashore because she was ill.

We know that much and little else. But, then, the chroniclers of the early Middle Ages disappoint in giving details of their journeys. Men and women of all sorts, not just royal, traveled extensively in those days; some making pilgrimages over the known Christian world, others flitting off to Rome—a journey that, from England, took only a few weeks. We find laconic references to crossing the Alps with little mention of the hardship that must have involved, especially as some of those climbs were made in winter.

So, in order to prefigure the growing and stultifying power of the Latin Church at that time, I have felt justified in taking that journey and running with it, adding even more drama to what must have been an adventurous undertaking, though I have taken care—I always do—to make sure that none of the historical people in it act out of character.

What I have done is some date fixing. In the story, Joanna still sets off at the age of ten, as she did, and arrives by the time she was eleven years old, again as she did, but I have put her trek to Sicily two years later—in 1178—than when it actually took place in 1176. This is to fit in with my fictional heroine's time line. In 1176, Adelia was busy elsewhere, so I have used a novelist's license to enable her to take part in Joanna's extraordinary journey.

HENRY, THE YOUNG KING. It would have been typical of that young man to desert his sister while he went off to fight in one of the tournaments to which he was addicted. Professor W. L. Warren, that fine historian of Henry II's reign, says of the Young King: "He was gracious, benign, affable, courteous, the soul of liberality and generosity. Unfortunately he was also shallow, vain, careless, empty-headed, incompetent, and irresponsible." He let nearly everybody down at one time or another. He died when he was twenty-eight years old of dysentery contracted while he was supporting rebels in Aquitaine in their fight against Richard, the brother with whom he'd once been in alliance against their father.

RICHARD THE LIONHEART. History's P.R., which so often gives good publicity to the wrong people, has awarded him an almost saintly aura through the Robin Hood legend. Nobody can deny that he was a fine general and a brave fighter, but he was capable of greed and cruelty. On crusade, he once ordered his Moslem prisoners to be slaughtered and their bellies slit open to see if they had swallowed any jewels.

He had no care for England, spending less than a year in that country in all his life. His coronation was a signal for a massacre of the English Jews his father had protected. He's said to have announced that he would sell London if, by doing so, he could raise money for crusade. It may be that his bisexuality—he seems to have done penance for sodomy at one point—drove him to try and placate his Christian God by his effort to win back Jerusalem from the Moslems. His death was caused by an inglorious arrow that hit him while he was in what is now France, besieging the castellan of Châlus who he mistakenly thought had unearthed some treasure.

HENRY II OF ENGLAND was damned by history for calling for the death of his Archbishop of Canterbury, Thomas à Becket. He was in France at the time and, in a famous rage at Becket's refusal to allow reform of a corrupt system, cried: "Who will rid me of this turbulent priest?" A few of his knights, who had their own quarrel with the archbishop, immediately took ship to Canterbury and assassinated the man on the steps of his own cathedral. Thus Thomas became a martyr and saint, and the king a sinner. But it was Henry Plantagenet who plucked England out of the legal Dark Ages by introducing the Common Law (i.e., a comprehensive system of justice available to all his people) and that wonder available to the English-speaking people—trial by jury. Until then, judgment on crime had been left to God, by chucking the accused into a pond, for instance, to see if he sank (innocent) or floated (guilty).

ELEANOR OF AQUITAINE. Not up to the intellectual weight of her husband, King Henry, she is still one of the few women of that time who emerge from the monk-written chronicles with a blazing character. She bore ten children, and she backed her elder sons' rebellion against their father, who imprisoned her for it (though quite nicely). After his death, she ruled England on Richard's behalf while he was away on crusade, as well as raising the ransom when he was held hostage on his way back. When he was killed, she spent her time trying to get the erratic King John out of trouble. Outliving all her sons except John, she died in her eighties, having had probably more adventures than any queen before or since.

At the end of her life, she took the veil at Fontevrault in Anjou, France (most beautiful of abbeys), where, despite their turbulent marriage, she was put to rest beside Henry Plantagenet.

FATHER ADALBURT'S pronouncements were made by naïve real-life clergy round about this time.

DOCTOR. For clarity, I have applied the title to physicians though, in fact, it was conferred only on teachers of logic and philosophy in those days.

CATHARS. That name for the sect, and "perfects" for its priesthood, were not what the Languedoc heretics applied to themselves but were given to them by the Church that wiped them out. I have used them because that is how both are now generally referred to. The full crusade against them, and its burning of thousands of Cathar men, women, and children, didn't begin until after the time of my story, but already one or two were being sent to the stake and enough cruelty inflicted on them by the Church to justify my account of what Adelia and her friends suffered in the fictional palace of a fictional Bishop of Aveyron, in order to demonstrate an Inquisition that was starting to flex its horrifying muscles.

Her subsequent enforced stay in the Cathar village is based on the classic *Montaillou* by Emmanuel Le Roy Ladurie (Penguin Books, 1980), which, because it, in turn, is based on the papers of the painstaking inquisition endured by that village's people, gives us insight into the lives of men and women of that region during the Middle Ages.

BAGPIPES. The *cornemuse des Pyrenées*, the *samponha*, was, and is, sufficiently like the Scottish bagpipes to make the Highlander Rankin feel at home.

THE APPENDECTOMY. I believe it is feasible that Adelia could have performed one, and for her patient to have survived. The existence of the appendix was known in very early times. Certainly, the Salerno School, with its practice of anatomy, would have been aware of it, and of its danger when infected.

ANESTHETIC. Man has been aware of the properties of opium since the days of the pharaohs, whilst laudanum, extract of opium—usually with wine—certainly appeared in the Middle Ages if not before, though its use for anesthesia was prohibited by the Inquisition as an evil, the Church not approving of interference with God-appointed pain, nor of the shedding of blood, thus reducing surgeons to the status of barbers.

SURGERY. The practice stretches back to the time of the Sumerians around 4000 B.C.—archaeologists have discovered sharpened bronze scalpels, knives, and trephines among Nineveh's remains. In the Hammurabi Code from that time, there's a list of what the physician should be paid if he "make a large incision with an operating knife and cure it," etc. In India around 600 B.C., an ancient surgical text describes procedures for surgery, even cosmetic.

Above all, we should not underestimate the hardihood of the human body. Neolithic skulls have been found showing that they underwent successful trepanning—the growth of bone inward from the operation site suggests that the patients lived for a considerable time afterward.

From what we can gather from early records, the survival rate after amputation was about fifty percent.

Fanny Burney, writer and diarist, lived for many years after having had a breast removed because of cancer in 1811 without benefit of anesthetic.

In September 1942, Wheeler B. Lipes, a twenty-three-year-old corpsman, was acting as pharmacist's mate on board the American Navy submarine USS *Seadragon* in enemy waters when, in the absence of a qualified doctor and without access to penicillin, he successfully took out the appendix of a nineteen-year-old shipmate.

In 1961, a Russian doctor, Leonid Rogozov, on an Antarctic expedition, cut out his own appendix under local anesthetic with the help of nonmedical colleagues, and lived to tell the tale.

HEMORRHAGE. In olden times, this was stemmed by cauterization—a risk in itself, but not an automatically fatal one.

SUTURES were in use from the first, though some early surgeons employed ants to bite the flesh of the wound together, cutting the insects' bodies away and leaving the teeth in place.

SEPSIS. A killer, of course, and one that Adelia would not have been aware of, as was no one else until the nineteenth century.

But though the Middle Ages are depicted as being unsanitary—and mostly were—cleanliness was prized by some. Jews and Arabs, of course, had it written into their religious rituals, and a Christian to be dubbed a knight had to take a bath before the ceremony. Medieval household accounts show considerable outlay spent on laundry and fullers—robes that took months, even years, of needlework to make had to be kept clean if they were not to disintegrate from sweat and dirt.

Also, though the infant mortality rate was horrific, a child that survived beyond the age of five probably developed an immunity that could carry it into old age.

PALERMO CATHEDRAL has been altered and restored so many times—and not, in the opinion of many, to its advantage—that it no longer has the splendor it had in the twelfth century, so I have transferred to it the wonderful and great mosaic Pantocrator of its more untouched rival, Cefalù, a building which John Julius Norwich describes as "not just the loveliest Norman exterior in Sicily, but one of the loveliest cathedrals in the world."

THE DISINTEGRATION OF SICILY. The glory of enlightenment that was the Kingdom of Sicily lasted only sixty-four years. The marriage of William II and Joanna was apparently happy, but also tragic in that it was childless. William himself was not statesman enough to preserve what his country had been, nor to pass it on to good hands. He died at the age of thirty-six and his kingdom descended into violence and medieval bigotry. For a while Joanna was virtually imprisoned by her husband's illegitimate successor, Tancred, and had to be rescued by Richard the Lionheart. In 1196 she was married off again, this time to the Count of Toulouse, to whom she bore three children, dying in childbirth with the third, aged thirty-four, outlived by the indomitable Eleanor of Aquitaine, her mother.

EXCALIBUR. Nobody knows what happened to it. In the upheaval that followed William's death, King Arthur's sword disappeared—like the great kingdom to which it had been given.

Acknowledgments

MY GRATITUDE, as always, to my editor, Rachel Kahan, for her excellent and painstaking judgment. And to my agent, Helen Heller, who, like Rachel, knows how a plot should be shaped. I rely on them both. And I would like to thank the whole team at Putnam for the work that makes my books look as well as they do. Also, the staff and stacks of the wonderful London Library provide me with everything I need for the immense amount of research that goes into every novel. Thanks, too, to my daughter, Emma, for taking so much secretarial work off my shoulders, and to my husband, Barry, the rock to which I cling.

About the Author

ARIANA FRANKLIN is the pen name of British writer Diana Norman. A former journalist, she has written several critically acclaimed biographies and historical novels. She lives in Hertfordshire, England, with her husband, the film critic Barry Norman.